The Ru

THE LIMARNI QUEST

Best wishes

John E Nicholson

John Ellwood Nicholson

ISBN 978-1-912145-60-7

Acorn Independent Press

Acknowledgments

I would like to thank family and friends for their support and great ideas in completing this book. I would also like to thank members of the Ringwood Writers Circle, Greyfriars, for their constructive comments and encouragement. None of this would have happened without them, or have been as much fun.

About the Author

John Ellwood Nicholson is a native of Cheshire who now lives with his wife in Dorset. He attended Kings School, Macclesfield and the University of British Columbia in Canada. A career in finance, spanning more than thirty years, took him to South East Asia and various sub-Saharan African countries including Liberia. His admiration of the latter in overcoming two brutal civil wars is undiminished.

For my wife Isobel
My editor in chief in all things

PROLOGUE
NEW YEAR'S EVE

Do I or don't I? If I hadn't just had my nails done, I'd toss a coin.

What am I on about? Of course I'll go. I'm used to going out as a *single* and why should I worry that most people at Paula's party will be *couples?* Most of my friends are married, many with kids, but Paula and I have ... well, we've stayed unattached. Anyway, I'm happy with my own company. Not lonely. In fact I lead an active life ... most of the time. But whatever I do, I'm definitely not going back to live with my parents. I'll never forgive them for the silly name they gave me ... and anyway, they argue all the time.

Sitting at my excuse for a dressing table, I stick a tongue out at my at my reflection and make a face. Hello, yes it's me, Penny Lane, polite, kind, considerate, and always doing the right thing ... well, almost always. I smooth out the few wrinkles round my eyes - laughter lines - forcing out a laugh to prove the point. And those round my mouth and forehead - not bad at all for a thirty-six year old - well, thirty-seven tomorrow.

New Year combining with my Birthday Eve is my established time to reflect and reminisce so ... let me think, how's my year been? Not brilliant, actually.

Toby *bloody* Dickson walked out on me in March, which hurt, as I'd thought he may be the one, but from the day he'd moved in, Paula had called him a *dickhead* and she was right. That mini-fling I had with married-man, Roland, was doomed from the start, so for the past three months I've been celibate. Oh well.

And ... why am I still in the same lousy job? Hazing the mirror with a deep breath, I stare persuasively at my image.

Go and register with agencies you've been promising to do for months. There, that's my New Year's resolution, a new job, a new life and maybe, a new man. And why not? I'm a bloody good catch.

Now then, time to do my make-up. Christmas present from Chloé at work and it's good stuff - thanks Chloé. There, all wrinkles gone ... who am I kidding? And now the new dress I bought in the sales. Standing, I pirouette in front of the mirror. Blue certainly suits me and the sequins and sparkly bits round the top may just attract the attention of a gorgeous young man who happens to be there. Ha, I'll be lucky. All good looking men in their thirties are either married or gay.

Time to go. Taxi due in ... oh hell, five minutes. No more time to add to my *sensational* appearance. I blow a kiss into the hall mirror, 'I'm off to a party.'

PART ONE
LONDON

Chapter One
New Year's Day

What the...? Desperately clawing my way out of a dark, frightening nightmare, I'm gripping the edge of the sheets as though my life depends on it. My heart's thumping and I'm terrified. But why - what of? Fighting off the last of the demons, I'm slowly coming round, waking up and ah ... thank God, my panic gradually subsides as the racket which scared me half to death is only the wailing siren of a police car screeching along Hook Road below my bedroom window, but - why did it freak me out?

I know why, *something is horribly wrong with me*. My head seems to have tiny bombs exploding inside and my mouth is as sour as a drain. I make the mistake of trying to rise from the bed, but sharp pain racks my skull and I groan. Hardly daring to open my eyes, I do so very slowly. They hurt. I close them and even that is painful. Carefully, I try again. Keeping my eyelids apart, I concentrate on trying to focus. At least I'm in my own bed with only Mr Ted next to me. Lying back, I cradle my throbbing head in my hands and, making a supreme effort, slowly uncurl my limbs and stagger out of bed, aching all over.

Last night - what happened? Can't remember, a complete blank. But two glasses of wine at Paula's ... ah, that's it, of course, it was Paula's New Year's Eve party.

Gradually recovering, I leave Mr Ted snug in his blanket and giddily make my way to the bathroom, holding on to the walls to keep upright. The harsh overhead light reflects ghoulish images off the black and white tiles and chrome fittings, one minute I look like a zombie the next like my mother. Can't decide which is worse. I lean my feverish forehead against the cool tiles then look in the mirror – shit,

I'm still dressed for the party. Splashing my face with cool water marginally revives me.

Swaying my way into the kitchenette, I sip two glasses of water and swallow three paracetamol tablets, then force myself to eat oats, mashed bananas and syrup, my dad's well-used recipe. Ugh, it's disgusting, I deserve a medal for that. Nauseous and full of aches and pains, I lie on the sofa, lulled by rain drumming on the living room window, the sound consoles me and I drift off into that gap between sleep and wakefulness. The noise suddenly increases, transforming into the incessant ring of the telephone.

Ah, wouldn't you know it? "Hello Mum, thanks for the birthday and gift card ... no, Mum, I'm not nearly forty ... okay. I know, still on my own ... yes, went to Paula's party ... no, I didn't meet a nice young man ... just a quiet day at home and ... what's that - croaky? Oh a bit of a sore throat, that's all ... and you went to the Rymer's as usual ... oh, that's nice, thanks Mum and same to you, love to Dad ... yes, next week, bye".

I could have told her about my massive hangover but she'd probably rather not know that. I've lived my life burdened by the expectations of being an only child, the apple of my parents' eyes.

Feeling a little better, I continue trying to dredge up the events at Paula's. Tiny bits begin to emerge like wobbly mirages in a heat haze. Ah yes, here we go, there was this guy, now who was it? Damn, it's gone again leaving me with a horrible feeling of uneasiness.

Last night's clothes feel like dirty rags and I need a bath. Running the hot water, I take off my dress and underwear and put them in the washbasin to soak. Before getting in, I examine myself in the full-length mirror. My once beautifully coiffed hair looks as if it's been through a hurricane and my black-rimmed, bloodshot eyes need sleep. The rest looks okay. Staring at myself, I have a gut feeling of what it was, the thing that happened last night, I'm pretty certain it was sex, somebody took advantage of me. Oh shit, who the hell was it?

Lowering myself gently into the bath, I close my eyes and sink to the bottom, the hot water soothingly covering my body before surfacing and swallowing a mouthful making me cough and splutter ... and sob. Putting my head back under to wash away the tears, I recover slightly and step out, wrapping myself tightly in a towel. I start to cry again.

Hey, hang on a minute, I never, ever, ever have more than two alcoholic drinks a night and never, never have a hangover so ... oh hell, my drink must have been spiked, the rape drug. It explains everything, my memory loss and why I feel so awful. But surely I'd know if I'd had sex ... or raped. I'm not bruised or bashed in any way so ... oh, no, all the evidence went down the plughole.

Deep breath, pull yourself together.

Slowly dressing, I eat a slice of banana and peel an orange, two of my five-a-day, followed by toast with marge and jam and more paracetamol. That's a bit better. I'll phone Paula and tell her some guy at her party spiked my drink and ask who it was. Should I tell her about being raped? No, maybe not, not yet anyway, just in case I'm wrong.

Pouring boiling water into a mug of instant coffee, I slouch back in my favourite chair telling myself to be calm, willing more pieces of the jigsaw to appear. Nothing. Apart from Paula, there's no-one else I want to confide in, especially Chloé and the girls at work - it would be round the office in no time. Sipping the scalding black coffee, I promise myself that *if* I was raped, then I'll get the bastard. Nobody can abuse me and get away with it.

Picking up the phone, I call Paula. It rings for ages before a disembodied, husky voice asks who is calling at such an unearthly hour.

'It's eleven and it's me, wake up for God's sake,' I snap.

'Oh, Penny, go away,' her faint voice tails off, 'I was in La La Land dancing with Ryan Gosling, so I'm going back to see if he's waiting.'

'Look Paula, it's serious. I'm ill and think my drink was spiked last night.'

There's silence for a few seconds and then I hear her clearing her throat. 'Fuck off. The way you behaved, you ought to be ashamed of yourself.'

'What do you mean?'

'You know very well what I mean, you were pissed and, when you were actually here, you acted like a, let me think ... like a tart.'

'What do you mean, *actually here*?'

'Oh, go away, Penny,' she yells. 'Ryan may still be waiting.'

'Paula, listen, are you saying that I wasn't there all the time?'

'I don't know where you went - off with that bloke I think.'

'Please, Paula,' I appeal. 'I don't know anything about last night, either leaving the party or being with a man. I must have been drugged because I'm sicker than I've ever been and have complete memory loss. And, if I behaved badly, I certainly can't remember.'

Disappointingly, she only laughs and says I'm crazy.

'Really,' I yell, furious at her attitude. 'And who was the man I'm supposed to have misbehaved with?'

Her laughter only increases before she slams the phone down.

Well, that's that then. But I'm not giving up, no way. I'll text her that I'm reporting her to the police. Ha, that'll make her tell me who the bloke was. And if someone did have sex with me, I hope to hell he took precautions. It makes my flesh creep just thinking about it.

CHAPTER TWO
JANUARY 24th

I hate my *daily desk drudge* of a job, and it shows. It's Friday afternoon and I'm looking forward to a quiet weekend, but before I can pack up my desk, fat Bossy Bunter tells me I'm on a disciplinary hearing next week. Damn, I didn't think anyone in their right mind would ever read those boring EU directive amendments I've painstakingly translated from French and German. The only way I could struggle through them was by adding a few choice swear words into the text which I expected to lie unnoticed in the archives till doomsday. Well, I was wrong.

Adding to my misery is the fact that my soddin' period's five days late. I felt sick earlier in the month but put it down to the drugs in my spiked drink. What's really driving me up the wall is that after more than three weeks, I still can't remember a thing that happened at Paula's party. On the way home, I nip into a chemist for a pregnancy test kit and then in the privacy of my bathroom, I do the test, twice, and I'm pregnant, twice. Hell. Lying on the sofa, I cry myself to sleep, only to wake up and cry again. What am I to do? I'll get rid of it, that's easy. I'm not having the kid of a rapist and I hate Paula because she's still blaming me for what happened that night, and won't tell me the bastard's name.

Over the weekend, I try to blot out the whole business but it's now Sunday evening and I know I should have done something about my *condition*. I phone Paula and this time I'm polite. 'Hello, it's me again.'

'Oh, hi.'

'Paula, I have a problem.'

'What sort of problem?'

'*I'm pregnant* sort of problem and it happened at your party.'

'Shit.'

'Look Paula, the drug slipped into my glass must have been strong because my mind's still a complete blank, but the sod who drugged me also raped me.'

'Oh fuck, this is *so* bloody embarrassing,' Paula sighs. 'I'll be honest with you, both Kelly Jones and Fiona Worthing told me that they were ill that night, their drinks had been spiked.'

'Aha, so I wasn't the only one!'

'No, *I'm so sorry.* It was a guy called Mike Burgess, Do you remember him?'

I screw up my face in concentration . 'Mike Burgess, no, but you've got to tell me where I can find the bastard because I'm going to cut his nuts off.'

Paula stays silent for a moment. 'But it wasn't Mike Burgess.'

'What do you mean, of course it was,' I yell. 'He drugged and raped me.'

'No, Penny, it wasn't him, he'd been thrown out long before your disappearing act.'

'My disappearing act! What on earth do you mean by that?'

'I mean that Mike Burgess made a complete arsehole of himself, so another man at the party grabbed him and hurled him into the street, and he didn't come back.'

'Are you trying to tell me that there must have been another pervert there?'

'Yes ... but no. Look, Penny, the man who threw Burgess out, his name's Charles, well after Burgess had gone, you and he were getting on well and although I was busy, I did notice that you were both missing for a while, maybe in a bedroom, these things happen.'

'Not with me, they don't'

'That's true but you definitely had the *hots* for him, and he you.'

'But how could I possibly forget a thing like that? That's crazy. Now, when was it that you say I misbehaved?'

'When you reappeared in the early hours. This Charles guy ... very nice by the way, had to leave as he was going overseas later that day and that's when you started staggering around, pissed to the gills.'

'Well, we now know, don't we, Paula, that it was drugs, not alcohol. So, it looks as if it was this Charles who got me pregnant.'

'Yeh, well, I guess so if er ... have you been with anyone else?'

'No,' I snap.

'Sorry, just thought I'd ask.'

'Well I haven't.' Calming down gradually, I say, 'Obviously, I'll get a termination but first, I want to meet him, where does he live?'

'Honestly, I don't know. I only met him for the first time at the office a couple of hours before the party and he told me he was due at his parents in Dorset for New Year but the roads and railways down there were flooded, remember?'

'Yes, I remember the flooding.'

'So I felt sorry for him and gave him an invite. The only thing I know about him is that he's with the Foreign Office.'

'Okay, that's easy. You work in the FO so find him for me.'

Chapter Three
January 27th

Sitting at my desk, my turbo isn't charged today and I laboriously begin my morning warm-up ceremony. A murmured incantation of "*I hate this job, I hate this job*" but a call from Paula interrupts my futile ritual. 'Speak softly,' I whisper. 'You'll have to make it quick, my boss is on the warpath.'

'Yeh, okay, but not much to report so far.'

My heart drops. 'Why's that?'

'Well, there's some silly Foreign Office regulation stopping me searching the files for his name and address but my friend, Helen, in HR, did me a huge favour and looked for me.'

'Go on then.'

'She was able to find out his surname is Temple but, and here's the strange thing, he doesn't work at the Foreign Office after all. Everyone Helen thought would know said they weren't certain where he worked or, for that matter, anything else about him.'

'That's weird, what was he doing in the FO then? Security must have checked him.'

'Oh yes, they did, but the officer in charge refused to give me any information. Evidently, I'm not ranked high enough. Charles Temple seems to be a man of mystery.'

'He does, doesn't he? But he did tell you that he was going overseas after the party so maybe he's not back yet.'

'That's true. By the way, have you seen a doctor yet?'

'No. I'll go to the clinic to get rid of it when I'm ready, after I've seen the mysterious Charles Temple.'

'Well, don't leave it too long.'

'No, er, sorry, got to go.' The obese, slightly menacing frame of William A Bunter looms over my desk as I stealthily replace the receiver.

'No personal calls, Miss Lane, you've been warned before.'

'It was my contact at MAF,' I lie. 'I had to get clarification on the situation in Bulgaria regarding agricultural output and the CAP.' I hold up a bunch of papers as evidence.

'Huh.' With a withering grunt, he swings his fat arse round and walks away. If he checks the incoming number he'll have me banged to rights, my final disciplinary hearing. I can't afford to lose this Home Office job, it pays well and the pension's fantastic *IF* I do my full thirty-five years. Oh my God, thirty-five years! I've only got another what? ... Twenty-four years, three months and, I glance at the chart pinned to the wall of my cubicle, seventeen days to go. The only break I've had in the last twelve years was a twenty month secondment to China to teach English to some of their upwardly mobile Mandarin public servants.

Watching the slowest clock in Christendom pedantically tick its lethargic way round to five-thirty, I breathe a huge sigh, tidy my desk and head for the lift.

'Hey, Penny,' it's Chloé, she gives me a nudge as the lift doors open. 'Are you coming out with the gang tonight?'

'I'd love to, but I've had a stinking headache all afternoon,' which is not a complete lie.

'Oh, too bad, we're going to a new place that's just opened, *La Tropicale*. Full of African beat music and *all that jazz*,' she laughs. 'It's brill.'

'Thanks Chloé, maybe next time.' Phew, that's the last thing I want right now, African jungle drums.

It's the first dry evening for ages. Stepping out into Marsham Street, I decide to get some much needed exercise by walking to Waterloo Station. I stare at the swirling traffic and huddled pedestrians shuffling towards the underground or bus stops, bound for their homes in Teddington and Maidenhead after another exciting day in the city. A man eating a bagette brushes past me as the clumsy sod trundles along in the opposite direction. All along Great Smith and Broad Streets into Parliament Square, I look at my reflection in successive shop windows but once I get onto Westminster Bridge, I feel the full force of the wind and wrap my fleecy scarf more tightly around my neck.

Big Ben's six o'clock chimes finish as I skip down the steps onto the Embankment, and walk quickly past the now empty, boarded-up booths. The London Eye is still doing business although the queue is considerably shorter than when I last passed. Hurrying up out of the cold, I take the steps two at a time before crossing into Waterloo concourse.

Luckily, the next train is to Alton, first stop Surbiton, which should only take fifteen minutes. My heart sinks as it's crowded and I have to stand crushed uncomfortably amongst fellow commuters. Getting out at Surbiton, I take a deep breath of fresh air and scan the sky, still no sign of rain. I go along Victoria Road, popping into Sainsbury's to buy a couple of ready meals, then walk briskly to my small (mum calls it cosy) one-bedroom flat in Albany Court, Hook Road. Annoyingly, the lights in the entrance hall and landings have fused yet again and I make a mental note to call maintenance, nobody else in the block seems to bother.

Holding firmly onto the handrail, I feel the way up, step by step, through the darkness to the second floor. It's eerily quiet. I have an uneasy feeling that I'm not alone and a shiver runs down my back. Mumbling under my breath and fumbling around in my handbag, I try to find my keys which are, as usual, tucked into one of the folds near the bottom. I blindly feel for the keyhole with my left hand, struggling to insert the key with my right.

'OH FUCK,' I scream. The shock is as if I swallowed dynamite and it had been set off. Someone has moved close behind me. The beam of a torch held high over my shoulder, is directed at the door lock.

The someone, who is now obviously male, says in my ear. 'I hope this helps.'

'WHAT THE HELL ... WHO,' I yell. 'Leave me alone, I'll call the police.'

'It's me, Penny, Charles, don't you recognise me?' The accent is vaguely familiar.

'Who?'

'Oh dear, I didn't make much of an impression, did I?' A teasing note in his voice. 'We were at Paula's New Year's Eve party.' He shines the torch briefly on his face. 'Does that help?'

My mind's all over the place, heart pounding and I'm struggling to get my breath back. Standing in the entrance with the door half open, I put the hall light on. Oh my God, I recognise him now. The part of my memory that had been lost for the last month suddenly snaps into focus. I remember his face, his smile and the scar on his left temple and how and where we made love. Just seeing his face has brought it all back in a flash, like a miracle. Strangely, I feel embarrassed and formally shake his hand as if we've never met before and yet ... he's the father of my unborn child.

'Hello Penny,' he doesn't seem to notice my confusion. 'It's great to see you again.' He's taller than me, with close-cropped brown hair, wearing a dark suit, white shirt and striped tie. His features are pleasantly craggy in a Daniel Craig sort of way, and his good-humoured smile melts any inner control I had. My knees wobbling like jelly.

'Oh, yes, hello.' I stand still. I feel like the air is alive and when I move, I'll push my life in a new direction. Pressure builds in my chest. 'Come in, Charles, the place is in a of a ...'

'I'm sorry to spring it on you like this but I tried calling, I think your mobile is dead.'

'Is it?' My memory isn't fully into focus yet but all the terrible things I'd imagined had happened to me have now been blown clear out of the water. Attempting to cover my uncertainty, I blurt out, 'How did you find me?'

'Ah,' his deep blue eyes twinkle mischievously. 'I have my ways.'

That's unnerving, but I decide not to challenge it for the moment.

'Listen Penny, how'd you fancy going out for dinner; there's an Italian restaurant just up the road from here, if that's alright with you.'

My watch shows it's already five-past seven. 'Thanks, that'd be great.' My brain's still racing but starting to gather my wits. 'I'll just go and get changed.' I point to the counter separating the kitchenette from the living room. 'There's an open bottle of wine over there, help yourself.'

'Thanks.' Taking a mobile phone out of his pocket, he eyes the bottle of Sainsbury's house Merlot suspiciously. 'Do you mind if I make a couple of calls?'

'No, go ahead.' Taking a few deep breaths, I'm slowly getting my emotions under control and recall that I was a willing participant in our love-making although the effect of the drugs must have played a part. I've never had a one night stand before, but on the plus side, I couldn't have behaved too badly or he wouldn't have come looking for me.

Casting aside my work garb, I step into a new dress, tights and heels. Luckily, I'd washed my hair first thing this morning and trust that the smell of something called mimosa-exotica might still linger. I muss it up then use my little finger to wipe smears of lipstick from the corners of my mouth. Taking one last look in the mirror, I look flushed but hey, not too shabby. Trying to look serene and calm, I stroll into the living room. He's still on the phone speaking sharply to someone, but on seeing me, abruptly finishes.

'Sorry about that, business matters, and problems.' He slips the phone into his inside jacket pocket and gives me a smile. 'You look very nice.'

'Well, thank you, kind sir,' I acknowledge gracefully and, knowing that I'll have to tell him about the baby, ask him to sit down for a moment, he'll probably run a mile when I tell him. 'Charles,' I try looking directly into his eyes but find it difficult. 'I have to explain something to you.'

'You're not throwing me out, are you?'

'No, no,' I laugh. 'Nothing like that.'

'Okay,' he looks at me guardedly. 'Go ahead.'

'You'll probably find this very strange and actually, it is, but after you left the party I was very ill. My drink had been spiked.'

'Fuck!' He's genuinely shocked. 'I hope you're not pinning it on me.'

'No. Paula found out later that it was the man *you* helped to throw out, Mike Burgess.'

'Oh him, yes, I remember. He was a weirdo. I saw him bothering you and a couple of others.'

'The trouble was that the drug - whatever it was - had a delayed action because it only fully kicked in after you left. I lost my memory of everything that happened from the time I arrived at Paula's until I woke up the next day, feeling like death. That whole period was a complete blank.'

'Wow, that's bizarre. How long was it before you got your memory back?'

'Twenty-seven days.'

Giving me an odd look, he mulls over what I've just said. 'But hang on, it's the twenty-seventh today.'

I nod. 'It was only now, when you crept up behind me in the dark and gave me the fright of my life and ...'

'Sorry about that.'

'That's okay,' I laugh. 'And I saw your face, you know, when I switched the light on, that's when everything suddenly came back to me.'

'What, just now?' His expression is one of utter amazement. 'Was it the shock or the sight of my ugly face?'

'I don't know, but whatever it was, it worked.'

He purses his lips and gives a silent whistle. 'Phew, I hope you don't mind but I need something strong to drink, brandy maybe?'

'Yes, there's half a bottle in the cupboard under the sink, help yourself.'

Heart still racing, I watch as he strides into the kitchenette, finds the brandy, and pours himself a large measure. 'Can I get you one?'

'No thanks.'

Settling back in the chair, he gives me a questioning look. 'I'm dreading asking you this but during your *blackout*, did you remember me and our time together?'

I shake my head. 'No, 'fraid not.'

His hand trembles as he takes a mouthful of brandy, grimacing as he does so. Ha, that cheap Spanish liquor has that effect on most people.

Coughing slightly, he continues. 'I remember *everything* that happened and can assure you that I didn't take advantage of you in any way. I *honestly* didn't know about the drugs.'

'It's okay, I believe you,' I say as composed as possible. 'We only found out about the drugs several days later when two other girls told Paula that their drinks had been tampered with. You see, at first Paula didn't believe me thinking I'd had too much to drink. But what happened to me wasn't your fault.'

He gives that attractive smile of his which makes me go weak again. 'Phew,' he gasps, 'I need some air, are you still game for that dinner.'

'Yes.' Standing up ready to leave, I realise that I still haven't told him about the baby. Damn.

Shrugging on our coats, we head for the door. Unlike most of my ex's, Charles is the perfect gentleman, holding the outside door open and carefully shepherding me to the inside of the pavement, before taking my arm as we manoeuvre around other pedestrians. His touch is gentle yet firm.

La Sentore is half empty and he chooses a booth against the wall near the back, away from the other diners. The decor is mainly red - red carpets (shabby), walls and even the table cloths and napkins (thankfully clean). Large, white framed pictures of Tuscany help to tone down the redness. Muted radio is playing Gold FM and Phil Collins comes on singing *"Against All Odds"*. I wonder!

Charles must have an air of importance because as soon as we're seated, a waiter wearing an unnaturally white shirt and bow tie with black slacks, glides silently to our table.

'I'll just have a small glass of red wine with my meal, please.' He shows the merest glimpse of surprise before ordering the same for himself. Quickly studying the menu, I ask for the anti pasta followed by spaghetti carbonare. Either out of politeness or joint compatibility, he has the same.

Glancing up, his smile is cautious.

'Charles, how did you *really* know where I live and my mobile number.'

'Ah,' he smiles sheepishly. 'I should have told you straight away, it was Paula who told me.'

'But I spoke to her this afternoon and she didn't say anything.'

'I know, because I rang her after you. You see, I've been out of the country since New Year only arriving back in Heathrow early this morning, and then spent the day at work.' The waiter brings our drinks and Charles proffers his glass to make a toast. 'It's good to see you again, Penny Lane,' he laughs, 'Paula told me your surname. Are you from Liverpool?' He half-sings, *"beneath the blue suburban skies"*.

'No, I'm not and I've been teased all my life.' I realise I'm smiling. Should I start by announcing I'm pregnant or shall I have a termination without telling him? I'll put that dilemma on hold until I know him better. 'So, do you work for the Foreign Office like Paula?'

'No, I don't.'

'Oh! But she met you there.'

'Yes, I know.' He doesn't volunteer any other information which I find a little annoying.

'You're not being very open with me, are you? Where do you work?' Out of sheer frustration, I almost add *for God's sake*.

Taking his time, as though mulling over what to say, he looks directly into my eyes. 'I graduated as a geologist from Sheffield Uni, but didn't take it any further. Officially, I'm a security consultant for the HESEC Corporation, you may have heard of them.'

'Yes, but what's geology got to do with security?'

Again he hesitates. 'I don't talk about my work openly but,' he looks around making sure no-one's within hearing distance. 'Ah, wait a minute, you work at the Home Office so you must be covered by the official secrets act and have all the extra security checks.'

'Of course.'

'Even so, I'd like you to promise not to repeat any of this. Would you do that for me?'

Curiouser and curiouser, what on earth can be so secretive? I have the distinct feeling he's not being totally honest with me but decide, for now, to give him my promise.

He looks reassured. 'To put it briefly, HESEC provides freelances for the FO - bodyguards, surveillance, special service forces with skills of close protection, clandestine entry in hostile foreign countries. But if anything goes wrong, they don't want the blame traced to them – we're deniable, off balance sheet, the dirty end.'

Almost breathless, I ask. 'Do you kill people?'

'Only bad people.'

'Only what?' I yell, freaking out. 'What the hell does that mean?'

He sighs and gestures for me to keep my voice down. 'It's not a regular thing, believe me. Only twice and it was a case of him or me – I had to do it.'

'Wow, like spooks,' unsure where this is leading.

'Well, sort of. HESEC has a ghost section that, to the world at large, doesn't exist. Neither MI5 or MI6 have any jurisdiction over us, we report to Downing Street through a small but secretive subdivision at the FO. And my job is to implement some of this, er, let's call it, *unregulated work.*'

This sounds like a script from a gangster film. 'I want to know why you're telling me this.'

A look flashes across his face, too fast for me to read. 'I hadn't planned to, not yet anyway, even my family doesn't know it all, or my friends.'

Noticing my look of scepticism, he awkwardly shifts in his chair before looking directly into my eyes. 'Penny, while I was away, I thought about you a lot. We had fun at the party, didn't we?'

'From what I remember, yes.'

He smiles that smile of his again. My heart skips a dozen beats this time.

'The first time ever I saw you face.'

'You're not going to sing, are you?'

'No.' He laughs. 'You'll be glad of that. I just liked your face, you know, when we met.'

'I'm trying to remember.'

'I can tell within a minute if I'd like to see a face again ... you I mean. Remember this picture?' He scrolls down on his phone and shows it to me.

'Oh God, I look rather ... '

'I took it on the night.'

'Yes, I can see that. It doesn't flatter me very much.'

There's that smile again. 'I love it. In Africa, I looked at it every night before going to bed. You're very special, you know.'

'Thank you very much, kind sir, but I've never considered my looks as special. The bridge of my nose is too thin and a bit stubby at the end.'

'Yes, I know.'

'My ears stick out but I try and hide it with my hair.'

'I had noticed.'

'And my eyes are too big.'

'A little, yes.'

'And my chin ... hey, you could argue, you know.'

'Why?'

'You're pulling my leg.'

'Not that I'd noticed, I like the way you are.'

'That sounds like another song title.'

'Just the way you are tonight,' he laughs. 'I'll arrange the music later.'

Can he be real? If he's making a play for me he's definitely succeeding. I wouldn't mind seeing his face every day – waking up in bed. 'I'm glad you came to see me tonight.' I give my well-practised, seductive smile.

'So am I.' His expression turns more serious and he fidgets in his chair. 'I'm thirty-four now,' he blurts out. 'I've had my fair share of girl friends ...'

I'm sure he has is my immediate thought.

'But none of them like you. It may seem crazy only having met you once but I want *you* to know *who* and *what* I am.'

Bloody hell, is he going to declare his love for me? He seems very pleasant. What am I saying, *pleasant*, he's brilliant and my poor crazy hormones must be in overdrive because I feel an instinctive sexual urge within me. I want to kiss him more than anything in the world. I'm aware of him looking at me, as a man really looks at a woman, noting different aspects: my hair, my make-up, my neck and the swell of my breasts beneath my dress. It excites me. I feel a physical urge to be in bed with him, his naked body against mine. It's not the sex act, I just want to hold him close, the father of my unborn child. Fantasy over, I'm going to ruin everything by telling him my secret before things go too far.

'You've gone quiet,' he pushes his empty plate away.

'Sorry.' My heart wants me to forget but here my head takes over and I blurt out. 'Charles, I'm pregnant.'

Open-mouthed, he looks at me to see if he heard me correctly.

I nod my head. 'Yes, I'm pregnant.'

Carefully putting his cutlery down, he points his index finger at his chest. 'Me?'

'Yes.' Unlike Paula, he doesn't ask about the possibility of other partners.

Before he can gather himself to speak, I say, 'You needn't worry, it's not your responsibility, it was my fault and I can easily terminate it.'

Choking slightly, a tiny strand of spaghetti sticks below his bottom lip, he's about to reply when the mobile in his pocket gives a couple of loud beeps. 'Excuse me a second,' he swallows and coughs. Checking the screen, his expression changes to annoyance. 'Hell, I'm sorry Penny but I have to go. It's urgent. He stands, finds his wallet and pulls out two crisp fifty-pound notes, waves to the waiter and leaves them on the table. 'I really am sorry about this, honestly I am, but I have to go immediately. If you've finished, I'd like to take you home. My car's parked at the back.'

Distrust bubbles inside me. Putting on a brave face, my sceptical mind believes he's rigged his phone to ring whenever he needs an escape. 'I understand,' I mutter. 'And yes, I'd like a lift.'

'Can we meet tomorrow for lunch. There's a restaurant in Henrietta Street called *The China Wall* and it's not too far from your work. I'll book it for twelve noon. Is that alright with you?'

I shake my head. 'That's a bit difficult, my boss won't let me go for lunch until one, and then I have to be back within the hour.'

The waiter, noticing the money on the table, rushes fawningly to open the door. Taking our coats, Charles leads the way to his car, an impressive Jaguar sports.

'What's your boss's name and title?'

'I doubt if you could help, Charles, but for what it's worth, he's William A Bunter, Home Office Foreign Services Controller.'

Nodding his head, he drives out of the car park and quickly takes me the short distance to my home. 'I'll fix it, Penny, and I'll see you at noon tomorrow.' He leans over and kisses me lingeringly on the lips. 'Until tomorrow.'

CHAPTER FOUR
JANUARY 28th

Amazingly, miracles can happen. It's eleven-thirty and just a minute ago, fat Billy Bunter told me that I can take the rest of the day off, no reason given. If that's not a miracle, then I don't know what is. Anyway, it's given me a real boost. From the world's leading exponent of face-folding misery on his vein-streaked face, who considers women to be ticking hormone bombs, I could tell he hated doing it, but old Fatso got in some retaliation by telling me in no uncertain terms that I'd better be at my desk by nine prompt in the morning to avoid a final warning. His reluctant benevolence must have come from on high. Could it possibly be Charles? If so, then, it's a bit scary, how could he have influence on the senior hierarchy of the Home Office?

Anyhow, whoever it was, my lunch date at the China Wall seems to be back on track but will *he* be there waiting for me? Feeling rather chuffed at this sudden change of fortune, I go to the cloakroom and tidy myself up. I've spent most of the last fourteen hours or so, wondering what Charles will say about the baby, but my reflection in the mirror provides no answer. Deliberately taking my time, I watch the foyer clock reach twelve before going out to hail a taxi. I'll arrive a fashionable ten minutes late because ... I'm worth it.

Damn, best laid plans et cetera. It takes over ten minutes just to get a taxi and, in heavy traffic, my ten minutes late has turned into twenty-six. Hurrying past the saluting Chinese warrior doorman at the China Wall, I rush inside hoping to catch sight of an anxious-looking Charles, nervously biting his nails in anticipation of my arrival. Who am I kidding? There's no sign of him.

Trying to look composed, I take in the resplendent interior of the restaurant, the plush red furniture, crisp white tablecloths and the indigenous artwork on the pale-grey walls, it has an expensive air about it. I approach the China doll behind the Reception desk, a flowery scent of perfume surrounds her. 'I'm meeting Mr Charles Temple for lunch.'

Her white, made-up face, with bright red lips is like a mask and I apprehensively watch as her long, red fingernail trace the printout of bookings. 'Madam, there is no reservation in Mr Temple's name.'

'Please check again. I was supposed to be here at noon, and maybe he's left thinking I wasn't coming.'

'No, Madam. There's nothing in that name all day.'

My heart sinks, broken into little pieces. He's dumped me and I don't even have his phone number. Should I stay or leave? Oh, hang on. I go back to *Miss Suzie Wong* at Reception. 'Could you check under the name HESEC?'

'No, Madam, nothing for HESEC.' From her expressionless painted face, it's impossible to know if she's sympathetic or smirking.

I ask myself, why am I here and what the hell do I do now? There's no point phoning the HESEC office because Charles told me he works for a department that *doesn't exist.* I could sit at the bar and order something very strong but what's the point? It's obvious he's not coming. I might as well leave and catch the first train home, tuck into some comfort food and have another good cry.

My shoulders sag, but as I make my way out, *Suzie Wong* suddenly calls. 'Excuse me, Madam, are you Miss Wane?'

My heart leaps. 'Yes, Miss Lane, that's me.'

'There a message for you, Miss Wane. Your lunch date will be fifty minutes late.'

'My lunch date! Do you mean Mr Temple?'

She holds up a memo pad with a message written on it. 'It doesn't say, Madam.'

Once again, my poor, suffering emotions are all jumbled up. What the hell is going on? The restaurant clock shows twelve-thirty five but will there be another disappointing twist?

My new friend, *Susie,* calls a waiter who shows me to a table and hands me the wine list. Out of a list of dozens, I choose a bottle of red priced at forty-eight pounds; it's one of the cheapest. He returns and pours me a glass. I take a sip without tasting. I'm not at all relaxed, only apprehensive.

My lunch date, and *it is Charles,* strolls in exactly fifty minutes late. His attractive smile makes me forget the doubts I've had, especially as he gives me a gentle kiss on the cheek, apologising profusely for keeping me waiting. He also apologises for leaving me so abruptly last night. There's a genuine look of concern on his face, or is it just an act?

'I thought you'd stood me up.' I try and make it sound as if I'm miffed. 'There's no reservation in your name.'

'Really?' He frowns shaking his head. 'Oh, it must be one of the secretaries again.'

I'm not completely satisfied. 'And was it you who got me off work this morning?'

'Ah,' he smiles. 'I have my ways.' Is he deliberately encouraging this air of mystery?

'And what was last night's crisis?'

'It's to do with a small package, an extremely important package I brought back from Africa. It went missing. Anyway, it's been traced to another office so, panic over.'

The waiter arrives to take our order. After asking for my preferences, I let him decide. It's a nice feeling and quite a change being out with a decisive man.

'Before we got interrupted last night,' Charles pours wine into his glass and tops up mine. 'You'd just given me the startling news about being pregnant. How are you feeling?'

'Apart from early mild morning sickness, I feel great.'

'You said you'll have a termination. Do you mean it?'

'Yes, after all, it's only biology.'

He nods and takes his time before speaking. 'Penny, I'm committed to a contract with HESEC for another two years but after that, I'd like to settle down and have a family.'

What am I to make of that? Crossing my fingers, I ask. 'And do you have anyone in mind?' If ever there was a leading question, then this was it. I hold my breath.

He shrugs as though regretting being so vague. 'Penny, what can I say? My contract will keep me out of the country almost all the time and sometimes there's danger involved. It would be wrong of me to ask anyone to wait that long.'

Disappointed, I mumble. 'Yes, I see.' Wondering what to say next, my brain must have flipped because I ask him straight out. 'Do you want me to keep the baby?'

He swirls the wine round his glass. 'I'll leave that decision to you, I can't make any commitments. I hope you understand.'

'That's okay, I do understand,' which isn't true because I'm not sure if he wants me to say I'll keep the baby and wait for him. I would if he asked.

Before we can utter another word, two smartly-dressed men stride into the restaurant heading directly for our table. Charles introduces me to one of them, Tim, who just grunts an offhand acknowledgement, whereas the second man, a muscular looking brute if I ever saw one, stands back a few paces. Tim deliberately turns his back on me while bending over to whisper something to Charles. At the same time, the other man unobtrusively sidles up to an adjacent table occupied by an Oriental-looking man, I'm astonished to hear them speaking Mandarin. The world of Charles Temple is full of surprises.

'Look,' Charles addresses Tim in his normal voice, 'I know it's bloody serious, of course I do, but there's nothing we can fix 'til morning. Arrange a meeting with Thrimby for eight o'clock, and then we'll get to the bottom of it.'

Tim straightens to leave. 'Okay, Holly, you're right, I'll see you then.' And with that, they leave as quickly as they'd arrived, although I have a strong suspicion that the second man tried to hide the fact that he'd been conversing with the Chinaman.

'That was all a bit strange.' I tensely finger my wine glass. 'What's it all about?'

'Oh, it's okay, Penny.' He replies casually. 'Tim and Hal are both colleagues of mine, and there's a bit of a flap on in the office.'

'Is it still to do with that missing package?'

Making sure nobody's within hearing range, he lowers his voice. 'Yes.'

'But when Tim spoke to you, you said it was serious.'

He raises his eyebrows mischievously. 'Oh, did I?'

'You know damn well you did. Look, Charles, I know you're in some kind of hush, hush security business and it's none of my concern, but I find it all a bit disconcerting.'

'You're right and I'm sorry.' He reaches across the table and gives my hand a gentle squeeze. 'There's skulduggery afoot amongst some of the top people at HESEC. That's all I'm going to say now, and remember the promise you gave me last night, not to repeat any of this, must still apply.'

'Of course I understand, but are you in danger?'

'I don't think so.'

Feeling reassured, I recall something Tim said. 'Oh, and why did Tim call you Holly - that's a girl's name!'

My question doesn't seem to register at first then, blinking a couple of times, he laughs. 'What? Oh that, oh it's just a silly nickname.' He gives my hand another squeeze. 'Would you mind if we don't talk about it anymore?'

Although I nod in agreement, I hate this ongoing air of mystery about him and his work, but if that's what he wants, then I'll keep mum. My head's full of conflicting thoughts and it's difficult to know how he truly feels about me, but if our relationship is going to develop in the way I hope, there'll be plenty of time to find out more about the *real him* and what he gets up to.

'Do you fancy a walk and a breath of fresh air?' He asks after settling the bill. 'I'll show you where I live, it's only ten minutes away.'

'Yes, I'd like that.' What's going on in his mind, I wonder? More sex? No, surely not. All the intrigue must be playing silly games with my brain.

It's another overcast day and Charles gently takes my arm as we stroll along Henrietta Street, avoiding Covent Garden which is heaving with people, into the quieter Tavistock Street. Delivery vans and taxis manoeuvre their way along the narrow road and a boy, balancing on a skateboard, weaves between the pedestrians. Passing a shop with a reflecting glass panel at the side - a bit like looking into a car's rear view mirror - I notice Tim and Hal stealthily following close behind, keeping a few people between us.

'Charles, do you realise we're being followed.'

He scowls, looking annoyed.

'It's Tim and the one who speaks Mandarin.'

Giving me a puzzled look, he asks, 'Hal? How do you know that?'

'I spent two years in China and learnt the language. While you and Tim were huddled together, Hal was talking to a Chinese man at the next table. He said something along the lines that *he'd get what he wants within a few days.'*

As we turn into Wellington Street, Charles is lost in thought, giving the impression that it's confirmed a theory of his.

'Here, we are.' He stops outside a double-panelled door set between *Suzanne's Boutique* and the *HotSpot Mobile Phone* shop. The name, St Ives Court 1887, is neatly chiselled in the stone mantle above the entrance, and there's CCTV cameras on either side. 'I'm on the first floor at the back.'

'How can you afford to live here?' I'm amazed that anyone, other than an Arab Sheik, could afford an apartment in this location.

'Oh, it's not mine,' he laughs. 'It belongs to HESEC. It's my pad whenever I'm in town and it's close to the office.'

'Lucky you, the rent must be cost them a fortune.'

'You're probably right anyway, come on inside.' He taps a security code into a concealed keypad hidden behind a pillar then, after hearing two confirming beeps, uses a key to open the heavy door. Before following him in, I check for signs of Tim or Hal. They're nowhere to be seen.

Charles leads me into an elegantly-decorated lobby which opens up to accommodate two lifts. The ride is incredibly smooth and there's only a slight *swish* as the door to the first floor glides open. It's very peaceful after the hustle and bustle outside, and small bright lights set into the ceiling illuminate the way along a blue-carpeted, windowless corridor to Apartment 3.

Suddenly, he stops in mid-stride, gesturing me to stay behind. I notice his apartment door is open a crack and, oh my God, he takes a gun out from his inside jacket pocket, just like a cop in the movies. Trembling, I stand well back while he carefully pushes the door wide with his foot. Holding his gun with a double grip, he slowly and silently steps inside. I faintly hear a man's voice – it sounds foreign – and the only word I can hear is *package*.

Charles shouts. 'Drop your gun'. There are sounds of a scuffle and furniture being smashed, then BANG, BANG. My heart's in my mouth as a bullet rips into the door frame, and I instinctively fling myself to the floor. And the other shot … oh no, Charles staggers backwards through the doorway, the gun falling from his limp hand. Turning towards me, his eyes are glazing over and there's a bullet hole in his forehead. He crashes heavily to the floor, bright-red blood oozing from his head onto the pale-blue carpet. I want to scream but my throat's seized up. I'm shaking, vomit is rising in my mouth and I feel dizzy then … darkness.

Chapter Five
January 28th

I must have fainted. Trembling like a leaf, my eyes slowly manage to focus, and what I focus on is Charles, lying motionless, blood oozing from his head. Hysterically, I scream and scream when suddenly I'm grabbed roughly from behind, an arm tight around my chest and a large, calloused hand over my mouth. Struggling to get free, I can't - it hurts. He's strong with dreadful body odour, his breath on the side of my face stinks.

Although watering, my eyes aren't covered and I see Tim creeping towards Charles's prone body. He feels for a pulse in his neck, then shakes his head. 'He's gone.'

Numb with shock, I watch as he takes a gun out of his pocket, just as Charles had a few minutes before, then silently goes through the open door into the flat. 'There's no one here, the window's open.'

I summon up all my inner strength and in one quick movement, twist my head a few inches to give out another scream. My head's sharply jerked back and I'm forced to stop.

'Get the bitch out of here,' Tim orders my captor, the side of his face now visible. It's Hal. Half dragging me all the way out of the building, he almost throws me into the passenger seat of a car with darkened windows, parked outside the front door. Running round, he jumps behind the wheel.

'You're going home.' Hal growls. 'No argument.'

I scream, and receive a vicious slap across the face.

'Shut the fuck up or I'll tape your mouth shut.'

I obey, still shaking uncontrollably. I can't understand, with the shooting and my screams, why nobody appears to see what is going on.

'But what about Charles,' I cry. 'He needs to be in hospital.'

Giving a frown, he asks, 'Who?'

'Charles, Charles Temple, he's been shot.'

'You must be crazy, woman.' He ridicules. 'You saw nothing. Nothing happened. Now, where do you live?'

'But the ambulance.'

'He's dead, you stupid bitch. Now, again, where the fuck do you live?'

There's no escape, I'm Hal's captive. I give him my address. Feeling shocked, shattered and scared, there's nothing to do but cling onto the faint hope that Tim will get an ambulance. As Hal's driving, I ask him what's going on but he yells at me to shut-up. I'm powerless. At least, the route we're taking is south-west along the A3, heading for Surbiton and not somewhere out in the sticks to quietly bump me off.

Arriving at my flat, I feel easier but to my dismay, Hal insists on coming inside. In my kitchenette, opening and closing cupboards, he finds my almost-empty bottle of brandy. Pouring the dregs into a glass, he hands it to me. 'Drink this.'

The first sip of rough liquor revives me slightly but I can't get out of my mind, the sight of my wonderful Charles, his life blood seeping away.

Hal pulls a small, leather box from his pocket and takes out a brown pill. 'Here, this'll make you sleep.'

Sleep! That's impossible. I take it with a gulp of brandy and then it dawns that it could be poison, like a cyanide pill. Oh hell. But I'm certain he'd use force if I refuse.

After emptying the glass, he sits next to me on the sofa. There's that smell again. 'Now listen carefully, you have to forget everything you saw today. If you blab your fucking mouth off, you'll be in deep shit.'

Raising my voice, I cry, 'Forget! How can I forget, Charles was my fiancé.' It's not true but it might make him more caring as he is supposed to be his colleague.

Frowning, he takes a paper from his inside pocket and thrusts it in front of me. 'Sign this, it's the Official Secrets Act, and that means you'll go to jail if you repeat anything you saw today.'

This is stupid, but I sign. My face is already sore and I don't want another slap. He doesn't know that I'm already subject to the Act.

'Now go to bed, sleep, and when you wake, forget everything.'

There's no point in arguing. He's a threatening looking bully and the cold grey eyes boring into me are cruel. Pocketing the signed paper, he leaves abruptly, slamming the door behind him.

I lie back in my chair and cry. For how long I'm not sure but I'm still awake. But ever so gradually, I'm starting to feel muzzy so that pill must be working, either making me sleep or ... oh God. I want my mum. I could phone her but what would I say? If the pill is poison, then she should find my body before anyone else. Taking a scrap of paper, I try to write a note but my hand's unsteady. I tell her to contact the police and that Hal from HESEC poisoned me and that, lover Charles Temple from er, oh, I'm woozy, er - shot dead in his er, can't remember - very sleepy, my eyes close and I drift away.

I'm awake. Wide awake *and* alive. Dragging myself slowly up from the sofa, I stretch to relieve the stiffness in my limbs. It's two o'clock in the morning so I've been asleep for around nine hours. Hal was right about the pill and thank God my wild imaginings were wrong - it wasn't poison. If the pill was intended to erase my memory of everything that happened then it hasn't worked. Charles's killing comes back to me in vivid focus, triggering trembling all over my body, and tears well-up in my eyes.

'I didn't know him that well.' I sob out loud, although there's no one here to listen. 'But he was special to me. Well, he would be wouldn't he?'

Wiping away the tears, I breathe deeply trying to pull myself together. Oh hang on, I'm pregnant, how could I forget that? What a terrible start in life for the poor little bastard - conceived in a sea of drugs, traumatised to the core when I witnessed its father shot, and then to cap it all, Hal's pill must have given those little baby-cells one hell of a jolt. I wonder if it's still alive? But, of course, I'm having a termination so it doesn't matter, does it? The way I feel, I wouldn't mind terminating myself. I stop crying, at least for the time being, and now have to decide what to do next. Hal made it crystal clear that I mustn't say a word to anyone on fear of ... God knows.

Feeling grubby, I have a bath and go to bed in the hope of getting a few more hours' sleep. The problem is, I'm not tired. Closing my eyes, I'm about to drift off but my mind's far too active and the image of Charles keeps flashing into my head. I get up and put the TV on; shopping channels but that doesn't matter.

I wake with the surprising realisation that I slept after all. It's five past six and the BBC morning news is on. I want to see if there's anything about yesterday's shooting. There are reports about Syrian refugees, revenge killings in the Central African Republic, flood damage in Somerset and more, but nothing about Charles. Maybe it's too soon. But no, shooting incidents are usually shown within an hour or two with TV cameras focused on the roped-off crime scene and reporters interviewing nearby residents.

Switching the set off, I want to do something but what? Telling my parents would be a mistake. Anyhow, mum would insist on me going to live with them. No thanks. I can't involve anyone at work, that just leaves Paula. She's trustworthy and, of course, she brought Charles and me together in the first place. I'll call her this evening.

So, should I go to work or phone in sick? I'll go, staying at home all day would drive me crazy.

Arriving at nine-thirty, I'm met by misery- guts himself, Bossy Billy Bunter. 'You're late again, Miss Lane. I've warned you before.'

'Sorry Mr Bunter, I overslept.'

With that, he turns his back and stalks away. I was expecting worse. For some reason, he doesn't give me the final warning he'd threatened me with. Has he been warned off? Well, the way I'm feeling, I wouldn't care if he did fire me.

Sitting at my desk I switch my terminal on but my brain is all over the place and I distractedly shuffle a few papers around. To do any serious work is impossible because I want to cry all the time. Why was Charles murdered? Is it secret hush-hush government business or could it be gangland crime? And what's in the package the killer was looking for? It must be very valuable if they had to kill for it. But Charles told me that it had been found so ... I'm totally confused.

No more messing around, I'm going to the police to tell them everything about the shooting in St Ives Court, how Charles was killed, and the role played by Tim and Hal, and to hell with Hal and his threats. When I tell Old Fatso I'm ill and going to the doctor, he flings his arms up in despair, his face as sour as a pickled egg, and angrily stomps away.

Surprisingly, the Reception desk at Charing Cross Police Station is fairly quiet even though there is much bustling activity. Uniformed and civilian people of all ages are rushing in and out of unmarked doors, many needing a keyed in password before opening. A large arrow indicates where I should stand. There are only four people in the queue. Peering at my reflection in the glass-covered notice boards, I make sure my mascara hasn't run again. After about ten minutes, I'm at the front.

'Yes, madam, and how may we help?' The desk sergeant is a heavy, rather ugly man with a broken nose, short grey hair, and large sticky-out ears.

'I witnessed the murder yesterday of Mr Charles Temple and I've come to give a statement.'

A look of suspicion crosses his face, probably reserved for crazy people. 'And where, madam, did this murder take place?'

'At St Ives Court, in Wellington Street, Charles Temple was killed – murdered – shot in the head. You must know about it.'

Staring straight into my face, he expresses each word carefully. 'Not at this very moment, madam.'

'But that's ridiculous,' I reply sharply. 'It happened almost twenty-four hours ago, right here, in central London.'

Arching his eyebrows slightly, he retorts, 'I'll check for you, madam. May I take your name and address?'

Turning to enter my data on his keyboard, his forehead creases in surprise when I tell him my full name, but I'm used to that and pass him my driving licence which brings the faintest hint of a smile. Using an internal phone, he cups the mouthpiece in his large, gnarled hand so I can't hear what he's saying. Finishing his conversation, he turns back to face me. 'Please take a seat in the waiting area, madam, and someone will be with you shortly.' Frustrated that I'm not immediately whisked into an interview room, I do as requested.

Feeling tense and emotional, I sit watching everyone around me. The man next to me loudly slurping coffee from a Styrofoam cup, a black woman cleaner languidly sweeping the floor between the aisles, a young lady sobbing against a man's shoulder, a group of Arabs talking heatedly amongst themselves - we're all waiting for something to happen. There's nothing to do but wait, my head full of conflicting thoughts. Maybe they're getting MI5 or MI6 to see me, Charles was probably on some secret government business. Twenty minutes passes before a fresh-faced young officer, Detective Constable Hythe, holding a clip board, escorts me to an interview room. He only looks about twenty-four or twenty-five.

'Is anyone else coming?' I ask. 'A senior officer?'

'No, madam,' he's clearly riled by the insinuation of my question. 'Now then, Miss Penny Lane, I'm informed that you are reporting a murder, is that correct?' His speech is as plodding as the desk sergeant's.

'Yes, that's right, yesterday, early afternoon, just before two fifteen. But surely you must already know about it.'

The look on his face is a cross between distrust and tedium as though he gets half a dozen of these reports every day. 'And *whom*,' like my old English teacher, he emphasises the 'm', 'Was murdered?'

'I've already told the sergeant, it's Charles Temple of HESEC, who works in a *ghost* department.' My inward sigh doesn't go unnoticed. 'With two of his colleagues,' I add, 'Tim and Hal they also witnessed his killing.'

Pen dangling in the air, DC Hythe gives me a searching look. He repeats what I've just said at the same pace as he writes it down. 'Let me see if I've got this right. Mr Charles Temple of HESEC's ghost department was murdered at St Ives Court, Wellington Street at around fourteen fourteen hours,' he's momentarily puzzled at his own interpretation of *just before quarter past two*. 'Witnessed by you and two of Mr Temple's colleagues, Tim and Hal, also of HESEC's ghost department. And their surnames are?'

'I don't know.'

'Surnames unknown.'

I nod my head. 'Yes, that's correct. And straight after that, Hal took me home, forcing me to sign the Official Secrets Act and making me swallow a sleeping pill.' This last piece of information adds to the bad vibes I'm already getting from the constable.

'Would there have been any space ships or aliens around at the time?' he smirks.

Seething with anger, I bang my clenched fist down on the table. 'How dare you,' I shout. 'It happened, exactly as I've described.'

He mumbles an apology. 'It's just that er ...' Shamefacedly looking at his notes, he hands the pad over, asking me to check that it's all correct. It is, nothing about space ships so I sign it at the bottom.

He now gives me a stern look. 'I have to inform you, Miss Lane, that no shooting or murder incident has been reported at St Ives Court, or anywhere in that vicinity. Before seeing you, I also established that there is nobody in HESEC called Charles Temple.'

'But that's because he works for HESEC's ghost department, it's kept secret from the public.' It sounds pathetically weak and this fact reflects in his expression.

'For your further information, I contacted the caretaker of St Ives Court who confirms that there was no shooting incident of any kind, either yesterday or, in fact, any other day.'

'But that's crazy,' I yell. 'I was there, I saw it for myself. Charles Temple was murdered. Shot dead with blood all over the floor and a bullet shattered the door frame, I'll show you.'

Putting his hand to his mouth, he gives a slight cough, 'I must warn you, madam that it's a serious offence to waste police time, carrying serious penalties.'

'But it's all true, I can prove it.'

'And how would you do that, madam?'

'By showing you the blood stains and bullet hole.'

Glancing at his watch, he says, 'I *will* come with you, because the caretaker of St Ives Court has kindly agreed to let us in. He'll be there for the next forty-five minutes so we should leave straight away.'

Angrily wittering on to himself that it's a waste of time, I follow DC Hythe out of a side door towards the car park, half-running to keep up with his long strides. It's a blustery, winter's day, a few light clouds are blowing across the cold sky while the pale rays of a watery sun struggle vainly to break through the gloom. Lights from the windows above reflect dimly on the damp tarmac. Although it would only be a fifteen minute walk to Charles's place, I'm relieved we're going by car, my first time in a police vehicle.

The mid-afternoon traffic is particularly heavy. 'Can't use the damn siren for this one,' he complains, sighing heavily as he's forced to wait for traffic lights to change.

'Hurry the fuck up,' he grumbles at the un-obliging inanimate objects. The expletive seems to dissipate his increasingly crabby mood and the traffic gods must have heard as the street beyond the green light suddenly clears. 'Ah, that's better.'

Arriving outside St Ives Court, he manoeuvres to park half on the pavement over double yellow lines, switching on the vehicle's blue flashing lamp to show it's official. We're obviously expected because the door of the apartment block is immediately opened by a squat, rubber-faced little man, swamped in a massive camel coat.

'Mr Pooley,' DC Hythe questions. 'Are you the caretaker here?'

'Building engineer, mate,' Mr Pooley corrects him emphatically. He looks at me out of the corner of his eye and his lips twitch. 'Is this 'er, then?'

'This is Miss Lane, yes.'

'What's it all about? A load of fucking nonsense if you ask me. A fucking murder and fucking blood all over the place! You must be fucking crazy.' Blotting out the repetitive expletives, my linguistic training easily picks up his feeble attempt at a Cockney accent.

'Thank you, Mr Pooley,' the DC's stern words endeavour to control his bad language. 'Kindly take us to apartment number three on the first floor.'

'Alright, mate, this way.' His head projects unnaturally from his voluminous garment, and as we're heading for the lift, his coat fleetingly flaps open revealing a smart suit and tie. Mr Pooley is not what he seems but, unfortunately, I don't think *PC Plod* noticed.

Inside the entrance area, everything is exactly as it was yesterday. We take the same lift to the first floor and Mr Pooley hesitates as if he's not sure of the way, before proceeding to Charles's apartment.

''Ere we are, mate, number *free*. It's been empty for weeks.'

Oh my God. My jaw drops and my heart pounds almost to bursting as I take in the scene. The pale blue carpet which was covered in Charles's blood just twenty-four hours ago, hasn't even the slightest discolouration.

'Now, Miss Lane,' DC Hythe peers down at me. 'Please show me where the blood stain is?'

Trembling in disbelief, I shakily point to the spot where it should be.

He stoops to take a close look. 'I er, can't see anything. Mr Pooley, can you?'

'No, mate,' he nods in my direction. 'This one 'ere's a nut case.'

'But it must have been changed,' I stutter.

'No it aint.'

Carefully examining the floor, DC Hythe agrees, pointing to signs of normal wear on the carpet. 'It hasn't been changed.' Straightening himself, he gives me a look of irritation. 'I warned you before about wasting police time, Miss Lane, you lied to me.'

'But I didn't,' I yell, tears springing to my eyes. 'This is exactly where Mr Temple was shot and his blood soaked into this carpet. I saw it, I promise.'

45

Shaking his head in annoyance, he goes on. 'And another thing, where might the bullet holes be?'

'Up there on the ... oh hell! It's gone.' The white door frame is intact and I look closely to where the damage was done. Nothing. 'Someone must have repaired it.'

'Don't be daft,' Pooley mocks. 'You're 'avin a larf.'

Checking his notes, DC Hythe asks. 'Who owns the apartment, is it HESEC?'

'I don't know, mate, I'm just the caretaker.'

'The building engineer?' the DC corrects with a wry smile.

Nervously running his hands through his hair, Pooley mutters. 'Yeh, whatever.'

The two men walk towards the lift but before joining them, I touch the door frame with my finger where I'd seen the bullet hole, it's tacky, white paint. 'Hey constable, look at this.' I hold up my finger to show him. 'It's wet paint, the frame has just been repaired.'

'Is it?' Pooley asks in what seems to be genuine surprise., 'Oh I know,' he quickly blusters. 'It's just regular maintenance,' but caught unawares, he forgets his Cockney accent.

DC Hythe nods, accepting Pooley's explanation. 'Let's go, Miss Lane,' he orders curtly. 'I can't spend any more time here.'

I'm close to tears once again as we return to the police station in silence. Am I going mad? With a multitude of thoughts flashing around inside my head, it feels as if it's only a matter of time before it shatters completely. Not only was Charles, himself, a man of mystery, but I saw him murdered and, within the last twenty-four hours, all the evidence has been removed and there's no report of him even being killed. What the hell can I do?

Back in the same interview room, DC Hythe takes out of his notebook and slaps it down on the table. 'You're wasting my time, police time, and ... '

Interrupting forcefully, I yell. 'Didn't you see? Mr Pooley is a phony. That ridiculous coat he was wearing, meant for someone twice his size - he was covering up a smart business suit, a caretaker would have had work clothes or overalls.'

'Are you sure?'

'And he was no more Cockney than you. His accent kept slipping, he's a fraud!'

'And how would you know that?' he smirks. 'Are you an expert?'

'Yes, in fact I am, it's my profession and I'm good at accents. I'd say he's from west Norfolk, just as you are from Manchester.'

'Hey, hang on.' Startled, he eyes me suspiciously. 'How do you know that?'

'I've already told you, I'm a linguist and amongst other things, the way you speak with a flat 'A' gives it away. I think there's been a cover up, everything at Mr Temple's apartment has been changed, making it appear as though nothing has happened, and Mr Pooley is part of it.'

DC Hythe frowns, deep in thought, rubbing his chin. I think he's beginning to have doubts. 'Wait here a moment, Miss Lane, I'll be back in a few minutes.'

Impatiently I wait, but in less than five minutes, he returns with a bad-tempered expression. 'Miss Lane, this is your final warning about wasting police time. I must caution you that if you pursue this matter here, or in any other police station, we will bring charges against you under section 5 of the Criminal Law Act and the CPS will seek the maximum sentence, which is six months imprisonment.'

It's as clear as a crystal hobnob that Detective Constable Plod has been over-ruled because he was starting to believe my story. But why would Charles's death be covered up? Maybe it was top security, just like in the *Spooks* TV series when top Home Office bosses made their own rules, including assassinations. But I work for that same Home Office and have never seen or heard of anything like it. Distraught and feeling my tears starting to flow again, I have a sensation that eyes are watching me as I leave the police station.

Outside, the cold air stings my face so I tighten the scarf firmly around my neck before deciding that there's no point going back to the office. I won't be able to concentrate on translating all that EU Directive rubbish or anything else. Paranoia sets in and I look around a couple of times, but can't see anyone following me. It's nearly four o'clock and already getting dark. At least there's light from street lamps, shop windows and the passing traffic. Taking the tube is an option, but since 7/7, I've avoided using the underground whenever possible, so a brisk walk to Waterloo would be better to clear the confusion in my poor brain.

The train is already on the platform and settling in a window seat, I watch an eclectic mix of passengers gradually filling up the compartment. As the train glides quietly out of the station, I concentrate on trying to make my mind a blank, but my pregnancy immediately jumps in to fill the void. What on earth am I going to do? There's a bit of Charles in me, unless I decide to get rid of it. Urgently needing someone sympathetic to talk to, I rummage through my handbag for my mobile phone to call Paula, and I now remember the battery ran down this morning. Shit.

As I open the door of my apartment, it feels cold and damp so I turn the feeble radiators onto maximum and switch on three bars of my electric fire, to hell with the cost. Holding my coat tightly around me, I stick a frozen meal in the oven and plug in my mobile to bring it back to life. There are two messages from someone called Adele Holbrook; she says it's urgent – extremely urgent. I don't know who she is or what she wants, but it worries me and adds to the psychological battering I've been through during the last two days. Whilst changing in my bedroom, the re-charging mobile rings but I'm too tired to rush back into the living room, so it goes to voice mail. It's that Holbrook woman again with the same insistent message.

I make a mug of tea and decide to return her call, just to get her off my back. It only rings a couple of times before the same voice answers. 'Miss Holbrook, my name's Penny Lane and you left messages for me to call but, if you're selling something, you're wasting your time.'

'Hello Miss Lane, thanks for calling back and no, I'm not selling anything. In fact I've something very important to tell you.' She has a pleasant, well-modulated voice and doesn't sound like a *cold-calling* sales person.

'OK then, what's so important?'

'I know we've never met,' she continues. 'But what I have to tell you is, actually, I'd rather tell you in person than over the phone. I know you live in Surbiton and I could come round to see you or we could meet somewhere else if you prefer.'

How the hell does she know where I live? This is starting to freak-me out. 'Miss Holbrook,' there's a tremor in my voice which I hadn't intended. 'I'd prefer you tell me now. I'm just about to join friends for dinner, and I'm in a bit of a rush.'

'Well, if you're sure. It's bad news I'm afraid.'

Shit, more bad news.

There's a silence and I can almost sense her apprehension through the phone. 'I think you'd better sit down.'

'I am sitting.' I lie again, rummaging in the fridge hoping to find a yoghurt dessert for later.

'Well, it's Nick.' The pitch of her voice softens. 'He's dead ... I'm so sorry.'

'Nick, did you say, dead?'

'Yes, I'm afraid so, he was in a traffic accident yesterday.'

'Oh dear, that is sad but I er, don't think I know anyone called Nick, you may have the wrong name or number. Are you sure you want me, Penny Lane?'

'That's the name Nick gave me with your address in Surbiton and the phone number. He gave me a package for you emphasising that it was for the baby.'

My throat tightens and my heart skips a few beats. This Nick died on the same day that Charles was murdered, and he left a package for me, there's that word *package* again, and it's for the baby. 'Would Nick have another name?' I ask.

'Holbrook. He was my brother, Nick Holbrook.'

This is weird. I'm not sure whether to take her seriously or if it's someone's idea of a sick joke, but from the tone of her voice, she doesn't sound like a crazy person. Just what's going on I haven't a clue but it's too much of a coincidence to tell her to go away. 'Miss Holbrook, where are you calling from?'

'I'm in Kingston, Kingston upon Thames, not far from you.'

'Have you had dinner yet? Because if you haven't, could we meet. Do you know *La Sentore*, it's an Italian restaurant on Hook Road? There's a car park at the rear.'

'I'll find it. But I thought you said you were going out with friends.'

'I lied.'

'Oh, I see. I'll be there in half an hour. Is that okay?'

'Yes, that's fine. Oh by the way, bring a photo of Nick with you.'

CHAPTER SIX
JANUARY 28th

The spray of hot water cascades over my body, easing the tension in my neck and shoulders. Reaching for a towel warming on the radiator, I reluctantly step out of the shower. Padding into the bedroom, I dress in my new purple cashmere sweater and warm trousers, and apply a minimum of make-up to my weary-looking face.

Wild thoughts are spinning round in my head - is the death of this guy, Nick, anything to do with Charles? I don't understand. She said it was for the baby and only Charles knew that.

It's raining outside so I pull on my old, shower-proof and hood and walk briskly to the restaurant. Hanging my dripping coat inside the entrance, I see a young woman, sitting alone near the back, giving a tentative wave in my direction. She watches uncertainly as I approach and ask if she's Adele Holbrook. She is. She doesn't look weird or threatening. Cautiously looking at each other, we haven't a chance to speak before a waiter appears and hands each of us the menu.

'Is red wine okay for you?' Her voice is low, with a hint of emotion. 'I can manage one glass without being over the limit.'

'Yes, that's fine, and how about something to eat, I'm starving?' I order the same safe anti-pasta and spaghetti carbonare that I had three days ago with Charles. I have to fight back tears just thinking about it. Adele says she'll have the same.

Sizing her up, she's not exactly glamorous but nevertheless, a pleasant-looking young woman, slim and trim with short dark hair, probably in her late-twenties/early thirties. She's wearing a smart, grey- tailored suit with a bright red and yellow silk scarf loosely tied around her neck.

As soon as the waiter leaves, she opens her handbag and passes me a photograph. 'This one is Nick.'

It's a group of three people. The one in the middle is clearly Adele but then, oh my God, my head feels like an explosion has gone off inside. The person she's pointing at is Charles. My heart is thumping so hard the whole restaurant must be able to hear it. The third man is taller than the others but has a strong family resemblance. Taking a couple of deep breaths, I stutter, 'I know him as Charles Temple.'

Abruptly, she stops speaking, pressing her hands either side off her nose and opens her brown eyes wide as if trying to suppress a sneeze. 'That's his brother's name.'

'Brother's name?' I exclaim, wishing my brain wasn't so confused and trying to focus on forming a coherent question. 'But that is Charles Temple ... isn't it?'

'No, Penny, that's my brother, Nick Holbrook. She points to the other man. 'That's Charles Temple, our brother, well, half-brother actually.'

My throat feels dry and I can hardly speak. I rock backwards and forwards in my chair knowing it's true.

Getting over her shock quicker than me, she sighs. 'Believe me, what I'm telling you is correct.' The words, the set of her mouth and her whole body are utterly convincing.

'But.' I croak. 'Why would he call himself by his brother's name, that's ridiculous.'

Adele wipes a stray tear away and slowly shakes her head. 'I have no idea, it doesn't make sense. Charles was sent to Africa weeks ago and hasn't been heard of since – he's missing.'

'Missing?'

'Yes, we don't know where he is and neither does his company.'

'Which company is that?'

'It's DfID, you know, the Department for International Development, part of the Foreign Office.'

Still pointing at the photo, I explain. 'I met this man at a New Year's Eve party and he told me his name was Charles

Temple. After that, we met on several occasions, but at no time did he say his name was Nick Holbrook. Why would he do that?'

She dabs her eyes. 'I honestly can't imagine.'

'I even met two of his colleagues and oh! ... wait a moment, when we were in the China Wall restaurant, I heard one of them call him Holly. Yes, and afterwards, he brushed it off saying it was just a silly nickname.'

'That's right.' Adele smiles. 'Everyone called him Holly at work.'

Our starters arrive.

'All the family were very upset when Charles disappeared. Nick went to Africa on business making enquiries and offering a reward for information.' The loud rumble of a heavy lorry stopping outside interrupts our thought processes for a moment. Adele pauses and looks directly at me. 'I've just realised something, you don't seem surprised to hear he's dead.'

'That's because I already know.'

'Who told you?'

'Nobody told me, I was with him when he was murdered.'

'What! Murdered!' She gasps, her face visibly pales. 'Of course he wasn't murdered.'

There's no point in beating about the bush so I relive the terrible events although, in a way, I find it therapeutic to be able to confide in someone. Briefly, I tell her the whole story, it isn't in sequence because I start with him being shot in St Ives Court, about Tim and Hal and then go back to when we met, the fact that my drink had been spiked, my loss of memory, our subsequent meetings and me getting nowhere when I reported his murder to the police. All the time I'm recounting the story, she's giving me questioning looks, trying to work out if it's true or if I'm just a weirdo with a vivid imagination.

'I think I believe you.' She acknowledges quietly. 'Nick was always vague about the specifics of his work and I know he carried a gun. Now I come to think of it, this traffic accident story they tried to fob us off with did seem unlikely, especially as they said it was a hit-and-run and there were no witnesses.'

'How did you hear about his death?'

'My father got a call from the police, or so he thought.'

'Do you know who Nick worked for?'

'He was with a security outfit, HESEC. From what we could piece together, it was government-related work giving security advice to foreign regimes. What we did know for certain was that he travelled overseas all the time, mainly Africa.'

We are quiet for a few moments, sipping our wine but leaving most of the food untouched. The waiter watches us with polite curiosity.

'Adele.' My voice is barely a whisper. 'There's one other thing I have to tell you.'

'Go on.'

'I'm pregnant.'

'Ah, so that's what Nick meant about a baby.'

Looking her in the eyes. 'It happened at the New Year's Eve party.'

'Are you trying to tell me,' her voice incredulous. 'That it's Nick's?'

'Yes, I am.'

'But hang on, you said you met Nick for the very first time at that party.'

Blushing slightly. 'Embarrassing isn't it? I think you deserve an explanation.'

'You're damn right I do.'

'Well, I already told you that my drink was spiked.'

She nods.

'The drug triggered my memory loss but, according to Paula, it was her party, I acted quite normally for a while, dancing with Nick, talking and laughing a lot, and then we disappeared upstairs.'

Giving me an odd look, she shakes her head. 'That doesn't sound like Nick.'

'And me neither.' 'It was that damn drug. Paula said Nick left around two in the morning saying he was going abroad on business later that day. Shortly after that, I reappeared swaying all over the place.'

'Were you drunk?'

'No, but I was as sick as a parrot the next day, the events of the party were a complete blank. It was three weeks before I found out I was pregnant. I thought the druggee had raped me.'

'But it wasn't him.'

'No, but what actually happened only came back to me four days ago when, out of the blue, Charles ... oh, I mean Nick suddenly turned up and, pow, everything snapped into focus – just like that.'

'Including your ... '

'Yes.' My voice quakes as I wipe away a few tears. 'Including that.'

'Oh, well that's ...' She hesitates. 'If you don't mind my asking, could it possibly have been anyone else?'

'No.'

'Then it's a sort of consolation for you and, of course, my family, Nick's baby. Have you seen a doctor?'

I look down at the table not answering.

'Penny,' Adele persists. 'You will see a doctor, won't you?'

My voice is unsteady. 'This is difficult for me. Thinking I'd been raped, I'd already decided on a termination.'

'Yes, but now you know it wasn't like that, you will keep it, won't you?'

'I'm not sure. Having a baby will change my life and I don't know if I'm ready for that - this is my life, and I'll deal with it myself. Life as a single mother isn't very appealing.'

'Of course, I understand.' She backs off. 'But we as a family will give you all the support you need. After all, it'll be the only part of Nick we'll have left. But what about your parents, won't they be pleased?'

'Pleased! Pleased that their only daughter has got herself *in the club* during a one night stand by a man who's now dead. Ha, they'll go ballistic.'

'Then we're here to help you, financially as well.'

'But they've never met me and anyway, I'm only four weeks gone so it's early days.' Tears are welling up again. 'Can we talk about something else?'

'Yes, of course.'

'Nick told me he was a geologist.'

'Yes, or at least his degree was in geology. But straight from uni, he joined HESEC and told us only a jot about his job; we soon gave up asking.'

'He told me about it being dangerous - I think that's why he was killed. And for some strange reason, someone high up, with a lot of clout, has gone to a great deal of trouble to cover it up.'

She shakes her head. 'But why, what was he involved in?'

'I don't know. Oh, by the way, did you bring the package Nick left me?'

'No, it's in a safe at home, we can go and get it now if you like.'

'Probably not. It's Thursday now, so could I come round to your place on Saturday morning.'

'That's fine. So what are you going to do now?'

'Ha, I wish I knew. There's no point going back to the police, I'd be arrested for wasting their time, and HESEC deny any knowledge of Nick. Have you any ideas?'

She shakes her head. 'No, I haven't at the moment, but I'd like to tell my family. They should know the truth about the way Nick died, shouldn't they?'

'That's up to you.'

'And my mother will definitely want to know about the baby.'

'Oh no, not yet, it's far too soon - you must wait for my *say so* first.'

CHAPTER SEVEN
JANUARY 30th

I'm forty minutes late for work, but why I'm here at all is another matter. Totally whacked after another restless night, my head is all over the place with unanswered questions. I'm frightened *and* I've been warned off by the police, *and* on top of that I'm pregnant, *and* I don't know what the hell to do.

'Miss Lane.'

Oh crap, fat Billy Bunter is hovering over me with that predictable, malicious expression on his fat, flabby face. I'm in trouble again.

'Despite my frequent requests, Miss Lane, you've failed to produce document EU/CAP/04178, the translation of the French minister's speech regarding the EU directive on increased levies on sugar beet production.'

'I'm sorry Mr Bunter, I'll attend to it straight away.'

'Too late, Miss Lane. It was removed from your desk and passed to Miss Levalle.'

'But I wasn't feeling well yesterday.'

'This, Miss Lane, is a gross dereliction of duty on your part. You've already had several warnings about your poor time-keeping and work performance, and this,' he slaps an envelope on my desk. 'You'll be called for your final disciplinary meeting.' With that, he turns on his heel and with his obese arse wobbling, heads back to his office. The bastard enjoyed that and he wants me fired. Next time, I *will* be out ... out of work and out of money. Desperately trying to blot out the turmoil churning inside me, I spend the rest of the day struggling to catch up with work but my heart isn't in it and I know there are mistakes. If Bunter checks it, he'll sack me. But I need this job and, as my dad always points out, the great pension that goes with it. But if I keep the kid then, God knows what'll happen to me.

At the end of a tiring journey, I drag myself home feeling miserable and collapse exhausted onto my armchair. Massaging my tired, aching feet and ankles, I close my eyes. What a rotten day - in fact, days. Damn, any chance of resting is abruptly halted as the door entry system buzzes. Who on earth can it be at this time? I press the top button.

'Hewo.' It's a tinny voice with a strange accent.

'Who is it?'

'Interfrora. I have frowers for you.' He's probably Asian, can't pronounce 'L'. But flowers for me, who would send me flowers? Anyway, it's cheered me up a bit and I press the second button telling the man to come up. After a minute, there's a faint knock on my door and I open it without checking the spy hole.

Bloody hell. My wrist is roughly grabbed by a large gloved hand and before I can scream, I'm yanked hard against the door frame and another hand is brutally placed across my mouth. Two men, wearing ski masks, push their way in, the second quickly checking each room. I'm petrified, shaking, are they burglars or rapists? They say a few words which sound like Cantonese. My heart is pounding so hard it feels as if it'll burst out of my chest and my wrist hurts like hell where the guy is holding me.

The other one, who is taller, drags a stool from under the kitchen counter and together they haul me onto it, taping my hands tightly behind my back and then across my mouth.

'You not do the screaming,' one of them says. 'Or kill you, okay?' Two sets of cruel, dark eyes stare at me through the slits in their masks.

Shaking uncontrollably, I feel my guts twisting and turning.

'Okay?' The man shouts again.

I nod my head, just staring at them, scares me out of my wits.

He rips the tape from my mouth. I yell out, it hurts and I think some skin came off with it. 'Don't hurt me. Take anything you want but don't hurt me.' The pain in my wrists is excruciating and, inhaling sharply, my voice almost breaks as I beg them to undo the tape. 'Please, they hurt.'

The larger man looks behind my back and must see that I'm not faking, because he pulls a knife from his belt and slices it.

'Not try the escape or kill you. Okay?'

Nodding, I massage my wrists and place a hand over my swollen mouth.

'Okay Miss Wane, where package?'

'Package?' Staring at them open-mouthed, my voice trembles. 'What package?'

The smaller man hits me so hard across my cheek it feels like my eyes are going to explode. Blood trickles down my chin.

'No pray games Miss Wane. We want package, where it?'

'I don't know anything about a package.' I whimper. 'You can search the place but I have no package.'

The man slaps me even harder this time almost knocking me off the stool. I cry out in pain, and I taste the metallic tang of blood in my mouth. Unable to stop trembling, I sob. 'I don't know about a package.'

Just as the man is about to hit me again, the entry phone buzzes loudly. He stops in his tracks and, for some reason, both men take a couple of steps backwards staring at the door. Now that they've moved, I'm closer to the entry phone than they are. Ignoring whatever the rational side of my brain is screaming at me, I jump off the stool, race the few yards to the door and press both buttons shrieking. 'Help, help me, please help me.' Crouching, frozen to the spot, I brace myself to be set upon but … nothing. Peeking over my shoulder, I see them run into the bedroom, but it's two floors up. Heavy footsteps are pounding up the stairs to my door followed by a loud bang and a man's voice shouting. 'Open up, now.'

Fearing that it might be another thug, I open the door cautiously on the chain. It's Hal. My hand shakes as I pull back the chain and let him in, pointing to the bedroom.

'They're in …' Is as far as I get before crumpling to the floor, crying my eyes out.

In three long strides, swiftly pulling out a gun from inside his coat, he rushes into the bedroom. 'The window's open.' He shouts from the doorway, making no move to go after them. 'Who was it?' He puts his gun away but I'm too traumatized to reply.

He examines my face. 'You alright?' Although his voice is sympathetic, his eyes are cold and his damned body odour is as strong as ever. Helping me into the chair, he goes to the kitchen, bringing a tea-towel soaked in cold water which he places against my swollen lips, wiping blood from around my mouth.

'Who was it? Do you know him?'

Slowly shaking my head but still sniffling, I tell him that it was two Asian men wearing masks, demanding a package.

At the mention of the word *package*, his expression hardens and he takes hold of me firmly by the shoulders. 'Where is it? Did they take it?'

I whimper. 'I don't know anything about a package.'

'Didn't Nick give you a package?'

'No, he didn't.' I don't know if I can trust this *Chinese-speaking* brute, it could have been HESEC covering up Nick's murder. 'What's this all about, Hal?' I sob. 'What is this package that you and the others want? What am I mixed up in?'

He doesn't answer but heads for the kitchen. 'I'll get you some tea.' Soon, I hear the comforting sound of the kettle boiling then mugs rattling on a tray as he carries them in.

I try taking small sips, the hot liquid stings my cuts and dribbles down my blouse.

'Take it slowly, I'll make a cold compress.'

Sitting quietly for a few moments drinking my tea, a sudden thought sets my heart racing again. 'You *are* with HESEC, aren't you Hal?'

'You know I am,' he retorts irritably.

'Then who were those two men who attacked me, are they the ones who killed Nick?'

'It's possible.'

'But why was there a cover up?'

'What do you mean?'

'You know what I mean. I went back to his apartment the next day with the police and all evidence of the shooting and the blood on the carpet had been removed.'

Anger flares up on his face making me flinch. He looks as if he might hit me. 'You stupid bitch, I warned you not to say anything to anyone, including the police.'

'But Nick, my fiancé was murdered, the father of my unborn child.' I place my hands on my belly to emphasise the fact. 'I have to find out why.'

He snarls. 'You've no idea what you're getting involved in. It's dangerous and people get hurt, even killed. So for your own sake, leave it.'

'But why? Are you another Spook in HESEC's ghost department?'

He laughs hollowly, but his attempt to smile immediately fades. 'I'm sworn to secrecy but, to get you off my back, I'll tell you what I can. Everything we do at HESEC is for the British Government and covered by the Official Secrets Act.' He pauses for a moment. 'You signed it, remember?'

I nod. 'So tell me, what's so important about this package?'

He sighs and pulls a face. 'We aren't sure. There's been a huge cock-up and we think Nick was the only one who knew its contents.'

'How's that?'

'When we travel overseas, we go as Queen's Messengers and often bring back files in the diplomatic pouch. Foreign authorities and even UK customs aren't allowed to open anything as we have diplomatic immunity, it's under the Geneva Convention.' He shifts uncomfortably and fumbles for a pack of cigarettes in his pocket. 'Do you mind if I smoke?'

I shake my head.

'When Nick arrived from Africa a few days ago.' He blows smoke out of the corner of his mouth. 'He brought some paperwork and the package with him. The next day, that package was missing.'

'Was that when you and Tim came to the China Wall Restaurant and took him away?'

'That's right. We rushed back to the office, searched everywhere, and then someone found that our section chief had signed for it.'

'So it wasn't lost at all.'

'We assumed he'd put it in a safe, so we stopped the search.'

'I don't understand. If your boss had it, why is everybody still looking for it?'

He sighs again. 'The chief had gone to one of those hush-hush Cobra meetings, completely incommunicado, so we couldn't contact him until the following morning. Then we found out that he hadn't got the package and someone had forged his signature, someone in our office. Shortly after that, Nick was killed.'

'So Nick was not the only the person who knew the contents.'

He purses his lips and shrugs, not drawn on my theory.

'Does that mean you've got a mole in your office?'

'A mole!' He snorts.

'You *know* what I mean,' I reply angrily. 'A mole or double agent or whatever.'

'Yes, okay, I know what you mean and yes, it looks that way.'

'Then I'm still in danger.'

'Not if those villains thought you were telling the truth.'

God, I hope he's right. Nick did tell me he was suspicious of some people in the office and that's probably why he took back the package. If the villains make the link with Adele, then she could be next. Suddenly, another question pops into my mind. 'By the way, Hal, why did you come round to see me? Did you know I was in danger?'

'No, of course not.' A catch in his voice makes me think he's lying. 'I was concerned about you – you know, bringing you home when Nick was shot. I happened to be in this area so thought I'd call and see that you are okay.'

He's lying. Stubbing his cigarette in my saucer, he stands to leave. 'I'll give you my phone number. You can get me twenty-four seven so call anytime. It's easy to remember - 989800. Don't write it down, just remember it.'

'Yes, thanks Hal, I've got it.'

CHAPTER EIGHT

JANUARY 31ˢᵗ

Another bad night. Disconnected thoughts whirling through my mind making my brain hyper-active. Groggily, I crawl out of bed and stumble to the kitchen. My throat is parched and I desperately need tea. Carrying a steaming mug into the tiny living room, I drape a blanket over my shoulders and cuddle up to the single radiator - I must get more heating. It's only six thirty but I daren't wait any longer before contacting Adele. I worried about her all night. A sleepy voice answers and confirms, rather irritably, that she's fine. I tell her about the two masked men and how Hal came to the rescue.

'Shit! Slow down,' she's wide awake now. 'That's fucking awful. Are you alright, and the baby?'

'Just about, a bit sore and swollen here and there but, we're okay - petrified but okay.'

'Tell me what ... oh hell!' She stops in mid-sentence. There's a disturbing silence for a moment.

'Adele, what's happened?'

'Your phone's bugged.'

'Bugged! How do you know?'

I hear her sharp intake of breath. 'Listen Penny, follow my instructions without question, just trust me, okay?'

'What are you talking about?'

'Don't say another word,' she commands. 'Go outside immediately, at least a hundred yards from your place, and I'll call you on your mobile.'

'But that's crazy. It's six forty-five and bloody freezing outside.'

'For God's sake, Penny, do it. Don't answer your house phone, in fact unplug it now. You must do as I tell you.'

'But ... '

'No buts.' She hangs up.

Stunned, I stand stock-still, looking numbly at the phone in my hand wondering what she's on about. My phone bugged, but how? I examine the receiver and base unit but can't see anything. But I know Adele's on my side, and just now, she's probably the only one so what choice do I have? Unplugging the phone, I spring into action throwing on some warm clothes. Outside, it's still dark and I shiver in the bone-chilling nippiness of the air. Trying to generate some internal body heat, I start to jog down Hook Road in the direction of *La Sentore* when my mobile rings.

'Adele?'

'Yes, where are you?'

'I'm freezing my butt off getting strange looks from every passing motorist. Anyway, how do you know my phone is bugged?'

'I'll explain later. Your mobile might also be monitored but hopefully, not yet.'

'Who would do this?' My breath gives out a mist of cloudy air as a gust of icy wind whips against my face.

'Never mind about that. Listen, do you know Canbury Gardens in Kingston?'

'Yes, I think so. Is that where the Boaters is?'

'That's it. Go back inside and grab your passport, call a taxi on your mobile and have them drop you off at the north end of Canbury Gardens, near the Albany. Have you got that?'

'Yes, but ... '

'Get on with it,' she orders, 'I'll meet you there and explain everything. Go right now or you'll be in even more danger.'

'Okay then.'

'Don't forget to switch off your mobile in the taxi and stuff it down the back seat.' She cuts the call.

Shaking with fear mixed with excitement, I quickly retrace my steps and shove a few clothes in a rucksack, stuffing my passport in my coat pocket. I phone for a taxi. Damn, I should have done that first.

'*It'll be there in five.*' A voice from the Indian sub-continent tells me, but that's what they always say. Looking at my watch every few seconds, time crawls by as I wait inside the main door ... and then, thank God, it arrives. It's starting to get lighter and as the roads are still fairly quiet, it only takes seventeen minutes to the dropping off point. Getting out, I turn and look around. The street and park are empty save for a couple of overweight, red-faced joggers puffing along the Thames towpath.

Brakes screech as a Ford Focus with Adele at the wheel comes to a sharp halt next to me. 'Get in.' I'm in the passenger seat in a flash and she zooms off along a side street before turning left on Richmond Road.

'Did you get rid of your mobile?' She sounds like a snappy headmistress.

'Yes.'

'Good, I have to go back home to pick up a few things and then we'll go into hiding until we figure out what to do.'

This is unreal – is this really happening to me? I've a hundred and one questions but decide to keep them for later and let Adele concentrate on her driving as she speeds along Richmond Road before sharply turning off to the right along a quiet, tree-lined cul-de-sac.

'We're here,' she breathes a sigh of relief. 'Get your bag and follow me.'

Her apartment is on the top floor of an ordinary looking two-storey block and the key she uses is really odd. As it closes behind us, there's a metallic *clang* and Adele places a heavy iron bar across two anchor points at either side.

'Wow,' I exclaim. 'What kind of a place is this?'

'It's my place, but Nick used it as his bolthole when he wanted to get out of the City – hence the heavy security. He kept a lot of his *special* equipment here and was able to unwind from the stresses of the job. There's a built-in strong room and our means of escape is ...'

'Escape,' I yell. 'Already?'

'Hopefully not yet.' Giving me a defiant smile, she points to a door off the entrance hall. 'It's through that bedroom window, onto a garage roof, then down into a narrow passageway and out onto Marsland Street where Nick's Jag is garaged, then away.'

'Bloody hell.'

She laughs at my reaction. 'One thing Nick taught me was that whenever he entered a building, the first thing he'd do was look for an escape route.'

Feeling exhausted after what had happened to me over the past hour, I steady myself against the wall. 'I need to sit down.'

Adele commiserates. 'Yes of course, have you had breakfast?

There's an unpleasant taste in my mouth as if my tongue is coated with something nasty. 'Only half a cup of tea.'

'You and the baby need more than that. I've got cereal and toast, but we've got to be quick. We're picking up a hire car at nine o'clock.' She checks her watch. 'It's just after eight-fifteen so we can't hang around.'

'I'll have toast please, and ... well, thanks for everything.'

'Hey, it's for me too, remember. Nick was my brother and I miss him like hell.'

'Yes, of course, it's worse for you and your family but help me out here, I don't really know what's happening. How did you know my phone was bugged, why dump my mobile, why leave my flat and go into hiding and, hell yes, why hire a car when you have your own?'

Acknowledging my questions with a wave, she brings two rounds of buttered toast and puts it on the arm of my chair. 'Would you like marmalade on that?'

My stomach heaves and I need a couple of deep breaths before declining.

She walks over to a side table by the front window. 'You see this gadget attached to my phone.'

I nod.

'Nick installed it. A red light comes on if the number calling is bugged. He was going to install an encryption device, if he'd lived.'

'I see.'

'Living with Nick and Charles taught me a lot about security and how villains operate. Landlines and mobiles can easily be tracked and even my car is probably known. I'll explain everything once we're in hiding.'

'And where's that?'

'I'll leave that till later, but it'll be safe, at least for a few days.' She frowns. 'Look Penny, what happened to you yesterday and the fact that this guy, Hal, was in the area to conveniently come to your rescue, well, it stinks.'

'How do you mean?'

'The two thugs, you think they're Chinese, are after the package Nick left with me, and clearly, Hal's after it as well, but I'm suspicious of his motives. Nick had told me he was doubtful of some people in HESEC. He must have known he was in danger and if anything happened to him, he wanted you to have it, whatever it is.'

I feel a bit better after finishing my toast. 'It must be valuable. My theory is that after handing it in, Nick must have changed his mind and taken it back, probably because something had happened that day to trouble him.'

'You're probably right, but one thing is certain, because of that damned package, we are both in danger.' All the time we've been talking, she's peering out between the slats of the venetian blind covering the front window. 'Shit, I think we have visitors.'

'What?'

'A car's pulled up on the road outside,' she shakes her head. 'I've not seen it before.'

Taking her mobile phone from a corner shelf, she zooms in and aims it through the gaps. 'Two men are sitting in the front seats, one is on the phone, aha, now they're getting out.' She takes several pictures. 'Oh hell, they're big, evil looking Asians. They must have tapped into up our phone call; they've been bloody quick.'

Scalp tingling, my blood running cold. 'They're not coming here, are they?'

'It looks like it. Grab your things, Penny, we're leaving. The security door will hold them up for a few minutes.'

A shot of adrenalin surges through my veins and Adele's presence makes me feel anything's possible, even getting away from those Chinese heavies.

With her bags ready, she dials 999 yelling for the police. 'I'm being attacked,' she screams hysterically, giving her name and address followed by another scream, then, giving me an impish wink, she leaves the receiver dangling. Suddenly, there's a loud clatter on the door followed by what sounds like attempts to jemmy it open. Quick as a flash, Adele places a small object the size of a cigarette packet against the inside of the door, then we scramble though the bedroom window. Adele helps me down Nick's pre-planned escape route to the garage on Marsland Street and his Jag. The engine fires, wheels squeal as we round two sharp bends into Richmond Road, turning left towards Kingston.

Scared out of my wits but trying to calm my racing heart, I shout, 'What was it you put under the door?'

'A smoke bomb,' she laughs, her voice amazingly controlled as though it's just a game. 'When they eventually force the door open, it'll explode covering them with purple dye.'

This is getting more like James Bond every minute. Holding on for dear life, I ask, 'Whatever next?'

'Listen, Penny, Jackson's Car Hire is less than ten minutes away. I'll do all the talking because they know me as Lesley Cork of Bargara Close, Ham.'

'How on earth did you ... ?' I shake my head, now is not the time.

She pulls into a bay next to Jackson's forecourt. Under strict orders, I wait quietly in the Jag for several minutes until Adele taps on the window and gestures me out, transferring our bags and into a greyish-blue Vauxhall Astra.

'All done, we're off.'

'What about the Jag?'

'I've arranged to have it re-sprayed then new number plates, and paid up front in cash. I'll collect it when I can.'

'Do you think we were followed from your place?'

'No, I double checked. Now we're away from possible eavesdroppers, I'll tell you where we're going. My parents have a cottage in the New Forest which they rarely use. I've got the keys.'

'But what about my job, and I'd have to tell my parents.'

'Fuck your job, you hate it anyway. I've got a new mobile for you to call your parents – you can do it when we stop for petrol in Sunbury. I've got plenty of cash for us to live on until everything's sorted out. As soon as we get to the cottage, you can open the package and then we'll know what we're up against.'

Seated in the passenger seat, trying to calm down, I can't help but marvel at Adele's driving skills as she weaves through busy traffic on Kingston's notorious one-way system, then over a bridge with the Thames flowing beneath and on past Hampton Court Palace with its views over the river.

Stopping for petrol in Sunbury, she hands me a new mobile. 'Call your parents and anyone else who may want to contact you. No more than five minutes, though.'

Doing as I'm told, I try my parents' number. Luckily, there's no answer, so I just leave a brief message that I'm taking a few days' holiday with a friend in Spain and will call when I get back. Ha, that'll send them into a tiz. My mother hoping I'm with a nice young man and my father cursing that I'm jeopardising my career. Arguing between themselves, as usual, they'll immediately call my old mobile which, at this very moment, is stuffed down the back seat of a taxi. Next, I phone Paula's home knowing that she'll be at work and leave the same message. I think about calling Billy Bunter to tell him he can stuff his job but I'll let him stew instead.

Adele, her back to me, has her mobile pressed to her ear, and when she's finished, takes the SIM cards out of both phones and uses bluetack to surreptitiously attach them under the roof gutter of a taxi about to head for central London.

'That should confuse them,' she laughs as we get back in the car and head for the M3.

'Does that mean they'll trace the calls to that taxi?'

She nods. 'I texted photos of the two Chinese men, who are now, hopefully covered in purple, to Kingston police station along with the number plate of their car.'

'How do you think of these things?'

'I already told you, I lived with a spook, but from now on, Penny, no more phone calls and don't, whatever you do, use debit or credit cards or go into any bank, they can track us down just as easily as SIM cards.'

My mind's almost spinning out of control. Do I understand what's happening? Do I hell as like. Do I know who *they* are? Do I hell as like. Up till six weeks ago, I led a calm, untroubled life which was boring but safe. I wasn't witnessing murders or being beaten up by Chinese thugs or having to run away and hide. Meeting and sleeping with Nick changed my life forever. I'm pregnant, Nick murdered and yesterday, I was almost killed myself, and I'm scared, bloody scared, but I've got this amazing woman who seems to have solutions to every problem, and takes danger in her stride.

We're passing fields and clumps of dense pine trees stretching away on either side of the motorway, reminding me how quickly the metropolis turns into countryside. It is mainly flat with a few rolling hills which are like a misty green ocean in the weak wintery light. I turn to Adele. 'I've a lot to learn about you.'

'Really?' she smiles.

'Yes, you're so ... I don't know, confident, so much in control. I don't know how you do it.'

'Ha, you're not the first one to say that. My father saw to it.'

'How do you mean?'

'I was brought up in a military household with strict military discipline, we all were, Charles, Nick and me. Stiff upper lip and all that bloody nonsense. He made us very competitive and it was especially hard for me as I was the youngest *and* a girl.'

'What did you compete in?'

'Everything. Athletics, martial arts, shooting, we all joined the local gun club as junior members as soon as we were twelve. Father gave the two boys a hard time when I won more trophies than them.'

'Wow, you must be good.'

'And unlike the boys, I can also run flat out for ten minutes before my hands start to shake.'

'Bloody hell, can you also leap tall buildings in a single bound?'

'Not yet,' she laughs. 'But I'm working on it.'

This time, I laugh with her. 'And what about a *fella*?' I notice she's not wearing any rings. 'Have you got a boy friend?'

'Oh, yes,' she briefly turns to face me, her expression softened. 'I've got one of those.'

'Who is he and why isn't he here?'

'His name is Rupert Shelley, and he's presently serving in Afghanistan.'

'Oh, I see. Is he in the army?'

'SBS, working behind enemy lines. He'll be away for another four months.'

'It must be difficult for you, for both of you. Are you in regular contact?'

'If we're lucky, once a week on Skype and the occasional text and call.'

We're both quiet for a few moments before she speaks. 'We were going to get engaged, but Rupert said we should leave it until his return – you know, just in case.'

'And will you go ahead, in four months?'

'You're fucking right we will,' she laughs.

After about an hour, we join the A31 at Cadnam and then take a right turn to Rufus Stone. Passing over a cattle grid, Adele drives expertly along narrow roads through the New Forest. 'There's a bit of history round here,' she says without elaborating. 'And a forty mile speed limit, partly because ponies and deer wander freely.'

Turning a blind corner, we suddenly see two brown and white ponies standing stock-still in the middle of the road. 'Ha, there you are, you see, any more than forty and I'd have hit those idiots.' She carefully manoeuvres around them and picks up speed again.

'You'll be pleased to know,' Adele checks the rear view mirror. 'That there haven't been any cars behind us since we turned off the main road.'

I sigh, wanting to believe that we have got away from ... well, whoever *they* are.

Eventually, we crunch down the gravel driveway of Pine Lodge, Adele's parents' weekend cottage. A bitter wind batters my face as she takes out a bunch of keys and leads the way past a few sorry-looking bushes and a bed of snowdrops to a door on the right of the property. Cursing under her breath, she fails to unlock it with the first and second key, but the third one works. The door creaks loudly like sound effects from a horror film. The loud beeps of the alarm make me jump, but Adele quickly taps in the numbers to immobilize it. 'By the way, the security number is double two double nine. Remember it in case you have to use it.'

It feels even colder and damper inside than out. Curtains are drawn at the small windows and she switches on lights controlled from a panel by the entrance. I look around the large living room furnished with various chairs of unrelated styles but all with a faded, well-used look about them. There's a fireplace with logs stacked either side, two crammed bookshelves against the wall, a couple of coffee tables, and a small television set. Following Adele into the kitchen, I notice that the solid-looking back door has four heavy bolts keeping it secure.

Through a gap in the curtains, I can see the branches of a bare sycamore swinging in the wind. The cold penetrates my winter coat. 'Is there any heating?'

'Just the log fire,' she replies. 'I'll light it while you make tea.' She strikes a match and puts the flame to the corners of exposed newspapers. 'I've got something else to tell you,' she adds as I carry a tray into the room. 'It's bad news so I decided to save it until we got here.'

Huddling in front of the freshly-lit fire with mugs of tea warming our hands, Adele gives a weary sigh. 'When we stopped for petrol, one of the calls I made was to my parents. My mother was distraught because last night, whilst they were out visiting friends, their house was ransacked. They, whoever *they* were, even found the safe under the floorboards of the master bedroom and forced it open, but as far as my father could tell, nothing had been taken. Not even jewellery or cash.'

'Oh God, it must be the same people, maybe it was lucky they were out. Oh, by the way, was there anything in their house referring to this place? Will they be coming here next?'

'I don't think so. The deeds are with our solicitor and the family always refers to it as *the Lodge*, and the Lodge could be anywhere.' Finishing our tea, Adele reaches inside her handbag and takes out a small package wrapped in brown paper, about six by four inches deep. *'THIS IS IT,'* she says with a touch of drama, placing it on the coffee table next to my chair. 'This is the package Nick left for you.'

CHAPTER NINE
JANUARY 31st

'Is this all it is?' I exclaim rather inanely, 'I was expecting something ... you know, something bigger.' My hands tremble as I sit staring at it. 'It's because of this,' I touch it with the tip of my finger, 'that Nick was killed.' Gingerly, I pick it up as though it might suddenly metamorphose into something weird. It only weighs about the same as a box of M&Ms and is tightly sealed with tape. The only writing on it is, *"for Penny Lane"* with my phone number and address written alongside. Holding it to my ear, I give it a little shake – there's a faint movement inside.

'You should open it,' Adele says. 'Let's see what's so bloody precious.'

From somewhere in the darkness outside comes the lonely hoot of an owl. Creepy.

Trying to pick at the edge of the tape, it's too firmly fixed, so Adele goes into the kitchen returning with a sharp paring knife. Very carefully, like attempting to diffuse an unexploded bomb, I insert the tip of the knife and gently run it along the four sides. Slowly, peeling back the paper, I find a sealed box inside addressed to *Sir Desmond Thrimby, Section Chief, HESEC, XFO Security*, with a loosely folded note on top. It's a hand-written letter addressed to me. Nervously, I read it out.

"Dearest Penny, I hope you never have to read this as it probably means I'm dead. Although I'd suspected it, I'm now certain we have a double agent in HESEC XFO and he, or they, know that I know. Recently I've become privy to a huge secret worth billions and they'll kill to get it. Take the enclosed to my friend, Axel van Damme, 232D Boulevard Emile Bockstael in Brussels

– you can trust him completely. Also, you can trust my good friend, Colonel Noah Tofa in Liberia. I'm sure my sister Adele will help you. But please be on your guard, there's a Chinese connection to all this and they're ruthless. Oh, and one last thing, it's your decision about the baby, whatever you decide, you have my blessing. Have a great life and think of me sometimes. I love you, Nick."

My throat catches, tears streaming down my face. 'Oh, Nick,' I say out loud, 'Why did it have to be you? I'll always love you, and our baby.' I crumple back in the chair, unable to stop crying, while even *super woman* herself is sobbing. We hug and cling on to each other until she gains some semblance of control.

Still snuffling, she reaches for a box of tissues, hands me a wedge.

I pick up the letter again. 'There's a PS.' Taking a couple of deep breaths to relax my throat.

"Just remembered. Sorry about all the confusion calling myself Charles Temple. He's my brother, missing in Africa on a FO/DfID mission and, for nefarious reasons which I haven't been able to fathom, no-one is making any attempt to find him. I thought by using his name when I went to the FO, it would cause a stir and let them know that I'm on to them. I've been chasing up clues in various WA countries, and on my next trip, I'll follow up on a good lead with Noah Tofa. I'm sure it's to do with Limarni."

Wiping her face, Adele gets up and opens the liquor cabinet. 'What we need is a stiff drink.' Finding a dusty bottle on the bottom shelf, she pours two glasses. 'How about a drop of fifteen year old malt?'

'Sounds perfect but I'm not sure it's good for me, being pregnant.'

'You're definitely going to keep it then.'

'If it checks out, medically I mean, then yes, I'll keep it. It's Nick's baby.'

'That's brill, and my mother will be over the moon. But you're supposed to cut back on stress, of course.'

'Ha, that's a joke,' holding up Nick's letter, I add. 'With this, my stress levels are through the roof. Do you know what Limarni is?'

'Limarni - no, never heard of it,' she wrinkles her forehead. 'It could be a person or a place, maybe. I'll ask my parents.'

'We haven't seen what's in the box yet,' I say. 'Maybe it's a Limarni. Anyhow, will you open it please, I'm shaking too much?'

Taking the knife, Adele slices through the tape and opens the lid. She gasps and whispers to me. 'You'd better see this.'

Seated on a bed of cotton wool are three odd-shaped objects looking a bit like lumps of glass. One roughly the size of a conker and the other two more like plum stones. Gingerly touching the big one, it feels cold and hard. Picking it up, I hold it in the palm of my hand. 'What the hell?'

'May I look?' Adele waits for a signal before picking up another piece. 'I think I know what they are.' She holds it up to the light. 'They're rough diamonds, see how it catches the light, blue and white inside a crystal, and they're big, especially that one. I saw pictures like this in one of Nick's geology books.'

'If they are diamonds, they're probably worth a few hundred.'

'Thousands,' Adele corrects.

'Well, even thousands, but in Nick's letter, he wrote about billions. These may be worth a thousand or two but not billions, and surely not enough to kill for.'

'You're right.' Adele rubs her hand across her forehead in puzzlement.

Slowly, I lift out the cotton wool and begin to loosen it with my fingers. 'Ah, hang on, there's something else.' Pulling out a thin slip of paper from the bottom of the box, I pass it to Adele. 'Look, it's a list of numbers.'

She takes the slip and reads out, '7.0150.92/11.2204.76. God knows what they are.' She carefully pulls the empty package apart. We study every fragment of paper and cardboard, even holding them up to the light, but there's nothing else.

I feel deflated. After all the mayhem of the past six weeks - Nick's murder, my beating, the attack on Adele's place and the Holbrook's house, all for this package containing three uncut diamonds and a list of numbers. 'Adele, are you sure these are diamonds?'

'No, but I can't think of anything else. All I do know is that you need special equipment to check if they're real. It's not just a case of seeing if they cut glass.'

I sit back in my chair, sighing at this anticlimax. 'It could be the numbers, couldn't it? A clue that'll explain everything?'

She picks up the list again, shaking her head. 'Could they be a code?'

'Yes, it's possible.'

'Or maybe, mmm, I wonder.' She scratches her chin, her expression more animated than before. 'What about a numbered bank account, or a safety deposit box? You know, the ones Mafia bosses have in Switzerland.'

'But surely there are too many numbers for one account.'

'Maybe there's more than one,' she gives her chin another rub. 'I'm clutching at straws here but, if it is a bank, then where?'

Lost in thought, we remain silent for a few moments.

'It *must* be the numbers.' My eyes rest on Nick's letter, the stones and the list, 'Maybe these diamonds are just samples of dozens more in a safety deposit box.'

'Well, it's as good a guess as any. Perhaps this Axel van Damme will know, Nick said you should see *and* trust him.'

'Did Nick ever mention him to you?'

'No, but as Brussels is the main diamond cutting centre in Europe, it supports the theory they're genuine.'

'And then there's someone in Liberia. Did he ever mention him?'

'Not to me, he didn't. I'm not even sure where Liberia is.'

'Questions, questions, but we're short of answers. I think I will go and meet Axel Van Damme, what do you think?'

'I'll come with you, but before we do that, you know the original package was addressed to HESEC. Let me see,' she sifts through the scattered papers. 'Here we are, Sir Desmond Thrimby, we should contact him first. He's bound to see me as I'm Nick's sister.'

'Thrimby, yes, I thought I'd heard that name, Nick mentioned him when he was talking to Tim in the restaurant.'

'And after Thrimby, we'll go to Brussels to see this guy, Axel van Damme.'

'That's settled then.'

'You know something,' Adele says, 'Here we are, running away from the world, supporting each other, but I know next to nothing about you apart from your brief relationship with Nick, and that you work at the Home Office.'

Shaking my head, I laugh. 'You're right. But as far as I'm concerned, there's not much to tell, having lived what must appear to most people, a boring life.'

'I don't believe it,' Adele smiles encouragingly. 'Let's hear it anyway.'

'Well,' I pause, giving the subject a little thought, 'I think I've already told you I'm an only child.'

'Yes.'

'And both my parents were only children also.'

'Oh dear.'

'They were both in their late thirties when I was born. So ... apart from not having siblings, I've never had an aunt, uncle or cousin, and for that matter, I only had one grandparent and she died when I was eight.'

'That's so sad,' Adele consoles. 'You've hardly got any family at all.'

'None, except for some distant first and second cousins. And I never met them.'

'Why's that?'

I sigh, reluctantly dragging up memories which I'd rather forget. 'I think it's because my parents didn't get on. There was always a ... how should I say ... an atmosphere throughout my childhood, especially when anyone came round socially ... which wasn't very often.'

'What was the problem?'

'They argue about pretty well everything – me included. First my schooling and then my job.'

'What do you mean?'

'My Mother wanted me to go to the local state school, but my Dad said no. He wanted me to go to a private school even though they couldn't afford it. Luckily, I ended up in a Grammar school which he reluctantly accepted, but insisted I had to start work straight after uni in a job with a good pension.'

'Do they still argue about you?'

'Oh yes. And when they realise I'm quitting the Home Office, my Dad will go into apoplectic fits of rage, but my Mum won't mind. Anyway, quarrelling about absolutely everything is almost compulsory with them. I hate it.'

'I'm sure you do.'

'That's why I moved out as soon as I could and rented my place in Surbiton.'

'Do you think it's your mother's or father's fault?'

'Interesting. I always thought the main instigator was my Mum as she nagged him all the time, especially when he went out to various societies in the evenings. But I changed my mind when I went back to Reading from uni one weekend – a friend of mine was having a hen party. I stayed with her and didn't tell my parents. Anyway, a group of us was in a pub when I saw my Dad chatting up a tart in a double D size red dress, saying he wasn't married.'

'Oh boy, what a shock,' Adele laughs. 'Do you think your mother knew about his shenanigans?'

'On thinking about it, yes, I think she did. Maybe that's why I've been unlucky in love. Every boyfriend I took home did a runner once he'd met them. There ... my life in a nut shell. I told you it was boring. And now that I'm feeling totally miserable, let's go to bed – I'm shattered.'

CHAPTER TEN
FEBRUARY 1ˢᵗ

Waking with a jolt, the room is dark but at least I know where I am and a rattling of pots coming from the direction of the kitchen means Adele is up. I'm parched and, wow, it's cold. I'm used to cool bedrooms but this is ridiculous. Wrapping a thick blanket over my pyjamas, I make my way into the kitchen. Adele is already dressed complete with quilted anorak and fur boots.

She gives a cheery smile seeing my comical attempt to keep warm. 'I'm sorry but the cottage cools down overnight and I won't relight the fire until we've done our shopping. I suggest you get dressed while I try and find something for breakfast.'

Teeth chattering, I return to the bedroom putting the same blanket back on top of my clothes. When I get back to the kitchen, there are only biscuits and two steaming mugs of tea on the table.

'I can heat some baked beans or spaghetti hoops if you want.'

My head's about to say *yes* but my delicate stomach firmly disagrees, supported by a nasty taste of bile in my mouth. 'No thanks, I'll stick with this for now.'

'Before we go out,' she takes a tin of Cadbury's biscuits down off a cluttered shelf, 'I'll hide the diamonds in our *special hideaway*. Charles added a false bottom to it years ago and it's better than a safe.'

Two mugs of tea and a dry digestive later, Adele sets the house alarm and we step outside into the cold, morning air, the weak winter sun casting faint shadows over the courtyard and shrubbery. She scrapes a fine coating of frost from the car's windows and I take a few steps down the drive to get a better look at the lodge. It's certainly a substantial residence, considering it's only a holiday cottage. The gravel feels soggy underfoot confirming the heavy rain I heard when trying to get to sleep last night. Out of the corner of my eye, I see a lone jogger - a lady, encased in blue and yellow lycra and wearing a red woollen hat, padding along the road at the end of the drive, followed almost instantly by a man whistling for a dog. Have they been sent to find us? Oh my God, I hope not. Surely the villains couldn't have got anyone here so quickly. Adele doesn't seem concerned, so it's just me being paranoid but who can blame me?

The nearest town to Pine Lodge is Ringwood, situated on the western edge of the New Forest which Adele tells me *has been moulded by the fads of monarchs and commoners for a thousand years.* There's a misty glow over the tree tops and, straining my eyes, I can see what looks like snow in the distance. We drive slowly along narrow, winding roads passing the stark outlines of deciduous forests, heathland, and oak woods, their bare boughs rimed with frost-covered lichen. Ponies and cattle graze on the sparse grass verges and every so often, Adele has to slow down and skirt those animals which believe they have the right of way over noisy, polluting vehicles.

It takes twenty minutes to reach Ringwood and on our approach down the A31, the town, with its prominent church tower, sprawls before us under dark, low clouds. Luckily, Adele knows her way around and finds a space in the Furlong car park. In the precinct, a French Tricolour heralds *Le Festival de France* with half a dozen stalls attended by a few warmly-wrapped, French men and women selling continental cheeses, cold meats and pâté as well as olives in an array of colourful jars and bottles. It's full of activity and there's a buzz of busy people, finding time to chat with friends and acquaintances. I see two mothers with their babies in pushchairs and my heart leaps thinking *that could be me in eight months.*

The sight of all the food makes me realise how hungry I am. I tap Adele on her shoulder. 'Can we get something to eat first, I'm starving.'

Giving me a grin, Adele points to Waterstones. 'We'll get something right here.'

Getting a table for two by the window, we both order soup and rolls followed by ham sandwiches.

Wiping a couple of stray crumbs from her mouth, she pushes her empty plate away. 'Feeling better now?'

'I am, but still hungry. How about you?'

'Hell no, I've had enough but there again,' she laughs, 'I'm not eating for two. What do you want now, cake?'

'No, I'll have the soup and sandwich again.'

'Okay, I'll send it over while I check out what books they've got on Brussels.'

Gazing out of the window, my poor tummy flips as on the opposite side of the square, a tiny Chinese woman in a bright red coat wheels a trolley load of shopping towards the car park. Could it be? No, I'm over reacting, she's the least looking thug I've ever seen. After clearing my plate and a second cup of tea, I feel warm and more like my old self. Adele comes back holding a bag. 'I've got a Brussels guide and map - you're not still hungry, are you?'

'No, I'm stuffed,' I smile.

'Good, let's get our shopping but no credit cards, I've got cash.'

Whether it's because I'm in a strange town or simply scared of the unknown, I stay close to Adele, hoping there are no more Chinese faces in the crowd. As I left home yesterday without a change of clothes, I buy underwear, tops and trousers from the shop next to Waterstones and a super winter coat and lined boots from another shop a few doors away. Satisfied we have everything, we get a few days' supply of groceries in Waitrose.

As we leave Ringwood, it suddenly gets very dark and snow is drifting, the lightest of flakes, swirling in the car's headlights, but fortunately, not settling. Reaching the lodge, we're relieved that everything is as we left it this morning. The tin of Cadburys biscuits hasn't moved.

Adele lights the fire then insists I sit down and rest. I don't argue, feeling more relaxed now that we've got food in the house and the two of us are alone.

'I'll prepare a meal later,' she throws herself into a giant armchair. 'We'll have sirloin steaks with oven-ready frozen chips and peas. That'll recharge our batteries.'

'Sounds good to me.'

Her expression becoming businesslike. 'I have a proposal.'

'That's good because my poor brain's too muddled to work out anything.'

'Right,' she says. 'After what you've been through, you clearly need a rest before we tackle Sir Desmond Thrimby at HESEC and then heading for Brussels. I'm confident we'll be safe here for a few days so let's think of everything we need answers to, you know, make a list, and plan our next moves. Oh, and I almost forgot, I'll show you Nick's stuff I brought from my flat.' She opens a large, leather briefcase and empties the contents on the coffee table.

My eyes almost pop out of my head. 'Did he rob a bank?'

'No,' she laughs. 'It's the standard issue for HESEC's agents.' She thumbs through three wads of cash. 'There's roughly, give or take, twenty thousand pounds, twenty thousand US dollars, and another twenty thousand in Euros.'

'What, just like that, but why twenty thousand of each?'

'I don't know. Anyway, there's enough to keep us going for a while.'

'But it's not ours, it belongs to HESEC.'

'Not now, it doesn't. Those *purple-dyed* Chinese must have taken it.'

'Oh, so they did,' I say catching on. 'The thieving bastards.'

'And here's Nick's false passport and driving licence, called himself James Moore for some reason, and these,' she holds up what look like aerosol hairspray cans. 'HESEC's special mace and pepper sprays. They're illegal, of course, but very effective.'

'Hell's bells, and what are those.' I point to another packet Adele holds up. 'Are they syringes?'

'They are almost certainly to disable people - knock 'em out.'

'Any guns? He had one with him when he was murdered.'

'No, there's no gun, which is strange.'

'What's in those little bags?'

'More SIM cards and, that's everything, except for his bag.'

'Don't tell me that's a lethal weapon too.'

'No, but it's a HESEC special design. With a false compartment with a special lining which, so he told me, is supposed to conceal everything from airport security x-rays.'

'Wow, that's handy.'

'Nick said it's unique to his department.'

Sitting back in my chair, frowning, I shake my head trying to drag my wayward attention back to Nick and all his gadgets. 'There's something strange here. Seeing all this stuff and knowing his background, what I find hard to understand is why was he killed so easily?'

She hesitates before answering. 'I know what you mean, Nick was a top man. From your description of his murder, I'd say it was a trap – a setup – because you're right, it *was* too easy. But who planned it? Was it the Chinese or could it possibly have been someone in HESEC, or even the police?'

'I don't know, it's a puzzle, but the fact that he was murdered in HESEC-owned accommodation, and it was covered up so professionally, would point to them, but there again, why was I warned off by the police? Also, the guy who shot him had a Chinese accent.'

'I know. We may get to the bottom of it eventually, but for now, what I suggest is, that the day after tomorrow, Monday, we'll go out somewhere, away from here and I'll use a new SIM to call Sir Desmond Thrimby and make an appointment. We may get answers to these questions from him.'

It's Monday morning and I had a much better sleep last night, almost nine hours of uninterrupted, dreamless sleep. The bedroom still feels like an icebox with delicate frost patterns on the inside of the window. Quickly getting out of bed, I get dressed adding my new heavyweight coat to my normal clothes. Opening the bedroom door, I pick up the enticing smell of frying bacon emanating from the kitchen. My stomach and tiny embryo happily agree that, on this occasion, I may partake of a fried breakfast. A good sleep followed by a greasy-spoon meal is a great start to anyone's day.

'You'll be interested to know,' Adele's busily adds dirty pots to others from last night. 'After you'd gone to bed, I checked out Sir Des's Who's Who.'

'Did you now?'

'Unfortunately, there wasn't much there. His brief entry tells us nothing except the posh public school he went to followed by three years at Cambridge, his wife is Lady Elizabeth and they have three sons, Tarquin, Toby and Tristan.'

'What a Wally!'

'The only mention of his current career was as a senior executive in HESEC, after fifteen years service at the FO. He got his knighthood in 2008 for *Services to British Industry*.'

'So he's an ex-Foreign Office man, like Charles. I wonder if they knew each other?'

Adele shrugs.

After stacking up the remaining dishes, we leave the icy cottage. Joining the A31 east, it soon merges with the M27 before connecting with the M3 just after Rownhams Services. Luckily, yesterday's snow flurry has already melted. Exiting at junction 6 to Basingstoke, Adele drives the car to the top floor of a multi-storey car park where she inserts a new SIM. After passing through a multitude of operators, she eventually get through to Sir Desmond's secretary, Miss Wannacot.

'Hello, Miss Wannacot, my name's Adele Holbrook, the sister of the late Nick Holbrook, and I'd like to arrange a meeting with Sir Desmond Thrimby.'

'Oh, Miss Holbrook,' there's an emotional catch in her voice. 'We were so sorry to hear about Nicholas, such a tragedy and we all miss him very much.'

'Thank you, it was a dreadful shock to all the family.' She gives me a wink. 'And his fiancée.'

'Oh yes, it must have been. I er, didn't know he was engaged.'

'Yes, just a short time before he died.'

'Oh, that's so sad. I'm afraid Sir Desmond is out at the moment, but he should be in within the next half hour. Can I reach you on the number you called on?'

Looking at her watch, she scratches her head. 'Yes, I'll be available for say twenty minutes and then I'll be driving so won't be able to answer.'

'Of course, I understand. I'll do my best, Miss Holbrook.' She hangs up.

'I don't want to stay round here,' Adele says. 'They may trace where we are, but Basingstoke is a good hour from London.' She takes the SIM card out for a couple of minutes before replacing it. 'I don't know if that'll work or not.'

Exactly twenty minutes later, the phone rings, it's Miss Wannacot.

'Sir Desmond Thrimby will be pleased to see you both on Wednesday morning, the 5th of February, and wonders if ten o'clock will be convenient for you.'

'Thank you Miss Wannacot and yes, ten o'clock is fine.'

'Phew, that seems too easy.' I smile. 'All you have to do now is get rid of the SIM. You could put it in that car leaving now. I heard them arguing about the best way to Derbyshire.' The BMW Z3 roadster, incongruously occupied by an old, quarrelsome couple, was about to reverse out of the next parking bay when Adele neatly stuck the SIM to the underside of the car's gutter. 'I wonder how long it'll be before they're pulled over,' she laughs.

Chapter Eleven
February 5th

We arrive ten minutes early at HESEC's offices, a shiny glass and steel block off Lower Thames Street with a view of the Tower of London. The early morning sun is low above the river, a perfect disc against a clear, wintery sky with no sign of the earlier clouds. The foyer is elegant with greenery everywhere. Palms and miniature trees, abstract paintings and light classical music playing softly from hidden speakers.

Our names are checked on a computerised register before we're ushered through an airport-type security system involving the contents of our handbags. Then, arms outstretched, every contour of our bodies is patted down by a grim-faced female security officer who eventually gives us the all-clear.

We are directed to the fifteenth floor where Miss Wannacot meets us. She's a formidable-looking, middle aged lady dressed in a neatly tailored navy suit, white blouse and pearl earrings. Following her along a carpeted corridor, I notice each door has a nameplate - none has Hal or Tim as a first name. Finally reaching a waiting room, she asks us to take a seat at a transparent coffee table spread with a selection of magazines, featuring luxury resorts, numerous ads for jewellery and speed boats. The outside walls are plate glass from floor to ceiling and the bright reflecting light gives me a strange feeling that I'm hovering, suspended between street and sky. Subconsciously, I fiddle with my late grandmother's engagement ring I'm wearing to maintain the story that Nick and I were to be married.

A soft-toned bell rings on Miss Wannacot's desk and, picking up the phone, she glances at us, and murmurs a few words before replacing the receiver. She comes over. 'I'm afraid Sir Desmond will be fifteen minutes late. He's been unexpectedly held up in a meeting.'

Smiling, I thank her. Hesitating, she turns to face us. 'Would you mind if I sit with you for a moment?' Her expression has softened and she glances at her watch, probably making sure she won't be caught fraternising.

'Please do,' Adele shuffles over and makes room.

'It's just that as I told you on the phone, I want to say again how sorry I was to learn about your brother, Nicholas. Such a tragedy, and they haven't caught the hit-and-run driver yet.'

'I'm hoping Sir Desmond will have some news on that,' Adele says.

Miss Wannacot shakes her head. 'Not that I've heard. And you too, Miss Lane. I didn't know that Nicholas and you were engaged.'

I fight back a few tears. 'Yes, we were. Did you know Nick well?'

'As well as one can in this job, you know, everything is so private and hush-hush. Nicholas was such a nice man, everybody liked him, especially the ladies,' she colours slightly. 'He was very professional and his special status was well deserved, especially appreciated by Mr Caldwell.'

'Mr Caldwell?' I query.

'Yes, he was the Section Chief before Sir Desmond.' From the way she says his name, I get the feeling she's not enamoured with her new boss.

'Oh, so Sir Desmond is only recently in the position.'

'Yes, he came here six months ago after four years as British Trade Commissioner in Beijing.'

My heart skips a beat and I notice Adele gives an involuntary movement. 'Beijing in China,' I add foolishly, as though I'm showing a teacher that I know where Beijing is.

'And he brought a colleague with him.' This time, it's not just her expression that's changed but also the tone of voice.

My heart beats faster as the image of Hal, speaking Mandarin, flashes into my head. 'Would that be Hal by any chance?'

'Hal? Oh, you mean Harold ... Harold Thomas,' she looks surprised. 'Yes, Harold was in Beijing with Sir Desmond and ah! I realise now, it was he who took you home after Nicholas's accident.' Her lips close tightly as if holding something back. I wish I could tell her that it was murder and not an accident. Her phone rings and she excuses herself to return to her desk. I give Adele a nudge and, without saying a word, she nods showing she's fully au fait with the *Chinese connection*.

From where we are sitting, we can see down the length of the corridor. There's the sound of a lift door quietly gliding open and a man emerges heading in our direction. Walking straight past us without a glance, he enters an office on the opposite side of Miss Wannacot's desk.

'That looks like him,' I whisper. 'Not very friendly, is he?'

'You can go through,' Miss Wannacot announces from the doorway. 'Sir Desmond will see you now.'

His office is luxuriously furnished with amazing views over London. Rising slowly from behind a large panelled desk, he shakes our hands with a firm but unpleasantly damp grip. He is tall, about six foot, with broad shoulders and white hair, his face grave with sharp grey eyes. He's probably in his fifties, but it's hard to tell as he has a noticeably large belly and a double chin that rolls outward over his collar.

'Miss Holbrook, my condolences for your loss.' His voice is deep, but I detect his cut-glass accent is not natural. 'I've sent a letter to your parents.'

She gives a slight nod in response. 'Sir Desmond, my brother was murdered and we want to know who did it and why.'

'I can't possibly comment on that.'

'But that's not good enough. Nick's fiancée, Miss Lane, met two of his colleagues before he was killed, Hal and Tim, but she didn't get their last names.'

'That's normal practice, Miss Holbrook,' he says without hesitation, as though he's said it a hundred times before. 'In our line of business, we give away as little as possible, I'm sure you understand.'

'No, I'm afraid I don't.' Adele crosses her legs slowly, his eyes taking it all in. She's wearing a tight skirt, shorter than usual. I think it's her way of dealing with men and exploiting any weaknesses they may have. She gives a little cough. 'Hal promised to let Miss Lane know when Nick's killer was caught.'

'Hmm, did he now?' comes a sceptical response, his gaze returning to her face.

'Yes he did. We'd like to see him please.'

'I'm afraid that won't be possible, Miss Holbrook.'

'Why not?'

'He's not authorised to communicate with members of the public.'

This meeting is not going well. We were hoping he'd be on our side but it's now clear that we're not going to get any help from him which makes me believe he's probably part of the cover-up himself.

'Sir Desmond,' Adele, continues. 'My brother was working for you when he was murdered, right in front of Miss Lane. It wasn't a traffic accident as you and the police state, it was cold blooded murder, and you know it. Since then, Miss Lane who, by the way, is pregnant, and I have been attacked by thugs demanding a package that Nick was supposed to have given her. We have no idea what they are talking about. My parents' house and my apartment have been ransacked and we're all scared. Miss Lane went to the police to report the murder, but they didn't believe her, saying that she was wasting their time.'

Going slightly red, he puts up his hands, palms forward. 'Just hold on a moment, young lady, you've no right to speak to me like ...'

'No, I won't hold on,' Adele refuses to give way. 'We want answers now, otherwise we'll be forced to approach the press and go viral on the web.'

This threat must have hit home. He exhales noisily, angrily steepling his fingers on the desk. 'I'll answer as much as I can, but please remember, and you too Miss Lane,' he glances briefly in my direction. 'We are a security organisation working in strictest confidence for the British Government, consequently certain matters of national security are off limits.'

'Bullshit,' Adele replies forcibly. 'My family deserve more than the lie that Nick was killed by a hit-and-run driver.'

He looks intently at Adele for a few moments. 'I'm sorry, Miss Holbrook, but the whole business regarding your brother's death is a matter of national security.'

'Is that it?' she shrills. 'Is that all we get?'

'There's nothing more I can say. I'm sure your father appreciates the situation even if you don't. He is a military man, after all.'

I take over from a fuming Adele. 'Have you caught the person who shot him? Hal, that's Harold Thomas, promised he would let me know, but I haven't heard from him since he *saved my life*.' I notice a reflex twitch on his face with my last revelation. 'You do know about that, don't you?'

His eyes almost bore into my head which is unnerving. 'When would this incident have taken place, Miss Lane?'

It takes me a moment to find my voice. 'He came round to my flat, arriving just in time to save me from two masked men.'

He drops his gaze to make some notes. 'You were being attacked?' he says it slowly as if speaking to someone who's mentally retarded.

'Yes, by two men who wanted this *mythical* package.' My heart is now racing like an engine.

'And did you give it to them?'

'No,' I shout. 'We've already told you, I had no idea what they were talking about.'

'I see,' he says simply. 'And what happened when Mr Thomas arrived?' He continues to intimidate me with his stare. Without Adele at my side, I would have probably caved in.

'They escaped through a bedroom window.'

He arches his eyebrows sceptically. 'And then?'

'Hal ... Harold, attended to my injuries and made tea. He was very kind.' My throat is dry and I have to swallow a couple of times before I can continue. 'He stayed with me for a while and gave me his private phone number saying I could call him any time, day or night.'

'What was the number?'

I try to look angry, but probably fail. 'You're testing me, aren't you? It's 989800.' God, I wish he'd stop staring at me. 'Hal also told me that there is a mole in HESEC.'

The mention of a mole must have hit a nerve, and he angrily snaps, 'And what the hell did he mean by that?'

'I don't know, do I?' I stutter, 'Maybe a double agent.'

'A mole and a double agent, my, my Miss Lane,' his temper quickly back under control, 'I think you've wandered into the realms of fantasy.' His eyes narrow and his hand gives the tiniest shake as he makes more notes. 'Did you call him on his private number?'

'No.'

'And do you think the death of Mr Holbrook and the attack on you are connected?'

'You're damned right we do,' Adele jumps in, her dander well and truly up. 'They all wanted this mysterious package. And the moment the police heard that my dead brother had been working for you at HESEC, they dropped the case accusing Miss Lane of wasting their time. Do you also control the police?'

Her accusation is ignored.

'National bloody security, is it?' she shouts. 'And there's my other brother, Charles Temple, missing in Africa, and you and the Foreign Office refusing to do anything to find him. What do you know about that?'

'Miss Holbrook,' he fixes her with a hostile stare, 'I object to your tone and we'll get nowhere if you continue in this manner. I will tell you what I'm permitted to reveal, but as far as Mr Charles Temple is concerned, I have no information on him whatsoever.'

'Is that from the Ministry of Lies or is it you?'

His face colours in anger, he stands and presses a button on the side of his desk. 'I'm afraid, ladies,' his voice is low and harsh. 'We'll have to end this meeting now.'

'Or is it to do with Limarni?' I hastily butt in.

From the lack of reaction to the name, I don't think it means anything to him.

'Lim what?' He queries.

Damn, what do I do now? 'Yes,' I quickly improvise in case Limarni might give him a clue. 'Le Mali, is it a country in Africa?'

He makes a hurried note before Miss Wannacot enters and asks us to follow her to the lifts, her mouth fixed in a firm line, but I'm sure her eyes are sympathetic. We thank her and I smile as we say goodbye.

As soon as the lift door closes, Adele pokes me in the ribs indicating a CCTV camera mounted in the top corner of the lift, she whispers, 'Well done, let's talk later.'

CHAPTER TWELVE
FEBRUARY 5th

A mist from the river has rolled in since we'd arrived at HESEC, blotting out the morning sun. We hurry to collect our carry-on bags from the hire car we'd parked earlier, and hail a taxi to St Pancras.

Clambering in, Adele says, 'From now on, we're not in hiding and I'm damned sure that someone - whether HESEC, the police, the bloody Chinese or *whoever*, will have a trace on us. Somehow, we've got to give them the slip before reaching Brussels.'

'I know.' Checking my watch, I add, 'We've got almost an hour before our Eurostar leaves.'

'Good, that's just about right,' she closes her eyes in thought. 'When we get to Brussels, I'm thinking we should go unannounced to Axel Van Damme's place.'

'Why's that?'

'So he doesn't disappear or notify the wrong people.'

'But surely he must be on our side because he's the one Nick said I can trust.'

'I know, but after what we've been through over the past few days, it's difficult to trust anyone, certainly without being very careful.'

'Thrimby didn't know about Limarni, did he?'

'No. Your bit about Mali was brilliant, where did that come from?'

I laugh. 'Mixing with you, I guess. It must be rubbing off.'

A cold easterly wind whips at our coats as we carry our bags into the station. The check-in proceeds smoothly, staff feed our tickets into an automatic barrier before approaching customs. Holding our breath when Nick's briefcase, with the secret compartment containing *the package* and his other gadgets are x-rayed, we let out a sigh of relief as it passes through with no problem, but panic kicks in when my handbag is placed to one side after passing through the machine.

'Over here, madam.' A lady customs official beckons me over. 'Please open your handbag.'

Adele stands slightly to one side.

The woman looks puzzled as, one by one, she takes the contents out obviously looking for something. After a few moments of rummaging, her eyes light up as she tugs at a small black metal object under the clasp. 'And what's this?' she holds it up in front of me.

'I don't know. Isn't it part of the clasp?'

'No, it triggered an alert in the machine.'

Suddenly Adele is by my side. 'I know what it is,' she gives a sly tap on my ankle. 'It's your father's hearing aid, the one he lost last week. We looked everywhere for it.'

I catch on quickly. 'Yes, you're right, poor Dad was lost without it, you know, it's a metal type from Switzerland.'

The lady frowns. 'But why would it trigger an alarm?'

'Well, it's bound to, isn't it,' Adele confidently expands, 'It's electronic with a tiny transmitter and er, it's er ...'

'It's magnetic,' I butt in. 'And that's why it stuck to the clasp of my bag.'

The official, taken by surprise by our concocted story, only hesitates a moment before tamely placing it in Adele's confidant, outstretched hand.

'Thank you,' I manage to give her a beaming smile. 'Dad will be so relieved.'

'Grab your bags and keep moving,' Adele whispers out of the corner of her mouth. 'Don't give her a chance for a rethink.' We quickly pass through immigration then take the escalator to the platform.

'Wait here for a minute,' Adele sidles off to where some cases are stacked on a trolley. Casually, she leans on a suitcase as she checks her make-up in the vanity mirror. She closes her bag and joins me. 'Let's board. That bloody hearing aid thing was a tracking device, which is now in someone's bag, on its way to Bray in Berkshire.'

'But how did they ...?'

'It must have been that security bitch at HESEC.'

At twelve fifty-eight, we board the two hour and one minute Eurostar express train to Brussels and make our way to our allotted seats at the front of the fifth carriage. There are two rows of two seats either side of the centre aisle. They are comfortable with high backs but the upholstery is a rather tired-looking, yellowish-grey colour.

'We can relax for a couple of hours but still must be careful.' She stands and looks around. 'Ah good, there's plenty of space, you stay where you are because if we've been followed, they'll know our seat numbers. I'll go back a few rows and watch.' She puts a scarf over her head. 'Disguise number one,' she cheerily remarks. 'It's probably nothing but don't worry, I can handle anything.'

All the symptoms of tension build up in my arms and neck muscles again. It's all very well Adele saying she can handle anything, maybe she can, but I know damn well I can't. Resting my head on the seat back, I try to relax and after a while, my breathing eases and the smooth ride helps me calm down.

Oh shit! A shiver snakes through me as I suddenly feel the presence of someone in the seat directly behind me - there was no-one there before. What should I do, yell for Adele? Not yet, it may be just a passenger changing seats.

'Penny Wane,' a deep male voice with a distinct Chinese accent, speaks through the gap between the seats, scaring the living daylights out of me. 'Where Miss Holbrook?'

'Who are you?' I stutter, my lips trembling.

'No matter, I want package,' his menacing whisper is totally controlled. 'I have gun pointing at centre your back and won't hesitate kill you. Listen.'

I have a sudden flashback to seeing Nick with a bullet hole in his head. I hear a metallic click. I've never known such fear as I'm feeling right now.

'You hear, Penny Wane? Safety catch off. Give me package and I weave you awone.'

'I er ... '

'Not fuck me around, where package - in your bag?'

Although I try to speak, my tongue seems to be stuck to the roof of my mouth. Paralysed with fear, I know something has to be done before a bullet rips into my back, but I manage a feeble nod. He must believe it's in my bag because I'm aware of him moving as he comes round to sit next to me. Turning to face to him, I feel something hard pressed into my ribs.

'Give me bag.' His face cruel and unshaven. 'Quick,' he snarls.

Shaking like a leaf, I reach under my seat and pass him my handbag.

Holding the gun in one hand, he uses the other to open it when, without warning, he makes a strange gurgling noise which seems to come from deep within his chest and, little by little, as though in slow motion, he topples over falling heavily onto my lap. Petrified, I look down and see a hypodermic syringe sticking out of his neck, his slavering, drooling mouth gapes open, and his whole body starts to twitch as though he's holding live electric wires.

'W…what the hell!'

Adele's leaning over him. 'Leave this to me,' she whispers, removing the syringe, shoving his gun into her coat pocket. 'He may only be out for a few minutes so we have to be quick.'

Horror-struck, I shake my head unable to speak and a tremor is spreading to my thighs, down my legs and into my feet.

Adele holds me with her eyes, her will is like iron. 'Get a fucking grip and help get him up,' she snaps, 'We'll take him to the loo, hurry.'

Pulling myself together, I somehow manage to stand and between us, we lever the man upright. Glancing back down the aisle, I see a few people peering in our direction, a couple of them stand to get a better view.

'Tell them in French,' Adele murmurs, 'That your brother is unwell and we're taking him to the toilet.'

There are some blank faces so I repeat it in broken English as a French person might. Their expressions vary but they all sit down. Adele places his arms around our shoulders and we stumble into the aisle. God, he's heavy. Although his head is lolling around, he's not totally paralysed and instinctively moves his feet with ours, bearing some of his own weight. We stagger through a sliding door into the corridor and push our way into the vacant Disabled Person's Toilet, the irony of which passes Adele by. It's cramped with three of us inside. With great difficulty, we manage to sit him on the closed seat.

'Keep him there,' Adele orders.

I hold onto him the best I can, my jaw's clenched tight and teeth are clamped together, but it doesn't stop them chattering. Pulling on a pair of gloves, Adele opens her handbag and takes out a plastic knife with a roll of gaffer tape. Quickly, she tapes his mouth and binds his legs and ankles together. Suddenly, his eyes begin to focus and he grabs my arm in a vice-like grip. Calmly taking the gun from her pocket, Adele smashes it down on his hand half a dozen times until he releases me. His screams are muffled by the tape over his mouth - only his eyes show the agony he's in. The cool, unwavering Adele grabs his other hand and binds them together, then over his face, around his head and mouth again.

'There,' Adele straightens, banging into me in the confined area. Our faces are only inches apart and I notice her eyes are pitiless. 'I think that's him taken care of, don't you?'

'What er, what happened?' I stutter. 'What was in the syringe?'

'It's one of Nick's, but I don't know how effective it'll be. It's probably a variant of corticosteroid which paralyses the muscles for between five and ten minutes.'

'So he won't die then?'

'No, but we can kill him if you want,' she says callously. This is the other Adele, she's like two different people and this one scares me.

'You can't kill him,' I gasp, 'But can we leave him here until we reach Brussels?'

'I don't see why not,' she answers matter of factly. 'Now, let me take a closer look at his gun.' She wipes blood off the butt onto the man's anorak. 'Fuck, I think it's an SM4, the Groza silent pistol, I've only ever seen a picture of one before.' She holds it out in front of her admiringly for a few seconds. 'Yes,

I'm sure it's the one, a silent pistol made for the Russian KGB, it's their favourite close range assassination weapon.'

'You mean it's actually silent when fired, without a silencer?'

'Yes, it uses some kind of special cartridge, SP something or other, which contains the gasses entirely when fired. Let's see if it does.' She aims at the man's thigh. 'Stand back as far as you can, just in case.'

'Just in case of what?' I yell. 'Please don't shoot.'

Ignoring my plea and using a double-handed grip, she fires. There is a blinding flash and muffled bang which would be barely audible in the corridor outside, but the man's leg turns red. His gagged scream turns my stomach before he loses consciousness.

The disgusting odour of blood mixed with cordite hits me and I retch several times over the washbasin. What little breakfast I'd had comes up. 'Why ... why did you do that?'

'Oh for God's sake, Penny,' she snaps, 'This man's a hired killer. He's under orders to get the package and then kill us - no question. Don't feel sorry for the bastard.'

Wiping away the last of the vomit from my mouth, I can't speak.

'Now, let's have a look.' Still wearing gloves, she pulls back his sleeve and points to a tattoo on his wrist. 'Aha, a Triad, that's not surprising.' Then going through his coat, she finds his wallet. 'He's got Euros and Sterling - must be five hundred pounds worth, so we'll confiscate that, thank you very much and, oh shit, look at this.'

I look at the sheet of paper she passes me, and my poor, suffering guts give another double summersault. Staring back are photos of Adele and me, and written underneath is our booking on this train with the seat numbers.

Shaking her head, Adele runs water into the washbasin.

There's a faint sound outside the door followed by someone knocking. 'How long will you be?' an English male voice asks.

Adele and I freeze. After a second's thought, she whispers, 'Tell him in French, or fractured English, or whatever, that your brother is sick, and tell him the toilet's broken and there's no water. Tell him that.'

Nervously, I repeat her instructions, adding that he should try the one in the next carriage. I hear him curse but the sound of his footsteps grow fainter as he moves away.

'Bloody hell, Adele, let's get out of here.' It's then I notice the man's eyes flickering. 'Oh, double shit, he's waking up.'

She gives a half smile. 'So he is - no matter,' she takes an ink marker out of her bag. 'Look outside and if it's clear, write "Out of order" on the door in French, German and English and then I'll tape it closed as best I can. I've got something to attend to in here while you're doing it.'

Cautiously looking both ways, no-one's in sight and I do as I'm told.

A minute later, she comes out, her eyes still have that uncompromising look in them. 'Everything's taken care of. Now, you return to your seat, you can tell any passengers who ask – not in English of course, that your brother is better and has gone back to his seat in another coach. I've got a few things to get rid of.'

PART TWO
BRUSSELS

Chapter Thirteen
February 6th

In Nick's letter, the address for Axel Van Damme is only a short way from several hotels in the Laeken District of North West Brussels. Adele gets the city map on her mobile and we chose the Brendtle Hotel so that we'd be as close as possible to the person Nick said I could trust.

After an early dinner, we go up to Adele's room to check the contents of the secret compartment in Nick's briefcase. It contains the cash, an unused syringe, two cans of mace and, of course, the package containing the diamonds. She gives a can of mace to me.

'I'd like you to hold onto the diamonds,' I say. 'We'll take it with us tomorrow.'

'Yes, but by the way, I've changed my mind about contacting Van Damme. I think we should phone him before turning up on his doorstep, what do you think?'

'Ha, we'll be in a mess if he's not there, but yes, I agree.'

Lying awake for what seems hours, I can't get the images of what happened on the train out of my head. I know Adele had her reasons for the brutal treatment she handed out to the assassin, but the unsettling thing was she seemed to enjoy it. What kind of woman is she – some sort of psychopath? I hope not but, I acknowledge, circumstances are such that I need to stick with her until I'm no longer the villain's target. I need her.

When I join her for breakfast, she's already ordered coffee. I'm worried my baby will be addicted to caffeine by the time the poor thing is born. With very little appetite, I only manage to eat part of my boiled egg and a slice of toast and jam, whilst Adele fills her slight frame with enough food to fill a supermarket trolley.

After breakfast, we go up to her room. Switching on the speaker, she phones Van Damme. Holding my breath, I sit on the bed next to her.

After five rings, a lady answers. 'Oui.'

'Good morning, I'd like to speak to Mr Axel Van Damme.'

'Who's calling?' There's a note of caution in her voice although her English accent is very good.

'My name's Adele Holbrook, Nick Holbrook's sister.'

There's a gasp. She must have put her hand over the mouthpiece as we hear some muffled whispering. 'Who's that again?' she queries as though she can't believe her ears.

'Adele Holbrook, my brother is a very good friend of Mr Van Damme's. I'm here in Brussels with Nick's fiancée, Penny Lane, and it's important we see him.'

There's a silence before a man takes over. 'Why should we believe you?'

'Mr Van Damme, we're staying at the Brendtle Hotel. We could meet anywhere you choose and you can check our passports. Penny has a letter from Nick giving your name and address.'

'Just a moment.'

Adele holds the phone away from her ear, murmuring to me, 'What the hell's wrong with him, why so suspicious?'

The man's voice comes back. 'You say you have my address?'

'Yes.'

'Come to the entrance, it's a fifteen minute walk from your hotel and put your passports through the letter box.'

'Thank you, Mr Van Damme, we're leaving now.'

Frowning, Adele says, 'He didn't even confirm that he is Mr Van Damme. Should we be worried?'

'I don't know,' I sigh, 'But we'll have to go. I'll take the mace with me – just in case.'

We walk briskly along Houba de Strooperiaan, our shoes crunching salt crystals recently spread on the pavement. The temperature is several degrees below zero and the wind bites into us as we turn the corner onto Boulevard Emile Bockstael, a busy dual carriageway with a wide tree-lined pavement. A bank of yellow *Boris Bikes* is waiting for customers who can brave this weather, but only two seem to be in use.

With my head bent against the wind, I try and keep pace with the measured click, click of Adele's shoes. I hadn't noticed before but she must have metal-tipped heels - knowing her, they're probably lethal weapons. I'm uneasy, even jittery about this meeting, praying it won't be as fruitless as the one with Thrimby but, what else can I do - we do?

The Van Damme's building is in a row of three and four storey apartments and its fading yellow-arched outer entrance badly needs repainting. Directly on the road outside is a blue-painted disabled parking bay and there's a CCTV camera over the door. Checking the names of inhabitants, Adele presses the button on Apartment 4D.

'Who's there?' It's the same man's voice.

'Adele Holbrook and Penny Lane.'

'Wait. I'll be down in a minute.'

Doing our best to shelter in the doorway, I stamp my feet trying to keep my circulation going but Adele seems immune to the cold. We have to wait four minutes before a shadowy figure appears through the obscure-glazed front door.

'Can you hear me?' It's the lady's voice again.

'Yes.'

'Put your passports through the letter box.'

'I'll put mine through, we'll keep the other for now.'

'Er ... that's okay for now,' she replies. Shortly, there's a loud click and buzz as the door opens. 'Please come in.' There's a look of misgiving on the woman's face and she nervously checks behind us to make sure there's nobody else. She's a tall, handsome woman who appears to be in her late thirties or early forties, smartly dressed in a bright red woollen top and neat pleated grey skirt. I notice her eyes are puffy as though she's been crying.

Relieved to be out of the cold, the foyer feels wonderfully warm but looks just as shabby as the outside. The Van Dammes don't seem to live in the lap of luxury.

'I'm Adele Holbrook and this is Penny Lane, we're here to see Axel Van Damme.'

She gives me an odd look and smiles giving Adele back her passport. 'What an unusual name.' Turning to Adele, she says, 'I'm Petra Van Damme, my husband is waiting upstairs. And you are Nick's sister.' Her expression has softened and her eyes fill with tears as she puts her arms gently around Adele's shoulders, holding her tight. 'Oh Adele, I'm so sorry about Nick. So, so sorry,' tears roll down her cheeks leaving a small damp patch on the shoulder of her coat. 'Please come this way, both of you.'

We take a clanking, old-fashioned lift to the second floor and step out onto a speckled granite-surfaced corridor, our steps echoing hollowly. Don't they have carpets in Belgium?

The Van Dammes' door has an iron grill over a fanlight and a tarnished brass sign above a bell push. There's a musty, unventilated smell, almost museum-like.

'You've heard about Nick then?' Adele asks Petra as we go into the hallway.

Sniffling into a tissue, she nods her head. 'Yes, Axel heard a couple of days ago.' Wiping away a stray tear, she gives a sad smile. 'My husband will explain.'

Their apartment, with two storeys, is larger than I'd imagined and we follow Petra up a flight of stairs to the top floor where she ushers us into a good-sized room with overflowing book-shelves on two sides and a well worn carpet covering most of the floor. A large window silhouettes a thin-faced, bespectacled man of indeterminate age, sitting behind a panelled desk, a walking stick leaning at the side. The weak morning sun picks out a vase of bright, yellow daffodils, contrasting with the dinginess of the room.

'Please take a seat, ladies, and forgive me for not standing.' His voice sounds weak and now that I'm closer, I can see his pallid skin and dark rimmed eyes. 'I'm just out of hospital after another operation on my leg, that's three in all.'

'His leg was injured in Cote d'Ivoire,' Petra looks at him worriedly, twining a strand of hair around a finger. 'But, thank God, the surgeon believes the damage has been repaired.'

Coming straight to the point, Adele speaks. 'Mr Van Damme, before we go any further, we want to see your passport to be quite sure you are, who you say you are.'

He frowns.

Petra asks. 'Why?'

'We need to be certain that you are Axel Van Damme, the man Nick told us to see.'

Raising his eyes in surprise, he hesitates before opening a drawer in his desk, moves a few papers around, produces a passport and slides it across. We look at it together. His name checks out and the photo, although taken several years ago, is definitely him.

'Thank you.' Reassured, Adele passes it back. 'I'm sorry about that, but we can't be too careful. And remember, you didn't trust me when I phoned - did you?'

He shifts uncomfortably in his chair. 'That's true and I can explain. I was discharged from hospital on Tuesday and tried to get Nick on his cell phone, but it was disconnected. Two months ago, he'd told us he would be here this week, so I phoned his company in London and was put through to one of his colleagues who told me that Nick had been killed in a car accident.'

Petra takes over. 'Since then, we've had three very odd, almost threatening phone calls ... strange accents demanding details of Nick's mine in Africa. That's why we were suspicious when you called.'

'But I didn't know Nick had anything to do with an African mine.'

'No, neither did we.'

I don't say anything but it must be something to do with those diamonds.

Adele turns to me. 'I think Axel contacting HESEC was when our cover was blown.'

'What's this?' he gives her a suspicious look. 'Cover blown! Are you in trouble?'

'Yes, we are,' Adele tries a reassuring smile. 'We'll tell you all about it but first, we want to know about your connection to Nick, it's very important.'

He pauses for a few seconds. 'We knew him very well,' he looks affectionately in his wife's direction. 'We owe everything to Nick Holbrook, you see, he saved our lives.'

'He did,' Petra confirms. 'But now he's dead and we can't repay him.'

'How did he save you?'

'It was like this,' Axel rubs his forehead with his hand. 'I was working on a contract in Cote d'Ivoire, that's the Ivory Coast in West Africa. I was heading a team doing oil exploration. I'm a geologist by profession. There were three expatriates and twenty locals. Oil reserves had been found off-shore and satellite images of the earth's gravitational map indicated there was also oil inland, but seismic analysis taken earlier was unclear, so it was necessary to go and do some test drillings and more seismic tests on the spot.'

'Was Nick with you?' I ask.

'No, he had nothing to do with our work. There had been a civil war in the country which kept flaring up, but we were not thought to be in danger as there were UN peacekeepers in that region, and we also had our own local bodyguards.' His frail voice begins to tremble as he takes a handkerchief out of his pocket. 'It felt so safe there that I arranged for Petra to come out for a week's holiday. God, I wish I hadn't.'

'Why was that?'

'Well, we were on the site when, without warning, a large force of heavily-armed rebels suddenly appeared – about forty in total, some of them boy soldiers. They were like wild savages, yelling and screaming, thrusting their weapons in our faces.' He glances upwards as if reliving the events. 'Whether they were drunk, on drugs, or both we couldn't tell, but they spoke to each other in a form of pidgin French so I knew they meant us harm.'

Petra goes and stands by his side and, their eyes meet and she gives him an affectionate kiss on his cheek. 'I can't even begin to tell you how scared we were. The leader demanded money. They took our wallets, watches, jewellery and cameras, all this was accompanied by ear-piercing shrieks while continuing to thrust guns at us. They said if we didn't hand over one million dollars immediately, they'd kill us.'

He's clearly finding it difficult to carry on so Petra takes over. 'Axel tried to explain we didn't have that amount but all he got was a rifle butt smashed in his face. Our so-called bodyguards were useless. They dropped their weapons and fled which made the rebels even angrier. They grabbed Vincent Morales, he was in Axel's team, a South African, and without any notice, they hacked him to death with pangas - you know, machetes, right in front of us. His dying screams still haunt my dreams.'

'It was barbaric,' Axel continues. 'Like your worst nightmare, and we knew we'd be next. Then, they grabbed the other expat, Jaroslav Baros, a Czech professor whom I'd personally recruited for the job. I begged them to stop.'

Adele butts in. 'Did they kill him?'

'No, they tied him to a post and beat him with rifle butts. He was in a terrible state, his face covered in blood. They laughed, shouting how they'd kill him and then ...' Axel stops, nestling his head in his arms, letting the rest of the sentence fade.

I want to say something comforting, but my mouth is too dry.

Petra places both arms around her husband. 'They left Jaroslav tied to the post and turned their attention to me, having something completely different in mind.'

Giving a sharp intake of breath, my clenched nails are cutting into my palms.

Petra murmurs. 'They tied my hands and started to rip off my clothes.'

'I tried to stop them,' Axel sobs. 'They chopped my leg with a panga, screaming they would kill me if I did anything. You see, they wanted me to watch what they were doing.'

Petra is now crying openly, tears rolling unchecked down her cheeks, clinging tightly to Axel's shoulders. 'And that was when Nick arrived.'

For a few seconds, there's a stunned silence. No-one speaks but my thoughts are racing, trying to visualise the horrific scene in that far away place, of Petra, about to suffer an unimaginable death and Axel being forced to watch, before being killed himself. Shakily, I wipe my face with a tissue. Only Adele seems unaffected, although I notice her fists are clenched in her lap.

Gathering herself, Petra takes a couple of deep breaths. 'It all took place in a blur. Nick and five uniformed men carrying submachine guns, burst into the clearing as if by magic.'

Axel, putting himself above the emotion, also seems to have recovered, as if the telling of the story has been therapeutic. 'It was so professional as though Nick's men had rehearsed this scenario a hundred times. Although outnumbered, the rebels were absorbed by the impending rape of Petra so, almost unnoticed, one of Nick's men rushed at the three thugs molesting her and, with short bursts of fire, shot them dead, just as Nick grabbed the leader who was holding me.' Pausing for breath, he takes a sip of water from a glass on his desk. 'The other four of Nick's men took up military-style positions aiming their weapons at the remaining rebels, a few clumsily tried to return fire but were immediately shot. The rest either dropped their weapons or rushed for the safety of the jungle.'

'God almighty,' Adele exclaims. 'How can you get over an experience like that?'

Petra gives a sad smile. 'I don't think we ever will.'

Axel leans across and gives her a gentle squeeze. 'After Petra and Jaroslav were cut free, Nick patched my leg with a field dressing, gave me an injection for the pain and ordered his men to get Petra and me into one of his Land Rovers. He stayed behind with his other men to prevent the rebels reorganising, and to give treatment to Jaroslav.'

Looking more relaxed now, Petra stands. '*Misschien*, I think it's time we had a drink, don't you? I'll make tea.'

'Thank you,' I reply, still shocked at her story.

'I'll let Axel tell you more.' Petra leaves the room.

'After making a quick call on his satellite phone, Noah drove us.'

'Noah?' I interrupt. 'Did you say Noah?'

'Yes, Noah Tofa, a colonel, he was Nick's right-hand man.'

'That's interesting because Nick mentioned him in his letter.'

'I'm not surprised by that,' he acknowledges, 'Noah was fantastic that day.'

'Anyway, please go on.'

'Well, Noah drove us through the jungle to a small grassy airstrip where we waited about ten minutes before a twin-engine, unmarked aircraft landed.'

'But what about your leg?'

'The injection must have numbed it, so it wasn't bothering me at the time, although blood was seeping around the edges of the dressing.' He stops as Petra comes in carrying a tray with tea and biscuits, and hands cups and plates round.

Cup in hand, Axel carries on. 'Noah told us we were heading for a small airstrip in the adjoining country of Liberia and that we had to fly low to avoid being picked up on the radar system at Robertsfield International, Liberia's main airport.'

'You must have been in a state,' I sympathise. 'Because you couldn't really be sure who your rescuers were and what they would do with you.'

'Yes, that's absolutely right,' he concedes. 'But we had no other choice.'

'So what happened then?'

'We flew for almost an hour over the jungle before landing on a very bumpy strip surrounded by rainforest.'

'Was that in Liberia?'

'Yes. While we waited for a vehicle, Noah changed the dressing on my leg, it was hurting, and they drove us about twenty kilometres to a hotel called Cleopatra's.'

'And did you feel safe?'

'*Safer*, certainly safer,' Petra smiles, refilling everyone's cups.

'Noah took me to a nearby private hospital where a doctor checked my leg wound, gave me a couple of injections and stitched it up – he did a good job considering his x-ray machine was broken. His German nurse came to the hotel each day to change the dressing and check for infection.'

As Petra takes up the story, it's almost like watching tennis as we keep swivelling around from one to the other. 'The hotel was right on the beach. We had a room overlooking a lagoon fringed by palm trees, which was separated from the sea by a small strip of sand. Such a contrast to our nightmare in the Ivory Coast.'

'Wow,' I say. 'What a terrible story. So you weren't exaggerating when you said Nick saved your lives.'

'If it hadn't been for Nick and his men.'

'Did Nick tell you why he was in Ivory Coast with his small army?' Adele asks.

'Well, he did in a way and yet, he didn't,' Axel rubs the side of his face. 'I could tell he was holding something back. He told us he was there training a contingent of Liberian security officers, but he didn't explain what they were doing in the Ivory Coast.'

'Yes, that's just like Nick,' Adele smiles. 'He never told us what he did, always too hush-hush.'

'There was something else,' Petra looks puzzled. 'He was trying to find someone. I think his name was Charles, but Nick wouldn't tell us anything else.'

Adele swallows nervously. 'Charles Temple is my brother and he ...'

We suddenly jump as the shrill sound of the phone echoes round the room. Axel gives a wary look towards his wife.

'Who is it – does it say?'

He looks at the handset. 'Ingehouden – damn – should I answer it?'

I whisper to Adele, 'Ingehouden means withheld.'

Giving a deep sigh, Petra nods. 'Darling, I think you have to.'

He picks up the receiver, his face grim, listening for a few seconds before shouting, 'I've no idea what you're talking about, go away and don't call again,' he slams the receiver down. 'It was the same man.'

'What the hell did he say this time?' Petra's expletive is in Flemish/Dutch.

'To tell Penny Lane that he wants the package. He obviously knows you're here but, what is this package?'

Before I can explain, Petra butts in. 'Axel, darling, we can't ignore the phone call. Leave the package for now because that call is a definite threat. I think you should call Dirk.'

For a second, Axel looks irritated, but relents. 'Yes, you're right, Penny and Adele may be in danger. I'll call him.'

'Who's Dirk?' I ask.

'Dirk van Vuuren, he's the ex *commissaris* of police in Brussels and a friend of ours. He has a security business and is also licenced to supply armed bodyguards, not cheap though.'

'That's alright,' Adele confirms. 'We're not short of money.'

Picking up the phone and speaking in Dutch, he briefly talks to someone exclaiming. 'It's urgent, very urgent, tell him to call me as soon you hear from him.' He replaces the receiver. 'He's out on a call but the girl thinks he'll be back in half an hour.'

Clearly satisfied, Petra nods. 'That's good, we can look in the package now.'

Adele takes it out of her bag and looks at me. 'Shall I?'

'Yes please.'

She reaches across the desk and places it in front of them both. 'This is the reason why we've come to see you. Nick left it for Penny the day before he was murdered.'

'Murdered!' Both Axel and Petra look stunned. 'We didn't know he was murdered, HESEC said it was a traffic accident.'

'Oh, he was murdered alright,' I explain, 'I was there.' Managing to keep my voice under control, I give them a summary of all the events from Nick's murder right through to arriving in Brussels, including the would-be assassin on the Eurostar.

'My God,' he cries giving us a curious look. 'There was a report on the radio this morning that a seriously injured man had been found on the Eurostar when it arrived in Brussels.' He looks questioningly at us. 'Was that anything to do with you?'

'Of course it was,' Adele coolly responds. 'He was the assassin Penny mentioned, so we dealt with him. I wasn't sure if he'd lived but - it doesn't matter.'

Petra and Axel gasp at Adele's attitude.

'I learnt a lot from Nick,' Adele states as if that's the only explanation needed. Whenever she reverts to her combative guise, the muscles around her chin tighten and her voice changes, a ruthless cold edge to it.

Axel looks worried. 'But this is serious, can it be linked to you?'

'No chance,' she pronounces emphatically. 'As I said, I learnt everything from Nick.'

Axel looks away quickly, but enough for it to register as awkward. 'Do you think it was my phone call to HESEC that gave the game away?'

'Probably, but you weren't to know,' Adele concedes. 'We're aware there's at least one mole in HESEC, but if he or they are in league with the Chinese men, or some members of the British police service, we don't know. Although we're not certain of the whys and wherefores, we believe Nick's murder and everything that's happened to us is linked with this damned package. His letter is on top.'

They hold hands and take their time reading it. 'A baby?' Petra looks quizzically at me.

'Yes, I'm pregnant, it's Nick's.'

Faltering slightly. 'That's er, wonderful, how many weeks?'

'About six.'

'But all the trauma you've had, it can't be good for you. Have you seen a doctor?'

'No, not yet, I haven't had time.'

'Penny,' Petra says seriously, 'I know it's none of our business but our friend Margit, she lives in this block, and she's a ... what's the English word, a sort of baby doctor?'

'A gynaecologist.'

'Yes, that's right, it's almost the same in Dutch. She's at the local hospital and I'm sure she'll give you a check up.'

Adele turns to me. 'It's a good idea, I think you should do it.'

'Well, if it's not too much trouble, would certainly help reassure me, one way or another.'

'That's settled then, I'll call her at one-thirty, that's her lunchtime.'

'What is Limarni?' Axel asks. 'Is it a place or person or ...?'

'We were hoping you would know.'

'I've checked with my family and googled it,' Adele says, 'But there's nothing with that spelling and Nick's writing was always precise. We think it might be something to do with Africa or the contents of the package. Take a look.'

Holding the package in his hand, he lifts the flap. 'May I?'

'Of course.'

Gingerly, one by one, he takes out the three stones, the large one first. He holds it up to the light. 'Do you know what this is?'

'We think all three are rough, uncut diamonds.'

'I think you're right,' he gives a whistle. 'This one is big, I've never handled one this size before. Where are they from?'

'Nick didn't say.'

Shaking his head, he turns to his wife and laughs. 'I wonder ... no, no, surely not,' he hints at disbelief. 'But do you think it's possible that Jaro may have been right all along? I thought he was, I think the English expression is barking mad.'

'Jaro?' I exclaim. 'What do you mean?'

Taking a jeweller's loupe out of his desk drawer, he puts it to his eye. 'Jaro, full name, Professor Jaroslav Baros. It will be a long explanation which I think should wait until I've checked them thoroughly. Do you mind?'

'No, not at all.'

He peers through the eye piece. 'It looks gem quality alright but it has two or three flaws, these can be cut through, of course and, you'll need a better man than me to say but, after cutting, there should be two good sized stones, possibly up to ten carat, and then there'd be a few smaller ones.'

'How much is it worth?' Strangely, the monetary value hadn't registered with me before.

'Just a moment.' Using his stick, he hobbles to the windowsill and places the stone on a white sheet of paper. 'I'm checking for colour, in daylight, it's erm, sadly not a blue-white, but not bad, probably a hint of yellow. Again, you need an expert but, in its rough state, it must be worth, I don't know, eight to nine hundred thousand Euros.'

'Bloody hell. That's a fortune, and there are still the two smaller ones.'

'That's right but ah! wait a minute, I assume the stones are unregistered. You see all mined diamonds are supposed to be registered in the country of origin and also the Kimberley Diamond Exchange so, the only way to sell them is not legit. That will bring the price down.'

Picking up the letter again, Petra says, 'But Nick talks about billions of dollars, not a few hundred thousand.'

'Yes, we haven't worked that our either,' I say. 'At the moment, selling the stones is the least of our problems. Our safety and sorting out the mess we're in comes first.'

'Yes, of course. Dirk van Vuuren should be here soon, and we can discuss your situation with him. He's a good man, very reliable and he'll hopefully come up with a plan.'

'Penny, was there anything else in the package?'

'Only a list of numbers.' I reach into my bag and pass him the slip of paper. 'We think it could be a safety deposit box but there again, which bank and in which country we've no idea.'

He and Petra study it for a few moments. Screwing up his face in concentration, he mutters, 'It *must* mean something. You could be right about a safety deposit box. Will you leave the stones and the paper with me until tomorrow morning?'

'Oh!' taken by surprise. 'I'm not sure.'

Adele takes over. 'Why do you need to keep them? As you're a geologist, we thought you'd know straight away what the stones are.'

'Ladies, I'm as sure as I can be that they are genuine diamonds although I must say I've seen some damn clever fakes in my time. But to be absolutely certain, I need to put them through a few tests, identification tests.' He rises from his chair and indicates we should follow him. Taking a key from a hidden panel at the side of his desk, he grabs his stick and hobbles for a door, partially hidden by a screen. 'Come and look in this room.' Carefully opening it, he nimbly enters numbers to disengage the alarm system. 'In here is my hobby.' We enter a large room with heavily barred windows, banks of cupboards, and numerous scientific-looking instruments. 'My real interest has nothing to do with oil exploration which is just to pay the bills, it's gemstones.'

'Ah, that must be why Nick told me to bring them to you.'

'I think so. Although I'm only an amateur, I can at least check if they're real. They're not synthetic diamonds, synthetics are not as big as this.'

'And how do you check if they are real?'

'To do it properly takes time. That's why I suggest you come back tomorrow morning.'

What choice do I have but to agree? The Van Dammes appear sincere, and in any case, Nick wrote that I could trust Axel.

Peering closely at some of the equipment, Adele asks, 'How do you test the gems?'

'The first thing is the scratch test followed by the thermal probe,' he points to a table-mounted piece of equipment near the barred window. 'Then a luminescence test under ultra violet light and finally, an x-ray defraction. At the end of all that,' he smiles, 'I'll be able to confirm if they're genuine, the quality, and a better estimate of the value.'

'Do you also cut the diamonds?' I ask.

'Oh no, that's highly specialised. In fact, there's no-one in Brussels I'd trust to cut this big one. It'll have to go to Antwerp, which is the centre for diamond cutting in Europe, it's the best in the world. I know of a couple of people who could do it.'

Just then, the phone rings. They exchange worried looks before Petra apprehensively picks it up, holding it a few inches away from her head. Straight away, she relaxes, heaving a sigh of relief. 'Hallo, Dirk, komen op maximaal.' Turning to us, she says, 'Dirk van Vuuren is on his way up.'

As an ex-police chief, he's shorter than I'd expected, but he's burly and muscular and enters with a steady, confident stride. Axel introduces us and we shake hands, his grip firm and his hooded, piercing blue eyes intimidating. Petra excuses herself to make coffee for him.

'You said it was important, Axel.' His English is good with a distinct Germanic accent.

'Yes, it is. Do you remember we told you about our *in de buurt van doodervaring* in the Ivory Coast when our lives were saved by an Englishman, Nicholas Holbrook?'

He shrugs unresponsively. 'Of course.'

'Well, sad to report Mr Holbrook was murdered a few days ago and Adele here, is his sister, and Penny, his fiancée.' He gestures in her direction.

Looking intently at us, his only noticeable reaction is a slight tightening of the lips.

Axel points to the package on his desk. 'The murder was linked to that, it contains three diamonds which Chinese thugs have attacked them for on several occasions. Penny tried to get help from the English police but they basically refused.'

The police comment brings a cynical smile to Dirk's face, but he still remains silent. Why doesn't he say something, or is this just *another everyday tale of villainy* to him? We are interrupted by Petra bustling in with the coffee, handing a mug to Dirk. He takes it without comment, drinking the hot liquid with his eyes closed, as if inhaling the steam will, like his fellow countryman, Hercule Poirot, help to solve yet another mystery.

His peculiar behaviour, however, doesn't perturb Axel. 'Since I spoke with Nick's employer, HESEC, on Monday, we, ourselves, have received three menacing phone calls, the last one just a short while ago, demanding the package that Penny Lane has.'

At last, Dirk speaks but in a derisible tone. 'HESEC eh? I know them.' Pulling out a note pad and pen he scrawls something down.

I feel like yelling - is that it? Taking a deep breath to soothe my agitation, I say, 'Mr van Vuuren, can you help us or not?'

Placing his empty mug on the floor, he nods. 'Of course I can. Tell me the whole story, leave nothing out.'

Somewhat reassured, and as logically as I can remember, I recount the whole story once again concluding with the assassin on Eurostar while he, scowling all the time, scribbles occasional notes on his pad.

When I finish, he asks, 'How long are you both planning to stay in Brussels?'

'We aren't sure.' I feel hot tears in my eyes at the seemingly hopelessness of our situation, and my voice catches as I continue. 'We had hoped to be out of harm's way here but we've been tracked to this apartment so, we haven't a clue what to do next. We're hoping you can help us.'

Dirk stands, and starts pacing the room. 'Okay, the first thing I'll do is check the numbers of those incoming calls that Axel received, they might lead to something, and I can put men to guard the Van Dammes here and also at your hotel. Where are you staying?'

'The Brendtle.'

'Okay. I'll get in touch with my contacts in police HQ to get the details on this man on the Eurostar, to check if there's a link to anyone here in Brussels. And I'll need two thousand Euros up front,' he adds abruptly. 'Is that acceptable?'

'Yes it is.' Without hesitation, Adele roots in her bag bringing out a wad of Euros and counts out the amount in fifty Euro notes.

Raising an eyebrow, probably taken by surprise, he pockets the money. 'I'll give you a receipt tomorrow. Here's my card and details,' he gives one to each of us. 'But for now, I'll take you back to the Brendtle. Do not leave the hotel under any circumstances and I'll collect you at ten o'clock tomorrow morning.'

CHAPTER FOURTEEN

FEBRUARY 7th

Rubbing grit from my eyes, yawning and luxuriously stretching, I peer at the blurred image of the bedside clock - seven thirty. What? I do a double take. Wow, I must have slept for nine solid hours. I place my hands on my belly. 'You enjoyed that rest, didn't you, little one?' But any feeling of inner calm is abruptly flushed away by a sense of foreboding about what the day will bring.

A quick shower, dress, and I'm ready for breakfast. I don't knock on Adele's door in case she's still sleeping, there's plenty of time before Dirk comes to pick us up.

The restaurant is half empty, but there's a noisy group of a dozen, smartly dressed Japanese men, shovelling and slurping food down their throats from bowls held up to their chins, while jabbering away at the same time. Disgusting. Brussels, being the headquarters of the EU, obviously brings in a constant stream of foreign business people.

Feeling ravenous, I help myself to a couple of boiled eggs, cold meats and cheeses, followed by tea, bread and jam. Taking my time, I eventually check the clock, it's almost nine, where's Adele? Swallowing the last of my tea, I go up and rap on her door. 'It's time to get up, Dirk will be here soon.' Hearing nothing, I wait for a few moments before placing my ear to her door. No sound of any kind, maybe I missed her on the way up.

I'm starting to feel uneasy. I try the handle and it's unlocked but, there's no Adele. Her handbag is lying open on her unmade bed, her purse and passport inside. A quick look into the bathroom reveals nothing.

I hurry to the hotel desk. 'Have you seen Miss Holbrook this morning?'

The receptionist thinks for a moment. 'I'm fairly certain she left the hotel about an hour ago.'

'Are you sure?' I cry.

Deep in thought, she says, 'Yes, I'm sure it was Miss Holbrook, I remember her from when you checked in,' adding, 'She left with a man.'

'A man!' I yell. 'What did he look like?'

'Ooh, I didn't see his face but he had his arm around her shoulders.' She fiddles with her hair. 'I remember he wore a very long coat, it was unusual - down to his ankles, and a woolly hat.'

Feeling myself start to shiver, I stare at her in desperation. Could Adele have gone willingly with someone without telling me? Maybe it was Dirk, but he's not due till ten. Damn. I phone the Van Dammes.

'No, she's not here,' Axel is also alarmed. 'Is Dirk with you yet?'

'No.'

'Penny, wait there until you hear from me or Dirk, is that clear?' His voice has that reassuring tone of masculine authority. I do as he says and stay in the lobby.

After anxiously pacing up and down for several minutes, my mobile rings, it's Axel. 'There's no sign of Adele. I've spoken to Dirk who's on his way to the hotel.'

Just as I switch off, Dirk bursts through the hotel door, his face like thunder. He comes over and grabs me forcibly by the shoulders. 'Is she still missing?' he barks.

'Yes.'

'*Schwachmat*, I told you both to stay in the hotel. Who saw her last?'

I point to the receptionist. 'She saw her leave an hour ago, with a man.'

He storms over to the desk and angrily starts to interrogate her. I can only hear her faint responses, as he aggressively throws questions at her. She starts to cry.

Cursing again, he turns back to me. 'Pack your bags and Miss Holbrook's. I'll take you to the Van Damme's for safety. We'll get nothing here.'

'But who would have taken her?'

'I don't know,' he snaps. 'Probably related to Axel's threatening phone calls.'

'But you put a guard on this hotel for us, where is he?'

Unwilling to look me in the eye, he pauses. 'I've er, brought him with me.'

Any natural reticence I had is now replaced by anger. 'Well that's no damn good, is it?'

'If she'd done as I said,' his yells back aggressively. 'And stayed in, she ...'

'She's been taken, abducted.' I scream. 'Hasn't she? She wouldn't have left under her own free will. If your man had been here, he could have ...' I'm too upset to finish the sentence.

His *man*, Fritz Stemper, a tall, slim older man, completely bald, comes with me up to our rooms. I grab Adele's purse then roughly throw our possessions into a couple of holdalls and hand baggage, and he helps carry them downstairs where I check out, before getting into Dirk's vehicle. Not saying a word, save for a few muttered obscenities, he races the short distance to the Van Damme's.

A worried-looking Petra lets us in. 'Any news, Dirk?'

'Nothing,' he replies angrily, as though we're all to blame and not him. 'I've had no word from the police, but they're watching the bus and railway stations as well as the airport. Give me her passport, I need her photo.'

Axel photocopies it, letting Dirk email it to his contacts.

I'm angry and frustrated that someone was able to take Adele, even though we all knew the potential danger. 'So what happens now?' I ask.

'There's not much we can do but wait,' Dirk replies brusquely. 'She should have stayed in the hotel.'

'Don't be so silly,' I yell. 'She must have been forced to go, and you bloody well know it. You let her down.'

Turning his back and ignoring my outburst, Dirk speaks quietly to Axel before heading for the door, tapping his mobile saying he'll keep in touch.

Seeing my tears, Petra suggests we all sit down.

'That bloody man, Dirk,' I sob. 'He didn't put a guard at our hotel as promised.' I hug my knees to my chest. 'No-one was there to stop Adele being abducted.'

Petra gives me another motherly embrace. 'Don't worry, and try not to get stressed, Dirk knows the crime scene in Brussels better than anyone. With abductions, there's always a ransom demand, so whoever took Adele only wants one thing in return, and that's the package of diamonds. Axel locked it away. And when they make contact, that'll be when Dirk comes up trumps. He's handled abduction cases before and *always* wins.'

'The hard bit starts now,' Axel sighs. 'The waiting.'

Feeling utterly desolate, I walk aimlessly round the room. Terrible images shooting through my mind of Adele being held by sinister Chinese brutes, rehearsing the worst possible outcome and trying to prepare myself for whatever might happen to her.

'Would you like some tea?' Petra asks, going through to the kitchen.

I try my best to smile, but find it difficult. 'No thank you.' I look at Axel. 'How long do we have to wait?'

'I don't know. Dirk promised to keep us informed. He's *very* upset you know, about what's happened.' Axel gives an even deeper sigh. 'I know he should have had his man at your hotel but he's doing his best now, and he has very good contacts in the area.'

'Yes, I know,' I concede, realising it's self defeating to labour the point. Slowly pacing another circuit of the room, I gaze out of the rear window which overlooks a small, central courtyard of the apartment building, a solitary winter-weary conifer sitting in the middle. Somebody must have put some scraps down, as a large variety of birds is excitedly pecking away on the icy ground.

Giving a light cough, Axel jolts me out of my melancholy. 'While we're waiting, I think you'll want to know that I checked the three stones last night and, as I'd thought, they are definitely gem quality diamonds. The problem is though that I'm fairly certain they are what we call *conflict or blood diamonds*, mined in West Africa where they're used to fund civil wars.'

'I don't understand.'

'I'm only assuming this because of something else I worked out last night.'

'What was that?'

'Those numbers you gave me, I'm pretty sure they're not safety deposit box numbers.'

'What are they then?'

'They're a map reference location, a very specific location, down to the nearest hundred metres. Nick omitted, maybe deliberately, putting the letters N and W, north and west before each block.'

'So where is this place?'

'It's on the Liberia/Sierra Leone border, here I'll show you.' I peer over his shoulder where a large atlas is open on his desk.

'You see here,' he points to the page. 'This is the country of Liberia and, if I trace along here to 7° 0150.92 North where it meets 11° 2204.76 West, we're looking at a spot just inside the Liberian border on this river, can you see it?'

Taking my time to take in the details of the multi-coloured map, and the longitude and latitude co-ordinates he's indicating, I ask, 'What do you think is there?'

'The best guess I can come up with is that it's where the three diamonds came from.'

'Like a diamond mine, you mean.'

'Yes, I think so.'

I chew on my bottom lip thinking. 'It would explain why Nick said he was privy to something worth billions of dollars.'

'Yes, that's ...'

The phone rings. Petra hurries in from the kitchen. Is it Dirk or the abductor? Tentatively, Petra picks up the receiver. 'Ah, hallo Margit,' the tension fades from her face and we collectively let out deep breaths. She cuts short her conversation and replaces the phone. 'Margit said she'd be happy to see you any evening next week to check on the baby. I told her I'd get back to her.'

'I'd forgotten about that,' I say. 'I don't want to do anything before Adele's safe.'

'No, of course not, I'll call her later.'

Sitting down again, I look at them both. 'There is one thing I can do.'

'Oh, what's that?'

'When Hal saved me from the Chinese thugs in my apartment, he gave me his contact number telling me to call him anytime, day or night.'

'But I thought you weren't sure if you could trust him,' Axel says. 'Especially as he's the son of Sir Desmond Thrimby.'

'Yes, that's true, but I can't sit here doing nothing, and he might be able to help.'

'But what about Dirk, he's the man on the spot. Hal is in England.'

'I thought of that. Obviously, our cover's gone and my first guess is that it's the Chinese who've taken Adele, not someone from HESEC.'

Axel and Petra only hesitate for a second. 'It's up to you, Penny, if you think it's a good idea then chance it.'

On the second ring, Hal answers my call. I quickly tell him that we are visiting a friend of Adele's in Brussels, and that she was abducted from our hotel this morning. He listens without interruption. I say nothing about the package or the diamonds.

'Give me your address and phone number,' he says. 'I'll be with you as soon as I can. Do nothing until I arrive and do not answer any questions from the police.'

'Okay,' I lie, knowing it's already too late for that. Getting a nod from Axel, I give him their address and my mobile number.

'Good, I'll contact you as soon as I reach Brussels.' He cuts the call.

'I hope I've done the right thing. I'd love some tea now, Petra, if you don't mind.'

Sipping our drinks, we continue the waiting, unable to concentrate on anything other than Adele. Wandering over to the front window overlooking Boulevard Emile Bockstael, I check both ways in the desperate hope that she's out there.

In one direction is a row of shops and office buildings with another busier road beyond. The other way is bordered by a row of trees behind which is a park with swings and roundabouts. It looks strangely empty. It starts to rain, large droplets spattering the window.

Suddenly, above the constant traffic noise outside, there's the sound of a powerful motorbike screeching to a stop outside the apartment. A short ring on the entry phone is followed by the bike loudly revving its engine and racing away. Rushing to the window, my view of the entrance is blocked by a canopy, but I manage to catch sight of the rear of the bike, the rider encased in black leathers, but there are no number plates.

While Petra runs downstairs to check their mail box, Axel checks the CCTV camera outside the entrance.

'Verfickter,' he curses. 'They've broken the camera.'

Petra, panting slightly, comes back holding a small brown envelope addressed to "Penny Lane".

'Open it carefully,' Axel orders.

My hands shake as I take the envelope and slowly lift the unsealed flap and pull out a folded piece of paper. The message is brief. *WE HOLD ADELE HOLBROOK. WE KNOW YOU HAVE THE PACKAGE. WE EXCHANGE THEM TOMORROW. IF NO PACKAGE, THEN WE KILL HER. DON'T GO TO THE POLICE OR WE KILL HER. INSTRUCTIONS FOR THE EXCHANGE COME LATER.*

CHAPTER FIFTEEN

FEBRUARY 8th

Waking in a cold sweat, I click on the bedside light and sit bolt upright, heart pounding, gasping for breath. Whatever my horrible dream was, has gone. My watch shows it's only half-past five. My brain is working overtime so getting back to sleep is impossible. Oh bloody hell, how did I ever get into this mess? Stumbling out of bed, I wrap a blanket round my shoulders and pace up and down the room.

What's the hells happened to my bloody life. Just over five weeks ago, it seems like a lifetime, all it took was one night and two dates with Nick to catapult me from my structured, boring life into this dangerous madness. And how to get Adele back? I could give up the diamonds but, who to? It's no good giving them to Hal or HESEC as it won't stop the Chinese, and the UK police seem to be hand in glove with the perpetrators. With so many thoughts sending me half crazy, I creep along the corridor to the kitchen. Axel and Petra are already there.

'We couldn't sleep either,' Petra pushes some card and tape to one side of the table to make room for me. 'We're having coffee, would you like some?'

'Yes please. Can I make myself toast as well?'

'I'll do it.' Shuffling along in her slippers, Petra goes to the counter. 'You sit there with Axel.'

'We didn't want to wake you, but half an hour ago, Petra was disturbed by the sound of a vehicle accelerating away from our building. She went down and found this note in our mail box.' He passes it over. 'It's addressed to you.'

'You should have woken me,' I cry, 'What does it say?' Without waiting for a reply I read the note for myself.

LEAVE AT 9.30. COME ALONE. WAIT OUTSIDE FRONT DOOR FOR A PRIVATE TAXI. DRIVER WEARS BLUE AND WHITE CAP. BRING PACKAGE WITH YOU. NO POLICE OR WE KILL HER.

I start to cry. 'Oh no.'

Petra comes over to comfort me. 'We left you to sleep because, as you see, there's no hurry. We've told Dirk,' she adds. 'He's coming here at seven-thirty.'

Wiping tears from my face, I read the note a couple more times. 'I'll have to go but what about the package?'

'Yes, we've thought about that,' Petra places coffee and toast in front of me. 'Dirk says we should make one up to look like the original, and put some false diamonds in it. As you see,' she points at the card and tape on the table. 'We've already started.'

'What do you mean, *false diamonds*?'

'I have a drawer of imitation, look-alike diamonds, mainly quartz,' Axel says. 'I can make look real to the untrained eye. We'll put those into the package.'

'But you don't know if these people have *untrained eyes*.' There's a note of exasperation in my voice which I didn't intend.

Looking uneasy, he says, 'Dirk thinks it'll work. The abductors would have to be experts with special equipment to know otherwise and they won't have had enough time to build up any sort of team.'

'You still have faith in Dirk then?' I ask apprehensively.

'Yes, I have. I know he slipped up earlier, but he has a good group working for him, many ex-policemen. He won't let you down again.'

'I hope you're right.'

Using the original box as a template, Petra continues to make the new package to the same dimensions. When it is almost finished Axel limps from the kitchen saying he will go and find some suitable stones.

Finishing my token breakfast, I go and shower, full of anxiety but determined to follow the task through. I don't bother with make-up, it would be inappropriate.

Back in the kitchen, Dirk has arrived, giving me a nod as he sips his coffee. He looks up. 'We have to plan this operation very carefully. Are you sure you're up for it?'

'Of course I am,' I reply irritably. 'I want to do exactly as the note says. That means I go alone and no police. If we try and pull any tricks, they'll kill Adele, that's if she's still alive.'

'Oh, she'll be alive,' Dirk replies confidently. 'She's their bargaining chip so they'll definitely not risk killing her.'

'Okay.'

'You're spot-on about the police though,' Dirk concedes. 'We won't tell them. What we will do, though, is use my men, they're better trained and better equipped than the police.'

'Well, if you're sure but please be careful, they may have people watching for anything suspicious.' Looking heavenward, I pray for some divine assistance, but all I see is the ugly-patterned artex ceiling with some yellowing stains near the light fitting.

'Please, Penny, leave it to me,' Dirk says, full of self-assurance. 'No matter how good these guys are, we will be better. Brussels is my town and they can only have been here a couple of days. Even if they've recruited local criminals, which I very much doubt, they won't be specialised in this sort of thing. I am.'

'So Dirk, what's your master plan?' He doesn't pick up the sarcasm in my question.

'I'll fix miniature tracking devices into one of your shoes and underwear so I'll know exactly where you are at all times.' He gives me an odd look. 'They might make you remove your shoes but it's most unlikely they'll make you undress.'

Undress? This last remark does nothing to boost my confidence.

'And I'll have motorcyclists and cars at various locations, all with radios, so they'll be able to follow without being seen. I had thought of using a helicopter but I can't do that without involving the police.'

God, I hope he's right. 'I'll give whoever *they* are the package, and hopefully bring Adele back safely,' I add with as much conviction as I can muster but, at the same time, doubting the outcome. The diamonds may well be found to be fakes and then where would I be? With any luck, rescued by Dirk van Vuuren and his men, they are our only hope.

Choking with emotion, the three of us embrace, Petra's hand lingering for a moment in mine. Pulling myself together, I take the lift and go and stand outside the apartment main entrance. I've stuffed the *all-important* package right at the bottom of my long-strapped cross-body bag. I'm five minutes early and it's so cold my breath mists in the air, and a few snowflakes waft around me like tiny, dancing fairies in the bitter breeze. I watch the traffic hoping to see a *private taxi* with a driver in a blue and white cap, but everything whizzes past without a break.

Time ticks by slowly. I've never felt so worried and so scared, not even when the two Chinese thugs attacked me in my apartment. That reminds me, I'd expected to hear from Hal, maybe he's still on his way. But for now, I'm on my own and saving Adele's life not only depends on Dirk's plan, but also on me playing my part.

Feeling more anxious by the minute, I check my watch again, it's already nine-thirty eight, they're late. Even though my adrenalin is sky high, the bitter cold is starting to seep into my bones. I stamp my feet to get some feeling back. Has there been a change of plan? Suddenly, a taxi pulls into the disabled parking bay and stooping, I can see the driver wearing a blue cap with a white brim ... this is it. Taking a deep breath, I quickly get in. Before I can close the door properly, the driver accelerates away at an alarming rate, taking the first turning on the right so fast that the car is almost on two wheels.

'You have package?' It's the same accent as the thugs who broke into my apartment.

'Yes.'

He nods. There's a satnav mounted on the dashboard which probably means he's not familiar with Brussels. Soon, I lose my bearings as he takes a series of rapid left and right turns, glancing in his rear-view mirror every few seconds, presumably to check he's not being followed. After about fifteen minutes of hectic driving, he turns down an unmade road and through open factory-type gates. Screeching to a stop, he hastily gets out and closes the gates, locking them with a large padlock. Damn, how will Dirk's men get round that?

He sets off again at a slower pace as the track is badly rutted. We are in what appears to be an abandoned, factory or warehouse complex, with rows of Victorian style industrial buildings, all completely dilapidated with gaping roofs and every window broken. He drives around the back of the last building and stops.

'Out,' he orders.

Clutching my bag hard against me, I get out and look around for any sign of Adele or her captors, but the place is deserted. Down a steep, litter-strewn slope on my right is a busy, very noisy motorway.

My heart's pounding against my ribcage. All he has to do is slit my throat and take my bag, there's nothing I can do to stop him, except I have the can of mace in my coat pocket but ... will it work?

'Here.' He orders me to stand by the car while he passes a hand-held gadget, like an airport security scanner, over my body, but it's not a metal detector as it only beeps near my middle where I'm wearing the tracking device Dirk made me wear around my waist.

The man roughly grabs at my coat but, through my panic, I have a thought. 'It's this,' I take my mobile phone out of my pocket and hand it to him. He passes the scanner over and it beeps. Seemingly satisfied, he fails to check me again, or my shoes.

Now, pointing down the slope to the motorway, he orders, 'Go, you climb fence and wait by quick road, now.'

'What?' I exclaim, 'I can't do that.'

He grabs me by the shoulders and pushes me towards the slope.

'Okay, okay, I'll do it.' What choice do I have? At least he's not slitting my throat. I assume by *quick road* he means the motorway so, with my heart in my mouth, I scramble down the embankment, but my foot slips and I roll headlong into the chain-link fence, my thick winter clothing cushioning my fall. Groaning, I pick myself up and dust muck and debris off my clothes, checking that my bag's intact. I'm shaken, terrified and want to cry.

'Quick, go.' The driver, still standing at the top, shouts at me.

The fence is about three feet high and I tear my coat pocket struggling to get over. Once on the other side, there's a gradual, stony gradient to the motorway where I immediately flinch from the noise and volume of traffic. I stand at the back of the hard shoulder, but even then, a truck swerves away from me, the driver honking his horn in anger. Looking back up the hill, the Chinese man makes a brief phone call before getting into his taxi and driving off.

Whatever next? I'm trembling with fright when a car pulls onto the hard shoulder and a different driver wearing a similar blue and white cap beckons me in. Amid blaring horns and screeching brakes, the driver forces his way into the flow of traffic, immediately moving into the fast lane. He also uses a satnav, keeping pace with the fastest cars while, at the same time, watching in his rear-view mirror. We head out of the city on the N1 motorway.

Travelling in silence, we pass signs for Vihroorde, then Zemst, and after about fifteen minutes, he slips into the inside lane and turns off at the sign for Tisselt. Crossing a long river bridge, we meander through the countryside and small villages. He negotiates a series of tight bends then turns onto a track which peters out at an open, high metal gate which he gets out to lock behind us. After about sixty yards, we stop outside a dilapidated building like a forester's cottage with several outbuildings, set in the middle of a large wood.

'Out,' the driver barks. In doing so, I get a good look at his face, a sallow-skinned, middle-aged Chinese man with prodigious thick, black eyebrows almost covering his narrow eyes. Of medium height, he has the broad shoulders of a wrestler.

A couple of sad looking pigeons squatting on the roof turn their heads to watch as I cautiously follow him along a rough path curving towards the main door, partly hidden by a large holly bush. We enter and walk down a corridor leading to a kitchen, furnished with several brown plastic chairs and two yellowing Formica-topped tables. There's an unpleasant smell of stale cooking fat, dirty pans and dishes piled high in the sink. The man roughly pushes me along another passage and gestures at me to go into the room at the end. It's large with pine-clad walls, a dining table in the middle and a couple of naked light bulbs hanging from the ceiling. With a shock, I see a bedraggled-looking Adele sitting awkwardly on a sofa, her wrists and ankles tied. Blood is smudged across her bruised face but, on seeing me, she gives a pained smile. She says nothing. Fixed to her chest with a couple of wires linked to a small black box, is an object looking suspiciously like pictures of suicide bombs I've seen on TV.

'Hello, Penny Lane.' The voice, sounding particularly chilling, comes from behind me – a voice I know. I turn to look - it's Hal, his eyes lit with a kind of madness.

My mouth falls open in astonishment, and the blood seems to drain out of me. I feel faint. Fear is constricting my throat and it's difficult to speak. My mind's all over the place. It's Hal, all the time it's been Hal, the man I phoned only yesterday to help us. But how did he get here so quickly? He must have traced us to Brussels, kidnapped Adele and he's working *with* the Chinese, not separately as we'd thought.

'What's all this, Hal?' I eventually stutter, at the same time noticing a second Chinese man standing by a side door at the far end of the room.

Hal takes a couple of strides towards me, a look of contempt on his face. 'You stupid bitch,' he spits out his rebuke. 'You've brought this on yourself,' and without any warning, he strikes me hard across the face.

Crying out, I stagger back as pain radiates from my jaw. Putting my hand to my mouth, I point to the two Chinese men. 'Are these the ones you saved me from in my apartment?'

'Of course, and they're also the ones who murdered your pathetic Nick,' he sneers. 'We didn't plan to, all we wanted was the package but the stupid fucker gave it to you.'

'But you saved me from them, why?'

'We weren't going to kill you,' he mocks. 'Until we had the package. They were going to soften you up so that when I rescued you, you'd tell me where the package was, but

133

you lied to me,' his expression softens for a fraction as if in respect. 'And I believed you.'

'B...but I didn't have the package.'

'No, but you knew Adele had it. If only you'd told me, then none of this would have happened.' He gestures in her direction. 'Now you and she are in deep, fucking shit.'

Although quaking uncontrollably, I inwardly seethe with rage. These are the men who murdered Nick, obviously on Hal's, or even Sir Desmond's orders. And now, damn it, I wish I hadn't brought the package with me, but I told the driver I had. Think, think, how do I bluff my way out of this? But I can't think, my mind's all screwed up. I wasn't expecting Adele to be tied up with a bomb strapped to her chest, so when Dirk's men force their way in ...

'Give me the package,' Hal demands. He puts the gun down on the table and picks up a small, square object. 'You see this?' he points to a red button in the middle of it, 'One press here and your girlfriend vaporises, *POW*.' Grinning sadistically, he thrusts his arms in the air demonstrating the effects of an exploding bomb. 'So hand over the fucking package and I promise to let you both go, it's as easy as that.'

'It's not here,' I lie, 'I don't have it with me, but it's yours as soon as you've released Adele, it's my precondition.' I want him to think that I have a bargaining position. Adele's arms and legs must be untied before Dirk's men arrive.

A tiny amount of spittle has gathered at the corner of Hal's mouth and he hits me again. I hear the sound of his hand against my face before I feel the flash of pain. He gives another contemptuous laugh. 'You're not giving orders,' he sneers. Turning to the Chinese men and using Mandarin, he tells them to check that I haven't been followed. Luckily, Hal has no way of knowing that I understand everything he says, and I pray hard that Dirk's men are keeping out of sight until they're ready to mount the rescue. Hal sits on a chair and lights a cigarette, leaving me standing in the middle of the room. The two men eventually return and tell Hal they've checked round the building and they are sure I haven't been followed.

I breathe a sigh of relief.

One of them goes back to stay by the front door. 'So Miss Lane, where have you hidden the package.'

'Release her now and then I'll tell you. I give you my word.' My voice has an authority which I certainly don't feel.

'Okay, I'll play along for the moment.' Placing the gadget on the table, he struts over to Adele but, before untying her, he gives her one last cruel backhander across the mouth. She gasps in pain, making Hal laugh again. Removing the explosive, he passes it to the Chinese man explaining in Mandarin that afterwards, he'll tie the two of us together then detonate the bomb, killing us both and destroying all the evidence.

'Now you bitch, he snarls at me. 'She's free, so where is it.'

I hesitate, trying to play for time. Adele vigorously massages her wrists. Where are Dirk and his men? Realising I'm gripping my bag too tightly, I carelessly look down and relax my hand, a gesture noticed by Hal.

'Aha,' he shouts in triumph, snatching the bag from my shoulder and emptying the contents on the table. His eyes light up when he sees the package. 'You bitch, you had it with you all the time.' He lifts the flap and takes out the three stones, giving them only a cursory inspection, then casually tosses them onto the table.

I can't believe it. He doesn't check to see if they're genuine. He searches inside the package for something else. 'Where's the fucking map?'

'Map?' I exclaim. 'What map?'

This time, he slaps me twice across the face. For the second time in a just over a week, I taste blood in my mouth. 'Don't come that shit with me, you fucking bitch,' he yells. 'You've taken it, haven't you?'

'I don't have a map,' I whimper, reaching into my pocket for a tissue to wipe blood off my face.

Furiously tearing the rest of the package to shreds, finding nothing, he comes at me again, this time with clenched fists. The tissues are next to something hard. The can of mace. As I back away, I try a distraction by shouting in Mandarin, 'Leave me alone.'

Startled, it fleetingly stops him in his tracks, giving me a split second to take out the can. Seeing it in my hand, he rushes at me but I thrust out my arm, pressing the nozzle straight at his head. Trying to duck, he's too late, as a fierce jet of liquid hits him square in the middle of his face. He gives an almighty shriek, screaming and gasping, covering his eyes with his hands before collapsing on the floor.

Swiftly taking a gun from inside his jacket, the Chinese man rushes to his assistance, but instead of targeting me, he tries to help the screaming Hal. Although suffering slightly from some of the mace which has blown back into my face, I look through blurry, smarting eyes, and see Adele move like lightning to the table. She grabs the gun, and in one smooth action, removes the safety catch, aims at the man who, realising his blunder, frantically tries to turn and shoot, but she fires first, hitting him in the chest. An incredibly loud noise echoes around the room. With a deathly gasp, he slumps to the floor, his gun clattering next to him, blood rapidly pumping out, soaking his clothes bright red. Amazingly, Hal pulls himself upright, still yelling in agony he lunges towards Adele. Calmly taking a couple of steps backwards, she's almost smiling as she coolly aims and fires three ear-splitting shots into his head, chest and stomach. His stunned eyes glaze over as he slowly sinks to the floor, taking an agonising look into my face, his last moment alive.

I'm paralysed with fear, unable to move or even think. Heavy footsteps pounding down the corridor warn us that the other Chinese thug is on his way.

'Get behind the sofa, Penny, and hide. Hurry.'

Heart pounding, I'm just about there when the man flings the door open and rushes in. Stopping abruptly, a look of sheer disbelief crosses his face as he sees his two dead colleagues. He looks around, Adele is pointing her gun directly at him.

'No,' he pleads in Mandarin. 'Please madam, no.' Dropping his gun to the floor, he starts to raise his hands, but before he can fully extend them, Adele, her face contorted with hate, screams 'This one's for my brother,' and shoots him right between the eyes. 'Rot in hell, you bastard,' she yells, watching him collapse to the floor.

136

Closing my eyes, I try to make sense of what I've just witnessed ... but I can't. My knees start to wobble and I feel sick. Vomit rises in my throat and I try to swallow it down but I can't stop myself throwing up the breakfast still in my stomach. Continuing to retch for a few seconds, I begin to think that yes, the first two killings were justified but the last one was murder. Adele didn't give him a chance, even though he'd practically surrendered.

'Are there any others?' Adele, remarkably cool, is still holding the gun at the ready.

'You've just killed three men,' I hear myself stating the blatantly obvious. There's no sign of guilt on her face, only a fierce determination.

'What the hell did you expect?' She's about to call me a name but changes her mind. Quickly, she sidles out of the room and I can hear creaking floorboards indicating that she's checking all the others. After a couple of minutes, she returns. 'All clear. Look Penny, I had to do it. All three were killers. Hal confirmed that. If I hadn't killed the last man what would we have done, arrest him and phone the police?'

'Well, yes, something like that.'

'But then we'd be involved in investigations and all sorts of crap and be stuck in Belgium for months. This way, we can probably get out before the shit hits the fan.'

'But ...'

'There are no *buts*. I acted as judge, jury and executioner. End of story.' Brushing all that aside, she asks, 'Do we have transport - did you come in a car?'

Feeling sick and confused, and trying to avoid looking at the dreadful sight of the three dead men, I mumble, 'The car's outside. But anyway,' I add, 'A rescue party should be here by now.'

'Well, they're not, are they?' she snaps, then pausing for a moment, asks, 'What do you mean, a *rescue party?*'

'A security expert, a friend of Axel's, and his men, are supposed to have followed me.'

'Huh.' Only half listening, she finds a bunch of car keys in the dead man's pocket and has the presence of mind to take the explosive remote gadget. Carefully picking up the bomb that had previously been strapped to her chest, she delicately drapes it on Hal's forehead. 'Come on, let's go.'

Once again, she transforms herself - like flicking a switch - from a softly-spoken young lady into a ruthless killer. In a daze, I follow her out of the building and down the path to the car.

'Let's see if this thing really works.' Still clasping the remote, she presses the red button. WHOOSH. There's a massive rush of hot air followed a micro-second later by such an enormous blast which lifts us off our feet and down on the path like two rag dolls. God, it hurts as I fall badly, but I instinctively protect my face with my arms as wood, plaster and other debris crash around us. Flocks of crows and other birds wheel around above our heads, scattering in all directions, their loud complaints gradually fading into the distance.

Gingerly, Adele sits up coughing and brushing fragments of wreckage off her coat and hair. 'Fucking hell, I wasn't expecting that? Are you alright and, oh shit, what about the baby?'

'Well, landing flat on my boobs didn't help,' I snort. 'They're very tender these days. I haven't thought about my baby since leaving the Van Dammes. How could I?' With Adele's help, I slowly stand and dust myself down and massage my ears. 'I hope the sound didn't travel through to my belly, because the poor mite will be half-deaf like me.'

'I'm sure you'll both be fine, but just think,' she says grimly, 'That could have been us in there. There won't be much left of anything ... or anyone for that matter,' she chuckles. 'Now, get in the car, I'll drive.'

At the end of the track, we come to the closed gate. She cries out, 'It's locked, any idea where the key is?'

Unable to control my trembling, I shake my head and start to cry, it must be delayed shock, I just have no idea of anything anymore. Avoiding my swollen lips, I wipe my face and watch Adele take the gun from her pocket and, standing back, shoots the lock away and opens the gates wide. Getting back in the driver's seat, she switches the satnav on. 'What's Axel's address, can you remember?'

A very cultured and comforting English voice comes on the car's satnav. Adele keys in the address and the direct route appears on the screen. The Doctor Jekyll part of her personality has returned, and she gives a smile, which is somewhat spoilt by her swollen lower lip and a brutal looking bruise developing at the side of her left eye. She's as calm as if she's just been out for a picnic in the countryside, instead of having a near death experience, and the *hardly worth mentioning* fact that she's just killed three men. How she manages to stay in control of the vehicle after the ordeal is beyond me.

'Don't worry,' she smiles again, 'I'll get us back to the Van Damme's, and we'll have quite a story to tell.'

CHAPTER SIXTEEN
FEBRUARY 8th

Leaving the car outside the front entrance, Adele rings the door bell and Petra comes rushing down to the foyer. It's almost like the ecstatic welcoming home of Olympic gold medal winners. Hugs and kisses only spoilt by our dirty, bruised faces. I'm overwhelmed with relief at being safely back and we're just entering the lift when two cars screech to a halt outside. Looking through the door's spy-hole, Petra sees Dirk and three armed men jump out, and she goes to let them in.

Dirk's arrival makes me see red. 'Where the hell were you?' I fume. 'We almost died.'

Ignoring my question, he says, 'I'm glad you're both alright.'

'Alright!' I holler. 'No thanks to you.' For the first time in my life I feel an intense desire to hit out ... to hit *him*, even my fists are clenched.

Seeing my anger, Petra intervenes, 'I think we should discuss this calmly upstairs. Dirk, leave your men here and come up with us.'

In the lift nobody says a word but I'm seething inside. Axel is overjoyed to see us but upset by our appearance and gently embraces me then Adele. I start to cry. Petra gently guides me into the living room where I flop utterly exhausted into an armchair. I wipe my face and take deep breaths, trying to bring my emotions under control.

'Why don't you girls come with me through to the bathroom?' Petra asks. 'You can wash and I'll attend to your wounds.'

Axel judiciously interrupts his wife. 'Darling, would you mind leaving that for a moment in case something urgent needs to be done now.'

'There certainly is,' Adele orders. 'Get rid of the car. It belongs to the villains and I've left the keys inside.'

Nodding, Dirk speaks quietly into a radio mike fixed to his coat. 'Okay, that's done. I think it's important to keep the police out of this.'

Adele concurs. 'But better still, set the damn thing on fire and destroy it.'

Axel turns to Adele. 'Good idea. Now, tell us what happened, briefly that is?'

I answer for her. 'We both will, Axel, yes, of course we will, but first,' I glare directly at Dirk, 'I want to know why you and your men failed to rescue us.'

'We lost you,' he feebly responds.

'I gathered that,' I rage. 'You had cars, motorcyclists, radios, and I was wearing your tracking devices, so how the hell could you lose me?'

He smooth's his bristly hair with both hands. 'When you were taken into the old Yuvark factory compound, the gate was locked behind you but one of my motorcyclists got through the fence and watched as you scrambled down onto the N1. As soon as the taxi left, he followed but,' he gives a diffident cough. 'He tried to lift his bike over the fence, but in doing so, he tripped and broke his leg.'

I shake my head in despair.

'The man radioed for help but I hadn't expected you would be going on the N1. I sent a car to the nearest slip road, but as luck would have it, there was a traffic holdup.'

'But couldn't you track me? I still had that contraption round my middle and kept my shoes on.' Snorting with contempt, I slip them off and kick them in his direction. He flinches.

'We couldn't pick up a signal.'

'Why?'

He hesitates again. 'The range is only about three kilometres and you must have been further away. My man drove all the way down the N1 and back again but couldn't get a signal. Not until just now, when you were on your way back.'

Looking disappointed, Axel doesn't comment on Dirk's failure. He glances at us both. 'So, you managed to escape on your own. What happened?'

Adele looks questioningly at me and I nod my agreement. 'For my part,' she begins, 'Hal took me by surprise at the Brentle, that was yesterday morning of course. He held a gun to my throat and I couldn't get away. He was very professional. I was tied, gagged, pushed into the boot of a car and ended up in that place where Penny eventually found me. She knows the rest.'

Thankfully, my emotions are now more or less under control and I carry on the story. Whilst I'm telling them, as succinctly as I can, it suddenly sinks in how amazingly lucky we've been, lucky to be alive, and that's due to the mace and Hal's mistake by untying Adele. When I finish the tale, there are open mouths and gasps from the others.

'Bloedige hel.' Catching her breath, Petra looks with incredulity at Adele. 'You killed three men and then blew them up.'

Unwavering, Adele stares back at her. 'Yes, they deserved it.' Her blunt, almost callous confirmation is received in amazement.

Axel breaks the silence. 'So it was Hal, Nick's work colleague, who was the villain.'

'Yes,' Adele gently rubs the bruises on her face as a sign of the brutal treatment she'd received. 'But we don't know if he's the main organizer, there's still at least one other Chinese man out there, the driver who picked Penny up from here, but I get the feeling the Chinese are more like lackeys and not the brains behind everything.'

'The brains, of course, could be Hal's father,' I add. 'Sir Desmond Thrimby. I'm sure he's involved but now, his favourite son is, ha,' I laugh. 'Let me think, yes, he's no more than a few grains of dust blowing in the cold wintery winds of Belgium.'

'And bloody good riddance as well,' Adele adds decisively.

Dirk gives a cough to get our attention. 'Do you know where you were held, the place? Because the explosion is bound to have been reported by now.'

I rack my brains trying to remember the places we passed. 'I think the last signpost I saw said "Tisselt".'

'But won't it show up on the car's satnav?' Axel asks.

'You're right, I'll get onto it straight away.' Dirk heads for the door, 'I'll find out what I can and maybe bend a few ears. If we don't keep the two of you out of this, you'll have to remain in Belgium for ages. Bureaucracy in the police here is a nightmare.'

'Do your very best, Dirk,' Petra sounds a little patronising as she sees him to the door.

Adele waits until Dirk has gone before pulling a face. 'He'll bend a few ears!' she mocks. 'What on earth does that mean?'

'Ah, it's a saying we have in Belgium,' Axel smiles. 'It means he'll try to convince the police to keep you out of any investigation.'

'Well that's good,' Adele acknowledges. 'And one positive outcome is that we've learnt something, like a breakthrough, and I'm pretty certain we can now piece together why Nick was murdered, and why Penny and the package were always the target.'

'Do you want to tell us about it?' Petra asks.

'Yes, I think so.' Adele looks over at me. 'What do you reckon?'

I've just been through the worst bloody day of my life and I feel knackered, but there's no point going to bed with so much crap going round in my head. 'Yes, go ahead, I might even find it therapeutic, for me and the baby.'

'I do hope so,' Adele sighs, settling into the armchair. 'Okay, let me start from just before we left London when we learnt our first important fact. Hal and his father, Sir Desmond Thrimby, who was Nick's boss, had lived in China for four years, hence the Chinese connection.'

Axel frowns. 'But what's that to do with the diamonds?'

'A lot and I'll come to that. As you know, Nick was, for the want of a better term, a *security expert* employed by HESEC, travelling in West Africa assisting friendly governments with security issues. HESEC is an independent organisation but it appears that its main paymaster is the British Foreign Office.'

'That's also what we understood,' Axel says. 'Because Nick was training Liberian border guards when he saved us over in the Ivory Coast.'

Adele nods. 'Right. In addition to this work, he was also unofficially trying to trace our brother, Charles, who went missing somewhere in Africa a few weeks earlier.'

'He told us that,' Petra confirms.

'I thought he would,' Adele manages a smile. 'But getting back to your question, Axel, I haven't worked out yet how Nick got involved with the diamonds.'

'And,' I butt in. 'The strange thing is that Hal only seemed to be marginally interested in the actual stones, he hardly glanced at them. What he wanted was a map.'

'And that,' Adele states emphatically, 'Is the crux of the matter. It's clear that Hal and the other villains knew there was a mega-rich diamond mine somewhere in Africa, but not the country. That's why he wanted the package, as the map would give the location. Because of that, Nick was murdered and we were attacked time and time again.'

'I understand it now,' Axel says.

'But for reasons we'll probably never know,' Adele continues, 'Nick handed the package in to HESEC, then something changed his mind so he took it back before it had been opened, forged Thrimby's signature, and gave it to me to pass on to Penny, for the baby. And thanks to Axel,' she nods in his direction, 'we now know the mine is located in Liberia on the border with Sierra Leone, but only we know that.'

Axel uses his stick to sit upright in his chair. 'I think,' he says slowly, 'that I can tell you how the diamonds are connected.'

Adele gives him a cautious look. 'How's that?'

'Do you remember when we were telling you about how Nick rescued us?'

'Yes, of course.'

'I also mentioned a member of our team, also saved by Nick, a man called Jaroslav Baros.'

'That's right' I reply. 'You said then you'd tell us more about him'

144

'Well, Jaroslav didn't leave with us but stayed behind in Liberia. He had other plans and I'm pretty certain those diamonds Nick had were something to do with him.'

'I'm afraid you've lost me, Axel.' I look round and Adele looks equally puzzled. 'I thought he was an expert on oil exploration.'

'He is, but like me, he's got other interests. But it all started with seismic, satellite and other tests for oil.'

'What did?'

He looks at his watch and then to his wife. 'Look, the explanation will take a bit of time so before I start, let's have something to eat. I don't know about you but I'm starving, and while we're eating, and you've both had a chance to clean yourselves up, I'll tell you about Jaroslav and why I think he's the reason, unwittingly of course, for the terrible events of the past few weeks.'

'Will ham sandwiches be alright?' Petra asks, heading for the kitchen.

'Yes, but do you have any pickles, Essigsobe,' I laugh, 'I've recently developed a taste for it.'

'Ja, of course, we Belgiums love our pickles.'

When we're settled with our refreshments, Axel sits back in his chair with a plate balanced on his knee. 'I first met Jaro or, to give him his full title, Professor Jaroslav Baros, during a conference at Brussels University a few years ago, where he delivered a paper on the earth's geological processes and gave his hypothesis on the explosive eruptions that brought various minerals to the earth's surface between two and three million years ago. His lecture wasn't well attended and several people thought some of his speculations illogical.' Axel pauses to take a sip from his cup. 'Unquestionably, he has a brilliant mind but like many people of his type, he tends to come up with extravagant claims, many of which are later proved to be wrong. But I thought one of his ideas was quite interesting and invited him to dinner that evening.'

'Ha,' Petra smiles. 'He came, alright, but he was quite rude and, I thought, a bit odd.'

Axel rubs his brow as if trying to recall exactly what happened that night. 'At first, we got on well but the more

I listened to him, the more peculiar he seemed. A very interesting character but rather eccentric. However, we kept in touch and as I've already told you, we worked together on oil exploration in various parts of Africa, but only because the pay was good.'

'But what was the idea of his that you found so interesting?' I ask.

He removes his glasses and cleans them with his handkerchief. 'I'll tell you in a minute, but what annoyed me was that he went back to Liberia many times and told me he'd found a very important, very influential contact who was ex-general Jacob Marcam.'

'Jacob Marcam, wasn't he the trouble maker?' Adele asks.

He nods. 'Yes, after starring in the Liberian civil wars, he's now in jail.'

'What for?'

'He's appealing against a twenty-year sentence for war crimes.'

'Oh, of course, I think I read about it somewhere,' Adele tilts her head, narrowing her eyes in concentration.

'Marcam's passion was diamonds, or at least what he could buy with them, and now he'll almost certainly spend most of the rest of his life in jail.'

'You say Jaroslav contacted people close to Marcam but, he's no longer powerful so what help will they be, or,' I suddenly think I can see where this is leading. 'Did Jacob Marcam know about this diamond mine?'

'That, I think, is definitely the key.'

'So he probably does know.'

'Ja, it certainly looks like it.' Leaning back in his chair, his thumbs firmly lodged in the sleeves of his sweater, he says, 'But it would help if I explained the basics of diamonds so you can understand Jaro's - let's say, *unusual* theory.'

'Okay.'

'Well, as you probably already know, diamonds are crystals of carbon formed over a billion years ago deep in the earth's mantle. A *mere* few million years later, massive volcanic eruptions forced magma to the earth's surface in geothermal vents, on the way picking up any diamonds in the area.

These eruptions could take several days, often settling below the earth's surface before a final violent eruption brought diamonds, embedded in volcanic rock, to the surface. As the magma cooled, it solidified into carrot-shaped pipes, called *kimberlite pipes*. Over the years, erosion has worn away the kimberlite exposing any diamonds near the surface. Okay so far?'

'Yes, but where are those kimberlite pipes?'

'Oh, they're all over the world, but only about two percent contain diamonds, the main concentration, the majority, in fact, are in Africa in areas of diamondiferous rock.'

'And would that include Liberia?'

'Yes, but only the western region close to the Sierra Leone border.'

'That's the lecture over, Axel,' Petra admonishes. 'Tell them about Jaro's theory.'

Looking slightly irritated at his wife, he continues. 'Jaro's theory, thank you darling, was that *if* the final eruption didn't have quite enough energy to make it all the way, then the kimberlite pipes must still be down there – just below the surface. Ergo, if you drill down in the right spot, you'll find a cache of diamonds.' He beams at us both. 'So that, ladies, is Jaroslav's theory.'

'But how would he know if these kimberlite pipes were there?' I ask.

'From 3D seismic imaging, ground-penetrating radar, vibrator trucks et cetera,' he smiles seeing the perplexed expressions on our faces. 'Basically, by using a variety of techniques, often used for oil exploration, we get a picture of the earth's substructure.'

'Does that mean to see what's under our feet?'

'In a way, yes, depending on the type of rock.' He scratches his head as another recollection comes to him. 'I remember Jaro showed me printouts of two examples where there were unexplained cone-shaped rock structures below the earth's surface, both of them in diamond rich areas which he believed could be kimberlite pipes. I thought he was wrong so didn't take much notice at the time.'

Starting to look excited, Adele asks, 'Was one of these images in Liberia?'

He nods. 'Yes, I'm pretty sure one was on the Liberia/ Sierra Leone border.'

'So he could have been right all the time.'

He shakes his head once again. 'I still find it hard to believe but with the map references being in the right place, plus those diamonds in Nick's package, there certainly is a possibility that he's found a diamond rich kimberlite pipe just as he'd predicted.'

'And, somehow or other,' I hear my own voice rising in anticipation, 'Nick must have found out about it, and that's why he wrote that he was privy to a huge secret worth billions and, of course, that's why Hal wanted a map. It all adds up, doesn't it?'

'Yes, but I'm the geologist here and I still find it hard to believe, but there again,' he frowns as though trying to dispel everything he'd learnt in his training. 'Another thing that made Jaro excited was that the underground cone would be protected from erosion.'

'So the unexposed diamonds would be in a relatively small area.' Adele says.

'Correct. Kimberlite pipes are very narrow, the diamonds wouldn't have dispersed.'

'He must be thrilled if his theory is right after all,' Petra says, 'Especially as his peers thought him a crank.'

'And that includes me,' Axel remarks thoughtfully. 'But here's the crunch and this is another reason why you've had all the troubles. As with any major discovery, he'll be scared that this information could be leaked to someone and he'll lose the mine and everything.'

'And that someone could be *the late* Hal, as well as Sir Desmond and the Chinese.'

'I guess you're right, Penny,' Axel sighs. 'But we're still talking about a lot of 'ifs' here. If the diamond content is anything like the Kimberley mine, and with the use of modern equipment, it would undoubtedly be worth billions'

We are silent for a few moments before Adele speaks. 'Axel, do you know if Nick and Jaro worked together?'

'Not that I know of. In fact, unlike Jaro, Nick and I felt the same about the importance of Africa's natural wealth being used to benefit the local people and not local dictators and their cronies, or foreigners.'

'So why then, would he help Jaro?'

'I can't think why.'

'Do you know where Jaro is now?' Adele asks. 'Is he in Liberia?'

'I haven't heard from him for, oh, it must be well over four months.' He shuffles through some papers on his desk. 'I have his email address and satellite phone number somewhere so I'll try to get him.'

'That would be interesting,' I say. 'And do you know if the Chinese are in Liberia?'

'No, but I'll find out. One thing I do know is that a relatively new diamond mine in Zimbabwe is now run by the Chinese, in exchange for funding Mugabe's new missile-protected mansion and his secret police force. They're taking hundreds of millions worth of diamonds for a pittance.'

'Poor Zimbabwe,' Adele sighs. 'Poor Africa.'

'You're right,' Axel looks downcast. 'Unlike government policy in the West, the Chinese have no objection to bribery and corruption as long as they can get what they want. China looks on Africa purely as an economic opportunity to strip out its natural resources in exchange for well, I don't know, anything from flip-flops to fighter jets.'

Adele gives a cheerless grunt. 'I'm sure the Chinese will be in Liberia. From what I've read, they're taking over the whole bloody continent.'

'But the question is,' I put in, 'Would Jaro work with the Chinese?'

Axel shakes his head. 'No way, he wouldn't trust them but hey, here's a thought,' he sits back in his chair, stretching his bandaged leg. 'I wonder if the villains know about Jaro?'

'That's a good point,' I nod. 'Maybe not, because if they did know, their men would be looking for him and not chasing us. You're right, Axel, if Hal and his cohorts knew about Jaro, they'd also know he and his mine are in Liberia.'

'I think you're right,' Axel's eyes narrow in thought. 'It seems that they were only aware that Nick knew about the mine, not who was behind it. And that's why Nick warned you about the mole in HESEC and also the Chinese, and why he wrote *billions* in his note. No wonder they were prepared to kill to get the mine's location.'

CHAPTER SEVENTEEN
FEBRUARY 9th

Another troubled night, keeping me awake with the dreadful images from yesterday.

My top pillow keeps getting damp with tears so I'm continually switching them around trying to find a dry side. Also upsetting me is the *big* question - are we safe now? The question is straightforward enough but almost certainly the answer will be *no,* there are still Chinese unaccounted for and I'm sure Sir Desmond Thrimby, back in London, is involved, probably even the ringleader. But thank God, his evil son, is *no longer* but Sir Des won't know that yet, in fact all he'll know is that his son has disappeared, vanished. My heart bleeds for him – not.

Still tormented, I join Axel and Petra for breakfast. They are both early risers unlike Adele who hasn't appeared yet. 'Are you sure you don't mind if Adele and I stay with you for a few more days? I feel safe here but we don't want to put you in any danger.'

'No, not at all,' Axel answers persuasively. 'We *want* you to stay. Remember, we owe our lives to Nick and will do everything we can to help.

At that moment, Adele breezes in and takes a seat at the kitchen table. The bruises on her face are starting to fade, save for one dark swelling at the side of her left eye.

'We were just telling Penny,' Petra says, 'That you can stay with us as long as you like, you're safe here, but it's important Dirk gets the all clear from the police. Your journeys to and from the villains' place will have been caught on camera and we don't want your pictures circulated as suspects, especially to border posts. It's Sunday today and our Belgium Gendamerie are not known for their productivity over weekends,' she laughs. 'It'll be a few days before Dirk can work his magic.'

'I hope he does,' I say grimly. 'He's not exactly covered himself in glory so far.'

Axel nods. 'No, and I'm sorry about that. I've used his services several times over the years and he's always been very good. Of course,' he smiles, 'I never asked him to rescue young ladies in distress before.'

'And let's hope you never have to in the future,' Petra embraces him.

'I'm sure he'll come up trumps this time,' Adele says positively. 'And thanks very much for letting us stay, you've both been brilliant.' Being more demonstrative than me, Adele goes over and kisses them both on the cheeks.

Axel looks a shade embarrassed. 'Before I forget, after Dirk left us yesterday, he contacted the Chief of Police, who happens to be a personal friend of his. He was told about a mysterious explosion near the village of Tisselt. As one of Dirk's ongoing investigations is to do with drug trafficking, he fed the Chief the story that it might be connected to his case.'

'Will that work?'

'I don't know,' Axel replies. 'But one thing Dirk found out from the Chief was that the building where you were held was used as a camping base in the summer, and ...'

'That sounds about right.' Adele interrupts.

Axel continues. 'The Chief also suggested there had been an argument between the traffickers, shots exchanged – that's to explain the gunshot wounds, of course, and the gasoline storage tank had been hit, exploding killing them all.'

'It's certainly a good story if the police accept it, but what about the roadside cameras we were caught on, did the Chief mention that?'

'No, but that'll take a day or two.'

'Well, in that case, should we leave today, before that happens?' Adele asks.

Axel looks questioningly at Petra and then at me. 'What would you like to do?'

'For my part, I'd like to chance it and stay here. I'm absolutely shattered and don't think I could raise the energy to do a runner.'

Looking concerned, Petra says, 'I think you're right. Have a couple of days rest, you definitely need it, Penny, and Axel and I do feel confident that with his connections, Dirk will keep you out of any investigation.'

I look at Adele. 'What do you think?'

'Yes, we'll stay. I could do with a good rest as well.'

'That's settled then,' Petra smiles. 'And Margit – Doctor Brabent, phoned last night to say that she can see Penny on Tuesday afternoon for a scan, to make sure the baby's fine.'

'That'll be a weight off my mind, thanks for that.'

'It's my pleasure and now we can all relax.' Strangely, after saying that, Petra's expression changes as she turns to look at Adele. 'Would you mind if I ask you something, it's been troubling me since you told us how you killed three men.'

'Go ahead, 'Adele says warily.

'Have you ever shot a person before?'

'But she had to do it,' Axel pipes up before Adele can answer. 'If she hadn't killed them, they would have killed both of them.'

Adele takes her time before answering. 'No, I haven't, that's the first time I've killed people, although the assassin on the train came close. When I used to shoot at targets at the gun club, I often wondered how I'd react if I had to do it for real. I think all club members think along similar lines. Would I freeze and make a complete mess of it?' She shifts uneasily in her chair. 'Well, I didn't freeze. Nick and I come from the same military family and the lesson we learnt from our father is very clear.'

'And what's that?' asks Petra.

'Assess the risk, and if against armed assailants, shoot first.'

I say nothing. Maybe I was silly thinking Adele shouldn't have shot the third man. Although he'd dropped his gun, he may have had another hidden somewhere.

'Of course you were right, Adele.' Axel says firmly turning to his wife. 'Just think, Petra, when we were hostages, if Nick and his men had hesitated to shoot first, we'd be dead now.'

Close to tears, Petra goes over to Adele and holds her in her arms. 'Of course Axel's right, and you were also right. I'm sorry I brought it up.'

'That's okay.'

Looking relieved, Axel says, 'And whilst we're talking about Nick saving us in the Ivory Coast, I have some news for you. Nick's right hand man, the one who flew us to safety in Liberia, Colonel Noah Tofa arrives in Brussels tomorrow.'

'What!' Adele frowns. 'That seems a weird sort of coincidence, him arriving just when we happen to be here. I'm always suspicious about coincidences.'

'No, it's fine,' Axel smiles. 'Noah comes here three times a year with a Liberian trade mission. He's one of their main negotiators. Remember, Brussels is the main EU parliament which foreign delegations visit all the time, so it's not unusual.'

I wasn't quite sure what to expect when Colonel Noah Tofa arrived. I haven't had much time to think about it with everything that's been going on but as he enters the room, I stare at him in astonishment. He's an attractively tall, well-balanced man having the figure of an athlete and dressed in an immaculate pin-striped, three-piece suit. His fine features and graceful stride bear a certain resemblance to Barak Obama bestriding the stage during the first America presidential race, although Noah is a shade darker.

Using our first names, Axel introduces us to Noah who only hesitates a second before approaching Adele. Holding both hands out to her, she unthinkingly places hers in his, probably as mesmerized by him as I am.

'Miss Holbrook, Adele,' his voice is deep and full of feeling, 'I was so terribly upset to hear about your brother's untimely death and I offer you and your family my sincere condolences.' His diction is that of an educated man with a distinct American twang. 'Nicholas Holbrook was a great man and did fantastic things for us in Liberia. Our President,

Mrs Henrietta Poltara, has asked me to convey in person, her deep sorrow at his passing.'

Adele's jaw stiffens but no tears; she's not the type. 'Thank you, Noah, that's very kind,' she says quietly, 'I'll convey your sympathies to my parents.' God, she's gone all formal.

Everyone is still standing as Axel introduces Noah to me, as Nick's fiancée.

Clearly taken by surprise, he says. 'Oh, I er didn't know - he didn't tell me.'

'No, he probably wouldn't,' I concede hesitantly, his deep brown eyes are like cocoa-rich chocolate. 'Actually, Nick and I weren't actually engaged.' Oh my God, I just put two '*actuallys*' together; what's wrong with me? Nervously, I clear my throat and muddle on. 'In fact, we only met six weeks ago but I am carrying his child.' Under his steady gaze, I feel myself blush. 'It was convenient to create this impression.'

'Yes, I see,' he says kindly, although I don't think he does. He pauses for a moment to register this latest news. 'Unfortunately, I wasn't in Liberia during Nick's visit to my country last month, I was at an African Union meeting in South Africa, so I'm now doubly sorry for you as well as the Holbrook family.'

There's no doubting his sincerity in paying this tribute to Nick, and the fact that it comes from such an unexpected source brings back with a vengeance, the heartache of loss for the man I wanted to love, at the same time rekindling my hatred for those bastards who murdered him. There's an awkward silence eventually broken by Petra who asks Noah if he would like a drink. He politely declines.

'May I ask you a question, Noah,' Adele says as she smoothes down her skirt. 'What exactly did my brother do in your country? He was always a little vague with my family.'

'Of course, Nick always worked on a *need-to-know* basis, mainly I think, to protect those close to him. I can tell you what he did in Liberia but he never revealed to me his work in other African countries.'

'That sounds like Nick,' Adele gives a faint smile.

'As you will all know,' Noah begins, 'Military coups are common-place in Africa, and when the British government considers a head of state is - how should I put it? A good guy -then they use organisations like HESEC, and men like Nick, to install security systems to try and protect the leader from being overthrown. So Nick created, trained and equipped a loyal guard for our president, Mrs Poltara, because she is in the *good-guy* category. He also worked with the Americans to ensure, as far as possible, that the Liberian army was led by trustworthy officers.'

Nodding her head up and down a couple of times, Adele says, 'I thought it would be something like that.'

'He did a brilliant job in very difficult circumstances,' Noah says, 'And selected me to be the overall commander of the programme.'

'Difficult circumstances? What were those?'

Noah raises his eyes and sighs. 'Mrs Poltara has done an amazing job since being elected to office but we still have an aggressive opposition, many supporters of Jacob Marcam.'

'But hasn't he been found guilty of war crimes?'

'Yes, but he's appealed the sentence, and many of his followers believe he'll be released anytime soon.'

'Is that realistic?'

'Marcam's crimes were serious, but I can point out a dozen current African generals who have committed much worse atrocities than he, and they haven't even been arrested. And that's why his supporters think he'll be freed.'

'But what do you think.'

'Almost certainly the appeal will be rejected because behind the scenes, the CIA is using its power to keep him behind bars. Marcam made the mistake of befriending terrorist groups. Once you give *the finger* to the CIA, it's never forgeten, and he's double-crossed them several times. Another complication is we've had UN peacekeepers in Liberia to keep the two sides apart. There were fifteen thousand of them at first but that's been gradually reduced over the years. I think it's about seven thousand now.'

'But why would peacekeepers be a complication?'

'Yes, why indeed!' Noah concedes. 'You see, they come from about thirty different countries of diverse religions, so it's not surprising there are conflicts between the various factions and orders by officers are not always obeyed.'

'Oh, I see.' Adele acknowledges. 'Very difficult.'

'And Jacob Marcam's supporters have made friends with many of the officers.'

'Ha, nothing is ever straight forward,' I sympathise, shaking my head. 'There's a piece of information I'd like to tell you.'

'Please, go ahead.'

'Just before Nick was killed, he wrote me a letter. It was enclosed in a package with some diamonds. He was very worried that there was a mole in HESEC's office and he was in danger from someone, but he didn't know who.' I pause before continuing. 'In his letter he said that if I had any problems, there were two men I could go to - two men I could trust. One of them was Axel and the other one was you.'

His jaw drops. 'Me?' he asks astounded.

'Yes.'

He nestles his head in his hands, elbows propped on the arms of his chair. 'I'm so ...' he sighs deeply. 'So honoured that he would name me,' his eyes are damp with emotion.

'Thank you very much for telling me that, and I give you my unconditional promise that I will help you in any way I can.'

'In Nick's letter, her mentions Limarni. Does the name Limarni mean anything to you?'

'Limarni?' He shakes his head slowly from side to side. 'No, I don't think I've heard the word before. It could be a Liberian word, though.'

'Could it be a person, or a place?'

Again he struggles. 'Yes, it could be either.'

Looking into his striking, dark eyes, I take a deep breath. 'We were hoping you'd know, anyway, I hope our problems, that is, Adele's and mine, are over.'

'But we can't be sure of that,' Adele interjects sharply. 'Although we've eliminated some of our enemies, we think there could be more, don't we, Penny?'

'Did I hear you right?' Noah turns to Adele. 'That you've *eliminated* some of your enemies.'

'Yes.'

'And by *eliminate,* do you mean you've killed them?'

'Yes, that *is* what I mean,' she hesitates before turning to me. 'Look, Penny, I think you should tell Noah everything, right from Nick's murder to where we are now.'

'Hey, hang on a moment,' Noah jumps up looking shocked. '*Nick's murder!* Are you telling me it wasn't a traffic accident?'

'That's right, my brother *was* murdered.'

Putting his head into his hands, Noah almost chokes, 'Oh no,' he sighs. After a moment he glances at his watch. 'Look, I don't have to be back at the Embassy for an hour so tell me what you can. If Nick was murdered, then I for one, definitely want to be involved.'

'I *do* want to tell you everything, Noah,' my voice catches in my throat. 'So much has happened. The last few weeks have been one long, continuous nightmare and I'm bound to struggle to sort out in my mind, you know, what's important.'

'Don't worry, Penny,' Adele says softly, 'I'll help. She looks at Noah. 'We've already told Axel and Petra and they've been absolutely marvellous.'

A tense looking Petra gets up from her chair. 'Can I get a drink for anyone?'

My throat feels dry. 'I'd love a glass of water.'

Giving me a sympathetic smile, she goes through to the kitchen.

With everyone focusing on me, I try to concentrate on my breathing and, flexing my shoulder muscles, I roll my head around to ease my neck. 'Okay,' I smile, 'I'm ready.' I start by explaining when I first met Nick and with some help from Adele, go through the harrowing events in sequence, up to and including two days ago when Adele shot Hal and the two Chinese thugs. Noah only interrupts a couple of times to get clarifications and Axel confirms the information on the diamonds. I was wondering if Noah would comment on the fact that I'm carrying Nick's child after only knowing him for such a short time, but I'm grateful he doesn't.

After I finish, Noah sits back in his chair, slowly shakes his head. 'This is one of the most incredible stories I've ever heard. Nick's well-intentioned gift placed you both in mortal danger, just for the location of a diamond mine.' There's a faint smile on his lips as he looks at Adele and me in turn. 'You are the two most amazing women I've ever met, but knowing that you, Adele, are Nick's sister, it's all perfectly believable.'

'Oh, just a moment,' I say. 'What I forgot to tell you is that we now know the diamonds are from Jaroslav Baros's mine.'

Noah gasps. 'Oh, you're kidding. Jaro has finally found his mythical diamond mine. Oh my God, do you know where it is?'

'Yes, we have the details. It's in Liberia virtually on the border with Sierra Leone.'

Still trying to get his head around this latest news, Noah says slowly, 'This is very confusing because recently, probably only six months ago, Jaro registered a new iron ore mine with the Ministry of Lands in Liberia. When I heard this, and being suspicious of anything Baros gets involved in, I checked at the ministry and found that his mine is located - guess where, close to the boundary of Sierra Leone.' Leaning back in his chair, fingers laced behind his head, he whistles through his teeth. 'The crafty devil is covering up the diamond mine, pretending it's just iron ore, so he won't get any unwanted attention.'

'Ha, when I worked with Jaro,' Axel snorts in derision, 'He was always up to some trick or other, I could never trust him.'

Noah stands to leave. 'Yes, that's also my opinion and I know Baros has made contacts with senior Liberians in the government, mainly those with a reputation for corruption and,' he suddenly stops in mid-sentence, an anguished expression on his face. 'Oh no,' he slaps the palm of his hand on his forehead. 'What am I doing?' he cries out, 'I almost forgot the reason for seeing you today. It was to give you some news, but what with listening to your incredible story, it's almost gone out of my head.'

'What is it?' Adele looks bewildered.

Noah lets out a sigh, 'I think we should all sit down again, I'm sorry about this.'

Curious, we do as he says.

'On this visit to Europe,' his tone is neutral but I can sense the tension in his voice, 'I was planning to nip over to London and see Nick but I want to tell you, Adele.'

'Tell me what?'

'You will know that since your other brother, Charles Temple, went missing, Nick has been meeting people all over West Africa hoping to find out what happened to him.'

'Yes.'

'Well, one contact Nick made, a Mandingo man called Bambara, approached me last week saying there is a man fitting Mr Temple's description being held in Guinea.'

'Guinea!' she exclaims.

'Yes, but he wasn't forthcoming as to the whereabouts, it's a huge country.'

'But I must go and find him,' Adele yells, a look of suppressed shock on her face. 'What is a, that word you used, a Manwingo?'

'No, Mandingo. It's a substantial tribe spread over large areas of West Africa and many of them are involved in trade. More than any other tribe, they are able to cross borders quite easily.'

'And is that man, Bambara, one of them?' Adele's asks excitedly.

'Yes, he'd just returned to Monrovia after doing business in the Ivory Coast and Guinea and knowing I was Nick's main contact in Liberia, he came to see me.'

'When can I go?' Adele begs. 'Please Noah, can you help me?'

'Of course I'll help you,' Noah says, 'I'll get you a visa from our embassy here in Brussels, that's no problem.'

'But is this man, Bambara reliable?' there's a note of caution in Axel's voice.

'It's hard to say,' Noah shrugs, holding his hands outward, his whitish palms contrasting strikingly with his otherwise dark skin. 'I was sceptical myself as there's a reward involved, but I did give him the third degree and think he could well be genuine.'

Biting my lip, I venture, 'I want to go to Liberia, too.'

Frowning, Adele she says touchily, 'But why? It's my brother, Charles, there's no need for you to go.'

'And you're pregnant,' Petra comes over and takes my hand. 'Don't forget, you're seeing Doctor Brabant on Wednesday, and Liberia will be too unhealthy, won't it?'

I have a sudden vivid memory of myself as a child, my mother sounding just like Petra. 'But what am I to do?' I cry, scowling at Adele, 'How can I go back to England alone with all those bloody villains after me?'

For the first time since we met, Adele and I are about to have a row but before she can respond, the phone rings leaving my question hanging in the air. No-one speaks as Axel picks up the receiver. 'Ja, Dirk.' He turns in his swivel chair so his back is towards us and reaches for a pen to make some notes. 'Ja, ja, verdammen,' he swears and lowers his voice so I can't hear his side of the conversation.

Finally replacing the receiver, he swivels back to face us. It's hard to tell from his expression whether it's good news or not. Giving a slight cough, he clears his throat. 'Dirk just told me that the police forensic labs have analysed the human remains, you know, from where you were held, and their initial findings are that the victims – they can't yet tell how many - are of Asian origin.'

Petra is the first to speak. 'Well, that's good news, isn't it? There are thousands of illegal Indonesians in Belgium and the crime rate is very high. Blame it on them.'

'And don't forget,' Adele adds to Petra's reasoning, 'I placed the bomb directly on Hal's head so there shouldn't be any Caucasian remains to change the scientists' minds.'

'You could be right,' Axel doesn't look convinced. 'But there were stores of gasoline and camping gas at the site which explains why the explosion was so *grosse*.'

'So are we in the clear?' I ask.

Gloomily, he shakes his head. 'There's also some bad news.'

Damn. My heart sinks and I realise I've clenched my hands into fists. 'You'd better tell us.'

'You and Adele, have had an NEP placed on you from London, that's a *Rapport de Notification europeen de Police* which roughly translates into a European Police Notification Order.'

'And what on earth's that?'

He sucks air in through his teeth. 'Your names and photos have been sent to central police forces in every European country and wherever you're identified, which could be a hotel, public transport, anything like that, they will notify the police in London.'

'They'll arrest us?'

'No, they'll just give them your whereabouts, that's unless you try to leave Europe and then you'd be stopped from leaving.'

'Oh shit,' Adele curses. 'This stinks of HESEC's dirty work.'

'So what can we do?' I shudder, a taste like acid in my mouth.

Axel shakes his head. 'I'm not sure but the Brendtle Hotel will, no doubt, report your brief stay there which will confirm you *are,* or at least *were* in Brussels.'

'Oh double shit.' Adele angrily slams her hand down on the chair arm. 'So how the hell do we go anywhere?'

'By changing your names.' Surprised, we all look at Noah who, so far, has remained quiet through these exchanges. 'Wherever you both decide to go, all you need are new names and fake passports.'

'Fake passports!' Adele yells, 'How do we get those?'

'Ha, I would think Dirk, your tame security expert could arrange those for you, don't you think so, Axel?'

'I guess so,' he replies slowly. 'Dirk does know the underworld better than most; I'll ask him to come round.'

'May I make another suggestion,' Noah speaks authoritatively. 'Tell him to get something like seven or eight year old Canadian passports because they weren't biometric in those days, easier to forge and cheaper.'

I look at Noah in a new light. 'How come you're such an expert in criminal activities?'

He laughs. 'My lips are sealed, but as long as this stays within these four walls, I can tell you that many foreigners arriving in Liberia have fake passports, escaping from something, but our immigration officers can usually spot them.'

'Are they refused entry?'

He laughs again. 'Oh no, as long as you slip them a large enough *dash* as our immigration officers are very wealthy. And don't worry, Adele,' he's still smiling, 'I'll meet you at the airport so I'll make sure you have no problem.'

Frowning, as though uncertain to accept Noah's solution, Adele asks Axel. 'Do you think it'll work then, false names, false passports and getting through Brussels airport without being spotted.'

'Probably,' he murmurs rubbing his chin, but lacking Noah's confidence. 'You could always alter your appearance, say a wig and glasses.'

'Oh, and one more thing,' Noah heads for the door. 'You can't come in on a tourist visa, we don't have tourists at the moment,' he smiles. 'You'll have to be a charity worker.'

Adele looks nonplussed. 'But which charity, I don't belong to one?'

'Then invent one. Create a charity on authentic-looking stationery of course, with a couple of forged letters of recommendation and say, ten million dollars for, let me think,' he scratches the side of his face, 'I know, education. That'll get you in the country.'

'But I don't have ten million dollars.'

'You don't have to,' he laughs. 'Just put it in writing and lie. I'll see you don't get into trouble.'

'You mean falsify everything.'

'Yes, I'm confident you can do that,' he checks his watch again. 'Look, I have to go but let me know what you choose to do. I fly out Friday afternoon, so if you decide to go down that route, I'll need the new passports by Thursday p.m. at the latest, with details of your charity. Make it a Canadian one, is that okay?'

Speechless, with her mouth wide open, Adele chokes. 'Thank you, Noah, I'll do that.'

'*We'll* do that,' I add stubbornly, glaring straight at Adele.

'We'll see about that,' she snaps back turning her back on me. 'Noah, you've given me new hope of finding Charles.' Standing on tiptoes, she kisses him on both cheeks. 'I'm *very* grateful.'

After the door closes, we sit silently for a moment, each with our own thoughts.

CHAPTER EIGHTEEN
FEBRUARY 13th

'So, are these your new passports?' Noah handles the two
scuffed Canadian passports and opens the top one. 'Okay,
let me see; issued to Gabrielle Rimmer, nice red hair,' he
laughs, looking at me with those *knee-trembling* eyes of
his. 'Born in Ottawa.' He flicks through the pages studying
numerous international entry and exit stamps. 'Very good,
now let me look at yours, Adele. Issued to Michelle Moore,
born Vancouver and oh!' he stares closely at her, 'I hadn't
noticed, you've had your hair cut. Good disguise, especially
with those spectacles. Yes, these will do nicely.' Putting them
down on the table, he looks at me speculatively. 'I take it then
that you are *both* going.'

'Yes we are,' I state stubbornly, looking at Adele to make
sure she's not pulling a face. 'That's thanks to Doctor Brabant
who confirmed there's no medical reason why I shouldn't go.'

'That's what she said,' Petra confirms. 'Although Margit
wasn't keen on her going, being pregnant.'

'She gave me an ultrasound and other tests on Tuesday and
the final results came through this morning so everything's
fine.' Pausing a second, 'I could just make out its head, arms
and legs and its little heart beating, it was amazing. I'm
supposed to have another scan in four weeks, hopefully back
in England.'

'Well done, you, I knew Nick's baby would be a fighter,'
Noah says with a sense of certainty. 'And oh, by the way,
I've given some thought about your journey to Liberia and
suggest you fly out of Brussels in six days' time, that's next
Wednesday, as long as Axel and Petra don't mind you staying
here till then.'

'That's no problem,' Axel answers. 'They'll be out of sight of anyone who might report them to London.'

'Good, and that will give me enough time to organise things in Liberia.'

With her arm around me, Petra says, 'Although Margit isn't too happy about Penny going to the tropics, fortunately, she's up to date with yellow fever and hepatitis jabs, as well as the polio booster. Margit's main worry is malaria.'

'That's what I thought,' Noah frowns. 'Is there anything safe you can take?'

'I'll take Chloroquine and Paludrine, it's better than nothing but it doesn't give the same level of protection as others.' I give a laugh, 'I'll have to use lots of stinky mosquito repellent.'

Noah playfully wags his finger in my direction. 'That makes sense, young lady, stinky or not, do as the doctor tells you.'

'Yes sir.' I give him a mock salute.

'Now here's what you both must do.' He takes a piece of paper out of his jacket pocket. 'Make bookings with Alitalia on 19th February to Casablanca, a change in Rome is necessary. Stay three nights in the Casablanca Aquitane Hotel before taking Air Cote d'Ivoire to Roberts International Airport, Liberia on Saturday 22nd. I'll be there to meet you. I've already checked and there's space on the flights and rooms in the hotel. But you must do the bookings in your new names. Once in the country, however, you can revert to being British as you'll no longer appear on any international passenger lists.'

While he's giving directions, I carefully write it all down. 'I've got all that, Noah, thank you. We've created our charity as you said. We've called it the *Pendelle Schools Charitable Trust* with ten million dollars funding for rural schools.' I pass him a folder with all the information, which he scrutinises carefully.

'You have been busy,' he looks impressed. 'I'll take this along with your old and new passports and write a letter of introduction to the Ministry of Education. If you could

166

arrange to collect them from the Embassy tomorrow, Petra, they'll be all set. How are you fixed for money?'

'We've got Nick's cash reserve, HESEC's actually,' Adele says. 'And we relieved the bloody assassin on the Eurostar of what he had, so all together we've got the equivalent of about two hundred and sixty thousand dollars, all in Euros, dollars and pounds.'

'That should be more than enough but in Liberia, it must be US dollars. Can you get the Euros and pounds changed.'

'I can arrange that,' Axel says, 'You'd be amazed at the volume of cash circulating in the Brussels gem trade.'

'Well then, if there's nothing else you can think of, I'll look forward to seeing you both at Roberts Airport a week on Saturday.'

'Before you go, can we have your phone and email address, just in case.'

He shakes his head. 'Sorry, can't do. Due to the unrest in Liberia, all internet and international phone connections have been blocked, but you can get me on this number,' he hands me his card. 'But only by satellite phone. Do you have one?'

'I can get one from Dirk,' Axel says.

'Okay.' We stand as he prepares to leave. 'Good luck with your leg, Axel, I expect to be in Brussels again late-April for an African Union summit. And ladies,' he gives the three of us kisses on both cheeks. 'See you soon.'

As the door closes, I suddenly feel drained and collapse into my chair. 'He's great, isn't he?'

'Yes,' Petra agrees. 'He's quite remarkable and such a gentleman.'

'To me,' Adele says, 'He's just *sex on legs*.'

We all laugh. 'You naughty girl,' Petra admonishes, grinning from ear to ear.

Axel looks circumspectly at Adele over the rim of his glasses, 'Be careful because I believe he's related to the President of Liberia, Mrs Poltara, and that means if there's any change of government, Noah would be out. He has his enemies.'

'I'll remember that,' Adele nods. 'Anyway, I do have a boyfriend, Rupert, fighting somewhere in Afghanistan, so I'll resist any temptation. Noah's quite safe,' she gives me a sly wink. 'And you can forget those smouldering eyes of his, we have serious business to attend to. Not only do I have a brother to find, but I also have to work out why Nick got involved with this guy Jaroslav Baros and his diamond mine.'

'I know that, and I'm sure Nick would want me to go.'

That night, Adele and I phone our parents, it's almost two weeks since I left a message on my mother's answer machine. Just in case their phones are tapped by HESEC, or whoever, Dirk uses some hi-tech gadgetry to route the calls through a colleague of his in Malaga, so we can't be traced to Brussels.

'Hello mum, I'm still on holiday in Spain and having a good time. I can't speak for long as I'm using a public phone, my mobile is broken.' I know my story is pathetically weak but I'm sticking to it and don't tell her anything that would trouble her and dad.

Mum's voice is tense. 'We've been worried about you, darling. Mr Bunter phoned twice saying you have to give three months' notice if you want to leave your job, and he's already passed your file to their legal department, official secrets and all that.'

Oh dear, I feel like crying but somehow manage to keep my voice calm. I tell her I couldn't care less about the job because I'd planned to quit in any case. She's not pleased but knows from experience that I make my own decisions in life, even the bad ones.

'Bye for now, mum. I'm going on a tour of old Spain with a friend and I'll call you when I can.' I quickly put the receiver down before she can protest. Poor mum, I'll eventually have to tell her that I'm pregnant but that will have to wait.

Ridding myself of the harrowing memories of the past few weeks will take time as my mind keeps racing between close encounters with danger and unravelling what the hell's going on. Petra assures me the horrors will gradually fade, she only has occasional flashbacks to her ordeal in the Ivory Coast. But she's wrong. The one thing I'll never be able to forget, never in a million years, is Nick's death and it's now fairly certain he was murdered for the location of Baros's diamond mine. I want revenge, for me and Nick's baby and, of course, for Adele and her family. That's why we're going to Liberia because the answer must lie there. And who or what or where is Limarni? Adele has already killed off Hal and the two Chinese men who shot Nick, but there are others. We want all of them.

PART THREE
LIBERIA

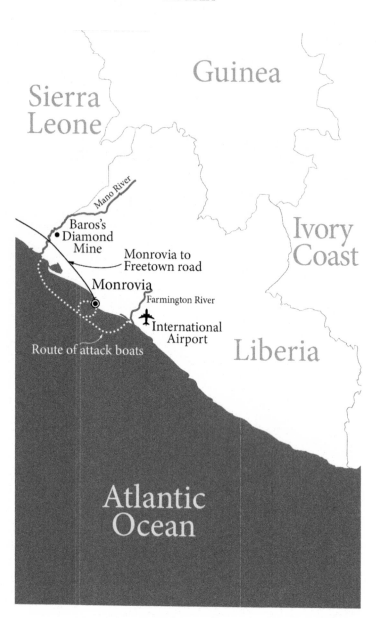

LIBERIA

Guinea

Sierra
Leone

Mano River

Baros's
Diamond
Mine

Monrovia to
Freetown road

Monrovia

Farmington River

International
Airport

Route of attack boats

Ivory
Coast

Liberia

Atlantic
Ocean

MONROVIA
LIBERIA

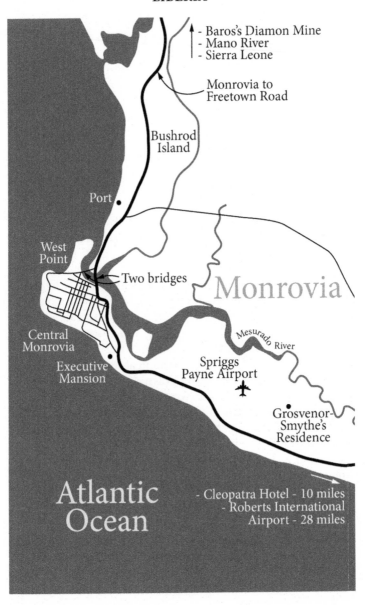

- Baros's Diamon Mine
- Mano River
- Sierra Leone

Monrovia to
Freetown Road

Bushrod
Island

Port

West
Point

Two bridges

Monrovia

Central
Monrovia

Mesurado River

Executive
Mansion

Spriggs
Payne Airport

Grosvenor-
Smythe's
Residence

Atlantic
Ocean

- Cleopatra Hotel - 10 miles
- Roberts International
Airport - 28 miles

CHAPTER NINETEEN
FEBRUARY 22nd

Our Air Cote d'Ivoire flight from Casablanca starts its approach to Roberts International Airport. I nudge Adele who's been fast asleep for the past half hour. The French pilot controls the bumps and skips as the wheels hit the runway and sharply applies the brakes, sending us straining forward against our seat belts. Prudently, I keep my arms between my body and the belt to protect my belly. We taxi past an old wrecked jet towards a partly derelict terminal building, and waves of shimmering heat are coming off the ground. An old-fashioned fire engine, a couple of tanker-trucks and a few assorted vehicles are the only signs of this being an *international airport*. No other planes are in sight, save for a couple of twin-engine Cessnas and a helicopter, all with UN markings.

A blast of hot air hits us as we make our way down some wobbly steps onto the tarmac. The heat and humidity seem heavy as if physically pressing down on me and by the time we reach the terminal, I'm sweating like a pig. Holding my bag in one hand, I do my best to wipe perspiration off my forehead and top lip, and there's an unpleasant trickle of moisture down my back. It's only marginally cooler inside the building. There's no air-conditioning nor fans and the air smells of mould and damp decay.

'Phew, what a stink,' Adele pinches her nose. 'Where's Noah?'

Looking around for any sign of him, my heart sinks. All the disembarking passengers are forced to queue in single file in front of the one, grumpy looking immigration officer perched high in an elevated booth. Angry exchanges between him and the first in line suggest we could be in for a long wait. I'm also alarmed on seeing half a dozen or so armed soldiers in shabby uniforms scattered around the arrivals hall, laughing and joking together and casually waving their weapons around.

Thank God, Noah appears marching smartly towards us in his dark green colonel's uniform, accompanied by two armed soldiers. He looks very smart smiling a wide, white smile.

'Good afternoon, Miss Lane and Miss Holbrook,' he speaks formally as if we're virtual strangers, 'My name's Colonel Tofa and I'd like to welcome you both to Liberia.'

'Thank you, Colonel.'

'If you'll follow me, I'll arrange the formalities for you using your *British* passports.' Fortunately, Adele has them near the top of her handbag and hides the Canadian ones. They served their purpose as we had no problems in either Brussels or Casablanca.

Escorting us to the front of the queue, he hands our documents to the immigration officer who stops what he's doing and, without even looking up, stamps our passports. Ignoring the Health and Customs desks as well as the baggage x-ray machine, Noah guides us through the security area, passing a group of Chinese men arguing volubly with an aggressive-looking uniformed Liberian officer.

Feeling a little disorientated, we follow him into an empty room at the back of the arrivals hall. He orders his two guards to find our suitcases and closes the door. Bliss, the room is cool. Opening a ice-box at the side of the desk, he passes us bottles of cold water.

'It's great to see you both again,' a faint musky, masculine smell of sweat comes off him. 'But it's best if we act formally while we're here.'

Adele gives one of her special smiles. 'It's wonderful to see you again, Noah, but it stinks like hell back there.'

'I know, sorry about that. This terminal is for civilian passengers and as you see, under repair. Next door is better but it's reserved for UN flights, you know, the UN peacekeepers. In fact there's a plane from Pakistan due later this afternoon.'

Desperate for news of Charles, Adele asks if he's heard anything about her brother.

He slowly shakes his head. 'No, I went to Bambara's house. His wife said he is sick with fever and he's gone for treatment from a native doctor.' Pausing for a moment, he adds, 'What you'd call a witchdoctor. She said he'd be back tomorrow.'

'Damn, I was hoping you'd have some better news.'

'Of course, but don't worry, Adele, I'm doing everything I can.'

'Yes, I know and thanks,' she sighs. 'It's just that ... '

'I know,' he sighs. 'Ha,' he suddenly grins at her, 'I see you've got Nick's briefcase with you, the one with the magic bottom.'

She laughs. 'Yes, it's *magic bottom* is bloody brilliant, stuffed with our cash and some of Nick's gear. It passed through every x-ray machine without the slightest problem. It's even got an alarm and tracking device hidden away.'

'I asked Nick to get me one,' Noah says. 'But he wouldn't. Its secret design is strictly for HESEC's senior people.'

There's a knock on the door and Noah's two men say they have our suitcases.

'We can go now.' Noah escorts us through the exit into the oppressive early afternoon heat towards a shiny new 4-wheel drive vehicle where an army driver holds the door open for us. 'I'm taking you to the Cleopatra Hotel,' he announces, getting in the front seat.

'Is that where Axel and Petra stayed?'

'Yes, and Nick also stayed there. Now, this evening over dinner, we can make plans, and I personally will be at your disposal while you are in Liberia. Your connection with Nick Holbrook makes you special guests, President Poltara has signed a warrant to this effect.'

'It's good of you to do all that for us,' I smile, although something is making me feel uneasy. Why it hadn't dawned on me before I can't imagine, but now that we're actually here, feet on the ground and totally out of our comfort zone, I realise we will have to rely on him, and only him, for everything. We haven't any other contacts and there isn't even a British Embassy to help us. Crossing my fingers, I pray that he will live up to our expectations.

Sitting in the sauna-like interior of the vehicle, I can imagine how a lobster must feel. I'd no idea anyone could feel this hot and live. Perspiring from every pore, a wet rivulet is trickling down my face and between my shoulder blades. Mopping my face, the little make-up I applied so carefully this morning is wiped away, I feel like a damp rag that needs to be wrung out to dry. Sweat is also beading on Adele's forehead and strands of hair are stuck to her brow. To avoid sticking to the seatback, we both sit bolt upright.

'It will cool down soon,' Noah says, turning the air-conditioner on full blast. 'It's very hot in Liberia just now, building up to our rainy season.'

There is a queue of vehicles waiting to leave the airport compound, many of them being searched and hassled by soldiers, but our official car is waved straight through. I think this VIP treatment must be a good sign that Noah is the right man. After a few minute's drive, we are in the heart of the country, a tropical, intimidating country.

Turning to face us, Noah says, 'Monrovia is twenty-eight miles away and the Cleopatra is just about halfway.' He pauses before adding, 'And let me introduce my men; Cooper here is my driver and the two other escorts are Moses and Jerbo, they've been with me for many years and totally trustworthy. Occasionally, I may have to leave you in their care so you'll be safe.' We nod and smile at them and I repeat their names in my head hoping I won't forget.

'We're just entering the Firestone Rubber Plantation,' Noah continues, 'It's the biggest rubber plantation in the world.'

Looking out of my window, I notice the plantation is geometrically laid out with rows of trees stretching away in lines from the road's verge. The closest similar looking tree in England would probably be the silver birch, but without the silver. The car is slowing to a stop and I can see construction work ahead as well as men in tattered, sweat-stained shirts and shorts toiling amongst the rubber trees.

'Those men are rubber tappers,' Noah explains. 'If you watch closely, you'll see they use knives to remove a thin layer of bark in a downward half spiral, then place the collecting cups underneath so that latex drips down into them. They empty the cups into their pails, and when full, take them to the processing factory. Firestone has around six thousand tappers.'

The nearest man to the car struggles to haul his bucket from tree to tree. 'The poor chap looks knackered,' I sympathise, 'Especially in this dreadful heat and humidity.'

'Yes, they have to work *very* hard and attend to three hundred trees each day, or they'll get no pay.'

Sighing and shaking my head, seeing first-hand how hard life is for many Africans. Moving off again, I'm surprised to see Asian faces under the workers' hard-hats and Asian drivers in the cabs of the earth movers. 'Are they Chinese?' I ask.

'Oh yes, most are Chinese criminals released from jail to work unpaid as labourers here in Liberia. There are *hundreds* of them.'

'More Chinese criminals,' I grumble. 'We've had more than our fill of them, in London and Brussels.'

'Yes, I know,' Noah sensitively replies. 'They're rebuilding the road all the way from the airport to Monrovia, taking our iron ore, rubber and timber in exchange.'

'It's not a free road then.'

'Ha, no way,' there's a noticeable lack of enthusiasm in his voice. 'Sadly, the Chinese as well as the Indians are taking over most things in this country. It's the same all over Africa.'

'When we arrived at the airport,' Adele says, 'We saw a large group of Chinese arguing with an official. What was all that about?'

'Yes, I saw that myself,' Noah says. 'They'd arrived without visas or work permits.'

'What will happen to them?'

'Oh, they'll get in eventually. Some big shot Chinese guy will arrive with a few hundred dollars and fix it. That's all the immigration man wants, government pay is poor and always late. If I hadn't been there to take you through immigration, you would have had the same problem, unless you had tucked twenty dollar bills inside your passports.'

'What, even though we're supposed to be from a charity?'

'No difference.'

The car is running smoothly on the rebuilt part of the road, the improvement is immediate, without potholes or rough patches. Leaving the plantation with its well-ordered rows of rubber trees, we find ourselves driving through dense, dark green jungle with various trees, vines, head-high ferns and flowering bushes. Groups of people, mainly women and girls, some with babies strapped on their backs, balance large bundles on their heads as they walk at the side of the road. Skeletal remains of old cars and trucks, bits of fridges and other discarded rubbish seem to be scattered all over. Every mile or so are groups of small rectangular mud huts, some with thatched roofs and others corrugated zinc, intermingled with concrete-block, one-room shops where trestle tables are loaded with fruit and vegetables neatly stacked in pyramids. The selling is clearly left to the women while knots of idle men sit in the shade of nearby trees, on what appears to be old car seats.

After a few minutes, Cooper gently applies the brakes and turns left along a rough track. On the corner is a large billboard with an arrow pointing to *Cleopatra's Beach Hotel*.

'The road will be bad now,' Noah announces rather pointlessly as we're already bouncing up and down on the backseat. We pass a pickup going in the opposite direction, the cloud of dust created almost blots out the road. The verges and roadside vegetation is covered in the same reddish colour. Before long, we arrive at a high, cinderblock wall topped with razor wire and a heavy metal gate. Cooper's long blast on the horn awakes a uniformed security guard we can see through the gates, dozing under a tree. Rubbing the sleep from his eyes, he rushes to open up.

Shouting something at the guard, Noah turns again as we drive up to the entrance of a Spanish style single-storey building. 'This is your home for the next few days. You'll be safe here but don't leave the compound or wander down the beach without me or my men, I want you to be clear about this.'

It's as we'd thought. We get out of the car and hear waves breaking on the shore, and through a cluster of swaying palm trees, I can just make out the ocean and a welcome sea breeze blows away the worst of the heat. The Reception area is cool and a stern-looking man stands at the desk.

'Gemayel,' Noah says coolly, 'I'd like to introduce you to Nick Holbrook's sister, Adele Holbrook and Penny Lane, Nick's fiancée.'

Gemayel's face softens as he warmly shakes our hands. He has the swarthy features of an Arab, probably in his forties, dressed in designer casuals. 'Bachir Gemayel at your service and please call me Bachir,' he gives a small bow. 'May I give you my deepest condolences about Nick, he was a very good friend. You are most welcome here at the Cleopatra and I've put you in our very best room with two single beds and a private bathroom; you don't mind sharing, do you?' His English is good but with a distinct American accent.

We nod our acceptance and I feel momentarily excited by the thought that Nick had stayed here. It's a strange feeling as though coming across his footprints in a foreign land.

'I'll leave you now,' Noah checks his watch. 'I'll be here for dinner at seven.'

As he leaves, Bachir gives a mock bow. It's hard to tell if he's being patronising. Picking up our bags, he leads us along a corridor to our room. Hesitating awkwardly by the door, he gives a nervous cough to clear his throat. 'I have to tell you this,' he blurts out, 'As I just told you, Nick was a good, good man, but I'm very worried that you are with Colonel Tofa.'

'But why?'

'Because he's a well-known rapist and murderer.'

'What!' we exclaim loudly together.

'If Colonel Tofa is looking after you in Liberia, it's important you know this,' Bachir says. 'He's protected by friends in high places. If you don't believe me, just ask around, everyone knows.'

Chapter Twenty
February 22nd

With legs like jelly, I close and bolt the door behind Bachir. 'What the hell do we do now?' I ask through ragged breaths.

'I don't know,' she mutters huskily, her face a picture of despair. 'I think we may have to go back to England, but no, we can't, we've got to find Charles and we can only do that by staying here.'

'And we have to locate the diamond mine to find out what Nick's connection was with this Jaroslav Baros fellow,' I add. 'We were almost murdered because of that, don't forget.'

'I can't forget that, but you should go home, Penny, because of the baby.'

My anxieties about being pregnant are still there, but the disturbing news from Bachir has pushed everything else into the background. 'I'm not leaving you on your own. Anyway, I got the all clear from Doctor Brabant.'

Adele straightens wearily. 'But aren't we jumping to conclusions here? How do we know Bachir is telling the truth? It was pretty obvious from their body language that there's no love lost between them, certainly on Bachir's side.' She screws her eyes tight in concentration. 'According to Axel and Petra, Nick got on very well with Noah and relied on him to help save them in Ivory Coast. He wouldn't have trusted Noah if he believed he was a murderer and rapist. Anyway, there's only one way to find out.'

'And what's that?'

'Ask him straight out when he comes for dinner.'

'Woo, that could be a bit awkward.' I can feel the embarrassment already. 'Anyway, I might have another idea.'

'Let's hear it then.'

'You know when we arrived, there was a bar next to the dining room.'

'Yes, go on.'

'Well, I'll bet most of the people staying in the hotel will be there before dinner. Let's quickly unpack, freshen-up and go to the bar. Someone will be bound to talk to us, two attractive young women,' I manage a smile. 'And see if they know about Noah. A man of his rank and influence is bound to be well known.'

'It's certainly worth a try,' she agrees.

Whilst not matching the splendour of the Aquitane in Casablanca, our room looks more than acceptable considering where we are. The white walls and ceiling have a few suspicious stains and dirty marks but nothing too awful. The sparse, dark-brown stained furniture looks crudely homemade but a nice touch is a small vase of red hibiscus on a coffee table along with four large bottles of drinking water and two cans of insect spray. A strong smell of disinfectant meets us as we check the bathroom, making my eyes water. It obviously works as there are half a dozen dead cockroaches near the drain. Oh yuk, they're so big.

The white cotton bed sheets smell fresh and clean and the two mosquito nets appear to be fairly new. The pièce de résistance is a small wooden terrace overlooking a palm fringed lagoon and a thirty yard sand bar beyond which ocean waves break lightly on the shore. A few people are swimming in the lagoon. They mainly look white skinned or light brown, not Africans. It could be a scene from an upmarket travel brochure.

Unpacking just enough clothes and toiletries for the next twenty-four hours, Adele places her *special* briefcase inside her suitcase and tucks it in the bottom drawer of the wardrobe which is fitted with a hasp and staple. Adele fits her own combination lock.

'I'll shower first, if you don't mind,' I say. The water is only tepid but refreshing and standing under the spray, I'm glad my hair was cut short before leaving home and the red dye is rapidly disappearing. Trying to avoid stepping on dead cockroaches, Adele takes over while I get dressed in one of my new summer outfits, the long sleeves of which will hopefully ward off any mosquitoes, helped by spraying myself with insect repellent.

I was right about the bar. It is crowded with principally European and Asian men, although I spot three rather butch-looking white women wearing Red Cross T-shirts, chatting together at a table overlooking the lagoon. Outside, the dusty haze is turning to an apricot colour by the enormous sinking sun, which seems to wobble as it slowly sinks towards the horizon. In different circumstances, this would be a perfect romantic setting.

Our entrance doesn't go unnoticed because, momentarily, there's a pause in the level of conversation and it feels as though all eyes are on us. Trying to ignore them, we find a small table at the rear of the bar and order our drinks. We only just have time to get our bearings before the first would-be Romeo approaches.

'Hi there,' says a drunken, lecherous voice with a strong North American twang. 'Who have we here then?' A young man, probably in his twenties and obviously the worse for wear, stands provocatively in front of us. We ignore him, we are looking for someone who's sober.

'Do you believe in love at first sight?' he slurs. 'Or should I walk by again?' He gives a silly giggle as inebriated young men invariably do.

'Just walk away, Sonny,' Adele snaps. 'As far away as possible.'

'Ooh, pardon me,' he sneers, taking the none-too subtle hint and, staggering away, telling anyone within hearing distance that we're a pair of lesbians.

The waiter, giving the young man dark looks, smiles at us and places our drinks on the table, a lager for Adele and plain tonic water for me. Trying to look relaxed, we chat together but at the same time, keep a lookout for someone who might know something about Noah. My heart sinks as an older man sways as he threads his way through the tables in our direction - just our luck that the bar drunk should pinpoint us.

'And a very good evening, to you, ladies,' he announces theatrically with a cut-glass English accent, at the same time giving a tolerable bow. Reaching into his breast pocket, he removes a monocle which, with practiced elegance, he places over his slightly bloodshot left eye. 'I can only apologise, dear ladies, for the appalling rudeness of the adolescent degenerate you just encountered.' Peering at us through his eyepiece, he continues. 'May I be so bold as to introduce myself, Reginald Grosvenor- Smythe, OBE, but please call me Reggie, at your service. And, if my antenna is tuned correctly, I believe you are both, like myself, from the land of the good Saint George.'

I was on the point of telling the old sod to buzz off when Adele blurts out, 'Reggie, do you know Colonel Noah Tofa?'

My heart skips a beat.

'Ah, so that's it,' nodding his head and giving a knowing smile. 'I thought it was you I saw with him earlier at Reception, and now you want to know if he's pukka.'

'Something like that,' I hesitate.

'Well now,' he pulls up a chair, furrowing his brow. 'If you are asking about Colonel Noah Masaquoi Tofa, son of the late Senator Eugine Shadarak Tofa of Nimba County and his second wife, Blessing Roberts, then yes, I do know *of* him.' He stares at us through his monocle as if awaiting the next question in a pub quiz.

Wonderful, it's like hitting the jackpot in one. Adele asks, 'Can we buy you a drink, Reggie?'

'That's extremely charming of you, dear ladies, but I insist on paying for our beverages.' A nonchalant wave of his hand instantly brings the waiter and he orders refills for Adele and me and a double scotch for himself. 'And Momo, dear chap,' he calls after the departing waiter. 'Top-shelf, none of that domestic rubbish.'

Adele, having already broached the subject, comes straight to the point. 'Reggie, what do you know about Colonel Noah Tofa's involvement in murder and rape?'

Like two furry caterpillars, his dense, bushy eyebrows shoot up like a pair of roller blinds. 'Ah! you want me to dish the dirt on the Colonel, do you?' He purses his lips in thought. 'Would it be a certain Mr Bachir Gemayel who put these thoughts into your heads?' Giving us no chance to reply, he answers himself. 'Of course it was.' Our drinks arrive and he passes the whisky glass under his nose, before giving a satisfied nod and emptying the contents in one, after which he examines it through his monocle as if it's a museum exhibit.

'Let me buy you another,' Adele smiles encouragingly, beckoning Momo again.

Simulating acute embarrassment, Reggie exclaims, 'Oh, dear lady, well, if you're sure, that's extremely generous of you but, before I get round to answering your loaded question, may I be so bold as to ask who you are and why you're interested in the gentleman.'

'Yes, of course, I'm Adele Holbrook and this is Penny Lane. We're here with the Pendelle Schools Charity to prepare a report for the investment of ten million US dollars in Liberian rural schools, and Noah has agreed to help us.'

Reggie rolls his eyes dramatically. 'Holbrook, eh! Could that possibly mean you are related to one Nicholas Holbrook?'

'Yes, he was my brother, did you know him?'

'Indeed I did.' He gives a token wipe to his monocle before adjusting it back into place. 'He stayed in these very premises on several occasions. My deepest sympathies to you, Miss Holbrook, and your family. Nicholas was a fine gentleman, unlike the Bacchanalian revellers you see behind me, wallowing in shed loads of money donated by naive western tax-payers. Nicholas did a great deal for Liberia without seeking personal gain, a very rare attribute.'

'Thank you, Reggie, his death was a terrible shock to us all.'

In no time at all, Momo arrives with more drinks, obvious that Reggie gets the very best service in this bar. 'I may be putting my *size tens* in it, ladies, but are you sure about this *so-called* charity with ten million dollars. I'll wager you're not being totally up-front with old Reggie on this one.'

I try and bluff. 'I'm not sure what you're getting at.'

He shakes his head giving me a sceptical look. 'Charities' generosity provides NGOs with a way of life far beyond their meagre capabilities which, as is the way, also enriches corrupt African nations. So take your money and give it to the poor in good old Blighty.'

'Can we leave that for a moment, Reggie,' Adele quickly changes the subject. 'The second reason, far more important in personal terms, is that my other brother, Charles Temple, disappeared somewhere in Africa several months ago and Noah was approached by a local person who said that a man fitting Charles's description was being held in Guinea.'

'Aha, so the charity nonsense is just a smokescreen.'

Adele hesitates. 'Yes, but please understand, Reggie, that Noah is our only lead to finding Charles and this is in strictest confidence as we're still using the charity as cover.'

He places a gold-ringed finger against his mouth. 'Fear not, dear lady, not a single word will pass my lips. Keeping secrets in this land of subterfuge is my stock in trade.'

'Thank you, Reggie,' Adele continues. 'It's because of this that we want to know if Noah can be trusted, or are we in danger? I'm sure you know what I mean.'

'Of course. I'll tell you what I know but, like you, I must also insist on strict confidentiality, otherwise I'll rapidly become persona non grata in this land of *little liberty*.'

I'm concerned that we're taking a big risk in opening up to Reggie so quickly because we don't know if he is a man of his word. My first impression, though, is that he's an English gentleman, but what the hell is he doing here in Liberia? Anyway, as things stand, we have no other choice.

'Well now,' Reggie settles back comfortably in his chair. 'First, I'll give you some of the background - this country suffered two civil wars during which at least ten percent of the population was killed.' He nods kindly when Adele orders him another refill. 'They were ghastly, barbaric affairs, the government on the one side, while numerous, ever-changing rebel groups were on the other. Combatants on both sides relied on drugs and magic to fortify themselves, the combination of which sent many of them barking mad.' He pauses to savour the contents of the refill. 'Our gallant, bold young Lochinvar, Colonel Noah Tofa, being a senior army officer, was obliged to fight for the government of the day.'

'We have heard about Jacob Marcam's involvement,' Adele says.

'That's good,' Reggie states. 'He was one of the key figures. Now, getting back to the good Colonel, it's somewhat ironic that in the first civil war, he fought against Jacob Marcam, one of the rebel leaders, and in the second civil war, he reluctantly fought for Jacob Marcam, no longer a rebel leader but the Head of the Liberian Army. Of course, this is a simplification of an incredibly confusing situation, but I think you get the broad gist.'

'Yes, thank you, we follow you so far.'

'Murder, rape and pillage were commonplace but, as things invariably happen, a Scandinavian television crew went into the town of Buchanan, filming the aftermath of one such atrocity, inflicted this time by government forces. It was so horribly graphic that it could not be shown on television. Colonel Tofa was the officer in charge of those soldiers and, unfortunately, a Lebanese lady, Mr Bachir Gemayel's mother, was one of the victims.'

'Oh my God,' Adele gasps, 'Noah was actually in charge of an atrocity.'

'Maybe yes ... maybe no,' Reggie pauses, studying his half-empty glass. 'Personally, I take Gemayel's accusation with a pinch of salt.'

I give Adele a quick look, she nods. 'Noah seems genuine,' I say. 'We had full confidence in him until Gemayel said what he did.'

'Yes, I'm sure,' Reggie smiles, 'But you're both brand new to Africa and in dealings with Africans, I have a little more experience. Do you ever realise the advantages a dark skin gives you? Most decent people, like your good selves, hate to be thought of as racists, and meeting them for the first time, you make a point of showing interest in what they say and believing them. You wouldn't necessarily act the same way with white people.'

'So do you think Noah maybe misleading us?'

Draining the last dregs from his glass, Reggie slowly gets to his feet. 'The answer to that, dear ladies, is that I don't know. Now, if you will excuse me,' he steadies himself against the back of his chair. 'It would be prudent for me to vanish before the Colonel arrives, because if you tackle him on this matter, he'll want to know who told you.'

'Of course,' Adele says. 'We'll definitely keep you out of it.'

'Before you go, Reggie,' I venture, 'Does the word Limarni mean anything to you?'

'Is this a kind of test?'

'No. Nick wrote me a letter before he died and mentioned Limarni as being significant.'

'Is it a Limarni, an object ... or maybe a person or place?'

'We don't know. We were hoping you might. Colonel Tofa said it could be a Liberian word.'

'It doesn't send a *ping* to any of my little grey cells at the moment, I'll work on it.'

'Thank you.'

Giving a courteous bow, he adds, 'If you need help in either or both of your missions, my humble services will be at your disposal. I don't live here in Cleopatra, but I come for Tiffin most evenings. *Illegitimis non carborundum.*'

Waiting until he'd exited the room, an open-mouthed Adele exclaims. 'W-what on earth do you make of him? With his monocle and flowery language and public school voice, not to mention his OBE, what's a man like that doing in Liberia? He's like a left-over from the Raj. And what was that *"illegit"* thing he said as he left?'

I can't help but laugh. 'My Latin is a bit rusty but it's something like, *don't let the bastards grind you down.* Not quite sure why he should say that. Anyhow, what he said about Noah sounded genuine and I like Reginald Grosvenor-Smythe and think we can trust him.'

'That's exactly what I think,' Adele smiles. 'But what are we going to say when Noah arrives?'

Feeling terribly vulnerable, I feebly respond, 'I don't know.'

'Well, what is certain,' Adele states vehemently, 'Is that we have to find out if there's any truth in the accusation. We can't put ourselves at risk.'

'No,' my mind is in a spin. 'But even Reggie isn't sure, and he seems to know most of what's happening in this country. Pity he hasn't heard of Limarni.'

'Yes, it is, but Nick wouldn't have put it in the letter if it wasn't important. Anyway, with regards to Noah you can leave it to me,' she says compellingly. 'During dinner, I'll carefully broach it in a roundabout way.'

'Good luck with that,' I murmur softly, unable to think of any roundabout way of asking, *"oh, by the way, Noah, have you raped and murdered any women recently?"*

Looking at my watch, it's only quarter to seven but already dark outside. Strolling onto the dining room veranda to get a breath of fresh air, we pick up the faint, sweet smell of frangipani, somewhat spoilt by fumes from mosquito coils set on the end rail. The light breeze makes the palms clatter dryly, clicking like knitting needles, and a billion pinpricks of stars shine brightly in the deep Prussian-blue sky. In the distance, the soft thud of waves on the beach is audible above the incessant sound of cicadas. If you could blot out the problems of Liberia, this would be an amazing place.

At precisely seven-fifteen, Noah strides confidently into the dining room just as the raucous noise from the bar is subsiding. Most of the heavy drinkers have already staggered away. Noah, with a friendly smile, shakes us cordially by the hand before raising his arm authoritatively to catch the waiter's attention.

'Drinks?' he enquires, settling himself comfortably at the opposite side of the table.

'Lager for me,' Adele replies.

Feeling anxious, I try to smile but my face won't let me. 'I'll stick to tonic water.'

Without looking at the menu, he says, 'I recommend the red snapper, if you like fish.'

Being too tense to think about food, we accept his recommendation. Adele somehow manages to chat about the weather, our room and the foreign aid workers in the hotel.

'Oh yes,' he gives a deep laugh. 'They consider this to be one of the safest hotels in Liberia, there's often a waiting list except in the rainy season. Very few foreigners come then.'

Nodding, Adele comes straight to her first point. 'Noah, can we talk about my brother?'

'Of course, I plan to go to Bambara's house tomorrow to see if he's returned.'

'Can we come with you?'

He rubs his chin thoughtfully. 'I was thinking of going on my own. West Point is a bad slum but, if you're prepared to take the risk, it would prove to Bambara that there would be money in it for him, whereas if it were just me, he could think it was a trap.'

Adele quickly agrees. 'How much should we pay for positive information?'

'It's up to you, but max ten thousand dollars. Not Liberian dollars, of course, as they're almost worthless. Anyhow, we'll have to negotiate ... start at a couple of thousand.'

Adele looks relieved. 'That's fine with me.'

'Good, that's agreed.' Looking satisfied, Noah takes a sip from his glass. 'I'll pick you both up at seven in the morning to get there before it's too hot.'

'We'll be ready,' Adele confirms. 'But Noah, as you know, another reason for being here is to find out from Jaroslav Baros why Nick had three large diamonds from his mine.'

'Yes, as soon as I can, I'll check if there have been any developments.'

'Thank you and oh,' she takes a deep breath. 'There's one last thing.'

I hold my breath and look nervously at the floor.

'Were you involved in murder and rape during the civil war?'

Opening his mouth wide in shock, he gasps, 'I beg your pardon.'

Shit! I'd thought she would be more subtle than that. It's more like a bull in a china shop than her *so called* roundabout way.

Adele's voice falters. 'We've just been told that you were involved in an atrocity.'

Furiously banging his fist on the table, he yells, 'Who told you that?' He looks around as though the source of this story may be sitting in the vicinity. 'Was it Gemayel?'

'No,' I cry out, a little too quickly.

190

'It was someone at the bar,' a quick thinking Adele lies. 'We were approached by a man who'd seen us arrive with you and wanted to know, you know, if we knew about it.'

'Which man?' he angrily demands, banging his fist once more on the table.

'He's not here now,' it's my turn to lie, trying to extricate us as butterflies swirl and surge in my stomach. 'He was drunk, a young American.'

'What's his name?'

'He didn't say.'

Noah stares fixedly into his drink saying nothing for a few moments. Eventually, his voice calmer, he lifts his head. 'It's obviously better known than I'd realised.' Anxiously, we watch as he finishes his lager and calls for another. 'It was many years ago,' his tone is stern, 'I was a young officer in the government army, and the country was in chaos, law and order had completely broken down. Jacob Marcam, was our senior general.'

We stay silent. I'm nervously fidgeting in my chair.

'I hated Jacob Marcam but I'd sworn to serve the president's senior command structure. As many of my fellow officers had quit, I was given more responsibility which made life difficult. I was up-country in Ganta when I was ordered to go to Buchanan to quell a rebel uprising. I got there within three hours, but it was too late. Everyone in the village, about thirty in total, was dead.' He takes his time as if the effort of remembering is too painful. 'My men, as high as kites on drugs and alcohol, had moved on to an adjacent compound of four expat houses and were in the process of looting everything of value. It was then that my immediate superior officer, General Matu, arrived with a television crew from Norway. He was furious and to save face in front of the TV cameras, he blamed me for the massacre. Matu was very close to Jacob Marcam so I didn't stand a chance.' Making direct eye contact with us, he articulates emphatically, 'Let me assure you I had no involvement whatsoever in those murders.'

During his upsetting account, our meals arrive and in a strained silence, we concentrate on eating, although my churning stomach has taken my appetite away.

Frowning, as if uncertain of what to say next, he carefully places his cutlery on his empty plate and looks up. 'Do you still want to come with me tomorrow morning?'

'Oh yes,' Adele anxiously runs her hands through her hair. 'Of course we've got to find Charles, and the sooner the better. That's okay with you, isn't it, Penny?'

I nod in agreement.

'Good,' Noah pushes back his chair. 'Now, if you'll excuse me, I'll say goodnight, and meet you both at seven.' Without a backward glance, he walks towards the door, all signs of the earlier swagger gone.

'Wow,' I gasp. 'Did you think his explanation sounded too well rehearsed?'

'No, I didn't,' Adele says. 'Don't forget, Nick thought very highly of Noah and I'm sure he must have been aware of the accusations.'

'Okay, you're probably right.'

The arduous day has finally caught up with us and, exhausted, we head towards our room. Passing by Reception, we notice Bachir behind the desk and go over.

'Oh, Bachir, thanks for the warning about Noah,' Adele says. 'But we've decided to go with him tomorrow to try and get through our business as quickly as possible.'

Bachir says, 'Well, at least you've been warned.'

'Yes, thank you, but there's one thing, Bachir,' I say. 'We met an American man in the bar earlier and wondered if there are many Americans here?'

He looks surprised at my question. 'No, we only have the one, Blain Tucker who works for Fowler Consultants, New York.' His face suddenly lights up and he chuckles. 'Ah, I see, was he trying it on with you? He can be very annoying when he's had too much to drink, which is almost every night.'

Shaking my head, I smile, 'No, it's fine.' Continuing along the corridor to our room, I wonder if telling Noah that it was an American who'd told us about the atrocity will land the poor sod in deep shit? Anyway, it would serve him right for telling everyone that we were lesbians.

CHAPTER TWENTY-ONE
FEBRUARY 23rd

Noah, who obviously believes in punctuality, arrives at the hotel on the dot of seven and ushers us into his car, again driven by Cooper. On the way to Monrovia, we pass through two checkpoints manned by UN peacekeepers, known as UNMIL. Unlike the majority of vehicles, we are quickly waved through, thanks to Noah's official status.

'What are they looking for?' I ask.

'Guns, the country is awash with them, and UNMIL are still here partly because Liberians don't trust our own army or police. We're too corrupt, they say.'

'Oh dear,' I sigh. 'Is UNMIL successful in keeping the peace?'

Noah exhales loudly. 'I guess so,' he acknowledges shaking his head. 'It's certainly better than it was when the Nigerian peacekeepers were here. They stole everything they could to ship back to Nigeria but ...'

'And the *but* is?' Adele asks.

'The but is that UNMIL are, how can I delicately put it, very active in buying sex, often leaving road blocks unmanned after dark.'

'Ha,' Adele gives a snort. 'Well some women obviously benefit then.'

Noah doesn't respond to her flippant remark.

As we approach Monrovia, huts and mud-brick shops appear along both sides of the road with hand-painted signs advertising their produce alongside garish posters for washing powder, malaria medicines and cigarettes. The traffic thickens, and clusters of buildings merge into continuous outskirts.

'We're getting close now,' Noah says. 'Keep your doors locked and windows up. Even in my car, you can't be too careful.'

Driving through the suburb of Sinkor, there is a sharp contrast between the large gleaming houses behind razor-wire topped walls and the shabby shacks in front of them. People walking at the roadside are wonderfully erect, but with splayed feet. Some women look smart with their elaborately coiled and braided hair and bright, coloured tie-dyed wrappers.

Noah points through the window. 'You see all the electricity poles? Plenty of poles but no electricity.'

'Is that because of the civil war?'

'Yes. The rich locals and NGOs in four bedroom villas and swimming pools manage okay, having their own generators, the rest have to use kerosene lamps and candles.' From the tone of his voice, I feel he's condemning the rich and yet surely, he must be one himself. He is still a bit of a conundrum.

It's obvious when we reach the city centre with its clamour of an overwhelming mass of people and the continuous din of car horns. Buses and trucks spew out clouds of black exhaust fumes. Store fronts are brightly painted, and hawkers gather to ply their wares. It seems the only decent vehicles are the ones sporting the markings of aid agencies, foreign consultants and charities. From the city centre, we drive down a hill towards a river.

'On that side is the Mesurado River,' Noah points over to the right. 'Those two bridges link the city with Bushrod Island and the road to Sierra Leone. On the left is where we're going, West Point slum, which is on a peninsula where the Mesurado meets the Atlantic.'

Cooper stops the car and Moses and Jerbo, both in combat uniforms, are waiting.

'We walk from here,' Noah says. 'Stay close to me and my men.'

I've stepped into another world the like of which I've never seen before. The ground seems to have been swallowed up by ramshackled, dilapidated huts, and the stench of rotting waste is so overpowering that short of wearing a gasmask, there is absolutely nothing I can do about it. I try not to retch.

Adele, made of sterner stuff, wrinkles her nose and shouts, 'It's bloody crowded, how many people live here?'

'It's anyone's guess,' Noah shrugs. 'Between seventy-five and one hundred thousand.'

'That's the size of a town,' I gasp, putting a handkerchief in front of my nose and mouth.

'I know that,' Noah responds curtly. He leads us further into the slum along a narrow, twisting path running with fly-covered sludge. Chickens, half their feathers missing, scratch in the dust. Men, balancing trays on their heads selling oranges, unshelled peanuts and dubious looking plastic bottles of water, weave their way through the masses. Gaunt looking women with protruding collar bones, their breasts hang without shape, the young children they carry are so malnourished I find it hard to look at them. In front of us, a woman with only one leg is walking gamely with crude crutches, much too short, and as she struggles along, her backside sticks out swaying alarmingly from side to side. We squeeze past, and after a further fifty yards, Noah comes to a halt.

'Wait here with Moses and Jerbo,' he orders. Throngs of noisy but cheerful children covered in snot and in grimy rags swarm around us wanting to touch our skin and feel our hair. Moses sends them packing. The braver ones extend their pale palms to us shouting 'Missie, gimme dash'.

Moses points his rifle, making them scatter, save for one young man, filthier than the others, holding a dirty plastic bag out to us. He opens his mouth, grinning, displaying stumps of teeth, mottled and black. Inside the bag is some rotting fruit, insect-covered fish heads and an open packet of powder. Waves of nausea roll over me.

''E say, Missie,' Moses translates, ''E eat good today. 'E crazy man.'

Feeling helpless, I wish now that I'd listened to Noah and stayed at the hotel.

Adele, who took Noah's earlier advice by hiding her money belt beneath her top, (supposedly, carrying US dollars, will resolve any trouble), turns her back on our two guards and surreptitiously takes out a few dollar bills, swiftly handing them to the nearest outstretched hands. Instantly, we realise it's a mistake. A mob of people materialise as if by magic, pushing, shoving and even climbing over each other to get to the money.

'Oh shit,' I yell, scared out of my wits. If it wasn't for Moses and Jerbo threatening to shoot them, I think we'd have been trampled to death in the madness but, thank God, hearing the uproar, Noah rushes from around a corner and immediately takes charge pointing his gun in the air and firing a couple of shots. The frightened crowd melts away as quickly as it arrived.

'What are you doing?' he rages, his dark eyes thunderous. 'For goodness sake, think before doing anything as foolish as that.' He looks heavenward in despair. 'You've made yourselves targets for every policeman in town when they find out you carry cash with you.'

We apologise. Taking a deep breath to stop my trembling, I somehow manage to pluck up the courage to ask, 'Why are these people hungry? We've seen dozens of charity vehicles in Monrovia and some expats in our hotel are from charities. I thought that was why they're here, to provide food for the poor.'

Still angry, he snaps, 'I'll explain later, but before you create any more trouble, I've found Bambara which is why we are here, not to cause riots.'

He guides us into a tiny dark room where the stink of human waste and sweat pervades everywhere. As if that isn't enough, the humidity is unbearable, lathering me in sweat. Adjusting to the dimness, I make out the form of a man lying on an old mattress.

'This is Bambara,' Noah announces. 'He's sick.'

A woman lifts Bambara into a sitting position to lean against the wall and a beam of light from the open doorway shines on him. The woman waves a tattered fly whisk to keep hovering insects away from his face. He has deep-set feverish eyes, sunken cheeks, and a thin hunched body, almost everything about him is recessed, but even so, I can detect a cunning look on his face. 'You got my big money?' he croaks.

Turning to Adele, Noah says, 'You tell him, speak slowly and he'll understand.'

Ignoring the filth and smell, Adele kneels next to Bambara, gently places both her hands on his shoulder and looks directly into his eyes. 'I promise you, Bambara, that if you take us to my brother, Charles Temple, I'll give you the money, but first, I want to know that he's alive. Did you see him?'

'He alive, Missie,' Bambara's voice is weak, but determined. 'I talk him, 'E say he Char Tempter fro' London an' 'e say, I go British Embassy for reward.'

Still kneeling, Adele looks up at Noah. 'How do we know if it's true?'

'Look, the names match. Charles and Char, Temple and Tempter. They are the same to him,' Noah sounds convinced. 'Before you came in, he told me that he spoke with the white man four weeks ago. He's being held near a mining town in Guinea, fifty miles over the border. As you can see, Bambara is too sick to go himself but he'll arrange for his brother to take us. Bambara knows we'll only hand over the money once Charles is found.'

Reassured to some extent, Adele stands and asks Noah, 'What's wrong with Bambara?'

'He says it's malaria, but it looks worse to me, maybe cholera. There's a lot like him, too sick to clean his hut but not sick enough to stay off his wife,' he growls. 'She's pregnant again. Anyway, you go with Moses and Jerbo and wait in the car. I'll be with you shortly.'

It's only a couple of minutes before Noah returns. 'Okay, I've also found out that Bambara's brother is in Yekepa near the Guinea border and he knows of an airstrip close to the mining town.'

'That's great,' I say. 'When can we go?'

Noah shakes his head. 'We'll need a plane and that'll take at least four or five days to arrange. I'll have to call in a few favours from General M'boyo.'

'Please do it as quickly as you can,' Adele says anxiously. 'Will money speed things up?'

'No, not yet, you'll have to be patient,' he murmurs, deep in thought. 'But before we can do anything else, you'll have to report to the Education Ministry. Remember, you're supposed to be here for charity education work. We have to do things by the book.'

'Of course, when can we do that?'

'We do it now.' He gives Cooper his instructions.

After seeing Bambara, any misgivings I had about Noah are fading, he's clearly doing his very best for us.

Cooper drives us into the centre of Monrovia and sets us down in front of a pock-marked door in the shell-damaged walls of the Ministry of Education. Every seat in the dingy waiting room is taken by a mixture of black, Asian and white people.

'Follow me,' Noah commands, marching directly through the waiting room, brushing aside the efforts of a secretary to stop us and enters a door marked *private*. He beckons us to follow.

'Good morning, Abel,' he says forcibly. 'This is Miss Holbrook and Miss Lane, the ladies I told you about.' Noah towers over the man seated at a desk which looks completely shambolic covered in files and papers, some of which have turned yellow with age. 'Sign and stamp these forms, Abel, and we'll be on our way.'

'I er, I can't, Colonel.' Looking intimidated, he almost chokes on his cigarette. 'Computer down, come back this afternoon, Colonel, please.'

Ignoring him, Noah makes a space by roughly pushing files away, some falling on the heavily stained carpet, and slaps two forms down in front of him. 'I don't care about your computers,' he snaps. 'Sign and stamp them now.'

'But where the ten million dollars from the charity?' Abel timidly asks.

Obviously expecting the question, Noah says, 'All in good time, Abel, the project has to be identified first, that's all you need to know.' Noah's authority continues to impress as the poor man does exactly as he's told. Picking up the completed forms, we leave the Ministry and Noah tells Cooper to take us back to the hotel via the central market and the Confucius Centre.

'Confucius Centre!' I exclaim.

'Yes,' he snorts contemptuously. 'It's a gift from the Chinese to bolster relations between our two nations. The Chinese are here in a big way.'

'Are you happy with that?'

He shakes his head, uncertain if he should say more, and checks there are no 'ears' close by. 'No, actually I'm not. Over the past few years, China has secretly bought-up most of the mineral wealth on the African continent, including Liberia, for nothing more than a pittance.'

'But that doesn't seem possible,' I say, 'I thought they were benefitting the country.'

'Ha. The only people who benefit are the African leaders – suitcases full of cash and overseas numbered bank accounts. And once the Chinese have them in their pockets, they get away with murder. Reduce workers wages, living conditions, health and safety and any previous human rights are gone. The money China invests they get back ten-fold, and it gives them the freedom to plunder the continent of everything that takes their fancy. There is an ivory ban all over the world except in China. Last year they had 22,000 elephants killed, paying $2,000 per tusk, the horns of 1,300 Rhinos for Chinese medicine ... and that's just for starters. You want to hear any more?'

'That's absolutely sickening, but not a total surprise.' I say. 'I know both Princes William and Harry have tried to do something about saving the elephants.'

'But the Chinese just smile and nod,' Noah butts in. 'And end up doing nothing.'

We continue to head into the market which is unlike others we'd seen along the roadsides, here they are selling mainly food. Although it is only ten o'clock, the heat is oppressive and the air smells of rotten fish and sweaty bodies. The babble of noise is incredible and everywhere, shoppers are crammed together, chaotically struggling in various directions. Amongst them are a few Chinese women. It's hard to believe that it's only three weeks since we were in the quiet, rather sedate Ringwood market, the contrast couldn't be more striking if we were on a different planet.

'Now Penny, look over there,' Noah points to a stall selling rice, tomatoes, greens, bananas and cans of USAID cooking oil. Behind the stallholder are sacks of rice stamped with the logos of UNICEF, the European Union and other aid agencies. 'You asked me where all the food aid went, well here it is.'

'But they're selling it. I thought donated food was free.'

He laughs cynically. 'You are correct but back in the real world, the food is now in the local economy and consumed by the rich who can afford to pay for it, not those it is intended for like the desperate children you saw begging in West Point.'

'But that's terrible,' I exclaim. 'Do the charities know this is happening?'

'Of course they know,' he says wearily. 'They can see just as well as you. But when they try to stop it, they come up against very powerful people who will, if provoked, arrange to have them deported on the grounds of insulting the nation. It happens.'

'Oh my God,' Adele shakes her head.

Noah continues. 'The charity workers happily stay at the Cleopatra having a holiday, sun bathing, swimming, wining and dining, all at someone else's expense, the British taxpayers, for example. And none of this gets mentioned in the international media which also knows full well what's going on. Instead, there are glowing reports sent back to the donors that all the food is being delivered to the needy.'

I sigh in disbelief, wondering if Noah could have his own agenda for smearing NGO's and charities, but there again, why would he.

'Ah, there's something else you should see,' Noah points to a stall at the end of the line. 'That's the closest thing to a pharmacy for most Liberians. Donated medicines marked *not for sale* are, in fact, being sold by people who have little or no idea what the drugs are, never mind what they're used for, to those who can't understand the directions printed on the packets.'

'That is so depressing,' I sigh heavily. 'Is it the same in other African countries?

'Yes, it is, and this is yet another scandal that most African countries face when trying to deliver donated food and medicines to the poverty stricken. The hospitals and clinics are desperately short of drugs,' he gives a derisive shrug. 'You'll be relieved to know that the Honourable Titus Sentali, the Minister of Health, travels around the country in a new chauffeur driven Mercedes Benz limousine, while his poor wife only has a Toyota Lexus.'

As we arrive back at the Cleopatra, Bachir scurries out of his office. 'Everything alright?' he looks at us inquisitively.

'Yes thank you, Bachir.' I'd almost forgotten our concerns about Noah.

'By the way,' he furrows his brow. 'You know that young American man, Blain Tucker, you asked me about yesterday?'

'Yes.'

'Well, he's gone ... deported. Two soldiers came shortly after you left this morning and took him straight to the airport. Would this have anything to do with *your* Colonel?'

'Er, I've no idea,' I stammer, trying not to show alarm.

Back in our room, we collapse on our beds. 'Wow, what about that?'

'It must have been Noah,' I say. 'He was fuming when he heard that somebody told us about the massacre. How could we know Tucker was the only American staying here?'

'Well, he's not here now but it's another sign that Noah has real power in this country. Anyway,' she gives a wry grin. 'It serves the silly Tucker right.'

'And what about Bambara? Do you think he was telling the truth about Charles?'

'Oh, I do hope so,' Adele sighs. 'But it does seem too good to be true.'

Kicking off my shoes relieves my aching feet. 'You know something,' I gently massage my swollen ankles. 'If we have

201

to wait a few days for Noah to arrange a plane, we should ask him to take us to Jaroslav Baros and his diamond mine.'

'I agree,' Adele lifts her bare feet up onto her bed and curls her legs beneath her. 'We should be able to go there without giving the location away. I'm confident that we left Brussels without being followed. By the way, I meant to ask you earlier, how are you feeling today coping with all this heat and humidity? Being pregnant must make it hard for you.'

'No, not really.' I get ready for a shower. 'Physically, I feel well, in fact better than I have for weeks, but emotionally, I'm all over the bloody place, you know, the slum.' I open the bathroom door and use my toe to push a couple of dead cockroaches out of the way. Standing under the shower, I suddenly find myself weeping, sobbing as my tears mingle with the shower water. What the hell's wrong with me? I stay under the cooling water for a couple of minutes before wrapping myself in a large towel and go back to the bedroom.

'Were you crying?' Adele looks concerned. 'Your eyes are red.'

I nod. 'I was back in the slum again, seeing all those children, begging, filthy rags and I couldn't do anything to help.'

Adele pads across the floorboards and puts her arm around my shoulders. 'I know, it was terrible and handing out money as I did almost caused a riot. Honestly, I don't think there's anything we can do. Let's take it easy this afternoon and later on, we'll go and have some drinks, hopefully, Reggie will be there.'

The hotel bar is crowded again. Apart from the three butch females sitting at the same table as last night, there are several other young white women mingling with the men. It reminds me of the International Singles Bar back in Surbiton. There's clearly money to be made selling alcohol to NGOs even in one the poorest countries in the world. We sit at a table near the veranda but before we can attract the attention of a waiter, Reggie, wearing colour-blind clothes, is making his way through the melee towards us.

'Greetings, dear ladies,' he carefully adjusts his monocle and gives a theatrical bow. 'I was hoping I'd have the pleasure of your company this evening. May I join you?'

'Oh, please do, Reggie.'

With Momo, our friendly waiter hovering behind, Reggie orders our drinks along with his own double scotch. 'Now tell me, dear ladies, how was your day with the good Colonel and, importantly, did you tackle the blackguard over the alleged atrocity?'

'Yes, we did,' Adele answers. 'We're fairly sure that his involvement was not as bad as rumoured. He said he arrived at the dreadful scene after the massacre. However, he was bloody furious that we knew about it and demanded to know who'd told us.'

'Oh dear.' Reggie empties his glass and mouth in almost the same movement.

'So we hinted it was a young American, remember, the one who'd insulted us, not knowing, of course that he was the only American in the hotel. He was deported this morning.'

Reggie's furry eyebrows shoot up and he gives a tut tutting noise with his tongue. '*Dei Gratia.* Thank you for enlightening me,' he gives a dry laugh. 'These young colonials need to learn better manners, don't you think?'

Smiling, we tell Reggie about seeing Bambara, going to the ministry, and visiting the market. 'Can you help us, Reggie? Is Noah right that free donated food and medicines are, in fact, being sold to the wealthy?'

Lost in silent contemplation for a moment, he absent-mindedly plays with his monocle. 'Mmm, sad to say, dear ladies, that it happens. It's a complete nonsense to keep pouring money into a scheme that doesn't work, but people want to help, it's their Christian duty.'

'Is there anything that can be done about it?'

'Very little, it's enough to make the angels weep,' he orders more drinks from Momo. 'The donors, God bless them, have tried many times, but throughout Africa it's the inner circle of mega-rich ministers and bureaucrats who decide. If you don't like it, then take your aid and you know where to shove it. They know perfectly well that another donor will come along in their wake offering more or less the same again.'

'What a mess,' Adele sighs. 'Reggie, you seem very well informed which leads on to a cheeky question, if you don't mind.'

'Fire away.'

'What are you doing here?'

He laughs and readjusts his monocle. 'I run an international consultancy firm. With all the aid and foreign money the country's receiving, many overseas companies get contracts here for the first time. They need help to set up offices, meet the right people and, most important of all, which palms to grease, and that's where I step in, for a modest fee, of course. It's a bit of a simplification but you know what I mean.'

'So you actually live here.'

'In Monrovia, for around eight or nine months of the year, but I flee to Europe for the most unpleasant part of the rainy season.'

'Can I be cheeky again and ask if you're married?'

'If you're proposing to me, young lady,' his animated eyebrows perform a little dance. 'And, indeed, why wouldn't you? But, I have to inform you that I have a wonderful wife, and therefore you're twenty-six years too late.'

'You've dashed my hopes, Reggie,' Adele feigns a grief-stricken sigh. 'But I'll learn to live with my disappointment.'

'Ah,' he smiles, '*La Coeur fauché*. It's good to see you have a sense of humour - like balm to one's soul. But you'll need it in gargantuan quantities if you're to stay *of sound mind* whilst you're here.'

Pondering that last thought, there's a silence, each waiting for the next response. Looking over the rim of my glass, I venture, 'Reggie, there is another question we'd like to ask.'

'Aha, I thought that might be the case, so Momo will have to recharge our glasses.'

Although Adele and I have only recently met Reggie, we'd decided earlier that we could confide in him, feeling we needed another ally besides Noah. Reggie seemed to be ideal. 'Before Adele and I left Europe,' I pause while Momo places our fresh drinks on the table, 'We spent a few days with Mr and Mrs Van Damme in Brussels, Axel and Petra.'

'Of course, the couple Nicholas rescued from insurgents in the fever-ridden swamps of the Ivory Coast. How are they?'

'Much better. Axel had to have three operations on the injury but is now well on the road to recovery. Petra is well but still a bit traumatised.'

'I'm not surprised, but I'm pleased to hear they're on the mend. At Nicholas's request, you may have heard, I was able to furnish them with the necessary documents so that they could legally leave Liberia, they were smuggled in without visas which could have been serious.'

'Oh, it was you who did that!' Adele declares.

'Yes, and I also did it for that scoundrel who was with them.'

Giving me a cautious glance, Adele says, 'Would that be Professor Jaroslav Baros by any chance?'

'Ha!' Reggie exclaims loudly. 'So that's the question you wanted to ask. You want to meet the mad professor with the make-believe iron ore mine, or is there something else?' Before either of us can reply, he continues, 'A word of advice, dear ladies, I've grown fond of you both over the past few days and you must be extremely careful. That bounder, Baros, is not to be trusted.'

'Why's that?'

'He's involved himself with rebel forces based near the border with Sierra Leone, the ones the UN peacekeepers are supposed to be guarding us against.'

'Oh dear, are there a lot of them - are they a threat to the Government?'

'It's hard to say how many, but yes, they're certainly a threat. Many of them were Jacob Marcam's men.'

'So what was Nick's connection with Baros?'

'That's a very good question, my dear, but I don't know the answer. Maybe the good Colonel does, he was very close to Nicholas.'

'Well, we'd like to meet Baros,' I say. 'Before Nick was murdered, I ... '

'Murdered!' Reggie bellows, cutting me off in mid-sentence. 'What on earth do you mean, murdered?'

'The car accident was what HESEC and the police wanted people to believe, but it was a cover-up. I was with him when he was killed by Chinese thugs.'

'Great Gods, that's absolutely appalling.' Reggie proclaims loudly. 'Were the Chinese fiends ever caught?'

My voice falters slightly. 'It's a long story but yes, we caught them and, how should I put it? They were eliminated. But there are still more out there and we're not sure who *they* are.'

Reggie sits open-mouthed whilst I give him a potted version of all the events in London and Brussels, that both of us are on the run and how, with Noah's help, we were able to leave Europe using false identities.

'Great Gods of Villainy,' Reggie thunders, vigorously polishing his monocle. 'You've been through hell, you poor gals but, if I may add, magnificently so. Nicholas would have been proud of you both.' Downing his whisky, he gestures again to Momo for refills. 'But what are these murderous, evil savages after?'

'We aren't certain,' I hesitate. 'Nick left me a letter saying he was in danger and thought someone in HESEC was involved. This turned out to be true. He also knew of a Chinese connection. The key to all this; the reason he was murdered and why we've been attacked and chased all over the place, is that Nick gave me some secret information which the villains were desperate to get and were prepared to kill for. We're deducing here, that it's something to do with Jaroslav Baros and this mysterious Limarni.'

'But nobody would kill for an iron ore mine that has no infrastructure to transport the ore to a port. Anyhow, there's a world surplus of the damned stuff.'

Exchanging glances, Adel and I had planned to hold back on telling Reggie about the diamonds as well as Axel's theory, but we've gone too far now and, fingers crossed, we can trust him. 'We think the mine is a cover for a new, very large diamond mine near the border with Sierra Leone. The villains somehow discovered that Nick knew its location, but he refused to divulge the whereabouts, that's why he was killed. As you know, Nick visited most countries in West Africa so the mine could be in any of them.'

'I see,' Reggie moistens his lips. 'Does Colonel Tofa know about this?'

I nod.

'Anyone else?'

'No. Except for the Van Damme's.'

'In that case,' he adopts a serious expression. 'We must be very careful what we say and keep our voices down. These walls have too many ears.'

I don't ask quite what he means, but take his advice anyway. I'm now confident it's good that Reggie knows that Noah is also in the frame, and later, we'll tell Noah that we've told Reggie.

'Momo, dear chap,' Reggie calls. 'Be a good fellow and bring us the same again, or maybe something a little stronger for the ladies.'

'Thank you, Reggie,' Adele smiles, 'I'll have a Scotch myself, but poor old Penny is off the hard stuff.'

'A religious thing is it?' he cautiously enquires.

'No, I'm pregnant, I'm carrying Nick's baby.'

'What!' Reggie exclaims, jumping to his feet. 'A chap can't take too many shocks in one night but, by all the Sages of the North, this is wonderful news. Heartiest congratulations, my dear.' He reaches out, rather clumsily, to embrace and plant a whisky-fuelled kiss on my cheek.

Chapter Twenty-Two
February 24th

In the dim light, I look over at Adele 's bed where she's sleeping soundly, lucky cow. I almost faint as I straighten up. Taking a deep breath, I stand there shaking before reaching out for support and slowly make my way to the window. I lift the corner of the curtain. Outside, it looks so calm and peaceful with the silver moon seeming to whiten everything. Trying not to waken Adele, I creep into the bathroom and wash the sweat from my face and body, ignoring a large cockroach which has set up home there, and gently pull a brush through my hair. Feeling steadier, I go back to bed and close my eyes.

'Wake up.' I must have dozed off. Adele is standing at the end of my bed, holding out a mug of tea. 'You've been dead to the world,' she remarks as I blink at the early morning light shining through the palm trees outside the window.

'Oh, thanks.'

'Take your time,' she says. 'When you're ready, we'll go for breakfast. Hopefully Noah will call soon with news of the plane.'

My restless night has not affected my appetite and we each eat a substantial breakfast of two small boiled eggs and toast, followed by another boiled egg and numerous cups of tea. There are a sprinkling of young people in the dining room, some of them looking the worse for wear after another night of booze and, I wouldn't be at all surprised, debauchery; what a life. Girlish squeals can be heard from outside, where those *hard-working NGOs* who are not hung over, are playing beach football, bikini clad girls versus boys in preposterously long shorts, but it gradually turns into rugby as the boys roll the girls in the sand before they all laugh and rush to rinse off in the lagoon. Oh! to be young and carefree and not carry the burdens of the world on your shoulders.

It's almost noon when our phone rings – it's Noah. 'Bad news I'm afraid, there's no plane available. I had to get authorisation from the President's office to hire one. Immediate approval was given but the first plane available is coming from Ghana and won't be here for five days.'

'Damn,' Adele curses, placing her hand over the mouthpiece while she relays the message. 'Is there another way of getting there, by road?'

'Impossible,' he replies. 'We have to wait.'

She closes her eyes deep in thought. 'Noah, what about Baros and the diamond mine? Should we try and go there instead and then we'll be back for when the plane arrives.'

'That's what I was thinking,' he replies. 'I'll contact my friend at the Ministry to make sure Baros is still at the mine and if so, we could go early tomorrow morning.'

'We'll be ready and thanks for all your help. Can we get there and back in one day?'

'We'll try but pack for a night away, it could take two days depending on the road conditions. We have to travel in daylight, it's too dangerous at night.'

Adele hangs up wiping her brow. 'That's all we can do then. I hope it's cooler there, I'm finding the heat and humidity hard to take.'

'I quite like the climate,' I smile. 'It's a pity we can't go now to find Charles but at least it gives us a chance to find Baros and his mine. We should keep a look out for Reggie to see what he thinks.'

Just as the light starts to fade, Reggie, dressed in a smart tropical suit and wearing a Panama hat, appears with Momo in tow, and heads straight for our table.

'Good late afternoon, dear ladies,' he elegantly tips his hat in our direction. 'I feel like a tailor's dummy dressed like this but the Japanese aid group I've just been with appreciate the panache and have given me a nice juicy contract. Momo, dear chap, drinks all round.'

'Congratulations, Reggie, you look wonderful.'

'And what are my two favourite British ladies plotting now?'

We tell him.

'What! that scuttlebut Baros,' he yells, the alarm in his voice is palpable. 'You're going with the Colonel to his mine?'

'Yes, we're going first thing in the morning.'

He purses his lips. 'Much too dangerous, it's the rebel stronghold. The peacekeepers are not here on a *kiss-me-quick* holiday you know, any attack on the government could well come from there.'

'What attack on the government?' Adele's startled voice exclaims. 'Are you talking about a coup?'

Raising his hirsute eyebrows, he places a finger in front of his lips. 'Don't let anyone hear you say the *coup* word. If you follow international news, you will know that military coups are numerous in Africa.'

'But that would take a big army, wouldn't it?' I question.

'No, not at all,' his monocle glinting in the late afternoon light. 'Just a handful of well-trained mercenaries. The blueprint for an African coup was set out in a novel by Fredrick Forsythe called *The Dogs of War*. If you haven't read it, I suggest you do.'

'But that was years ago, wasn't it?'

He shakes his head vigorously. 'You must remember the attempted coup in the Equatorial Guinea in 2004, allegedly funded by that numbskull, Mark Thatcher. It would have succeeded if the mercenary chappies hadn't been so incredibly stupid as to refuel their plane in, of all places, Zimbabwe. No, dear ladies, mounting a coup, especially in darkest West Africa, can happen at any time, and that's why I'm surprised Colonel Tofa would think of taking you there. The latest news is that Jacob Marcam has lost his appeal against war crimes so his supporters amongst the rebels know he won't be returning.'

'I think that's one reason why Colonel Tofa isn't worried, but is bringing two armed guards with him,' Adele tries to reassure Reggie. 'Surely he knows the risks.'

'He should,' Reggie stares through the bottom of his empty glass. 'But please be very careful, dear ladies, especially you, Miss Lane, in your er ... you know.'

'We have to go, Reggie.' I reach over putting my hand over his. 'We appreciate your concern but it's all to do with the note Nick left me, it's very important.'

CHAPTER TWENTY-THREE
FEBRUARY 25th

The outskirts of Monrovia are still in darkness but I can make out faint lights from paraffin lamps in the shacks whilst the large, opulent houses are flooded with bright security lights. The more eager stall-holders are already opening their businesses as arthritic old taxis, mini-buses and trucks, many with broken headlights, ply their trade. I close my eyes to the early morning beggars, but what can I do? Leaving the town centre, we glide down a steep hill onto one of the two bridges over the Mesurado River.

Noah, sitting in the front next to Cooper, says. 'This is Bushrod Island on the Freetown road.' Adele and I are in the two middle seats whilst Moses and Jerbo, with AK47s, are seated at the back, facing the rear. All four of them are dressed from head to foot in green jungle camouflage. I find having an armed escort very disconcerting.

Another roadblock. Noah hands a TAD travel authorisation document to an Asian UN peacekeeper who checks it carefully, shines his torch on our faces, salutes, then waves us through. Heading in an easterly direction, the first signs of dawn appear on the horizon, a pale orangey-pink tinge gradually expanding to light up the sky.

'This side of Monrovia had more fighting during the civil war,' Noah says. 'The roadblocks will be tighter the closer we get to Baros's mine.'

'Is it because we're heading in the direction of Sierra Leone?' I ask. 'And what about rebel soldiers, are they round there.'

'Ha, you are clued up,' he gives a short laugh, 'I think you've been talking to Reggie.'

'Yes, last night. He also told us Jacob Marcam has lost his appeal.'

'That was always going to happen, once the CIA got involved, the verdict was bound to go against him.'

'The CIA, out here?'

'They're everywhere, believe me. I'll tell you more about them and Marcam later but what's certain is the rebels will be weakened knowing Marcam won't return.'

After about four miles, we cross a road and rail bridge over the St Paul River after which the road gets rougher with very few buildings of any kind. Driving slowly for another hour, sometimes at crawling pace due to massive potholes, we see wrecked cars and trucks littering the sides, like dead animals. Every so often, columns of women walk in Indian file along the edge, unwavering and steady, with bundles of produce balanced on their heads,

Cooper stops the vehicle to stretch our legs at a market clearing where a side road on the right has a large sign pointing to the The National Iron Ore Mine, twelve miles away.

By now, the sun is fierce, it's humid, and the land seems to glisten and drip with steam. On the ground, a dog lies shaking with a fever. Three zinc-roofed shacks, selling a variety of fly-covered fruit and pastries are patronised by Moses and Jerbo. We stick to bottled soft drinks. Amongst the handful of customers, I'm shocked to see a Chinese man talking to Moses.

'Noah,' I point at the man. 'Does this mine belong to the Chinese?'

He shakes his head. 'No, it's owned by an Indian consortium.' He calls Moses over and asks what they were talking about.

'The China man, he ask if two Missie are English, so I say no, they Canada.'

Before setting off again, Adele and I need the toilet but the smell from the designated hut several yards away is so revolting that we decide nearby bushes are preferable. Modesty is something we have to forego if we're going to get anywhere with our mission.

After another half an hour of driving, Moses calls to Noah that we're being followed, but the dust thrown up by our vehicle makes it difficult to see who it is.

'Keep your eye on it,' Noah says.

After about twenty minutes, we arrive at the next road block and Noah has a quick word with the officer in charge while slipping him a small parcel. When the following vehicle arrives, the officer orders the two occupants out, one being the same Chinese man. He searches the inside of their vehicle and quickly produces a packet containing white powder.

'Cocaine!' the officer shouts. The two surprised men argue that they are innocent, but are arrested, handcuffed, and marched away. A smiling Noah shakes hands with the officer.

'It will be weeks before they're released,' he laughs. 'It was only flour.'

Over the next few miles, we are delayed at two more road blocks before Noah instructs Cooper to leave the road and follow what proves to be a badly rutted, narrow track. We bounce up and down for another half hour before a small, newly-painted sign next to an empty, three-sided shelter announces: "Baros Minerals Incorporated. Stop and Report".

'Keep going,' Noah orders Cooper, 'There's nobody there.'

We drive on. Towering trees on both sides lean over the track so that above is only a strip of blue sky. It seems peaceful when, SHIT, my heart jumps as the side window next to Adele shatters followed immediately by the sound of two gunshots.

'Oh, fucking hell,' Adele screams.

'Hit the floor,' Noah shouts.

Although paralyzed with fear, I somehow manage to push Adele down and lie on top of her. Struggling for breath, I feel a chill spreading through my limbs. My shaking hands are covered in blood; is it my mine or hers? I don't feel pain but maybe you don't at first.

'Are you hurt?' Noah's peeks over the front seat, his voice is tense, but controlled.

'I, er,' is as far as I get before a wave of nausea hits me.

'I've been shot in my fucking shoulder,' Adele curses.

'How bad?'

'Bad enough.'

'Okay, I'm getting out. Keep down and Penny, patch her wound. Cooper, stay with them.' He, Moses and Jerbo carefully sidle out of the vehicle.

For a moment, all goes quiet except for my own ragged breathing. 'Are you alright?' I ask Adele, immediately realizing it's a silly question.

'Apart from the fucking pain in my arm,' Adele continues to swear. 'And your knobbly knees poking into my ribs, yes, I feel fucking great. Now, for fuck's sake, get off me, you're like the weight of a pregnant elephant.'

Still queasy, I carefully shuffle backwards keeping my head down and helping her off the floor. The wound is high on her left arm, just below the shoulder. Half lying on the seat, she tries to see her injury. 'Fucking hell,' she snarls, 'Penny, find something to wrap round it.' She's like a foul-mouthed sergeant major giving orders to an underling.

Fumbling with my bag's zip, the first thing that comes to hand is my cotton t-shirt.

'Hurry before I fucking bleed to death.' Her continuous cursing reassures me that she's not in any immediate danger of dying. Boosted by a surge of adrenalin, I manage to tear the shirt into strips and bind a piece around her wound. She gives a sharp intake of breath but grits her teeth in silence. Blood seeps through the material. Wrapping two more strips over the first and tying two loose ends together, the make-shift bandages are free of blood. That's a good sign.

Outside, voices are shouting but too faint to hear what's being said.

'I'm going to sit up,' Adele announces, warily placing her right hand over her bound arm. 'It's not too bad.' She moves it up and down a couple of times to prove the point.

A volley of shots nearby makes us jump.

'Give me your gun, Cooper,' Adele snaps.

'Wait, Adele, look!' Noah and his men are coming back. Walking ahead of them are three men in dark blue uniforms, their hands held high in the air.

'There were four of them,' Noah announces looking very worried. 'We injured one and he's tied up by the compound gate. Are you alright, Adele?'

'Yes, but it'll need attention soon.'

He nods. 'We have an even bigger problem now. These are rebel soldiers, staunch opponents of the government, and it won't be long before more arrive.'

'So, what do we do?'

He shakes his head. 'I'm not sure. We could try and go back but they've probably blocked our way out.'

The decision on our next move is taken out of our hands as a convoy of half a dozen 4 x 4s, trailing huge clouds of dust in their wake, hurtle straight for us, skidding to a halt at the last minute. The dense dust has its own momentum and for a few seconds everything is blotted out. Gradually, as it clears, a couple of dozen heavily armed soldiers emerge wearing the same dark blue uniforms. Aggressively, they point their guns at us and, hopelessly outnumbered, Noah and his men put their weapons on the ground. As if choreographed, the soldiers part slightly to allow a white man to walk to the front. He's stocky, aggressive-looking with broad, muscular shoulders, long hairy arms dangling at his side, standing feet apart. Wearing a short sleeved shirt and khaki trousers, his hat white bloomed with sweat. Menacingly looking at us and bellows. 'Well, look who it is, what you doing here, Tofa?' His guttural broken English is spoken with precision. 'Who these women?'

Noah defiantly folds his arms across his chest. 'Hello, Baros, meet Nick Holbrook's sister and his fiancée. They've come a long way to see you.'

'Nick Holbrook's sister, eh?' he gives a humourless smile. 'I glad to see you. Where my money?'

What answer he's expecting I've no idea, we stare at him and say nothing.

'So what you here for and how you find me?'

'We've come to see you,' I say.

'And not get bloody well shot at,' Adele adds loudly.

He laughs. 'Just like your dumb brother. Now, where the money? He owes me. Even dead people have debts.'

'You bastard,' Adele shouts.

'Oh, you aggressive type, Holbrook? Who your pretty friend?'

'This is Nick's fiancée, Penny Lane.'

'Penny Lane!' he guffaws. 'No, that silly name?'

'I am Penny Lane,' I say defiantly. 'Nick was my fiancé and your men have shot Adele, she needs treatment.'

'Okay, we see. Now one more time, why you come here?'

'To talk to you,' I reply. 'We have information about your mine that the whole world wants, and we're wondering whether to release it or not.'

Any earlier banter quickly disappears. 'You make me nervous, Penny Lane,' he scowls, 'I take you in, including Tofa and his men, you now my prisoner.'

I look at Noah. He hasn't said a word since his fraught introductions and calmly gestures that we should not put up any resistance.

Clearly in command of the rebel soldiers, Baros barks out a series of orders. At gun point, the smirking soldiers violently thrust out their weapons as they round up a compliant Noah and his men, putting them in one of their vehicles. Another group pick up their guns and take Noah's sat phone out of his pocket.

'You two,' Baros roughly points at us. 'You with me, get in. Call me Jaroslav ... no, Jaro is better.'

Gently holding her wounded arm, I help an infuriated Adele into the back of Baros's vehicle. He takes the wheel and drives along the rough track deeper into the jungle, singing out loud, *"Penny Lane is in my car, beneath the green jungle skies"*, he laughs. I say nothing, I've had it all my life. After a couple of miles, we reach a clearing where a couple of dozen barrack-type buildings are set amongst trees, their roofs covered in palm leaves. A large crowd of blue-uniformed soldiers stare at us, silently eyeing us up.

'You stay with me,' he shouts as we stop outside a smaller but more robust building. Turning round, I see Noah and his men being roughly shoved into a windowless barrack block.

'Right, get in. You got explaining to do.'

Our sudden arrival has clearly troubled Baros but, to my relief, he immediately sends for his medical officer. Inside the hut is a large table covered in papers, a few crudely built wooden chairs, metal shelves with files of differing shapes, multi-coloured charts on the walls, and an unmade single bed in one corner. The door and windows are open through which a slight breeze cools the room to marginally less than oven temperature. Jaro wipes his brow, scratches his crotch and gestures us to sit down. Earlier at the hotel, Adele and I had agreed that if there was any trouble, we should be as truthful as possible, even telling him about the package and diamonds. There's no point in beating around the bush because we have to know what Nick's relationship was with Baros and why the mine's location is so important.

Very soon, a young black officer arrives carrying a medical bag. 'Hi there,' looking surprised when he sees us, he gives a big grin, 'I'm Doctor Duke Tyler and hey, what have we here?' His accent is pure American, straight out of the movies. 'What have you girls been up to?'

'Okay Tyler,' Baros angrily snarls. 'Not try your charm, fix this bitch's arm and then go.'

Tyler's eyes narrow as if he's going to react, but changes his mind and sits next to Adele carefully cutting away the improvised bandages. Using something strong-smelling out of a bottle, he gently cleans the wound which is still seeping blood. Adele, obviously in pain, screws up her face, but doesn't say a word. She's tough.

'Luckily,' Tyler announces as he puts new bandages around her arm, 'The bullet passed through the flesh without damaging any bones or tendons.'

'Thanks Doc,' Adele says when he finished. 'Give the bill to Baros here.'

'I will and it's my pleasure, Ma'am. Are you up to date with tetanus and do you have any allergies?'

'Yes I am, and no allergies.'

'Great, I'll give you a jab, you know, antibiotic, to be on the safe side and I'll check by in the morning.' Standing to leave, he gives Baros a wary look, probably to make sure he's not said anything out of line.

'Okay, let's talk,' Baros says as Tyler leaves. 'How you find me?' his voice is threatening and there's no trace of compassion on his face. 'You and Tofa are in big danger until I decide what to do with you.

'But why?' I challenge angrily. 'It was Nick and Colonel Noah Tofa who saved your life in the Ivory Coast, so why are we in danger?'

He gives an indifferent shrug. 'That was years ago,' he says. 'Give me my diamonds or money, at least ten million dollars.'

'We don't have your bloody diamonds or money,' I shout at him. 'Nick was murdered before he could do anything with them, and he left me a note to contact Axel Van Damme if I had problems, and also Colonel Tofa.'

'You lie,' he snarls aggressively, 'Nick wasn't murdered.'

'Oh yes he was and it was because of you, your secret diamond mine.'

'Did he tell you that?'

'No, he didn't. We worked it out with Axel.' I decide to tell him how Nick was murdered, the involvement of HESEC, and that Adele and I have been chased round half of Europe by Chinese villains trying to get the location of the mine.

He nods his head. 'Did you tell anyone?'

Will it endanger us if I do? 'We have kept it a secret from the villains but the Van Damme's know and,' I try and bluff but I don't think he believes me. 'A couple of other people, friends.'

'But not the Chinese, it's important, do the Chinese know?'

I shake my head. 'No.'

'But Tofa does.'

'Yes, but he's on our side. He was Nick's friend and wants to help us. Anyhow, what is it about the Chinese?' I ask him. 'Why are they after the mine's location?'

Baros tosses his head in exasperation as if I'm stupid. 'You should know why,' he snaps, 'China work with HESEC men and that why, as you tell me, they murder Nick Holbrook. The story that I find big diamond mine in Africa was leaked in London, I think by Holbrook, and China want to know where it is so they can grab it.'

219

'But if the mine is valuable,' I say, 'The Liberian Government won't let them have it, they'll want the revenue themselves.'

'You stupid woman,' he rages. 'The Chinese buy leaders of every African country, it corruption, you ever hear of it?'

Raising my voice in return, I say, 'President Poltara is not corrupt.'

Irritably, he shakes his head. 'You silly woman, Penny Lane,' he angrily bangs his fist on the table. 'Of course she corrupt. China corrupt all leaders and take gold, iron ore, copper, bauxite, land for food, everything. Now they take diamonds. In Zimbabwe, they mine millions of diamonds and give that mad man, Mugabe, useless weapons in exchange, and they not use African workers, oh no, they bring Chinese men, they not trust local people.'

The tension in the room isn't helped by the overpowering, muggy heat and the constant drone and whine of insects. I feel clammy, my clothes sticking to my body with sweat and there's a horrible stink . Looking at Adele, she appears to be slightly better and is sitting upright in her chair, although she must still be in pain. For what seems minutes, but is probably only seconds, no-one speaks then Adele asks, 'How did Nick get involved with you?'

'You not know this?' Baros is a bit calmer now. 'Last month, he come from up country, from Sierra Leone and Guinea looking for his brother; he not find him. Ha, he laugh at my invented iron ore mine, said it a joke and knew about the diamonds. He promise to keep it secret and sell three large rough diamonds in London for new equipment and ship here but,' banging the table again with his fist, 'He lie because he crook and he keep them.'

'He was never a crook,' Adele shouts back.

Baros sneers. 'He always crook, and spy. Why you think he in Ivory Coast when he rescue Van Dammes and me?'

'Training Colonel Tofa and other Liberian soldiers.'

'Ha, you joke, yes? He spying to see if we find oil and then he sell information to British Oil Company. It was Tofa and his men who save us, not Holbrook. Everywhere he go, he use locals to spy and make money for himself.'

The fury inside Adele breaks and she screams. 'It's you who lie,' she slaps her hand on the table forgetting about her injury. It take's a few moments for the pain to subside before she adds, 'Nick was a good man.'

Smirking, Baros shrugs his shoulders and holds his hands, palms up saying, 'Okay, okay, you his sister and his girlfriend say he good guy, but me, I see him in Africa and know he a greedy crook and spy. Say no more, change subject, no more.'

Realising we'll get no further, I take a deep breath to try and calm myself.

'But question is,' Baros frowns, 'What I do with you now?'

'Let us go back to Monrovia with Colonel Tofa and his men.'

'No way, you know too much. Maybe I keep you prisoner or,' he grins cruelly. 'Or I kill you.'

Feeling my stomach dropping away, my heart beats violently.

Seemingly unaffected by his callous threat, Adele's voice is as calm as ever. 'If we don't return to Monrovia, the army will come looking for us, they know Colonel Tofa has brought us here.'

'No chance,' he scoffs. 'The Liberian army not even try, they not ready.'

'Oh yes they are,' Adele confidently states without hesitation. 'Colonel Tofa arranged it before we left. Anyway, you're not going to kill us as we're too valuable, we left full details of the mine's location with Mr Grosvenor-Smythe, you know him, and he'll let the government and Chinese know if we don't return. Then you won't be able to stop the Chinese getting your stupid mine, it'll be all over.'

Expressionless, he stands behind the table and uses a grubby piece of cloth to wipe his brow, then theatrically breaks wind and goes to the door calling for Laylee.

It's getting dark but there's no discernible reduction in the oppressiveness of the room, the only sound is the cicadas outside, gearing themselves up for the night.

'I stop Liberian army and Chinese with MY army,' he calmly announces. 'So, you see, I don't need money from Holbrook. I sell more diamonds in Sierra Leone last month. I get plenty money to overthrow the corrupt government and put my man in as president. I hoped Jacob Marcam would be back but I have someone else, as you say in England, a puppet. I make him president instead of Poltara.'

Looking stunned, Adele, still comforting her injury gasps. 'A coup, you plan a coup, are you serious?'

We are interrupted by a youngish woman shuffling in, swaying her beefy hips as she scuffs her flip-flops along the concrete floor. This must be Laylee, wearing a long wrap-around skirt and her generous, unfettered bosoms sway disconcertingly inside a colourful top. Stopping near Jaro's chair, she gives him a flirtatious smile through heavily painted lips, rubbing her hands intimately over his shoulders.

Ignoring her attempts of affection, he roughly orders her to bring food and drinks and to tell Saul to get the generator working. Sulking at his brusque command, she shuffles out, looking daggers at Adele and me.

'Please give food and drink to Colonel Tofa and his men?' I add, wondering in what conditions they are being held.

'They'll get something,' he replies unconvincingly.

A cranking noise outside signals the generator starting and two bare light bulbs flicker a couple of times and then burst into life, highlighting the flying insects above us. The shuffling Laylee, now in a bad mood, brings in a tray with three tin mugs, a bottle of Johnnie Walker whisky and water, plonking it down on the table so hard that water slops out of the chipped jug. Her task completed, she leaves and Jaro unscrews the cap of the whisky and pours out three large measures into the mugs, taking one himself, which he drains in one, and then nods to us to follow suit.

'Just water for me, Jaro, I'm pregnant.'

Wiping his mouth on his arm, his face screws up disbelievingly. 'You can't be! What you doing here for God's sake.'

'I'm only two months, it's Nick's baby and I'm alright.'

He sniggers refilling his mug. 'Pregnant or not, whisky good for you and it keep fuckin' mossies away. Whisky and garlic better than sprays. Come on, both of you, drink up.'

'I'll have some of that.' Adele rises from her chair, deliberately taking the attention away from me, her eyes have got that steely glint again. It's always there when she senses danger. But what can she do with one arm in a sling? Passing a mug to me, she takes the third one herself, coolly knocking it back in one go without even blinking. How did she do that? It's probably a lesson from the Holbrook military training manual. She refills Jaro's mug and then her own before saying, 'Penny and I need the toilet and shower.'

Clearly amused, he says, 'Where you think you are, Claridges?'

'We know where we are, Jaro, but we still need them.'

He points outside. 'There hut at the back, you find it. Laylee will bring bucket of water, it river water but she put medicine in. And for peeing and shitting, go to bushes before dark and don't step in my shit.'

With a look of disgust on her face, Adele says to me, 'Let's go, and we'll take our bags so we can change.' In the dim evening light, we head for the bushes. As we stumble across the rough waste ground, we lend support to each other in case one of us trips. Although the sound of the cicadas is almost deafening, even more scary are the strange, unearthly screeches and croaks in the deep shadows of the trees. I pray to God there aren't any snakes or other nasties lurking in the grass. We reach the edge of the bushes and what seems to be an unsoiled area.

'We'll have to be quick,' Adele says. 'And we need a plan of escape, any ideas?'

'God no. He's not going to kill us, is he?'

'No, of course not, it's just his sick humour. Don't worry, I'll beat that bastard, Baros, you know I will.'

We take it in turns to crouch and carry out the necessaries before heading back to the building. In the gloom, we find the tin shack with the promised bucket of water which smells faintly of dettol. The room is no more than eight feet by six and has a horrible smell. In the cramped area, I wash the best I can, but at least I feel fresher.

'We've got to be ready to defend ourselves,' Adele whispers. I help her open the secret compartment in her bag. Taking out a tiny flashlight, she rummages through the contents. 'This is all I've got left,' she fingers a small phial. 'These are knockout drops,' and pushes it deep into the crevice of her sling. 'And these,' she holds a couple of syringes in the dim light, 'I think are similar to the one I used on that bastard on the Eurostar, but probably stronger. I'll keep one out as well, see how things develop.' She also takes out a wad of dollars. 'There's a couple of hundred, put them in your pocket and I'll do the same.'

Back in the room, the first thing I notice is a second bottle of whisky on the table, the first one lying empty on the floor and our bleary-eyed captor finishing off the dregs. A plate of fried chicken, boiled sweet potatoes and raw sliced garlic seems to be our meal tonight.

Slurring his words, he says, 'Help *yourshelf.*' He's getting drunk. Is it a good thing or not? Suddenly feeling famished, I wipe my plate with a tissue, and tentatively take some of the food. Adele does the same. There's no cutlery so we use our fingers. What's concerning me is that Adele seems to be keeping pace with Jaro in the consumption of whisky, and keeps topping up his mug as well as her own. She gives me a sly wink to show she knows what she's doing.

'What I got here,' Baros expands, giving an enormous belch followed by a loud fart, 'Make me richesht man on earth.' He's slurring almost every word now and his huge grin reveals disgusting teeth. 'Think about Kimberly mine in South Africa. It lost value through erosion. It still had diamonds weighing over two thousand kilos. My mine,' he shakes his head vigorously. 'No erosion.' He takes another large swig of whisky and Adele immediately refills it for him. She gives me a signal to get his attention. I bend down to scratch an insect bite on my ankle so he can see down my cleavage, which he ogles lasciviously while Adele expertly tips a few knockout drops into his drink. 'But 'til I get more equipment,' he continues, leering at me. 'All I want is good fuck, and not my African whore, oh no,' he points directly at me. 'You the one, Nick Holbrook's whore.'

Oh God, I feel sick. I'm covered in sweat and my chest's heaving. Have sex with this filthy, stinking excuse of a human being! Is he kidding?

Before I can say anything, Adele jumps to her feet. 'Hang on a moment, Jaro,' she stands just behind him. 'You're not going to have sex with Penny unless she wants to.'

What! Did she actually say that? I exhale noisily ... slow down, I tell myself, slow down ... ah, Adele signals to me to go along with her.

From his sitting position, Jaro turns and looks blearily up at Adele as the combination of whisky and knockout drops starts to take effect. 'I want fuck with her.'

'She'll agree on one condition, won't you Penny?'

I can't believe she said that, of course I won't. Behind Jaro's back and grimacing while comforting her wounded arm, Adele frantically nods her head at me to agree. I'm clearly the bait in a trap she's setting, but whatever it is, the plan must NOT involve me having sex with Jaro. They both look at me waiting my response. My head reeling. 'Well, I might if ...'

'If,' Adele takes over from my stuttering. 'You let Colonel Tofa come here. We need to discuss things with him.' While Jaro is trying to absorb that, she slips a few more drops into his drink.

It looks as if his brain is starting to play tricks on him. 'If Penny *promishes*,' his bloodshot eyes eventually focus directly at me. 'Then I let Tofa come, for two minute.' Although slurring his words, he still looks a long way from collapsing.

'Yes, we promise.'

My poor old heart is beating like a drum. Bloody hell, don't I have a say in this stomach-churning agreement? Obviously not.

Going to the door, Adele calls Laylee who's plainly been eavesdropping. 'Go and tell Saul to bring Colonel Tofa here,' Adele says, carefully slipping some cash into her hand, 'Professor Baros wants to talk to him.'

Fingering the notes, Laylee hesitates for a moment, and I watch her scarlet-painted toes nervously grip and ungrip her red flip-flops as she looks at Jaro for confirmation.

'Go get him, fasht,' he slurs loudly.

Pocketing the money, she shuffles off into the darkness.

Feeling physically sick, I instinctively cross my legs tightly. While we wait, I take a drink of my whisky and water and chew on a couple of slices of raw garlic, it's bloody horrible but a million times better than having a naked Jaro on top of me. Adele takes the opportunity to refill both their mugs. I hope the knockout drops work soon, because although he looks as if he's been on a forty-eight hour bender, his reddened eyes are still full of lust.

Abruptly, the door is flung open and Noah, arms above his head, enters followed by two soldiers holding guns to his back.

Noah angrily stands facing Jaro. 'What the hell is going on, Baros? We came here in good faith and all you've done is shoot Adele and lock me and my men in a shithole.'

'Because,' Jaro struggles to keep his head upright. 'You steal my diamonds.'

'You know that's not true,' I yell at him. 'We've kept the location of your mine secret so you owe us, not the other way around.'

Just how much of it he takes in I can't tell, but his gestures or those of a blind man, revealing sodden, sweat patches under his arms. God, he gets more revolting by the minute.

'Hey, Saul,' he calls out, 'Get rid of Tofa, take him back.' Jaro's voice is worryingly clearer now, 'I got other things to do.' Leering at me, I can smell his stink from here, all of eight feet away.

Adele thrusts a bag into Noah's hands before a befuddled Jaro can intervene. 'Here's food we haven't eaten, share it with your men.' Taking the bag, Noah tries to say something, but the soldiers grab him roughly and march him into the night.

'You go to, Laylee,' Jaro commands, 'And close fucking door.' Looking thunderous and giving me the evil eye, she slams the door so hard it makes the lights flicker.

Jaro's lustful smile has become twisted. *"Penny Lane is in my bed"* he laughs, pointing at me. 'Take off clothes.'

For a second, I've lost the feelings in my arms and legs and my brain is befuddled by fear. 'Not yet,' my panicky voice has gone up a couple of octaves, 'I'm not ready.'

'You promish, do it now.'

Standing behind Jaro, Adele anxiously nods at me demonstrating, like in the game of charades, that I should start to undress. 'Slowly does it,' she attempts a sexy voice, as she fumbles in her sling for the syringe. I have to distract Jaro so that she can jab the syringe into him. But, hang on ... Adele's starting to panic as she searches in her sling and bends low looking round the floor. Oh shit, *she's lost the syringe.*

Hastily changing tack, Adele improvises and pours more whisky into his mug. 'Come on, Jaro, drink up.'

'No,' he yells. 'Piss off, Holbrook.' Thrusting out his arm, he smashes the mug to the floor. 'Now, Penny Lane, *you whore,*' he angrily reaches to grab my arm but my reflexes are hyper with adrenalin and I twist to avoid him. 'Get clothes off ... we fuck now.' Oh, why hadn't I listened to the little voice in my head telling me to stay in the safety of the hotel?

Adele has unhooked her sling and is looking everywhere, scrambling on the floor, but can't find the damn thing. She mimes to me that she needs more time.

I'm experiencing pure terror, like a trapped animal, but as it's part of Adele's plan, I have no choice. To make matters worse, now shirtless, his chest, arms and back are covered in hair. He's like a grisly bear.

Adele is still frantically searching. Oh God, I feel as if the top of my head is about to explode. Ah well, here goes. Taking another deep breath, I start to remove my T-shirt, but it's sticking to me and it's a struggle to lift it over my head. Suddenly coming away, I cast it aside. I'm now in my bra and skirt.

Still no syringe. Damn.

Sitting on the side of the bed, Jaro clumsily removes his trousers. Any moment now, I think I'll throw up, in fact, I wish I could. He seems oblivious to Adele's frenzied searches behind him. 'Come, come Penny Lane,' he snarls, 'I ready.'

Frantically playing for time and trembling uncontrollably, I slowly unzip my skirt and let it slip to the floor. I'm down to bra and pants. His breathing is more laboured and saliva is starting to dribble down his chin.

Inwardly I scream and scream, Adele, hurry up.

What next? I slip the strap of my bra down over my left shoulder, it just hangs there, and Jaro's eyes are sticking out like two, blood-veined marbles. I guess it's how a strip-o-gram must feel. I'm just about to undo the bra clasp when Adele, almost jumping in the air like a triumphant gold medal winner, holds up the syringe.

Still unaware of Adele's antics, Jaro is just about to remove his filthy boxer shorts when Adele quickly moves to the head of the bed. 'Lie down, Jaro,' she says encouragingly. 'Penny will join you.' Slowly, he settles back, his pants tenting upwards and Adele plunges the syringe into his neck. As if by magic, his head, and his manhood, immediately slump, as every part of his body goes limp.

Collapsing onto the floor, I roll side to side, tears streaming down my face. 'What – what- what was all that?' I cry. I crumple onto a nearby chair.

Adele comes over, giving me an embrace and massages my shoulders.

'I'm okay,' My voice is barely a whisper as she passes me my discarded clothing. 'Is he dead?' I'm not sure whether I want a yes or no answer.

Adele takes his pulse. 'No, he's sleeping and hopefully, he'll be out for a few hours.'

'A few! what the *hell* does few mean?' I try to keep my voice down, not wanting to alert Laylee. 'Is it one hour, two or, I don't know, ten?'

'At least five and probably more considering the knockout drops and alcohol he's taken. I'm really sorry about putting you through that, you know, losing the syringe and all that and you having to, you know.'

'Yes, I do know and I'll kill you later, but what happens when he wakes up? He'll want to know why we haven't had sex.'

Shrugging her shoulders, she purses her lips. 'Just tell him he has.'

'But won't he know?'

'Not if I kick him hard in the balls, he won't.'

'How do you know that?'

She gestures vaguely as if it's a well known fact, and goes over to the unconscious Jaro, kneeding him sharply in the groin a couple of times with her good elbow. 'Ha, I enjoyed that.'

'I hope you're right.' Maybe having brothers and military training has taught her far more than most young women, myself included, should know.

Thankfully, my nerves are starting to recover. 'What was in the bag you gave to Noah and should we try and escape now?'

'No, it's too dark and we don't have a vehicle. I put all my money and a note in the bag telling Noah to get his men and vehicle ready for one-thirty tomorrow afternoon.'

'To escape?'

'Of course to escape.'

'But how will he do that?'

'He's a smart guy and will use the money to bribe, remember, he's Liberian like the rest of them so he should be able to work something out.'

The door abruptly bursts open and Laylee storms in holding a can of mosquito repellent like a weapon. 'Wha' 'appen to hi'?' she asks, the consonants at the end of words being dropped.

'He's drunk.' Adele points to the two empty bottles of whisky, then takes some of the money out of my pocket. 'Here's another twenty dollars for you, Laylee, leave the spray with us and kindly bring coffee and breakfast in the morning.'

Looking uncertainly at Jaro, Laylee hesitates, looking down at the twenty dollar bill again.

'There'll be more tomorrow,' Adele places her arm around her ample shoulders and leads her to the door. 'We'll make it worth your while and don't worry about Mr Baros, he said he wanted to sleep without interruptions, so we must all keep quiet.'

CHAPTER TWENTY-FOUR
FEBRUARY 26th

'Wake up.' Adele's hand clamped firmly over my mouth. 'Shh, don't say a word,' she whispers into my ear, 'Jaro's stirring.'

Taking a deep breath, I try to shake myself awake.

'You've got to get up now,' she whispers again.

Groaning, I shift my aching body and rub the sleep from my eyes. The faint, early morning light shines dimly through the window, the air a little fresher than last night.

Sitting on the side of his bed, Jaro rubs both hands over his unshaven face, a grumbling noise emanates deep in his throat, like the starter motor of Mr Smether's old tractor. 'What ...?' his voice, thick and rasping. 'Go get Laylee, I need coffee.'

On cue, Laylee appears as though she's been listening since first light.

'Good morning, Laylee,' Adele says brightly. Without Jaro seeing, she hands her more dollar bills which immediately lights up her previously grim face. 'Please bring coffee for Professor Baros, and breakfast for all of us.'

'Yer wan foo?' Laylee gives her rear end a less than dainty scratch.

'Yes please, coffee and food and another bucket of water for us to wash in.'

With a happy nod, she skips off, this time lifting her flip-flops clear of the ground. I think we've made a useful friend at last.

Like an old soak, Jaro struggles to his feet, scratching, burping and farting like an ill-mannered peasant, not in any way resembling an educated man, a professor. Struggling into his old, grubby trousers, he looks at me suspiciously. 'What happen last night?'

230

Luckily, I'm ready for this. 'I kept my side of our bargain – that's what happened.'

Nodding his head a couple of times and gently holding his crotch, it looks as if he's beginning to believe that we did have sex, but with all the drugs Adele pumped into him as well as the whisky, it should be a blur. 'Okay, okay,' he scowls, 'I keep my promise so I let you see Colonel Tofa again, but he and his men stay here.'

'But we need Colonel Tofa to help rescue my brother,' Adele snaps. 'Remember, he only knows about the iron ore mine, not the diamonds.'

'Huh, I not sure. Anyway, I not risk it so everyone stay, end of story.'

The door opens and Laylee, accompanied by a timid young girl, carry in two trays with our breakfast, mugs of a hot, dark liquid (presumably coffee), an unopened packet of white sliced bread, a tub of margarine, a pot of jam, some green skinned oranges and small bananas.

'Where plate and knife?' Jaro snarls.

'Eh?' She frowns and looks at the girl. 'Stupi' girl, go bring 'em now.'

I'm starving, and even though the coffee is strong and heavily sweetened, the bread stale and the jam tasting like it's ninety percent sugar, I tuck in with the others, although poor Adele grunts as she can only use her good arm. The insides of the oranges are surprisingly sweet and juicy.

'Jaro?' Adele asks, wiping her mouth on a tissue. 'Can we leave this morning? Just Penny and I.'

No answer. He seems to be making a quick recovery from the effects of the drugs and whisky, eating half the loaf and calling for more coffee. Eventually, he lifts his head. 'You keep Nick's secret, that good, but I put my life in this mine and have to keep fucking Chinese out. So you stay.'

'But we hate the Chinese just as much as you,' I counter. 'They killed Nick and tried to kill us so we promise to keep your secret. Please let us go.'

'No,' he bangs the table with his fist. 'If you go, Tofa tell President Poltara about the rebels and my plan to change government. She in pocket of Chinese.'

'Look Jaro, we'll make Noah promise,' Adele tries to sound convincing, but it doesn't wash with me, never mind Jaro.

'I let you go *only* when we take over government,' he shouts. 'Not till then, no argue.'

'But when will that be?' I plead. The thought of staying with him for even one more day makes me feel sick.

'Soon enough,' he gives that twisted grin again. 'Now,' he barks angrily. 'No more.'

Adele signals to me that we shouldn't continue, for now, anyway. Instead, she tells Jaro. 'We need to use the toilet.'

'Okay,' he nods. 'And after you been, I take you to my mine - it eighteen miles from here.'

Outside in the stinking shack, I tell Adele, 'He won't let us go.'

'Not willingly,' she agrees. 'So we'll have to escape.'

'But how? You've only got one syringe left, and what do you think he meant by *soon enough*?'

'I don't know,' Adele shakes her head grimly. 'I'm wondering if we could escape while we're at the mine but, there again, it would be bloody difficult knowing that the rebel army would be watching us. Anyway, we'll just have to see how things work out, trust me.'

'And another thing,' I continue, 'Why is he taking us to the mine? There's something not right here and I can't work it out. What's he planning?'

'I know what you mean. Whatever happens though, we must be back here by one-thirty because hopefully, Noah will have bribed someone to provide a vehicle for us.'

Shaking my head, I don't say anything but I can't believe it will be as easy as that.

'One good thing though,' Adele winces slightly, gently placing her hand over her bandaged arm. 'My injury's no worse and won't stop me doing whatever it takes to get out of this hell hole.'

Inside the disgusting washroom, our new friend, Laylee, has provided a bucket of disinfected water and we complete our basic ablutions the best we can. Feeling a bit fresher, we go back into Jaro's room only to find he's not there.

'Where's he gone?' Adele's question is immediately answered by a vehicle screeching to a halt outside. Jaro gets out. I stare at him open mouthed. He looks completely different wearing a clean check shirt and jeans, his grotty trainers replaced by polished cowboy boots, and now clean-shaven, there's a whiff of cologne in the air. His expression, normally horrible, has changed to a grin clearly directed at me. Bloody hell. Ominously, he's wearing a gun belt with firearms low down on both hips, but the silly Stetson perched cockily on his head, coupled with sweat streaming down his face, somewhat spoils the cowboy image.

'Let's go,' he orders, 'I take you to Limarni mine.'

'WHAT?' we yell in unison.

Looking alarmed at our outburst. 'What so strange?'

'Limarni,' I yell, uncertain if I should say anymore. 'What does it mean?' I ask feebly.

'It village name,' still looking strangely at us. 'It gone now.'

Adele takes over. 'It's just that Nick mentioned Limarni in his letter and we've been trying to discover what it meant.'

I feel frustrated, what an inti-climax. All this time we've been trying to find out what Limarni is, and now we know. And that's why Nick put it in his letter, not realising that nobody else knew. I was hoping Limarni would be the key to everything but ... maybe it is.

'Come,' he orders again.

Adele and I climb into the back of the 4 x 4. It must have been left out in the sun and inside, the humidity is unbearable. Jaro clambers in behind the wheel and opens all the windows. Because of the oppressive heat and lack of proper washing facilities, I had earlier decided not to wear a bra, but now I'm awkwardly conscious of the tightness of my T-shirt which doesn't go unnoticed by Jaro.

The thought of miles of bumpy roads to the mine fills me with dread, not least because of my pregnancy but, thank God, as we leave the clearing and head towards a thickly forested area, the laterite road is surprisingly wide and smooth. The cooling breeze through the open windows makes the temperature more bearable and putting on some speed, we leave a massive cloud of dust in our wake. Abruptly, the sun is blotted out by tall trees on each side of the road, like entering a tunnel of dark green vegetation.

Jaro, seeming to have recovered from his drug and drink overdose, starts humming to himself. Oh no, I screw up my face trying not to hear.

'Penny Lane is in my car. Here under the green jungle skies'. Turning to me, he gives me one of his nauseating grins, God, he must be in love. At least there's no doubt now that Adele's plan worked and he believes we had sex last night.

Still driving through dense jungle, we come across a clearing with a large settlement. The buildings are spaced out in regular rows with zinc roofs covered in palm leaves and dozens of kids of all sizes, running and playing, whilst women and girls are cooking, bathing, and waiting at a hand pump, balancing jerry cans on their heads.

'This family accommodation for soldiers,' Jaro points to the buildings. 'Not bad, eh?'

'It's better than West Point.' Adele leans out of the side window and some children jump up and shout in excitement seeing our white faces. Others look horrified and run away.

'Who pays for all this, surely not the government?'

'Course not,' he laughs. 'They not know of this place. I pay for everything.'

'But how can a white man like you have an army at his disposal?'

His smile vanishes. 'They Jacob Marcam supporters and know they get share of diamond money, but fucking American CIA bring fake charges against him for war crimes. He lost appeal because of CIA.'

'From what I've heard,' I say cautiously, 'Marcam's gone to jail for twenty years.'

'Ha, maybe not, 'cos I pay for his escape.' he replies defiantly.

Adele gasps. 'You're actually paying people to get him out of jail in South Africa?'

He holds his hands up saying no more, maybe he regrets telling us.

'And then what?' Adele asks. 'What will happen if he did come back?'

'We have coup,' he says smoothly. 'By replacing CIA puppet, President Poltara, with Jacob Marcam. Our army bigger and got better weapons than government and we beat them in short time, maybe one week.'

'You're talking about another civil war,' Adele's horrified. 'You can't do that.'

'We can ... we must,' he shouts. 'That only way I keep Limarni.' He shrugs his shoulders as though it doesn't matter. 'That why Colonel Tofa stay here.'

'But please, Jaro,' Adele implores. 'You say the coup won't start for a few weeks - we must have Colonel Tofa with us tomorrow, he's the only one who can get my brother released from captivity in Guinea. Please let him go. We'll make him promise you, on oath, that he won't say anything. I've just got to save my brother.'

'No, he stay.'

'We'll do anything if you let him go.'

'Anything?' I can almost hear the cogs going around in his brain. 'Maybe if I have hostage to keep him quiet.'

'Hostage, what do you mean?'

'I tell you what, Holbrook,' he faces her. 'Leave Penny Lane with me and I let Colonel Tofa go. If Tofa not keep mouth shut, you never see Penny Lane again.'

'Hey, hang on just a moment,' I yell.

Adele gives me a sharp kick on the shins. 'How long would you keep Penny for?'

'Two months.'

'One month,' Adele counters, giving me more kicks.

'Six weeks, take it or leave it.'

Adele turns to me. 'Look Penny, please do this,' her fierce eyeball to eyeball means she's up to her tricks again and she speaks loudly for Jaro's benefit. 'You know that the only chance of getting Charles free is with Noah's help, without that he's as good as dead. Please agree to it, please. It's only six weeks for you, but it's life or death for Charles.'

Why am I always the bait in her schemes? I guess I've got to go along with her plan but I can't think we'll be able to pull the wool over Jaro's eyes that easily. I just wish I knew what her plan is. I feel a creep of dread inching up the nape of my sweaty neck, but I have to put on a pretence. 'No, Adele, I can't do that, I'm two months pregnant for God's sake.'

'But you'll be alright.'

Damn her, but oh God, what can I do? Is it love or lust with him? He's probably been starved of white, female company for so long it must have addled his brain. I make one last attempt to find an obstacle. 'But what if I have problems, you know, with the baby.'

'No problem,' Jaro grins. 'You already meet Doctor Tyler, he take good care of you.'

A voice in my head is screaming refuse, but I hear myself saying, 'I'll think about it.'

Seemingly satisfied with the suggestion of me as a hostage, especially now he believes we had sex last night, we head further on through the jungle. He said he'll let Adele and Noah go, oh yes, but not me, no, I have to stay so he can have his evil way with me. Sweat drips down my face and chin onto my T-shirt, I'm in a whirl of fear and anxiety. I know Adele has a plan to get me out of it so I'll try and calm down, relax, breathe slowly to become at one with the heat.

We pass a clearing where women and girls are bent double, toiling in the morning sun tending crops, not even looking up as we drive by throwing up dust over those nearest the road whilst men and boys shelter under a huge mango tree.

'Jaro, why is it that only females do the farm work?' Adele asks.

'It the culture,' he replies in a matter of fact manner. 'Men do fighting and put world to rights, women do the rest.'

I shake my head in despair.

'We grow food,' he continues. 'In this field onion, tomato, pepper, cassava, sweet potatoes. Over at far end, chicken houses.'

'I thought rice was the staple diet in Liberia.'

'It is, rice grow by river, Asians get three crops a year but,' there's a hint of sarcasm in his voice. 'We get one.'

'What else,' I ask, not understanding why I want to keep the conversation going.

'We got banana, orange, fish from river and bush meat.'

'Bush meat?'

236

He laughs. 'Anything that move. Like deer, monkey, rats, reptiles; they all go in pot.'

'But not bread, butter or coffee,' Adele says mockingly.

'Okay, okay, we buy some food from Sierra Leone,' he admits. 'But big problem is getting fuel and mining equipment.'

As we head further inland, undulations are beginning to form, and the colour of laterite gradually changes from a reddish brown to dark burnt umber. He stops at the crest of a hill. 'Down there,' he points, 'Mano River and in distance, Limarni, we be there soon.'

Looking out over a vast green basin, it's steaming with equatorial heat. The high temperature and humidity are relentless, worse than in Monrovia where there's a sea breeze. A glint through the trees turns out to be the broad, gleaming curve of the river, a heat haze rests on the far bank, merging into the tree jungle. Unfortunately, every time he stops the car, clouds of dust from our wake overtake us, making breathing difficult and my throat sore. As if reading my thoughts, Jaro passes over bottles of water.

Driving around a tight bend, we come upon a large area cleared of all trees and vegetation. It's completely different reminding me of a science fiction film where people are on the barren surface of the moon, navigating around hundreds of craters.

'You see this place?' he sighs, shaking his head. 'This African alluvial diamond mine, each crater dug by hand and people sift the Kimberlite hoping to find diamonds. It belong to Jacob Marcam, but diamonds found here in last twenty years not fill the pocket of my jeans. Ha, Marcam not know he was five miles from the richest mine ever.'

We arrive at a barrier manned by heavily armed, blue uniformed soldiers who immediately wave us through. 'Are these road blocks anything to do with UN peacekeepers?' Adele asks.

'You joke with me,' he laughs out loud. 'My men better trained with better weapons than Pakis or Bangladeshis.'

A pair of large steel gates fringed with razor wire is the final obstruction before entering the complex. We are faced by a large compound covering several acres, the size of it takes me completely by surprise. Four large concrete block buildings and a tall steel construction which, I guess, is the mine shaft, looking like a giant Meccano set.

'Welcome to Limarni.'

An articulated truck, packed with crates, is presently being unloaded by two forklift trucks, and three tankers are parked next to a large fuel container. It's obvious now why the road is kept in such good condition.

'It's huge,' I say, 'This must have cost a fortune. We thought you were short of money.'

'I have other diamonds than the ones I give Nick Holbrook.' He's clearly extremely irritated by this. 'CIA and stupid *blood diamonds*. I forced to sell for a knock-down price to South African crooks in Sierra Leone, that where I get all my supplies. But I still short of heavy machinery like hydraulic shovels, crushing and milling equipment, x-ray fluorescent sorters and more, it on the shopping list I give to Nick Holbrook.'

Two white men, wearing hard hats and overalls walk over to the vehicle.

Jaro gets out. 'You stay.'

Now that the vehicle's stopped, there's no breeze and the sun pounds down with unbelievable force, roasting us inside.

Adele sighs turning to me. 'How are you feeling, you and the baby?'

'Apart from basting in my own sweat, I'm okay, we're okay. Let's get out of this mobile oven but first, I want to know what plan you've hatched.'

'Plan, what do you mean?'

'You know what I mean,' I try to stop myself shouting, 'I am not, repeat not, staying with Jaro as a hostage while you and Noah flit back to Monrovia. What's your plan to get me out?'

'Oh that, I don't have one yet,' she says dismissively. 'This infernal heat is boiling my brains but, not to worry, something will crop up.'

'Something will crop up!' I yell, starting to panic. 'That's no good.'

She puts her good arm around my shoulders. 'It will, it will, I promise,' she looks directly into my eyes, 'I won't leave without you.'

Watching our little drama, Jaro makes what looks like a snide remark to the two men who promptly burst out laughing. I shudder to think what vulgarity he's come up with.

He approaches, frowning. 'You have problem?'

'No, we're okay,' Adele puts on a forced smile. 'The heat is getting to us.'

Removing his Stetson, he wipes his brow in token sympathy and nods in the direction of the men. 'These two guys, Erik and Hans, run this place on a day-to-day basis, they South African.' Both touch their hats with their forefingers but don't come over. 'I've got business to do, so you wait in shade.' He points towards some trees near the river.

Wearily, carrying our half empty bottles of water, we make our way to the comparatively cool air under a row of tall trees knitted together, like a veil, with creeper vines.

While we're still within earshot, we hear Hans telling Jaro that the rain is now heavy in the highlands and the river level is rising.

'Yes, I notice,' Jaro replies. 'It good, so I bring plans forward.'

'Plans, what plans are those?' I whisper to Adele.

'Shush, a second,' she murmurs, coming to a halt and craning to listen to what else he's saying. His back is towards us making it difficult to hear until he says plainly, "*We pass around*", the rest of the sentence is inaudible.

My heart does a double flip. 'What did he say? Pass around. He's planning to pass me around to the others. I'm going to be gang raped.'

'Don't be silly,' Adele snorts. 'You're getting paranoid. He's not talking about you but something at the mine, probably passing round some process or other. Get a grip of yourself, I've already told you I'll get you out of here.'

'But you don't know how, you've no plan.'

'Look, I've never let you down,' she states firmly. 'And I won't this time. Noah should have a vehicle ready by one-thirty and, by hook or by crook, we'll get away. Now, let's get out of this bloody sun.'

'Okay,' hoping to God she's right. We flop down in the shade. 'By the way,' I say, holding my nose and peeling my damp T-shirt away from my body, 'I stink.'

'I know you do,' she laughs, 'I'm within smelling distance, but you're not as bad as Jaro, he really does stink.'

'And I feel a complete mess. What on earth do I look like?'

'A complete mess, that's why Erik and Hans didn't bother shaking hands with you.'

'But Jaro loves me,' I wince.

A flock of large, dark brown birds with red beaks is perched in the top branches above us while glossy open-billed storks dry their extended wings on the river bank. A flurry of white catches my eye as a flock of egrets flies down river which is a murky, greenish brown waterway meandering through the rainforest.

'Phew,' Adele, her face flushed, uses a cloth to wipe up the sweat observing that this must be the hottest day since we arrived. We both jump as two huge spiderlike creatures fall onto the ground near our feet. 'Fuck,' Adele yelps, quickly getting up. 'Look at those damned things, they're almost man-eaters.'

Mockingly, I say, 'Is superwoman frightened of spiders.'

'Oh, ha ha, get you,' she replies as three more giant arachnids join the others, creeping slowly towards us, swaying on their back legs, pointing their crablike claws at us. 'We're too close to these damned trees,' she cries, darting away.

Holding back my laughter, I follow her scurrying figure to some light shade near the river. A boat, manned by several local men, cruises slowly past and one of the crew gives a brief wave in Jaro's direction.

'Is that a fishing boat?' I look questioningly at Adele.

She shakes her head. 'I don't think so, no it's too sleek and the throttled-down engine sounds like a power boat to me. But what the hell is it doing here?'

We watch it until about a hundred yards down river, it pulls over to the side and ropes are thrown to the bank.

Bushes partially obstruct our view. Grasping my wrist, Adele leans out and can see at least half a dozen similar boats tied up in a line along the bank. 'That's weird, surely there can't be tourists here?'

'No chance, but it could be that Jaro uses them to bring goods in and out. After all, he did say that when the rainy season starts, the roads are impassable.'

'Could be.'

Beckoning, Jaro calls us to join him. 'You like Limarni, Penny Lane?' He stands feet apart, admiring his mine complex. There are large damp patches on his new shirt and jeans, and a garlicky odour whiffs over me.

'Yes, it's nice.' I move aside so that Adele is standing next to him.

Looking self-satisfied, he points to the steel structure. 'The shaft, it go down only three hundred metres to where, millions of years ago, the volcanic pipe ran out of steam,' he laughs. 'It never reach the surface. Every expert say I crazy but they wrong, all wrong. I best expert in geology and seismology, not them.'

'Yes,' Adele confirms, 'Axel Van Damme told us your theory.'

He points to the next building. 'The rock is crushed and put in cyclone machine to spin off waste, then mix with water from river to make slurry. And over there, the diamonds, which repel water, pass through grease beds to trap them, checking a second time under x-rays machines.'

'Does that mean you get a lot of diamonds?' Adele asks.

This hits a sore spot as he stamps his foot in frustration. 'Not enough,' he snaps. 'The equipment keep breaking, it old and your brother, he promise to sell diamonds and send new machines and special computers to run everything automatically, with suction tubes guided to suck up all the diamonds, but I get nothing. Instead, he give stones to Penny Lane.' Angrily, he turns to me. 'You owe me, bitch.'

I hold my tongue. I owe him nothing and I'm certainly not going to be his bitch.

'But when we get rid of President Poltara, I take money from Government Treasury to buy new equipment and then ha,' he continues, more calmly, 'Then I make *billions* and thieving Chinese are thrown out of Liberia.'

His rant is interrupted by shouting behind us. Two men, protesting vigorously, are being roughly frog-marched by security guards towards the tree line where there's a partly hidden steel barred cage, similar to the ones used for zoo animals. The two men are hurled violently inside, and locked in. They look terrified and continue shouting, desperately grasping and tugging the iron bars.

'What's going on?' I ask.

'The men work in mine and guards say they swallow something before they come out, that how diamonds are stolen.'

'So what will happen to them?'

'The juju witchdoctor will find if they guilty. If they are, they be killed to recover what they swallowed.'

'But they can't do that,' I yell. 'That's murder.'

'Nothing I can do,' he shrugs his shoulders as if he couldn't care less. 'It native law.'

'But it's your mine, you're in charge, not a witchdoctor.'

'Get in vehicle,' he orders brusquely, 'I explain on way back.' Taking a last look at the two men who are still thrusting their arms through the bars, screaming something incomprehensible, we go back to the car.

'You got to understand magic and witchcraft in Africa,' Jaro explains. 'A top witchdoctor is like Pope and Buddha, rolled into one, and people believe him. If I intervene, I get big trouble.'

'So, you'll just let those men be killed?'

Unperturbed, he continues driving back to the base camp. 'You see,' he eventually makes clear, 'Jacob Marcam has stake in the mine, so those men steal from him, and that make other workers very angry.

'But the court found Marcam guilty of war crimes.'

'Ha, I already tell you, he setup by CIA,' he almost spits the words out. 'He found guilty because they say he *instigated* – remember that word, *instigated* other people to do crimes so he get diamonds.'

'And you think it was wrong?'

'Of course it wrong. Many world leaders *instigate* wars. Example is war in Congo for seventeen years and six million people, women and children killed, it biggest genocide since World War Two, *instigated* by America. You know about this?'

'No.'

'Ha, exactly, that my point. They hide evidence and stop international media reporting because US control world media.'

'Really?' Adele sounds doubtful.

'Oh yes,' Jaro exclaims loudly. 'The US weapons industry need important minerals and can only get from Congo. But Congo Government play awkward, so US *instigate* a war but not send any American soldiers, oh no, they get Rwanda, Uganda and Congo rebels to do fighting. And is America guilty? No, of course not.'

Adele shakes her head. 'Are you sure of the facts?'

'One hundred percent,' he yells. 'Marcam get twenty years in jail and biggest criminals, US presidents are free. That why I pay mercenary men to help Marcam escape, so don't you two bitches tell me it can't happen,'

Adele, persistent as a terrier, won't leave it alone. 'But if, for argument's sake, Marcam does escape and gets here to Liberia, what happens then?'

'With my help,' he blurts out, 'We have coup and I make Marcam, as you say, *Figurehead President*, and his soldiers get rid of corrupt Liberian leaders and throw out Chinese bastards who take all the wealth from this country.'

'But you want to overthrow a democratically elected president.'

'You stupid women; you can fuck your democracy.'

'Why's that?'

'Because, you silly bitch,' his voice is rising to hysterical levels. 'In 1980, seventeen low ranking soldiers had a coup here, only seventeen, that all, and only people killed were the corrupt president and corrupt ministers.'

'And you expect to make five billion dollars from your mine?' Adele taunts.

'Of course, and it not take more than five years.' Thankfully, his voice is becoming quieter. Maybe he thinks he's won some sort of argument. 'Then, at the age about, well under fifty,' he continues, 'I retire. That make me very interesting person, hey, Penny Lane? After six weeks with me, you never want to leave.'

Under my breath, I'm screaming every swear word I know. How on earth have I got into this nightmarish situation?

Silently, we drive back into the base camp. Waiting for the dust cloud to clear, he hustles us inside and yells for Laylee. 'Bring chop, you lousy whore and make it good.'

Adele, who has remained remarkably cool through all of Jaro's ravings, addresses him in a controlled voice. 'Jaro, I want to leave with Colonel Noah Tofa and his men straight after lunch. We have to get to Monrovia in daylight.'

Like someone possessed, his face livid, he hurls his silly white Stetson to the floor and, with a shaky hand, takes one of the guns from of its holster, pointing it directly at Adele. 'No way, you bitch, you're going nowhere, you know too much.'

Even with this direct threat, Adele's unruffled demeanour is amazing. 'But you gave your word of honour as a gentleman, and you know I can't say anything about your plan while Penny is your hostage.'

Blinking a couple of times, as if trying to understand her logic, he lowers the gun, but only slightly, and then looks threatening at me. He can probably hear or see the thumping of my heart. The tenseness in his shoulders eases and he gives me another of his loathsome grins. 'Okay Miss Holbrook,' he eventually relents lowering his gun, 'I'll let you go as long as I hold onto my beautiful hostage.'

I bite my lip. The door is flung open by Laylee, who sullenly sashays her way in with a tray of food and a bottle of whisky. The sight of Jaro holding a gun doesn't seem to surprise her. Watching us both like a hawk, he taps the gun for us to sit at the table and then holsters it. Despite all his boasting about the extensive array of food at his disposal, lunch is a repeat of last night's dinner, except that the chicken is cold with congealed fat sticking it to the plate. I thought we'd bought Laylee's support; surely she could do better than this.

No-one speaks and I eat as much as I can stomach while Jaro downs a glass full of whisky. His rapid alcohol intake makes him more relaxed because after ordering us to stay, he leaves the room and shouts to Saul to bring Colonel Tofa's vehicle round. I whisper to Adele in no uncertain terms that she has to implement her plan before I'm left behind. Unperturbed, she places her hand on my arm assuring me not to worry.

Trying to keep my voice down, I seethe. 'Of course I'm bloody well worried.'

As if it's suddenly dawned on her that time is running out for me, she places herself flat against the wall behind the door, awaiting the unsuspecting Jaro who enters muttering to himself. She gives a sharp, targeted kick to the back of his knee, at the same time, deftly removing a gun from his holster. Taken by surprise, he stumbles and grunts but swiftly regains his upright position and springs round to retaliate. Unfortunately for him, his own gun is pointing directly at his head, the audible click is the safety catch being removed.

'You make one move, Professor Jaroslav Baros,' her voice is as menacing as a TV gangster. 'And I'll blow your head off. I've killed villains like you before and, believe me, I'll enjoy doing it again.'

I can almost see the cogs behind his eyes going round as he struggles to grasp what's happening to him. 'Put gun down,' his temper's rising, 'I already say you can leave.'

'We're all leaving, including Penny.'

'No, not Penny Lane,' he rages. 'You promise me she stay.'

'We've changed our minds.' The steel edge to Adele's voice is the same as when she killed the villains on Eurostar and in Brussels, she's in her 'terminator' mode again.

'We've found what we wanted,' she continues aggressively. 'My brother was murdered because of Limarni, your damned diamond mine,' he can see her index finger tightening on the trigger. 'You make one false move, and I'll happily blow your fucking head off.'

Not knowing Adele as well as I do, he doesn't recognize the danger he's in.

'It the Chinese who murder Nick, you stupid bitch,' he fumes, reaching for the other gun in his holster. Quick as a flash, using her martial arts skills, she lunges forward, brutally pistol-whipping him across the face, followed immediately with a vicious kick to his crotch.

'Penny, grab his gun, give it to me.'

Nervously inching towards the groaning Jaro, bent double in agony, I gingerly take the gun from its holster and pass it to Adele. Examining it briefly, she tucks it into her belt.

'Now, Penny, get the tape out of my bag,' she points to the back of the room. 'Be quick as Saul may be here any minute.'

From his bent position, Jaro makes a sudden grab for Adele's ankle, but her reflexes are much quicker than his and she smartly steps aside, bringing the gun down hard on top of his head. He grimaces in pain, putting a hand on his latest injury which unwittingly gives Adele the opportunity to kick him in the groin again. With a horrifying yowl that would awaken the dead, he collapses in a foetal position on the floor. A few seconds later, a vehicle screeches to a halt outside the hut.

'Damn.' Holding the gun at her side, Adele slips quickly behind the door. 'Penny, hurry and tape Jaro up, I'll take care of the rest.'

Saul enters with an AK-47 slung over his shoulder. Seeing me taping up the prone Jaro, he halts in his tracks, but before he has chance to react, Adele steps behind him, placing the pistol barrel on the nape of his neck.

'Stand still,' she orders. 'Or you're dead.'

A mask of confusion crosses his face but on impulse, he turns to strike back at his attacker. She doesn't pull the trigger but swipes him hard across the side of his head. Crying out in pain, he reaches behind, grabbing her gun-hand, forcing it away from his head. Struggling together, chairs and tables clatter to the floor, their arms locked for a few seconds. But as Adele only has one good arm, his superior strength slowly forces the gun towards her. Moving sideways, she tries using her injured arm to reach the second gun tucked in her belt

246

but her hand gets snagged in the material. Leaving Jaro taped up, I see that Saul's about to overpower Adele. I know I must to do something, but what? I grab the nearest thing to hand, the whisky bottle. Whilst Saul is concentrating on wrenching the gun from Adele, I rush over and crash the bottle down on the side of his neck. It doesn't break but Adele has the chance to release his grip. She brings the gun down sharply on his head, not hard enough though as he immediately manages to grab her gun-arm again.

'Hit him harder,' she shouts.

In their frenetic struggle, it's difficult to find the right target. Sizing up my dilemma, Adele twists and attempts a kick, so that he briefly takes his eyes off me. I slip behind him and, using all my strength, whack him on the back of his skull. He staggers under the blow enabling Adele to free her arm, hitting him brutally with the gun. He slumps on the floor.

Breathing heavily, she shrieks. 'Quick,' and points at Jaro who's sitting up struggling to remove the tape from his wrists. Now I've got the hang of this *bashing business*, I bring the bottle down square on the top of his head. With glazed eyes full of hatred, his movements are sluggish so, for good measure, I aim again, this time the bottle smashes to smithereens. Gasping, he sinks to the floor, his blood, mixed with whisky splashes my face and chest.

Panting for breath, Adele and I look at each other, then at the two men. A triumphant smile briefly flickers across her face as she gently massages her injured arm.

Puffing like a steam engine, I manage to ask, 'Are we safe now?'

'Are you kidding?' a note of sarcasm in her reply. 'We've still got to get out of this fucking place and let's see, two men down, only a thousand to go.'

The squeak of the door handle turning makes us jump and Adele, holding both guns, stands behind the door which slowly opens. Noah pokes his head round.

'Is everything alright in … oh my God!' his eyes almost pop out of his head as he takes in the scene of the two men groaning on the floor while Adele's and my sweat-stained clothes are splattered with blood. 'Are you …?'

'We're okay, just about,' Adele replies.

'We've been waiting,' he stutters. 'We were told we could take Adele back to Monrovia but Penny wanted to stay and then we heard a noise and, er, what happened?'

Adele looks as if she's about to blow a fuse. 'You mean to say that you've been sitting outside whilst we've been fighting for our lives!' She looks heavenwards. 'God help us!'

Noah, looking anxiously at the enraged Adele, mumbles, 'What do we do now?'

'We get the hell out of this place,' she hollers. 'That's what we do now. Have you got the vehicle?'

Pulling himself together, he nods. 'Yes, Cooper and my men are outside.'

'What about your weapons?'

'No,' Noah shakes his head looking very uncomfortable. 'They took them.'

'Damn,' Adele scowls. 'We've only got Jaroslav's two revolvers and Saul's AK-47,' she curses under her breath. 'So with only three weapons between us, we have to somehow break out of this base.' She is seething, and an air of tension is developing between her and Noah.

In order to take the initiative, Noah thrusts back his shoulders as though being male and taller than us gives him indisputable authority. 'Before we leave,' he says, 'I think it's important that I take charge.'

'Hang on one fucking moment,' Adele's anger has reached boiling point. 'First of all, you brought us to this place not realizing the danger you were putting us in. Reggie knew and he warned against it, but oh no, you knew better. Secondly, while you and your men have been sitting on your fat arses timidly handing over your weapons, Penny and I have disabled Professor Baros, and got you released. So why would we put our faith in you?'

For a moment, he recoils from this bitter attack but, quickly gathering himself, straightens to his full height. 'Okay, things should have been handled better and I'm sorry for that, but I know the people and country and this is where my military training comes in. Don't forget, Adele, I was trained by your brother.'

'For God's sake you two,' I hastily intervene. 'Stop wasting time and let's get out of here, and,' looking directly at Adele, 'Noah should take charge.'

Taking her silence as a 'yes', he opens the door and calls for Moses and Jerbo to come, telling them to bind and gag Baros and Saul. He looks around for something useful to help our escape, but there's nothing. When Jaro and Saul are secure, he passes the AK-47 to Moses, and Adele gives Noah a hand gun.

'I've only got one good arm, so I'll keep this,' she states firmly, 'I'm certainly a better shot than any of you.'

It's Noah's turn to seethe but when he sees the tenacious glint in her eye, he prudently holds his tongue. Keeping his voice under control, he tells us to collect all our belongings and get in the vehicle very calmly as though nothing is amiss.

Picking up our bags, I lead the way out of the hut but, damn, Laylee immediately confronts me.

'Wha' happen? Why you leave now? Where my boss?'

'Everything is fine, Laylee.' I block her view into the room and try to give a relaxed smile, while the others close the door and get in the 4x4.

'Where my boss?' she repeats, her voice rising in alarm.

Climbing into the vehicle and practicing my Liberian English, I reply, *'e say, 'e sleep now. 'E call you when 'e wan' you, so you go now and we see you soon, Laylee, okay?'*

Cooper's instinct is to speed away, but Noah places his hand on the wheel telling him to drive without causing suspicion amongst the curious soldiers who are milling around.

Fingers crossed and holding my breath, I wave farewell to Laylee who ignores my gesture, not moving from the hut. As we drive off, she's knocking on the hut door shouting loudly, and after a few seconds, she opens it giving an almighty scream.

'Cooper,' Noah yells. 'Foot down hard, NOW.'

We race towards the camp exit at a breakneck speed, amidst a clamour of shouting and gun shots.

'Everyone down,' Noah barks as a direct hit shatters Cooper's side window. A trickle of blood runs down his face and he doesn't flinch as Noah leans across to pluck a shard of glass from his cheek. Nobody else is hurt but the sound of gunfire increases as we accelerate away.

'Colonel, we're being followed,' Moses shouts, unleashing a burst of fire at a pursuing vehicle. Our 4x4 is a hard-top convertible and to make it easier to get our shots away, Noah unclips the catches and pushes powerfully to loosen the roof, which immediately catches the wind and flies off with a *whoosh*.

Cooper, driving like a man possessed over the badly rutted road, skidding and swerving round every bend, kicking up vast clouds of dust, makes it impossible to get an accurate shot at those chasing us. Noah shouts to Moses to shoot only when he has a clear target, but the continuous sound of gunfire from behind keeps everyone, except the brave and bloodied Cooper, crouching on the floor.

I'm petrified. Holding on for dear life as we bounce up and down, this nightmarish journey continues for another fifteen minutes before Cooper performs a sliding left turn and we're once again on the paved road to Monrovia. He leans heavily on the horn, scattering pedestrians, cyclists and other vehicles in all directions. The dust has cleared and, peeking over the tailgate, I can see two jeeps full of armed soldiers gaining on us. I pray we can get to the first roadblock before they catch up.

I glimpse Moses exchanging fire with them, but with no effect. Cooper swerves erratically from side to side, which probably only serves to slow us down. Yelling at Cooper to drive straight, Noah keeps low using his handgun, but the combined fire-power has no result. They're now close enough to see the whites of their eyes.

'Penny,' Adele shouts. 'Hold onto me.' I grab her tightly around the waist as she opens her door and leans out, a revolver in her good hand. She fires three rapid shots and I look up to see the leading jeep's front tyre exploding into shreds. The driver, unable to control its momentum, screams as it hurtles off the road into a ditch. Pulling Adele back into the vehicle, she curses loudly as I haul on her bad arm.

'We nearly there,' Cooper shouts excitedly and turning, I see the heavily fortified roadblock in the near distance. The remaining chasing vehicle stops. Relief floods over me and I burst into tears.

'Well done, everyone,' Noah calls. 'They aren't equipped to tackle the UN peacekeepers.'

Still panting and clearly in pain, Adele, summoning up a mischievous smile says to me. 'There, I told you it would be easy.'

'Easy!' I holler, 'Easy!' I've never felt like strangling anyone in cold blood before but I do now. 'We could have been killed,' I yell even louder at her. 'They were shooting at us or didn't you notice that you, you ...'

Before I completely lose it, Noah diplomatically butts in. 'We'll be safe from hereon so you can both relax.' He checks his watch. 'We should be in Monrovia by seven, Cooper can drop me off at the Executive Mansion and then take you on to the Cleopatra. I suggest you both get a good night's sleep and we'll have a recap, a council of war at ten tomorrow morning. Will that be okay?'

'Yes, Noah,' replies the unruffled Adele. 'Ten will be fine.'

CHAPTER TWENTY-FIVE
FEBRUARY 27th

Lying in bed, punching and turning my pillow, the constant whine of insects circling over my mosquito net is driving me crazy. I've just had the two most traumatic days of my life, nothing has ever come close to what I went through. Questions won't stop buzzing around my brain but, in the next bed, a gentle, soothing snore is emanating from Adele so, lucky her, she's clearly untroubled.

One of the many worries keeping me awake is, strangely, not being Jaro's hostage. Noah will be able to reveal to the government the location and value of Jaro's diamond mine, not paltry iron ore. The mad bastard will panic now, frightened he'll lose his mine and quickly mount his promised coup which will result in innocent people becoming that oft-used cliché, *collateral damage*, in other words, dead.

Anyway, to hell with all that, I've had enough. All I want is to get out of this place as quickly as possible and, oh, I don't know, probably go and hide away with my parents and try to blank out the last couple of months. Ha, they don't even know I'm pregnant ... that'll be a nice surprise for them, not.

I must have nodded off for suddenly, I'm shaking from head to toe, tears are streaming down my face soaking my pillow. What's wrong? Taking a deep breath, I wrap my arms tightly around my body trying to control my quivering, but it won't stop.

'Adele,' I call softly, so as not to startle her. There's no response, so I reach under her mosquito net and poke her shoulder. 'Adele, wake up.'

Her drowsy answer is unclear but I manage to pick out something ending in *off*.

'Adele.' This time, I give her a thump.

Rubbing her eyes, she moans. 'What are you doing?'

Through chattering teeth I stutter, 'I'm ill, look at me, I'm shaking all over.'

It takes a few more seconds before she puts on her bedside light, staggers out of bed and looks at me. 'Bloody hell!' she exclaims, her eyes wide open now. 'What's the matter with you?'

'I don't know.'

'Have you been taking malaria pills?'

'Of course, never missed.'

Still in a mood, she places her hand on my forehead. 'You don't feel hot so it's not a fever. Have you got a headache or any other aches and pains?'

'No, I just feel poorly and,' I sob, 'I'm crying for my baby.'

'Oh no!' now she looks alarmed. 'You haven't lost it, have you?'

'No, but what's all this doing to the poor little blighter? Do you think I should see a doctor?'

'A doctor!' she exclaims. 'At two o'clock in the morning? I could wake Bachir but I don't think he'll be able to help at this time of night.' She gives me an embrace. 'It's probably post-trauma survivor euphoria, soldiers get it, delayed shock after all you've been through. I'll make you a cup of strong, sweet tea to see if that helps.'

Still quivering with the shakes, Adele helps me hold the cup to my mouth.

'Look,' she says, sounding reassuringly calm. 'This is what we'll do.'

I sit on the edge of the bed listening.

'We'll get a doctor first thing. I'm sure either Bachir or Noah can arrange something, and after that, you can get the first plane back to England.'

'Yes please,' I whimper, feeling better just knowing I can go home.

'Get back into bed,' she orders. 'Try to get some sleep.'

I do as I'm told. Within a couple of minutes, she resumes snoring but I only manage to drop off sporadically. After half-dozing for a time, I check my watch, it's ten-to-six, at least I must have slept for a bit. My shivering is not so severe, thank God, but I'm wide awake and there's no way I'm going back to sleep. Quietly, getting out of bed, I totter unsteadily to the window. Moving the curtain to one side, I'm bathed in the light of the pale morning sun, burnishing the red and purple bougainvillea into a blaze of colour. The dawn chorus has started with chirping weaver birds flitting into the towering palms, whilst other birds of various hues and brilliance are busily searching for a breakfast of insects. In different circumstances, I would marvel at this scene but all I want to do is turn away, protecting my swollen eyes from the glare.

Placing both hands on my belly, I wonder how my tiny baby is coping. As soon as I get back to England, I'll see a doctor; it's not too late for a termination if it's damaged. I know I keep thinking that but I like the idea of having Nick's baby - I must have maternal feelings after all. Anyhow, whatever it is, it'll be stuffed full of Holbrook genes which will definitely make it a fighter.

My restless moving around the room wakens Adele. Pulling back the mosquito net, she stretches making a face as her left arm still hurts. 'Hey,' she says, 'I think you're looking a bit better. I'll get dressed and go and ask Bachir to get a doctor. You go back to bed.'

Less than fifteen minutes later, the door opens, revealing not Bachir but Adele, followed by a self-conscious Noah. Hastily, I pull the sheet up to cover my gaping nightgown.

'Penny, out of the blue, the plane's arrived to take us to Guinea,' she says. 'Noah and I are leaving with his men in half an hour.'

'But what about Jaro and the coup?' I stutter. 'That should come first?'

'No, it's all right,' Noah confirms. 'We'll go now and return quickly, we only have the plane for two days. Last night, I reported everything to the President and her senior military officers, so mobilization of army contingents is already underway along the Freetown road and Bushrod Island. Even if Baros is planning a coup, it will take him at least a week to assemble his forces and weaponry. Logistically, it's a big job.'

'Will you manage without me?'

'Of course we will,' laughs Adele. 'You're in no state.'

Giving a polite cough, Noah says, 'I'll ask Bachir to arrange for you to see my doctor. Hopefully, we'll be back this evening but it may take a second day to find and rescue Charles Temple.'

'And I'll phone you by satellite when we get there,' Adele says as she packs her special bag. 'A day of rest will do you and the baby a lot of good.'

With the hurried farewell, they rush away on what is, after all, the other reason for us being here in Liberia - to rescue Adele's brother, Charles. That's if he's still alive, of course, and if Bambara's information is correct. I think it's all a bit flimsy but it's got to be tried. I'm disappointed I won't be with them but that's me being silly. Almost three months pregnant and feeling unwell, I would definitely get in the way. I'm not a *force of nature* like Adele.

Jolted awake by the creaking of the bedroom door, Bachir, holding it ajar with his knee, carries in a breakfast tray. 'Mr Grosvenor-Smythe is sending his car for you in half an hour,' he announces, 'to see his doctor.'

'Reggie!'I exclaim. 'But Colonel Tofa said he would arrange that.'

Bachir shrugs indifferently. 'That's the message.'

I was going to tell him that I'm feeling better and don't need a doctor, but he's gone.

I'm only a couple of minutes late. Standing in Reception is a uniformed chauffeur who, clearly trained by Reggie, doffs his cap, bows and politely asks, 'Miss Penny Lane?'

'Yes.' A few yards behind him is one of the most elegant women I've ever seen. Having the stylish bearing of a model, she is dressed in a shimmering emerald green silk dress, short enough to show shapely calves, teamed up with high-heeled sandals. She has aquiline, almost European features and her jet black hair is held in place with an elaborate headpiece in the same colour silk. Matching eye shadow completes the remarkable image. Most Liberian's skin tones vary between mid to dark brown, but this lady is startlingly black which serves to enhance the brilliant colouring of her outfit.

She graciously extends her hand. 'Good morning Miss Lane, I'm Coralie Grosvenor-Smythe.'

Trying not to stare, I mumble. 'Yes, I am she.' Oh my God, if it's possible to grimace internally, then I just did. Gathering my composure, I continue, 'Yes, my associate, Adele Holbrook and I have had the pleasure of your husband's companionship here at the Cleopatra.' God, here I go again, what on earth's wrong with me?

'Reggie told me you've not been very well and he asked me to take you for a check-up to the Marguerite Clinic. One can't be too careful with one's health, and after that I'd be delighted if you join me for a drink and chat.'

Whilst the contrast in appearance between Reggie and Coralie couldn't be more different, in fact chalk and cheese doesn't even get close, her manner of speaking is so like Reggie's that it could be cloned ... if that's possible.

Feeling exceedingly scruffy, I follow the driver as he leads us out of Reception. The vehicle is parked in the reserved shaded bay and I know I should be flabbergasted but, with all that's happened to me recently, I'm way past the *surprise-stage* with anything. The car we approach is a silver-grey Rolls Royce. Feeling a bit awkward, I sit at the back on the cool, leather seat next to Coralie, whilst the chauffeur, unsurprisingly called James, silently glides the limousine towards the hotel's heavily guarded exit. I was half expecting her to say, *"home James and don't spare the horses"*, but that's me - put it down to the fever.

Sneaking a sidelong glance, I see she isn't quite as young as I'd first thought. Judging by the light wrinkles around her eyes and mouth, and a slight slackness of her neck, I guess she's probably in her late forties, but still fantastic looking.

'Reggie tells me that you and Miss Holbrook have had some exciting moments since you arrived,' she gives a pleasant laugh.

'I'm Penny and yes, we've had a few incidents and I think that's what caused my health problems last night. Too much excitement giving my nervous system a battering especially as my hormones are all over the place. I'm pregnant.'

'Congratulations,' she gives my arm a squeeze. 'But please take more care now, it would be a tragedy to lose Nicholas's child.'

My mouth gapes for the second time. 'I didn't realize you were so well informed.'

'Oh yes, Reggie has many sources and he may have already told you that Nicholas was one of the very few foreigners who genuinely tried to help Liberia, unlike those expat parasites you see most of the time.'

Creasing my brow, I say, 'I'm not sure I follow.'

'You will have seen expats at the Cleopatra,' she smiles. 'What do you think of them?'

It's my turn to smile now. 'Oh, I see what you mean, yes, most of the time they're either on the beach or drinking at the bar.'

She nods. 'Yet they are well paid *so-called* experts sent out by aid agencies, charities and foreign businesses to get Liberia back on its feet after the two civil wars. They're supposed to be highly skilled and motivated, but poor Reggie despairs at times.'

'So what's the problem?'

'Mainly that the calibre of expats is so poor. Liberia has such a bad reputation and it doesn't attract the best people, except the Chinese unfortunately.'

'Oh dear, poor Reggie and poor Liberia.'

'Because he's a westerner and has built up a solid reputation, many overseas agencies employ him to coordinate their activities and steer them towards the right people, mainly in government. At least he's well paid for his troubles.'

Aha, hence the Rolls.

'Over six billion dollars has come into the country since Mrs Poltara became president,' she continues, 'Reggie, how should I put it, receives handling fees to make sure the money goes to the right cause.'

I nod to show I understand, which I don't really, but it appears that although Liberia is losing out on that development, Reggie at least is a winner.

'To me,' there's a slight catch in Coralie's voice and her enigmatic smile could mean anything, 'Nicholas was one in a million.'

Mmm, interesting.

'And I'm so pleased he found love with you before his untimely death. Reggie and I were devastated.'

'Yes, we all were.'

Still apparently lost in a far-away memory, she continues, 'Nicholas was one of the few people, the like of which you only meet once or twice in a lifetime.' Slowly, her eyes well-up. 'He was an English gentleman,' she romanticizes then, quickly regaining control, adds, 'I was lucky to marry Reggie, one of the best,' she says demurely, 'And you also with Nicholas.'

'Did you know Nick well?' I ask, wondering just how well.

Hesitating for a fraction, she explains, 'Reggie brought him to the house I think, oh, maybe three or four times, and I also met him at the Cleopatra once or twice.'

I try to hide a smile - Coralie and Nick! It's pretty obvious she had the *hots* for him, maybe it was mutual. Ooh, I wonder if Reggie knew?

Coralie seems to realize she's said too much and quickly asks. 'How did you meet Nicholas?'

I don't want to shatter her illusion by saying I'd only had a drug-induced *one-night stand* with him, followed by dinner and two luncheons before he was murdered, so I lie. 'It was last year sometime, a special kind of evening and our eyes met across the room and somehow I knew we'd get together.' Bloody hell, I'm almost singing excerpts from *"Some Enchanted Evening"* Ah, but that's how I wish it had been.

Still a little tearful, Coralie sniffles. 'That's a lovely story but I, er, mean *we* miss him very much.' Poor Coralie, she most probably knew him better than me.

'We here, madam,' James fortunately interrupts what was becoming a tricky conversation by bringing the car to a stop outside a small, whitewashed concrete building with *Marguerite Clinic* in large, peeling letters above the door. Set back from the adjacent properties, the small front garden, more like waste ground, is strewn with litter. James rushes round, vainly trying to shoo away the cripples and beggars patiently waiting for handouts. Opening the car doors lets in the hot, humid air with its dank, fusty smell enveloping us like an old, clammy blanket.

'Thank you, James.' Coralie reaches into her designer handbag and thrusts one US dollar bill into each grasping hand. I feel awkward as I'd left my money belt in the hotel. 'The poor Liberian dollar,' Coralie sighs, shaking her head. 'It's devalued so much that now, the American money I've given will feed them for a week.'

Initially, I'm impressed with her generosity but then think maybe she could do more. I've often questioned myself on the morality of being one of the privileged in a world full of poverty, but never come up with a good enough answer. Already perspiring, we walk the few yards to the entrance. Coralie takes my arm as we enter the clinic's overcrowded waiting room. It's unpleasantly oppressive, combining an aroma of stale, body odour blended with antiseptic. At the end is a Reception desk manned by a harassed uniformed nurse.

'Tell Kit we're here,' Coralie announces regally, not missing a step while proceeding to a door marked 'Private'. Without waiting for permission, we go into a small, cool, anteroom. 'Have a seat, Penny, Kit will be here in a second. He's very well qualified, you know, trained in Berlin,' which probably is her way of giving me confidence in a local male doctor.

After just a few seconds, a side door opens and a distinguished-looking man wearing doctor's garb enters, deferentially acknowledging Coralie's arrival.

'Now then Kit,' she says, turning to me. 'This young English lady, Miss Penny Lane, wasn't very well last night and I want you to give her a thorough check. She's a special guest of ours and we want her back to full health as soon as possible. We're in a hurry for an important luncheon engagement, so kindly attend to her straight away, there's a good chap.'

With a slight bow, he gestures me to follow him into a nearby office; thankfully, Coralie has the good manners not to join us. At first, I find Dr Kit agreeable and we are soon joined by a young, white, buxom nurse, Gretchen. After describing my symptoms, including the pregnancy, he seems to lose interest and only spends a couple of minutes asking questions, some of which seem pointless.

He speaks to Gretchen in broken German. 'Another of that woman's deadbeats,' using the word *miststuck* to describe me. I'm about to angrily object but, just in time, realize that the stupid man assumes I don't understand what he's saying, so I stay silent.

He casually checks my blood pressure, wires me up for an ECG while managing to fondle my bosom through my bra and then, using his stethoscope, sounds out various parts of my upper anatomy, again concentrating on my breasts. All the time he's fondling away, Gretchen stands smirking in the background. It's then her job to take a blood sample, I think she deliberately hurts me, and he finishes by saying a full report will be sent to me at the Cleopatra by noon tomorrow. Rudely staring as I fasten my dress, he probably makes the biggest mistake of his life, speaking again in German to a simpering Gretchen. 'She is an English *miststuck* and can *lutsch meinen schwanz*. I've only gone along with the charade to satisfy the pompous English buffoon and his ludicrous wife.'

Gretchen giggles.

Outraged, I can't resist telling them, in fluent German, that the '*miststuck*' is leaving and they will, no doubt, hear from the Grosvenor-Smythe buffoons in due course. As I stalk out of the office, the two horror-struck individuals stand rooted to the spot.

On the way to the Grosvenor-Smythe's house in the Rolls, I tell Coralie everything Kit did and said, particularly the German conversation.

'The absolute stinker,' she says contemptuously. 'So that's how we're viewed by Herr Doctor Kit and his assistant. Reggie always felt there was something not quite pukka about old Kit, and thanks to you, we now know the truth. So you speak German?'

'Yes, that was my job in England, I'm a linguist.'

'Oh marvellous,' she smiles. 'What other languages do you speak?'

'I'm equally fluent in French and I can converse moderately well in at least eight other European languages. And then there's Mandarin Chinese.'

'What an amazing young lady you are. That makes you a polyglot.'

I laugh. 'Yes, that's right, languages are the only real gift I have. I struggled at school with everything else but foreign tongues have always come easily to me.'

'Ah, but how about Liberian English?'

'I'm doing quite well, partly because I know from my studies that most African words end in soft vowels, whilst the hard English consonants are dropped.'

'You do learn fast,' she laughs. 'Oh, by the way, what with everything else we've been discussing, I forgot to ask how you're feeling.'

'A little drained and lacking sleep, but I'm sure Kit was genuine when he confirmed that my temperature is normal, my blood pressure is spot on and he found nothing wrong with my ECG so, I feel a bit of a fraud.'

'Nonsense,' she says. 'The results of the blood test may show something. It's a big mistake to ignore any kind of medical problem here in the tropics. Many people do and every year we hear of expats dying through their own carelessness. And with you being pregnant.'

'For what it's worth, Kit didn't find any problem in that area, he was more interested in feeling my boobs than my belly.'

She squeezes my arm, it seems to be her favourite gesture of giving reassurance.

Turning sharply off the main road, James manoeuvres the Rolls down a curved driveway and two security guards salute as they open the heavily-barred gates. 'Ah, here we are,' Coralie says as we glide to a gentle halt outside a substantial two-storey house; so much for their *modest dwelling*. Two Corinthian pillars support a vivid blue tiled canopy, under which a short flight of steps leads to the front door, promptly opened by a liveried servant. It reminds me of a scene from *The Great Gatsby*.

Entering the spacious hall, I'm surprised to see a stack of chests and wooden boxes.

'I'm leaving Liberia tomorrow,' Coralie explains. 'Off to our villa in the South of France, and we're putting all our valuables into storage. Reggie will follow as soon as he can.'

Thinking it strange that she hadn't already mentioned it, I ask, 'Is it anything to do with the rumour of a coup?'

She confirms this by nodding. 'We always leave Liberia for several months around mid-April to avoid the rains, but Reggie decided to bring it forward, you know, just in case. Coups and civil wars can break out without warning and the next thing you know the airports are closed.' Pausing for a moment, she takes my hand in hers and, looking directly into my eyes says, 'Penny, you should leave Liberia as soon as possible.'

'Yes, I will, Adele said the same thing to me this morning.'

'Good, I'm pleased about that.'

Passing untidy piles of chests and boxes in the entrance hall, Coralie leads me through into a living room with four ceiling fans whirling around at high speed. Straight ahead, shaded by a pale blue awning are French windows, opening out onto a colourful garden. Exotic, flowery scents drifting in on the light breeze. Looking around the room, I'm amazed to see a sunken area in the centre, roughly twelve feet square with padded benches on three sides.

Unintentionally staring at the *hole*, Coralie watches me with a look of amusement. Taking my arm, she guides me down the three steps. 'We call it our conversation pit,' she gives a tinkling laugh. 'It's actually a very cosy place to chat to friends and have a beverage or two. And talking about drinks, what would you like? Our steward makes delicious lemonade which is very refreshing on days like this.'

Sitting in the *pit*, waving an arm, pointing or resting her chin on her hand, all her movements are graceful. The conversation turns to Adele and the mission to rescue her brother. How much of the story Reggie has told Coralie I can't be sure but I tell her that every time Nick came to Africa, he'd search from the Congo, through central and West Africa for any trace of Charles, a couple of leads in the past turning out to be false.

Sighing, Coralie agrees. 'I know a bit about this and the many lies people tell to claim reward money without producing any firm information.'

'Yes,' I sigh, close to tears. 'Poor Nick. On his last visit to Liberia earlier this year, he received what he thought was positive information that Charles was being held in Guinea. Noah questioned the informant thoroughly and it appeared to be genuine.'

Frowning, Coralie takes a few seconds before speaking. 'Your friend Noah, Colonel Tofa, has a checkered history in Liberia, especially while Jacob Marcam was commander-in-chief. So please be careful.'

'Yes, we heard something along those lines from Bachir Gemayel at the Cleopatra, but in his last letter to me, Nick said I should to trust Noah completely. In fact, Nick was in charge of training an elite force similar to the SAS in UK, with Noah as the senior officer.'

'Reggie feels the jury's still out on how effective that will be,' Coralie comments dryly.

'Well obviously, Reggie will know more than me but anyway, Noah used his influence with President Poltara and was granted the use of a plane. He, his men and Adele should be arriving in Guinea any moment now, after making a stop at a place called something like Yakapoo, to pick up the brother of the informant, a Mandingo called Bambara.'

'It's Yekepa, a big iron ore complex near the Guinea border.'

'Yes, that's it, so I'm now anxiously waiting for some news. Adele said she'll phone me this evening.'

Emptying her glass, Coralie says, 'I do hope Adele is successful in finding her brother. Please let Reggie know the minute you have some news.'

'Yes, of course I will.'

Elegantly smoothing down her dress, she smiles. 'You and Adele like Reggie, don't you?

Is this a leading question? 'He's been brilliant in helping us, especially today,' I cautiously reply.

'I'm so pleased to hear it. Meeting you both has meant a lot to him, particularly as you're both Holbrooks ... if you see what I mean. It's been such a change from the business people he usually meets.'

'I'm glad.'

Wavering a second, her smile turns into a giggle. 'Did Reggie tell you how he got his OBE?'

'No, he didn't, but we were both impressed.'

'Well,' she giggles. 'He won't mind you knowing. About ten years ago when the British had an embassy here, the Ambassador, Randolf Coker, affectionately known as Randy Cock, was caught, pants down, in a seedy downtown bar, with a young lady claiming rape.'

'Oh, my gosh, the Ambassador!'

'Yes. The police were there and he would have been for the high jump, end of career sort of thing, but Reggie was able to pull a few strings and everything was swept under the carpet. At the end of that year, Reggie got his gong for "Services to the British Industry".'

'What a wonderful story,' I laugh. 'So that's how these things work.'

'Yes, but keep it under your hat.' Still smiling, she puts a finger up to her lips.

She stands. 'Unfortunately, my dear, I have a lot of last minute arrangements to make. I apologize for cutting short our extremely pleasant meeting.'

Walking with her to the door, I ask what could be a cheeky question. 'Coralie, if you don't mind my saying, you look different from all the other Liberian ladies I've met.'

This makes her chuckle. 'That's because I'm originally from Ethiopia. My father was their ambassador to the Court of St James in London and I was educated for eight years at Roedean. After university, I joined the Ethiopian Foreign Office and was part of a delegation to Liberia, and that's when I met Reggie and, well,' she laughs. 'We fell in love.'

'So it was love at first sight, just like Nick and me.'

Smiling, her voice falters again. 'Yes, it was,' she says wistfully, 'Just like you and Nick.'

James, lolling drowsily against the Rolls, smartly comes to attention. Coralie kisses me on both cheeks, thanking me again for giving her the lowdown on the deceitful Dr Kit. 'Now, Penny, let me say once again that you should go home as soon as you can but don't forget, you and Adele Holbrook have an open invitation to our villa in the South of France or, probably more conveniently, our apartment in London.'

Wow, I think to myself, they really are filthy rich. 'That's very kind of you, Coralie. You and Reggie are two of the most amazing people I've ever met.'

I wave from the back seat as James drives out through the gates past dilapidated shacks. The phrase *a country of contrasts* shoots into my thoughts because what bigger contrast can there be than here in Liberia with the innumerable cripples, beggars and the squalid slums, compared to the phenomenal wealth of the likes of the Grosvenor- Smythes. I find it hard to get my head round. Africa receives billions in aid from the developed world, but instead of it spreading wealth throughout the population, it only magnifies the gulf between rich and poor.

CHAPTER TWENTY-SIX
FEBRUARY 28th

Although the Cleopatra's shower is refreshingly cool and is helping me to unwind, I feel alone and uneasy without Adele. I can't help worrying about her and only hope that Noah knows his stuff on this trip to Guinea, especially as he didn't cover himself in glory during our ordeal at Baros's mine. Anyway, I know there's no stopping Adele.

The water is now running lukewarm which is perfect for shampooing my hair and soaping myself from head to toe. Taking time to dry off, I let the towel slip and look at myself in the floor length mirror. Was it only two months ago that I'd prided myself on a trim 34, 22, 36, figure which I've kept for the last fifteen years? Now my boobs have suddenly grown and what had been my diminutive waist has definitely started to thicken. I fervently hope that the poor little blighter in there thrives on adrenalin because it's had far more than its fair share. Turning round, I'm not surprised to see a large, angry bruise on my bum, the result of bouncing up and down on the floor of the 4x4. I smile - my bum suffered to protect my bump.

The phone rings, it's Bachir telling me that Reginald Grosvenor-Smyth is in the hotel. Reggie, and now Coralie as well, seem genuinely concerned about us.

Feeling clean and refreshed, I enter the bar just as the tropical sun is setting, dramatically turning the sea to orange. A few people are sitting at the bar and Reggie, in splendid isolation, is overlooking the darkening garden.

'Good evening, dear lady, I trust you are in fine fettle.' Screwing his monocle firmly in place, he gives his customary bow. 'My dear wife enjoyed meeting you today.'

'It was very kind of you both to arrange my medical check. I'm sure Kit is a good doctor but, as I discovered, not a very nice person.'

'Indeed, I feel I should apologise for that rapscallion, he's as two faced as Ludlum's dog.'

Outwardly Reggie, as always, appears friendly and eccentric but I sense a certain tension in him. On cue, Momo arrives with a bottle of whisky, water and an ice bucket. Reggie pours a generous amount for himself and, for me, ice and water with a splash of whisky. 'Coralie informed me that you're planning to leave Liberia soon which, giving consideration to your condition, is a very wise move.' Sitting back in his chair, nursing his glass, he rubs his chin in quiet deliberation. 'It is also my understanding that you, Miss Holbrook and your devoted Colonel were involved in a spot of bother with Professor Baros.'

'Yes, we were.' Once again, he seems to know everything that's happened to us.

'Importantly, did you have a debrief after the heroic act?'

'A debrief? Oh, I see, no. Noah had planned to meet us this morning but, unexpectedly, the plane arrived to take them to Guinea, you know, to find Adele's brother, so we had to delay the debrief for a day or two. However, he has filed his report with the top brass.'

'I see,' he takes a large swallow from his glass. 'I'd be grateful if you'd kindly humour me for a moment, dear lady, as I have the feeling that there's more to your trip to Liberia than you first revealed and, if the ominous distant rumblings I'm picking up are to be believed, then I suggest you enlighten me now, before un-foretold events have dire consequences.'

I blink at him, unsure of what to say. 'We have been honest with you, Reggie,' I falter, 'Er absolutely, but we might have missed out, well, not told you everything we knew about Professor Baros's mine, the potential value of it, diamonds, if you see what I mean.'

His eyebrows give their routine jig as he fiddles with his monocle. 'Pray continue.'

Feeling a little uncomfortable, I recount the events of the last thirty-six hours, even the sordid, but failed sex encounter with Baros, his plan to hold me hostage, and concluding with our breakneck escape. Throughout my story, he watches me carefully, one hand cupping his chin while trailing his stubby index finger across his lips.

'Hmm, quite an adventure - *Acta est fubula*.' Removing his monocle, his eyebrows droop as he closes his eyes in thought. 'So Professor Baros's so-called iron ore mine is a cover for a diamond mine?'

'Yes, he says it'll be far more valuable than the Kimberley mine.'

Pursing his lips, he asks, 'Is he barking mad?'

'No, I don't think so. Considering he's hardly scratched the surface and already mined rough stones worth several million dollars, we think it's right. After all, he is an internationally renowned geologist.'

Reggie gives a silent whistle. 'And that,' he murmurs more to himself than to me, 'Answers the question of why the Chinese are poking around. The Professor clearly believes the Chinese would bribe ah, that's an ugly word, would encourage the country's leaders to pass the mine over to them for a suitable consideration. Knowing the Chinese track record in other countries, he's almost certainly right.'

'Yes, and Nick felt the same way too,' I add.

'Did he?' Reggie smiles at this last statement. 'And you are saying the Professor has already sent mercenaries to spring Jacob Marcam out of jail so that together, they would mount a coup and take over the government with the sole aim of protecting his mine.' His voice sounds worried although it's difficult to tell from his impassive expression. 'As long as the South Africans keep Marcam in the high security prison, then it would be extremely difficult but, if his terms of incarceration are relaxed, then they may well have a chance.'

'That's what Baros told us. Do you think it's possible?'

'Mercenaries will carry out their evil deeds for the piper who plays the tune ... and pays them well.' Downing another whisky, he absentmindedly refills my glass. 'But now that Baros knows that you, Miss Holbrook and the good Colonel are onto his secret, he'll be reluctant to wait for Marcam. And judging from your story which, you say, the Colonel has reported to his chiefs, your inopportune intervention may well be responsible for him *unleashing the dogs of war*.'

'The dogs of, oh! I see what you mean yes, that's what we fear, and it's partly my fault. If we hadn't gone to find Baros's mine, we ...'

'No, no, it might be a blessing because it will push the professor into acting sooner than he would have liked, his plot will not be as well organised because, no doubt, he was planning a surprise attack. However, it won't be a surprise now and the Liberian army contingents, limited though they are, can nail their colours to the mast and seal off the only road leading to Monrovia.'

The peace in the bar is interrupted as half a dozen noisy young men, accompanied by two giggling women burst in. I recognised this crowd as they prop-up the bar most evenings.

Grimacing, Reggie rises to his feet. ''Tis time I left you, dear lady, in the doubtful company of these heroes of the aid industry, and return to provide my inadequate assistance to Coralie before she departs these shores.'

'Of course, Reggie, please wish her a safe journey from me.'

'I most certainly will, thank you. You have my home number so please keep me informed on the fortunes of Miss Holbrook.'

Going to my room, I glance at my watch for the umpteenth time, ten past nine, damn, I'm giving up hope of hearing from Adele. There are probably a hundred and one things that could go haywire with their plans and I'm beginning to fear the worst and ah, hang on, my Sat phone rings. Snatching it up, all I can hear is few seconds of shattering static then very faintly, Adele's voice shouting down the line.

'We're camped at the edge of an airstrip in Guinea,' she yells. 'With Bambara's brother and he's told us a white man is being held at a nearby mining project and, guess what? It's operated by the Chinese.'

'Is it definitely Charles?' I shout back.

The reception again goes awry, and although I can hear a distant voice, I can't make out anything before the line goes dead. Well, at least they arrived safely but still no proof that Charles is alive or even if he's where Bambara says he is. I'll have to wait until tomorrow, no good worrying now.

Waking up refreshed after a good night's sleep, I put on some make-up and do what I can with my hair before appearing for breakfast. Surprisingly, the restaurant is quieter than usual. I wonder if the word is out about the expected coup? I sit at my favourite table on the balcony overlooking the palm-fringed lagoon, and the choppy blue sea beyond. It's a *view to die for,* which I've always thought was a silly expression. Anyway whatever, it is beautiful.

Bachir strides towards me just as I'm finishing breakfast, curtly announcing that I'm wanted on the phone, before scurrying off without saying who it is. Damn. It can't be Adele because she'd use the Sat phone. Maybe its Dr Kit saying my blood test shows I've only a few days to live ha, he'd love that. Lifting the receiver, I'm relieved to hear Reggie's voice greeting me with his usual eloquence.

'May I be so bold as to ask your general state of health on this happy morn?'

Happy morn? With his wife leaving today coupled with his fear of an imminent coup I don't think so. Trying to sound positive, I say, 'Thank you, Reggie, I'm feeling a lot better.'

'And pray tell me, what news of the brave duo seeking out Miss Holbrook's brother in the Republic of Guinea.'

'I heard from Adele late last night. She and Noah have arrived in Guinea near to where Charles is supposedly being held. Unfortunately, it's too early to know whether anything Bambara's brother said is true.'

'Yes, I understand,' his voice is suitably sombre.

'Reggie, do you have any news about Baros and his planned coup?'

'All I know is that there's a lot of activity around the mine compound and the powers that be are taking it very seriously, marshalling their brave troops at various stages on the Freetown Road, and vainly trying to get the UN peacekeepers to play their part.'

'But isn't that their job, to keep the peace?'

'Yes indeed, that's what any normal person would surmise, but our valiant, blue-bereted warriors think otherwise. They see their role here as more or less bluffing, posturing, carrying big guns and deflowering young virgins and, most importantly, collecting a generous bounty from the UN. Any idea of laying down their lives for Africans is, I'm afraid, way off beam.'

'But that's crazy, Reggie, and you make it sound, well, distasteful.'

'Indeed, they don't see Africans as a noble race worth fighting for. In fact, they have a well stocked library of excuses for such occasions, so they'll probably say that they can't get involved in internal politics. From past experience, I know they'll make their own carefully-edited film showing their UN paymasters just how bravely they've tried to keep the peace, the fabrication of which will reach Oscar levels of fiction.'

Condensing his diatribe, I say, 'So what you're saying is that they'll just stand by and let the rebel army take on the government troops and march into Monrovia.'

'That would be my assumption.'

'And who do you think would win?'

'That, dear lady, is a hard one to call, but your contemptible acquaintance, Professor Baros is, I believe, smart enough not to attempt an offensive if he thinks he'll lose, he'll choose his timing carefully and use Marcam's supporters lying low here in Monrovia, to act as fifth columnists when he decides to attack.'

I shake my head, trying to imagine the carnage that could start at any moment.

'If I may change the subject,' I hear a throaty chuckle on the other end of the line. 'My beloved Coralie informs me that you are a skilled linguist and suggests that if you're ever in the market for an interesting and rewarding career, you are exactly the person I'm looking for. A great many of my business transactions are with, how should I delicately phrase this? I know, pesky foreign wallahs.'

This makes me laugh. 'That's probably the best offer I've ever had, Reggie, but I'm sure you'll understand there are a few pressing matters to attend to first.'

'Of course, dear lady, of course. These are the worst of times.'

'Thank you for calling, Reggie. As soon as Adele and Noah return, I'm sure he'll be able to find out what's happening from a military point of view.'

'You are correct,' he then hesitates slightly. 'That's on the basis that he returns safely.'

Concerned by that, I ask what he means.

'Your bold young Colonel is taking a huge risk. If he's caught by the Guineans, he will either be shot or incarcerated for life. He knows this as well as anyone and he's only taken on this hazardous mission because of his loyalty to the late Nicholas Holbrook.'

Distressed and deep in thought, I leave Reception and without thinking, find myself strolling down the narrow path leading to the beach. Kicking off my shoes, enjoying the warmth of the sand between my toes, I make my way towards the sea, leaving footprints which, I pretend, are being left by the first person ever to walk here. I'm brought back to the present by the heat of the sun bearing down harshly on my uncovered head.

Distracted by excited voices, I turn towards the lagoon where the young people who were whooping it up in the bar last night, are swimming and sunbathing. The two young women, wearing skimpy bikinis, look as though they haven't a care in the world, flirting with the men as they race into the lagoon, splashing and spraying each other like children. I wonder to myself which charity or aid organization is paying for their exotic holiday, yet a part of me feels jealous of these girls and the lascivious attention they are receiving. Deep down, something within me would love to rip off my dress, and join in the frivolity, casting each care away with every splash of water that sprays high into the bright blue sky, blotting out the fact that I'm getting old and carrying the unborn child of my dead lover.

Heading back to the hotel, I wistfully concede that my chances of carefree frolicking have no place in my present world of worry and dread.

CHAPTER TWENTY-SEVEN
MARCH 1st

Worrying about Adele, I have an early night but lie awake questioning what the hell's happening to me. I keep thinking back to my dreary existence in a boring job translating mind-numbing French and German bureaucratic crappage. Chloé, forever the joker in the office, defined crappage as mindless EU directives, translated into thirty national lexicons, and never to see the light of day - and that summed up my fifteen year career in a nutshell.

Closing my eyes trying to drift off to sleep, the Sat phone rings, setting my nerves jangling in the silence of the room.

'Penny?'

'Yes,' I shout against a background of static.

'Listen,' Adele yells, 'do not interrupt. We've made contact with the Samla tribe. They were forced off their land by the Chinese-backed Guinea army. The Chinese built a huge copper mine on Samla land and it's poisoning the environment, the waterways, everything. The Samla will help us get into the mine before dawn tomorrow and we'll rescue Charles if he's there, then the Samla will destroy the whole complex.'

'Destroy it, why do that?' I forget I'm not supposed to interrupt.

'That's all, I'll call tomorrow.' The line goes dead.

The drummer in my head plays a five stroke roll against my temples as I mull over what Adele said. I had hoped they'd be on their way back by now.

It's not yet six-thirty but I'm hungry. Showered and dressed, I have breakfast and then call Reggie from Reception with Adele's news. Even in my troubled state, I can't help smiling as his distinctive voice asks, *"may I know who is calling at this unearthly hour"*? I picture him seated in a deep leather armchair placing his theatrical monocle into his wonky eye.

'Thank you for your update, dear lady and, unsurprisingly, as in the whole of Africa, it is the Chinese once again. They've got their hands on high quality copper ore in exchange for supplying the Guinea government with weapons to keep the dictator in power. As the Samla tribe wants its land back, their presence is an inconvenience.'

'That sounds right, Reggie. Anyway, all being well, I'll receive some positive news from Adele later today.'

'It would, indeed, be fortuitous if the whole party, with the addition of Miss Holbrook's brother, returns unscathed.' He pauses for a moment. 'Now for the other matter', the tone of his voice more serious. 'My contacts tell me that the US Embassy in Monrovia twisted someone's arm in the Pentagon who sent one of their drone gismos linked to a military satellite, to see what preparations are being made by Baros and his band of merry men. Strangely, there is no sign of their battalions heading for the Freetown Road which is the only route to Monrovia. Trying to bypass it is impossible as it is bordered by impenetrable jungle and treacherous swamps teaming with all kinds of nasties. The military bosses, who are scratching their heads at this very moment, have rather foolishly assured our lady President that there is no threat to her.'

'So does that mean Baros has changed his mind?'

'I hardly think so, dear lady. As I told you yesterday, Baros will be well aware of the build-up of government troops on the Freetown Road, but as he's been planning the coup d'état for sometime, he is bound to have Plan B up his sleeve, waiting for the right moment to launch the Four Horsemen of the Apocalypse onto an unsuspecting population.'

'And yet,' I say, 'Baros did tell us he was certain to succeed, his billion dollar haul completely depends on his man taking over as president.'

'Yes, which makes me believe the Liberian army chiefs have got it wrong. *Cul malo.* Now that the President is aware of the mega-rich diamond mine lying within her domain, and believing the advice she is getting from her high command, she is determined the mine will become government property.'

'That would be amazing and was exactly Nick's dream before he was murdered.'

'And on that note, dear lady, I have a little surprise for you.' I hear his unique chuckle on the end of the line.

'A nice one, I hope, Reggie.'

'It will be as long as Baros's coup fails. Amongst the President's advisers is Dr Alpho Hert who, wanting to ensure the mine is operated correctly, approached me asking if I could use my wise counsel in solving their dilemma.'

'That's encouraging, Reggie and,' I laugh, 'I'm pretty sure you will not be recommending any Chinese involvement.'

He chuckles again. 'Yes, on that score you are absolutely spot on. Luckily, I know the ideal person, someone who is an internationally recognized expert on the diamond trade, a person who knows Africa very well, and more importantly, someone of absolute integrity.'

'He sounds perfect, Reggie. How do you know him?'

I sense a beaming smile coming through the telephone line. 'I met this gentleman a few years ago, introduced to me by a certain Nicholas Holbrook after he'd rescued him and his group from murderous rebels in the Ivory Coast.

It's now my turn to pause, my head racing. 'You wouldn't be referring to Axel Van Damme would you?'

'Indeed I am.'

'Has he agreed to come?'

'As a matter of fact, he has, which makes it even more important that Baros's planned coup fails. But here's the irony. Axel Van Damme's co-worker in the Ivory Coast, also rescued by Nick Holbrook and Colonel Tofa, was in fact, the very same Professor Jaroslav Baros. He and Axel Van Damme are well acquainted, although possibly not the best of friends.'

'Yes, I remember. Do you think he'll have any influence on Baros?'

'None whatsoever, I'm afraid. It'll be a couple of weeks before he arrives and hopefully by then, Miss Holbrook and her retinue will be safely back from Guinea, enjoying the peace and quiet of the Cleopatra Beach Resort.'

Dragging myself slowly along the corridor, my head is reeling from a kaleidoscope of events and I'm worried sick about Adele.

Silently sidling from a side room, Bachir stops me in my tracks. 'Miss Lane,' his manner as usual is unfriendly, 'do you know anything about the start of a new civil war?'

Damn, what a question? I feel my hands beginning to shake and force them into my dress pockets. I'm not really sure what's supposed to be secret and what isn't. I play for time by saying, 'what do you mean?'

'I *mean* that some of my guests are cutting short their business trips and, my Lebanese contacts tell me that the Liberian army is moving in large numbers along the Freetown Road,' he glowers suspiciously at me. 'Why is that?'

'Bachir, why ask me? I haven't heard of any civil war.' Deliberately being economical with the truth, I continue, 'But I heard from Colonel Tofa that a rebel army near the Sierra Leone border is angry that Jacob Marcam's appeal failed.'

Although Bachir has always been offhand with me, he's not the enemy but, even so, I don't think I should be the one to tell him. As he considers my response, I get the feeling that he already knows more than he's letting on. 'Where is Miss Holbrook?' he asks.

'She's away, you know, looking for her missing brother but she'll be back tomorrow.'

He looks irritated. 'When she arrives, I want a word with her and Colonel Tofa.'

'Okay, I'll tell her.'

He hesitates by the door. 'Oh, and one other thing, you'll have to move out of your room first thing in the morning.'

'But why? If Miss Holbrook's brother comes back with her, we'll need an extra room.'

'I'll find you other rooms but they'll be smaller.' He's about to close the door then has second thoughts adding, 'Be out by ten. The Minister of Mines has booked my three best rooms for some VIPs arriving in the afternoon.'

'But … '

'No buts, Miss Lane. The Minister is very important. I have no choice and his VIPs include two Brits and also Mr Chan of the Sino Mineral Company.' With that, he stalks away.

Thoughts are whizzing around in a totally uncoordinated way and now I have Bachir's news to add to the mayhem. The Sino Mineral Company sounds like diamonds to me, which probably means that the location of Jaro's mine is out of the bag. And who are the two Brits coming with Mr Chan? And why would the Minister ask anyone to come to Liberia when a coup could start at any time?

Chapter Twenty-Eight
March 2nd

Yet another anxious night. I sit at the dressing table looking at my tanned face in the mirror, it's three-way reflecting back into itself and my likeness recedes from me - is this a metaphor? Unsurprisingly, I've developed dark bags under my eyes and ... and nothing, the Sat phone shrills and I grab the receiver.

'Penny, is that you?' I can just make out Adele's frantic voice over the fierce static.

'Yes, it's me, speak up.'

'Thank God, I've been trying to get you for ages,' she yells. The static eases slightly, but it sounds as if she's sitting inside an amplified sound box. 'We're on our way and expect to land at Spriggs Payne at about ... hang on,' I can just make out her muffled voice talking to someone nearby 'At fifteen-twenty hours, and we need two ambulances. Did you get that?'

'Yes, I heard but what's happened?' I yell back. 'Have you got Charles?'

'Two injured, and yes, Charles is with us but, Penny, get the fucking ambulances there and arrange a hospital for surgery. It's bloody urgent and you...' the line goes dead.

Damn. I try dialling her back but the noise is deafening and there's no response. What was it she said? *It's urgent and you - you what?* Shit. They're arriving at fifteen-twenty hours. Now, calm down and think, that's twenty past three. I look at my watch and it's already one thirty-five. They'll be landing in, er, one and three quarter hours. Ambulances, hospital, surgery. Oh bloody hell. And what was the name of the place they'll land at? Something '*pain*'? It could be anywhere.

My panic button is pressed down as far as it'll go. I rush to Reception but Bachir isn't there and the girl, Sadie, doesn't know when he'll be back.

'Sadie,' I ask desperately. 'Have you heard of an airport, something, something pain?'

'I t'ink you mea' Spriggs Payne, Missie, 'E for small plane.'

'Yes, that's it, Spriggs Payne, where is it, is it far?'

'No Missie, Spriggs Payne, 'e abou' half one hour fro' here.'

'Ah, thank God, and is there a hospital near it, with ambulances?'

'Yea Missie, JFK. 'e not far, 'e what we call, general hospital.'

'And is it good, Sadie, you know, private?'

She gives a puzzled look. 'E where we all go, Missie, we have to pay, bu' jus' small, small money.'

Damn, I have visions of filthy hospital beds covered in insects. I know, I'll phone Reggie, he's got all the contacts. I use the Reception phone. It rings and rings for what seems ages but I keep holding on, desperate for him to answer. I wait a couple of minutes and then the receiver is picked up. 'Mr Grosvenor-Smythe's residence.' The deep male voice is calm and clearly well-trained.

'I want to speak to Mr Grosvenor-Smythe,' I say loudly. 'It's very urgent. My name is Penny Lane. It's very, very urgent.'

'Mr Grosvenor-Smythe is resting and not to be disturbed, madam.'

'Listen you,' I just manage to stop myself swearing, 'Mr Grosvenor-Smythe's best friend is dying and I need his help now.' I try not to bellow in case he slams the phone down.

'And whom may that friend be?'

God, I could kill the supercilious bastard. 'Adele Holbrook, Nick Holbrook's sister is dying,' I lie, losing control and yelling my head off. 'And Mr Grosvenor-Smythe,' God, I wish he had a shorter name, 'Is the only one who can save her life.'

After a pause, the sonorous voice continues. 'Kindly hold for a moment, Miss Lane.'

Holding on anxiously watching the second hand of my watch tick, tick, my heart is beating like a demented tom-tom until I hear Reggie's distinctive, but drowsy voice. 'Is that you, Miss Lane?'

'Reggie,' a sense of relief floods through me.

'Is it correct that Miss Holbrook is dying?'

'Yes Reggie, I've just had a frantic phone call. They are all on the plane arriving at Spriggs Payne at twenty past three this afternoon and she and two others are seriously injured and need two ambulances to meet the plane and take them for urgent surgery.' I know I'm lying about Adele but hope he will forgive me later.

He's wide awake now. 'That does sound rather serious, let me get this clear,' he gives a couple of light coughs. 'The plane bringing Miss Holbrook and party is due to land at twenty past three and she wants two ambulances. She, plus two others, need urgent surgery. Is that right?'

'That's right Reggie, can you help,' I plead, 'I just don't know what else to do.'

'This is extremely short notice, dear lady, but I'll do what I can.'

'Oh, thank you, Reggie, that's ...'

'Now listen carefully,' he interrupts my blathering. 'Get Bachir Gemayel to send you by car to Spriggs Payne airport immediately. Take as many sheets and towels as you can find. Then using my name, and also that of Commissioner Ganta, make a note of that, Commissioner Ganta, tell the officials of the impending arrival of the plane and you stay there. I will do my best to arrange the ambulances and medical facilities. Is that clear?'

'Yes, Reggie, I'll do exactly as you say.' I decide not to mention that Bachir is out as it would take too much time to explain.

'Go now,' he commands. 'Stiffen the sinews for what lies ahead.'

He can't help it, can he? Feeling relieved that Reggie is helping, I turn to Sadie who's gaping at what she's overheard. 'Sadie, I need a car to take me to Spriggs Payne airport now. Is there one available?'

Pulling a face as she swallows hard and shakily replies, 'I don' t'ink so, Missie.'

'It's very urgent, a matter of life or death and Mr Grosvenor-Smythe says you give me a car.' I'm hoping the mention of the hotel's best customer will jolt her into action.

'I jus' check for you, Missie. Wai' here.'

I don't wait but follow her outside, urging her to hurry. Within seconds, sweat is clamping my dress against my body. I can see three empty vehicles of varying types in the yard but no drivers.

'There no car free, Missie.'

'Get me a soddin' car.' I'm red faced and frantic which scares the poor girl half to death. She stands rooted to the spot, tears rolling down her cheeks. Desperately looking around, I notice a hotel guard sprawled on an old basket chair by the gate. 'Sadie, listen, who's in charge of security? I want to see him, now.'

Still sobbing, she runs to the guard who points to a dark stained wooden hut, roughly the size of a small garage, about twenty yards away. 'Now Sadie, you go and get me ten clean sheets and ten clean towels, now, you hear?'

'You mea' now, Missie, one time?'

'Yes,' I bawl at her. 'One time.' I've already learnt that the expression *one time* in Liberia means *immediately*.

Wiping tears from her eyes, she hastily scuttles off back to the hotel.

Rushing over to the guard hut, I throw open the door. The windows are covered with tatty cloths but, in the dim light, I can just make out two men asleep on a dilapidated sofa, one only wearing underpants. The air stinks. Ignoring the smell and the half-naked man, I walk nervously towards them feeling so tense, my face might crack at any moment. Taking a deep breath almost makes me gag, but I manage to yell, 'Who's in charge?'

Jerking themselves awake, looking stunned, they plainly wonder what this crazy white woman is doing shouting at them. The fully dressed man stands and announces he's in charge.

'What's your name?'

'Sunday, Missie.'

'Right Sunday.' Trying out my best commanding officer voice. 'Take me to Spriggs Payne now, Mr Gemayel insists.' I'm getting used to lying but the only response is a blank stare, whilst the other man hurriedly starts to dress. Damn, that didn't work, I'll try my Liberian English. 'Sunday, you got car?'

'Yea, Missie.'

'You get car right now, one time, and take me to the place where airplane land. It called Spriggs Payne. You know the place?'

'I know the pla', Missie. But car, 'e no belong me, 'e belong bossman.'

'I know that. Mr Gemayel, he say to me, take car with security man who in charge, man call Sunday, and go Spriggs Payne. You wait with me till plane arrive. You hear?'

'Yea, I hear, Missie,' looking apprehensive. 'Wha' ti' the airpla' arrive?'

'Very soon.' I point at my watch. For whatever reason, it does the trick. Picking up a bunch of keys on the way, he follows me out of the hut, pointing towards a white Toyota 4x4.

'Car short o' gas, Missie.'

He means petrol. I take two twenty dollar bills out of my money belt and hand them over. Just then, the amazing Sadie rushes out of the hotel staggering under the weight of a pile of clean linen. Opening the car door, she places the bundle on the grimey back seat. I give her a beaming smile and thank her.

'We go now,' I shout at Sunday. 'One time.'

He calls out something to the other guard, now fully dressed, who rushes over carrying a jerry can which, worryingly, doesn't appear to be very heavy. Between them, they empty the limited contents into the Toyota's fuel tank, then Sunday gets in the driver's seat and I scramble in next to him, praying there's enough fuel to get us to the airport. With a gleam in his eye and skidding rear tyres, he switches the aircon on full blast and races out through the gate and down the rough track, heading towards the main road, scattering pedestrians, chickens and dogs, covering them in clouds of choking dust. I hold my belly as he hits almost every pothole along the way before we reach the main road. He does a rally-type-sliding left turn towards Monrovia and Spriggs Payne airport. It's ten past two, we have just over an hour before the plane is due.

Cursing vociferously, Sunday squeezes past slower traffic using the offside verge. 'Missie,' he says, 'We ha' to pass thru' three roa' blocks.'

'Yes, I know that, Sunday,' tension is already cramping my stomach. 'But we have to be at the airport in one hour, you hear? one hour.'

'Yes Missie, I try my bes".'

All the time he's weaving in, out, and around other vehicles, he's pressing hard on the horn. I bottle up my screams at every near miss while constantly checking my watch. Reaching the first road block, Sunday screeches to a halt at the end of a long queue and, like most other drivers, uselessly leans on the horn. Taking a deep breath, I get out despite feeling as though I'm about to frazzle in the heat, and jog past a dozen cars and trucks to the barrier where UN soldiers are checking every vehicle. I push my way into a small, open-sided office where the Asian officer in charge is leaning back comfortably in a chair reading a paper, oblivious to the mayhem outside. He gives a surprised look at my sudden arrival. I'm a real mess with my dress stuck to my body, hair uncombed and using a soiled cloth to wipe the sweat off my face.

'Hello,' he smiles. 'Aren't you Colonel Tofa's friend? Remember, at the Mano River road block, two days ago.'

'Yes, that's right,' I gasp, recognizing him now. I sneak a look at the name tag above his tunic pocket. 'Major Altaf.'

'That's right, and you are, oh, of course, I remember, Penny Lane. How could I forget a name like that?' he jokes, 'I hope you're not being chased again, are you?'

'No, but I'm trying to get to Spriggs Payne as quickly as I can. Colonel Tofa and his men are due there at three-twenty and several of them are injured. I'm arranging ambulances and hospital treatment.'

His smile fades, a look of unease crosses his face. 'Ambulances, hospital treatment?'

'Yes, can you help me please?'

He gives me a suspicious look. 'What have they been doing and where are they coming from? I hope they cleared everything with the UN.'

Damn, I've put my foot in it. 'They've been up near the border,' I reply, conscious that I'm rapidly becoming a consummate liar. 'Their trip was sanctioned by the President.' I'll probably get into deep shit over this, but that's the least of my worries.

'Well, if it's for Colonel Tofa, I'll do what I can.' He calls to one of his blue-beretted UN peacekeepers and gives him instructions. The man runs off, and a couple of minutes later, amidst raucous complaints and honking horns, he guides Sunday to the front of the queue.

'My man, Corporal Anjum here, will go with you,' Major Altaf says. 'He'll take you quickly through the other roadblocks. But I'll want a full report from Colonel Tofa on where's he's been and how he and his men got injured. All incidents of a military nature have to be reported to UN HQ.'

'Of course, and thank you.' With that warning ringing in my ears, we set off again with Corporal Anjum sitting in the front next to Sunday, and me in the back. I check my watch again, it's ten-to-three. For the next half hour, my insides somersault with worry and the fear of what's to come. Sunday, with the invaluable help of Corporal Anjum, makes good but hair-raising progress, and with only ten minutes spare, turns right off the main Tubman Boulevard opposite a sign featuring a bikini clad girl pointing to Bernard's Beach. Unfortunately, the sheer number of people forces Sunday to drive tortuously along the narrow paved road into the airport compound. It's exactly three-fifteen. Two armed soldiers shout for us to stop and Corporal Anjum and I get out. I'm shaking like a leaf. An official opens an office door to see what the commotion is all about. Remembering what Reggie told me, I mention his name and also Commissioner Ganta and tell him that a plane is due any minute and that two ambulances will come to take the injured to hospital.

He doesn't seem to register their names, but the presence of the UN peacekeeper allows us through. But the place looks deserted. Apart from two men pushing wheelbarrows full of rubbish, the place is empty. Looking round, there are half a dozen shabby single-storey buildings and three small single engine planes.

'Is this the right place?' I ask Sunday, anxiously looking for any sign of activity.

'Yea, Missie, this the pla', 'e always quiet like this.'

'But they were supposed to be here now.'

'Missie, look see,' Sunday's finger is pointing far to the right. 'Look there.'

Squinting into the bright sun, I can just make out a tiny dot of a plane approaching. It's a few seconds before I hear it. As it gets closer, it barely misses the tops of a line of trees before gracefully losing height and making a smooth landing. Taxiing to the end of the runway, it turns and heads back towards the terminal hut. Concentrating on the plane, I jump as loud honking horns herald the arrival of two army mini-trucks with large red crosses fixed to their sides, closely followed by a Range Rover. I can just make out Reggie in the passenger seat.

The plane comes to a halt and switches off its engines at the same time as two stretcher- bearers from each ambulance rush towards it. I'm about to follow when a firm hand grabs my arm.

'Good afternoon, Miss Lane,' it's Reggie. Carrying a silver-topped cane, he's clad in a cream-coloured suit, white shirt and regimental tie, topped off with a Panama hat, the ribbon matching his tie. 'I strongly recommend that we stand well back and be ready to deal with the bureaucratic nonentities who'll appear at any second.' He notices that I'm staring at his outfit. 'Ah, there are occasions when dressing like an ageing Lord Fontleroy impresses the natives -style is all important.'

As the plane door opens and steps are lowered, Noah jumps down. He at least looks uninjured but I want to know which of them needs urgent surgery. Noah is starting to organize the stretcher bearers when two uniformed officials, one with *immigration* across his back and the other *customs*, race out of the hut, waving their arms, shouting that everyone stop. This must be what Reggie expected. Openly grasping a wad of dollar bills in his hand, he orders James to bring the two officials over. They must be used to this kind of thing because after a few words, they turn and see Reggie's commanding appearance. After hesitating a second, they edge their way over, their eyes fixed only on one thing.

Reggie, standing upright, shoulders back like an aristocratic potentate, deliberately embarrasses the two money-grubbers by making them stoop before slowly handing the bills over, one by one; their positions as immigration and customs officers clearly forgotten.

Turning towards the plane, I can see the paramedics trying to manoeuvre two laden stretchers through the plane door and down the steps onto terra firma, accompanied by a great deal of cursing. Only the heads of the injured are visible above the sheet coverings. With the sun directly in my eyes, I can only see them in silhouette. I'm about to run over when Reggie grabs my arm again.

'Try to control your emotions, dear lady,' his voice firm and authoritive. 'I fully understand your nervousness, but don't do anything to delay them.'

I know he's right. After depositing the first two injured, the two stretcher-bearers run back to the plane and my poor heart skips a dozen beats when I see that the third person being carried off is Adele, with a blood-soaked dressing covering one side of her face. She turns her head catching sight of me and gives a thumbs-up. I breathe a huge sigh of relief. Finally, Moses, Jerbo and the pilot climb down, they seem to be okay. Moses looks around and then walks in our direction.

'Missie, Colonel Tofa say you follow the ambulance.'

'Yes, we'll do that Moses, but who are the injured, besides Miss Holbrook.'

'That can wait,' Reggie interrupts and firmly guides me towards his Range Rover. 'I've arranged for those needing surgery to go to the Marguerite Clinic. The operating theatre is ready and I've been assured the x-ray machine is working.'

'But that's Doctor Kit and his dreadful nurse.'

'Yes but don't worry, dear lady, because the appallingly-behaved doctor and his nurse are in no doubt that their professional conduct over the next few days will be the key to their future. I have made it abundantly clear that if any of our valiant heroes fail to make the best possible recovery, then the wrath of Reginald Grosvenor-Smyth, OBE, will descend on them like the Fearsome Lions of Albion.' He pauses for a few seconds to screw his monocle in place. 'I've also arranged for two American doctors from the JFK Hospital, with whom I am acquainted, to help Dr Kit.'

Once again, Reggie seems to have influence over so many people in Liberia. I sit next to him as James follows the wailing ambulances onto Tubman Boulevard. The crowds that had earlier slowed our progress are now keeping well out of the way.

'Reggie, I think one of the seriously injured must be Adele's brother, Charles Temple.'

'We'll soon find out,' he replies. 'At least Miss Holbrook didn't seem to be in any danger of dying.' James drives up to the clinic's entrance and I notice a satisfied look on Reggie's face as he points to a sign on the door saying *closed*. 'At least Kit's done that right.' He pounds on the door which is immediately opened by the receptionist I saw during my first visit. Struggling to keep up, I trot in Reggie's wake as he strides purposefully through the building to where Noah is waiting.

'What's the latest communiqué, Colonel?'

Noah motions us to sit on nearby chairs. 'Charles Temple has two gunshot wounds to the chest. We did our best to staunch the flow of blood on the plane and he remained conscious the whole time. An American doctor is with him. Bambara's brother, Elkin, has a chest injury. He's alive but lost consciousness, a doctor is also attending to him.'

'And Miss Holbrook?'

'She was wounded on the side of her face but I don't think it's life threatening.'

Just then, a harassed Dr Kit, looking sheepishly over at Reggie, comes out of one room. 'Both men are suffering hypovolemic shock, ' he says. 'We've stabilized them the best we can, giving them oxygen, blood and liquids. The x-rays reveal no serious internal damage to Mr Temple. Two bullets went through him without hitting vital organs, but Mr Elkin is much worse as a bullet is blocking an artery which will leak when it's removed.'

Reggie nods his head, satisfied that Kit is on top of the situation. The doctor returns to the ward just as a shaky Adele totters out of another room.

'I thought I heard your voices,' she says weakly, her voice restricted by the bandages and plasters covering half her face and head.

'Shouldn't you be in bed?' I scold.

'Don't be silly,' she says disdainfully. 'You ought to know that a few scratches won't keep me in bed. No, I've come to take a look at Charles.'

'Well, before you do that, thank Reggie for organising everything.'

'Oh, Reggie, thank you so much,' she declares. 'What would we do without you?'

'It is my pleasure, dear lady.' Doffing his Panama, he gallantly bends and brushes the back of her hand with his lips.

Doing her best to smile, Adele takes my arm. 'Come with me, Penny, I want you to meet my brother.'

Carefully, she opens the door to another room. The blinds are drawn but there's sufficient light to see a nurse attending to a prone body with an oxygen mask over the face, connected to numerous tubes, bags of plasma and a clear liquid. The nurse is Gretchen who turns and gives me an embarrassed look. 'Ve think he out of danger,' she says in her guttural English.

'That's good,' Adele says. 'Please remove his mask for a second.'

Gretchen loosens the mask's strap and slips it to one side. I can see his face clearly now and, *oh, my God*, my heart stops and my stomach turns over, I can't breathe or speak, I can only stare - it's Nick.

Dizzy, a flood of memories come back - memories of my time with Nick. I fight back a sense of panic. People are reaching out to me and I hear voices, but they're too distant. Against my will, my eyes close and I'm descending into a deep, deep darkness and I ...

'Ugh, what the!' I cough, retch and choke as fumes of ammonia invade the inside of my head. I'm lying on the floor, spluttering and coughing with tears streaming down my face like mini-waterfalls. Through the fume-filled nausea, I hear Adele's angry voice telling someone that they overdid the smelling salts.

'You're alright now, Penny,' Adele wipes the tears from my face and props me up into a sitting position.

Reeling from the assault on my senses and, through blurry eyes, I see Adele's bandaged face looking intently at me.

'Penny, you fainted. Just stay where you are and drink some water.' Holding a hand over my stomach until the queasiness recedes, I try to expel the fumes from my lungs and grab the glass, gulping down as much as I can. Another deep breath and I'm feeling better, but then the shock in my memory returns. 'It's Nick, I've just seen Nick.'

'No dear, 'Adele gently helps me to stand. 'You saw Charles, Nick's brother.'

'But ... '

'Yes, I know. As soon as you are up to it, we'll go and see him again.'

My eyesight clears and there's a small audience anxiously gathered around me. Apart from Adele and the immaculately attired Reggie, there's Noah and a guilty-looking Nurse Gretchen holding a glass bottle to her chest; it's obvious she gave me the overdose.

Steadying myself against Adele, she takes my arm as we go back into his room. Barely breathing, all I can hear is blood pounding through my ears. Gretchen opens the blinds then moves the oxygen mask to one side and I gaze down at the calm, sleeping face. The shape of his head and cheek bones are exactly like Nick's but there's no scar on his left temple and his other features, mouth, chin and nose, confirm that they are, indeed, different men. Gretchen replaces the mask and, feeling a bit like a zombie, I allow Adele to lead me out of the room.

Reggie looks anxiously at me. 'How are you?'

'Fine, thank you Reggie. I'm sorry I …'

'Not at all, dear lady, not at all. It must have been quite traumatic. Now, Colonel Tofa will take you back to the Cleopatra and you should try and get a good rest. You'll be able to hear about all the heroics tomorrow.'

'The Cleopatra, ah, hang on a moment,' I say. 'We have a problem. Bachir told me that we have to vacate our room tomorrow morning to make way for one Chinese and two British VIPs. The Minister of Mines has demanded it.' I look at the three of them in turn. 'The Chinese man is from the Sino Mineral Company.'

'Mineral Company!' Adele cries. 'Does that mean what I think it means?'

'It's diamonds, of course,' Reggie snorts. 'Those dastardly Chinese bounders are after Liberia's diamonds.'

'I think you're right,' I say. 'The location of Baros's mine must have been leaked.'

'Well, first things first,' Reggie announces. 'Forget the hotel, you two ladies can stay at my place, I insist, you'll be more comfortable there and I know an excellent nurse who'll live-in until Miss Holbrook's medical treatment is complete.'

'But we can't put you to that trouble, Reggie.'

'Tosh. You're staying with me and I'll enjoy the company. Miss Lane, let Colonel Tofa take you to the hotel, pack everything, and bring your bags to my house. No arguments.'

'That's very kind, Reggie, I think both of us would appreciate some peace and quiet.'

During the drive to the Cleopatra, Noah is reluctant to talk about the rescue save for the fact that they were successful in freeing Charles and the only serious injury is Bambara's brother. After dropping me off, he'll go and see Major Altaf to try to placate him and then he'll come back and take me and our belongings to Reggie's house.

The first thing I do at the Cleopatra is apologize to Bachir for borrowing his vehicle as well as a bunch of hotel linen but, I emphasize, it had been an emergency. I tell him how

Sadie and Sunday behaved wonderfully and I would be rewarding them for their help. He doesn't reply straight away so I also tell him that Nick's brother has been rescued and is recovering in hospital. He looks pleased with this last piece of news but tells me that all the costs I incurred with the vehicle and the linen will be added to my bill. I agree to pay everything.

'Miss Lane,' his attitude towards me is still indifferent, 'I informed you that you and Miss Holbrook would have to vacate your room tomorrow but you'll have to do it now, immediately. I've just been informed that the VIPs are due here within the hour and the minister is insistent his guests get the best rooms.'

For his benefit I sigh, shaking my head, to show this change is an imposition, neglecting to mention that it's what we were planning to do in any case. I'm on the point of going to my room when he holds out a note and asks, 'Can you help me. You are English so tell me how to pronounce this name, I want my staff to get it right. Is it Sir Alfred Beauchamp?'

Puzzled, I look at the card. 'Ah, I know it's strange, Bachir, but it's actually pronounced Beacham and he should be addressed as Sir Alfred.' He writes Beacham down and shows me. 'Yes, that's correct.'

He then shows me the second card. 'And is this pronounced Sir Desmond Thrimby?'

Oh my God. My throat tightens and it's hard to swallow. I put my hand on the wall to steady myself, my heart beating a frenetic tattoo. That evil, murdering bastard, Sir Desmond Thrimby is coming, *Verdammt und Verfickter.*

He looks suspicious. 'Do you know this man?'

Pulling myself together, I plead, 'Look Bachir, Miss Holbrook and I met this man once and he is NOT a friend.' Taking a deep breath I add, 'Please, for Nick's sake if nothing else, don't tell him we've been here or even mention our names.'

'I do understand,' Bachir frowns. 'I've survived in Africa a long time and know that there are certain secrets that have to be kept. In England you say *my lips are sealed* so Sir Desmond

Thrimby will not hear from me or my staff that you and Miss Holbrook are here in Liberia.'

'Thank you very much,' I believe him. The first thought when I'm in my room is to phone home, not having spoken to my parents for weeks. The last I told them was that I going on holiday for two weeks but not that it would be in the tropics of West Africa. Thankfully, the answer phone kicks in because I'm dithering about what on earth to say, that's without telling too many lies. I keep it brief. *'Hi, Mum and Dad. Just to let you know I'm having a good time and will be away for another week or so. Hope you are both well; I'll phone when I arrive home. Must rush, lots of love, Penny.'*

That done, I quickly throw clothes and sundries into our bags. After paying the bill and telling Bachir we'll be staying with Mr Grosvenor-Smythe, I sit just outside the entrance in the comforting shade of a flowering tulip tree, waiting for Noah to return with the vehicle.

Feeling an irritating itch on my ankle, I absent-mindedly reach down to give it a scratch but my hand touches something alive and hairy. Oh God. I jump as a huge brown and yellow spider climbs up my leg. An involuntary shudder courses through my body. Giving the blighter a good swipe, I send it flying. As I try to see where the horrible creepy thing has gone, the hotel's security gates open and a black Mercedes limousine enters the compound. The chauffeur rushes to open the rear doors and I can vaguely see three white men getting out, accompanied by a smartly-suited Liberian wearing the customary wrap-around sunglasses. My breath catches as the unmistakable figure of Sir Desmond Thrimby comes into view.

Panicking, I quickly move inside, trying to make myself invisible by crouching behind a row of large, potted palms at one end of the bar. Bachir is doing his well-rehearsed fawning act as he meets the VIPs, confidently addressing Sir Alfred Beauchamp and Sir Desmond Thrimby as if they were everyday names to him. The Lebanese seem to be the masters of obsequiousness. Sir Des suggests they take a drink at the bar before going to their rooms which puts me back into panic mode. The local man, with rings on all eight fingers and two thumbs, must be the Minister and says he'll collect them in the morning to go through the formalities at his office.

Bidding him farewell, the three men walk the few steps into the bar and sit on chairs directly at the other side of my palm-shielded hideout. They couldn't be closer but thankfully, their backs are towards me. My bum's half on the floor, my shoulders and arms awkwardly resting on a seat, my legs wedged between the table legs which has two empty glasses on it. The slightest movement will send them crashing to the floor.

'So Mr Chan,' Sir Des says with an air of self-importance. 'What's the programme?'

There's a moments silence before he mutters something I can't make out. 'I don't think Mr Chan speaks very good English,' Sir Alfred says. 'I suggest we use Mandarin, and then if we're overheard,' he smiles. 'Nobody will understand.'

At least I know my Mandarin is better than Sir Des's so, as long as I remain unnoticed, I'll be able to hear what they say. I hope Noah doesn't arrive soon, I'll be in trouble if he does.

The men are quiet as the waiter approaches with their drinks. Trying not to move a muscle, I listen to Mr Chan speaking slowly in Mandarin for the benefit of the two knights of the realm. *'The first thing we have to do is agree the size of the minister's sweetener, but obviously nothing will be paid into his Swiss bank account until the rebels are cleared from the mine site and neutralised.'*

Neutralised! God, what does that mean?

'I agree, Mr Chan,' Sir Des responds. *'I suggest we promise the minister five million US dollars in staged payments, as long as the mine proves to be as lucrative as expected,'* he laughs. *'This bribe will definitely get his total support.'*

There are some comments I can't follow, then Mr Chan continues. *'The minister must also wait until the first three diamond shipments have been made and the quality confirmed,'* there's a note of levity in his voice. *'Of course, the payments will never reach five thousand dollars, never mind five million.'* They all find his remark amusing.

Covered in sweat, my heart's pounding and worse, I'm starting to get cramp. I move my limbs slightly to get into a more comfortable position.

'The second thing,' Mr Chan tells them, 'Is to sign the agreement with the Liberian government that they will receive half the proceeds of the wholesale value of the diamond sales.' I can sense they are grinning in the knowledge that it will never happen.

Suddenly, I feel something making my leg itch. Twisting my head round, I can see it's that huge spider again. My stress levels reach nuclear proportions and I'm in my own living nightmare. My arms are on the wrong side of the table legs so I can't swat it and my mind is taken away for a second as Mr Chan says 'The cargo ship, the Shenzhen Yong.'

Oh shit, the spider's reached the edge of my dress, please don't go under, please … it disappears under, oh hell. My dress rises slightly marking its progress further up my thigh. I still can't reach it. Somehow, through my near hysteria I hear Mr Chan. 'In four days' time with a consignment of weapons.'

The creature is nearing my pants but now it's got this far, I can just about reach it by painfully bending my right arm back as far as it will go. But what do I do? It might bite or be poisonous. Mr Chan's voice calmly drones on. 'Two attack helicopters, armoured vehicles, missiles, plus a seventy-strong attachment of Chinese military advisers who …'

Whether it's instinct, self-survival or what I don't know but something makes me push my hand down, as hard as I can on the lump under my dress. Squelch. It squashes, a dark red stain appearing on my dress. I feel sick and my whole body shakes in revulsion.

Now I hear loud footsteps entering the hotel. Stretching my neck, I see Noah, dressed in his colonel's uniform.

Seeing the army officer, Sir Alfred says, 'I think, gentlemen, we should go to our rooms and continue this discussion later.' Finishing their drinks, they go to Reception just as Noah appears round the side of the potted palms, looking non-plussed seeing me crouching on the floor. I put a finger to my lips. He takes in the situation perfectly, turning his back and sitting at the table the men have just vacated. He loudly orders a beer from the waiter. The VIPs get their keys and move away.

'Okay, Penny, you can come out now,' Noah whispers. 'What's this all about?'

Gasping with the release of tension, I stand lifting my dress not caring that Noah is watching and find the revolting squashed spider stuck near the top of my thigh - like a lump of blood-filled phlegm. Poking it with my finger tip, I almost puke as it falls to the floor.

'What have you done?' Noah stares at the stain on my dress. 'Are you injured?'

'No.' I'm shaking violently. 'Noah, I'm in a bit of a mess,' I sob. 'Please let's go. It was a soddin' spider that crawled up my leg and ...' is as far as I get. I feel faint. Without hesitation, Noah picks me up like a baby and carries me out to the car.

During the drive, I manage to tell Noah everything I overheard whilst hiding under the table. He is clearly shocked. By the time we arrive at Reggie's house, a pitch blackness has descended almost as quickly as flicking a light switch. The house and grounds are flooded with bright lights, reflecting onto the surrounding trees and shrubs like tiny fairy lights. Looking up, I'm faced by the awesome wonders of the tropics, the sky bursting with shimmering stars which seem almost close enough to touch. The sound of croaking frogs and cicadas is all around and a phrase from somewhere comes to mind - a poem maybe about hearing the *voice of an African night*. As we climb the front steps, it suddenly dawns on me how dreadful I must look. Sweaty, dishevelled and my dress blood stained.

Reggie opens the door greeting us in his usual effusive manner, politely ignoring my scruffy appearance. 'Good evening and welcome to my humble abode, your bedchamber awaits, Miss Lane, and you may desire to freshen-up before dinner - say in one hour?' He courteously awaits my nodded agreement. 'The Colonel and I will converse on recent events.' Even in such a state, I still can't help smiling at Reggie's old-fashioned mannerisms. My guardian angel has definitely worked overtime, providing both Reggie and Noah to look after me.

After lingering in a soothing shower, I reluctantly drag myself out, drying my hair and pushing it into something that resembles a style. Rummaging through my make-up, I find lipstick and an almost dried-out mascara. Unfortunately, the dress from my bag is creased but – no matter, a few added accessories make me feel almost human again. Just being away from the Cleopatra gives me a boost, but I can't forget the arrival of that murdering bastard, Sir Desmond bloody Thrimby. Carefully negotiating my way down the elegant staircase, an inviting aroma wafts upwards reminding me how hungry I am.

Sitting at a polished bamboo bar, Reggie and Noah stand as I enter. Reggie, with monocle in place, is now wearing a red silk smoking jacket with a cravat, like a caricature of a Dickensian English gentleman. 'You look most charming, my dear,' he takes my hand giving it a light kiss. 'I hope you are feeling refreshed after your unfortunate experience this afternoon.'

'Thank you,' my smile encompasses them both, 'I feel much better now.'

'Colonel Tofa was just telling me how you were attacked by one of our native arachnids while crouching under a table listening to some very distressing news discussed by Mr Chan and his cohorts.'

'That's right. One of the men is Sir Desmond Thrimby, who was Nick's boss. He's almost certainly behind his murder and the numerous attacks on Adele and me.'

He looks grim. 'This is a matter of great concern but please be comforted that he's on my territory now so the advantage is most definitely in our court.'

'By the way, Penny,' Noah is trying unsuccessfully to hide a smile. 'The spider you squashed this afternoon is what we call a Palm Beetle. You'll be pleased to know they're harmless and children even keep them in little boxes as pets, so you weren't in any danger.'

'But it was a spider,' I protest. 'I saw two of them, eight legs like spiders.'

Reggie calmly intervenes. 'Strictly speaking, they are spiders, as you quite rightly point out, but Liberians, for some reason, call them beetles. I have quite a few in my garden.'

Feeling a bit silly, I'm about to pursue the matter further when the doorbell chimes.

Reggie scowls, commenting that it's rather late for uninvited visitors. From the hall, we can plainly hear Adele's voice.

Reggie hurries to greet her. 'Please enter dear lady.' He takes her arm and guides her to a comfortable chair which she sinks into, half her face and head still covered with bandages.

'I discharged myself as I only have a few scratches on my face. Charles and poor Mr Elkin need medical attention far more than I do. Of course, Dr Kit tried to dissuade me but I told him to ... well, let's say I told him I was leaving, whether he liked it or not, but I am going back tomorrow to have my dressings changed.'

'In that case,' Reggie beams. 'Come and join the party. Dinner will be served in ten minutes. Your luggage is already safely stowed in your bedroom.'

After the first course of a delicious lobster salad, Reggie surveys us all. 'I think it important to agree an agenda for this evening and therefore suggest, Miss Holbrook, that your exploits and the rescue of Mr Temple from the Republic of Guinea, absolutely splendid as they are, be left until we have covered more looming issues.'

'I agree, sir,' Noah says. 'We have imminent coup threats on two fronts now.'

'Go ahead, Colonel, you are the expert here.'

'First,' Noah takes a sip of soda water. 'There has still been no movement from Baros's rebel army which is extremely puzzling. During our forced stay there, I found out they are very well equipped with armoured vehicles, mortars, bazookas, sub-machine guns and other modern weapons. They may well be able to defeat the Liberian army but it would be a long, bloody battle with many casualties. But Baros's only chance to exploit the diamond mine for his own benefit is to install one of his men as president. So, why has nothing happened? What's he waiting for? The rainy season starts soon and by then it will be too late.'

'It is strange,' Reggie agrees. 'But there is now another dimension regarding the Chinese which Miss Lane heard earlier today. What do you know about this, Colonel?'

'Adele interrupts looking curiously in my direction. 'This is news to me, tell me more.'

Noah speak first. 'A few months ago, President Poltara entered into an agreement with China to bolster the capabilities of the Liberian armed forces with some new weapons. This is linked to iron ore sales, but there was definitely no mention of military advisers.'

'And by military advisers,' Reggie snorts. 'Substitute highly-trained combat troops.'

'And also,' I add, 'Mr Chan believes that the shipment of weapons, including attack helicopters and missiles, will quickly neutralise the rebels.'

'A potential powder keg,' Reggie says. 'But the Colonel here has already informed the President of this development. Unless prompt action is taken, I'm in no doubt that the Chinese will take command of the Liberian army,' he looks directly at Noah. 'Firstly to destroy Baros's army after which, under some pretext or other, they'll craftily replace President Poltara with a puppet leader, most probably their friend, the Minister of Mines.'

'I'm meeting with the army council later this evening,' Noah states.

'Very good, Colonel. But is it possible to stop the Chinese ship from berthing?'

'Yes, the President can instruct the harbour master to ensure it is made to anchor five miles offshore until further notice. It's an international law and can't be ignored.'

'Ha, that would scupper Sir Desmond's and Sir Alfred's plans,' I smile.

'What!' exclaims Adele. 'Sir Desmond, our Sir Desmond Thrimby is actually here, why didn't you tell me? And did you also mention a Sir Alfred, that wouldn't be Sir Alfred Beauchamp by any chance?'

'Yes, that's him, why do you know him?'

'I know *of* him,' she retorts sharply. 'He's Charles's boss in the Foreign Office.'

CHAPTER TWENTY-NINE
MARCH 3RD

In a cold sweat, I awake to the sound of my own sobbing, oh no, not another bloody nightmare. My mind is going round and round but first and foremost, I'm still trying to understand what the hell is going on. The two *British knights* are plotting with the Chinese to wrest Baros's diamond mine from him, that much is clear. Sir Des knows that Nick had a connection with a mega diamond mine but not its location, and that's why he, his late *unlamented* son, Hal, and their bunch of villains gave us all that grief. But how does Sir Alfred Beauchamp fit into all this? And the fact that he's Charles's boss makes matters even more confusing. I wonder if they're aware of Baros's plans and yet surely, the Minister of Mines must know, being in the cabinet ... or don't things work like that in Liberia? Either way, whether it's Baros or the Chinese, a coup is about to happen and what's even more frightening is that we'll be stuck in the middle. Even with all the confusion swirling around in my head, I must have dozed off because I'm abruptly woken by Adele giving me a poke telling me she's on her way to the clinic.

As I come downstairs, subtle flowery scents are borne on a breeze blowing gently through the open French windows. The air-conditioning is replaced by ceiling fans, under which Reggie is seated in an armchair facing the garden. On hearing my footsteps he turns and asks me to join him for a coffee.

'Coralie and I like to sit here most mornings in the dry season,' he muses reflectively. 'Just taking in the beauty that Mother Nature has graciously bestowed on us.'

I'm far too polite to suggest that Mother Nature would have got nowhere without the labour of half a dozen lowly-paid Liberians, but that's just me being small-minded. 'It is beautiful, Reggie.' A mug of coffee is discreetly placed at the side of my chair.

'Well, my dear, when you come to work for me,' he smiles mischievously, raising one of his amazing eyebrows. 'When all the troubles have been put to bed and you and your baby are ready for another great adventure, you can expect something similar to this.'

This is the second time he's offered me a job, but I think it's probably more in jest than being serious. 'That's very kind of you, Reggie, bearing in mind you hardly know me.' I don't want to rubbish his proposal because the last thing I want is hurt his feelings.

'For someone like you, visiting a developing country for the first time, it must all seem rather strange,' he chuckles. 'Here I am, a rather eccentric Englishman in the wilds of tropical West Africa, making an exceptionally bountiful living.'

'I don't care if people call you eccentric, in my book, you and Coralie are the best.'

Sipping our coffee, we both pause taking in the scene. Eventually, he breaks the silence. 'I'm sure you'd like it here. You see, international agencies tasked with apportioning vast amounts of tax payers' hard earned cash often haven't a clue how this country works. Put in simple terms, they don't know who to contact, which ministers are corrupt and incompetent or who can be trusted. That's where I come in and, with your language skills, you could as well. Coralie and I have become adept at keeping a close watch on, I think the modern parlance is *movers and shakers,* whilst keeping well clear of politics. After thirty years, I couldn't live anywhere else, not in a large, dirty city, the cold, taxation, no, I like the Africans and their way of life. I don't patronise them and have learnt to respect their traditions,' he smiles. 'Like sharing a bottle of cane juice or, better still, a twelve year old malt with them.'

'You're absolutely right when you say it would be an adventure to live here, but I'm sure you appreciate there are too many uncertainties in my life. In a year's time though, I may well come knocking on your door.'

Before Reggie can reply, Adele arrives back from the clinic. She's really angry. 'I've just found out those bastards in Guinea shot half my bloody ear off, my head's been shaved and I've lost spoonfuls of flesh from my left cheek. Why didn't they tell me before?'

I go over and give her a hug. 'You could always have plastic surgery.'

She's got that steely Holbrook look in her eyes again. 'No, no way. I got these scars rescuing Charles and I'll keep them just the way they are, even my half ear.'

I can tell she's not in the mood to change her mind.

'But Charles is doing well,' she smiles. 'He's sitting up in bed, but it's bad news about Elkin - the doctors removed the bullet and now his internal bleeding is severe and they are struggling to control it. Dr Kit has given him less than a fifty-fifty chance of survival. The next twenty-four hours are critical.'

'That is sad,' Reggie sighs. 'It would have been a miracle to do what you did without someone sustaining serious injuries.'

'Oh, one more thing, Penny,' Adele gives me a wink, 'Charles has asked to see you, so will you go now?'

'You can take my car,' Reggie says gallantly. 'But don't forget we have another meeting here with Colonel Tofa at noon and it's vital we all attend.'

Knocking lightly on Charles's door, I feel a small tremor of excitement as a faint voice calls me to enter. The morning sun is streaming into the bright, air-conditioned room. A small vase of red flowers is placed on a table next to a jug of water and a drinking glass. Sitting in bed, propped up by several pillows, Charles smiles and, gosh, it's a mirror image of Nick's smile, my heart beat accelerates. Our eyes meet. I know it happens between people all the time but why does this seem more meaningful to me?

'Hello.'

'Hello, Charles.' A tingling under my scalp spreads slowly to my face.

'You're Penny Lane, then.'

I nod.

A look of amusement crinkles his eyes. 'You're name really is Penny Lane!'

'My dad was a Beatles fan, well more Paul McCartney really.' I'm keen to change the subject as my name has been a millstone all my life. At least he thinks it amusing.

I feel his eyes looking closely at me and wish I'd made more of an effort with my appearance. Pointing to a chair next to the bed, he says, 'I understand that the last time you saw me you fainted, so it's probably better that you sit while you can,' he flashes me a mischievous smile. 'You know, just in case it's a permanent reaction.' His voice is Nick's voice, deep and warm and, I remember now, droll.

'It's just that I'd had a stressful day, and was exhausted, anyway, how are you?'

'Oh, okay, thanks. I've been pumped full of some lovely new blood, antibiotics and I don't know what else and yes, I'm on the mend. The doc says I'll be fit to fly home in four days or so, back to dear old Blighty.' His bright blue eyes, Nick's eyes, regard me shrewdly. 'Adele told me everything you'd done for us,' he puts his hand on mine. God, it takes my breath away. 'Penny, you helped save our lives, thank you.'

For a second, I feel self-conscious. 'I only helped to arrange the transport, that's all.'

'You did a lot more than that. Without you, I'd still be rotting away in Guinea.'

'But it was Nick, indirectly I guess, who gave us the clue on where you were being held, through Bambara, and, of course, Noah.'

At the mention of Nick's name, his expression becomes grief-stricken, the earlier playful atmosphere has gone. 'I only found out from Adele two days ago.' Tears well up in his eyes and I give his hand a squeeze. 'We were as close as any brothers could be.'

My heart gives a surge filled with an aching tenderness.

'I'm told you were with him when he was murdered.' He glances at me and I nod.

'And now you're expecting his baby. That really is good news, a baby to keep his spirit alive.'

303

'Yes. I'm worried that all the ... I guess trauma is the appropriate word, I've been through might have affected it.'

'Oh, it'll be fine, Penny,' he snorts dismissively. 'It's a Holbrook remember; it'll probably come out doing somersaults and carrying an AK-47.'

I smile, that's not quite the image I want to think about.

'Did you know Nick long, were you engaged?'

'No, nothing like that. I only met him on New Year's Eve, a month later he was dead.'

His expression changes again. 'A whirlwind romance. Did he know about the baby?'

'Oh yes, he seemed pleased.' My voice surprises me, it's perfectly steady, 'But he couldn't commit to a relationship for a couple of years; something to do with his job.'

Charles sits quietly for a moment. 'You did like him, though, didn't you?'

I feel myself smiling, not embarrassed now. 'Oh yes, I liked him a lot.'

His face is impassive and I realize we're still holding hands. 'Just meeting you now for the first time, Penny, I'm sure you are the girl he'd been looking for all his life.'

Wow, what an amazing thing to say, my heart is starting to race again as I'm taken aback by a sudden rush of love for Charles. Love! Don't be ridiculous, no-one falls in love like this, it's obviously my over-active hormones. Thinking about the past with Nick and now the present with Charles, I'm trying to join the dots between what happened then and what's happening now. Is it possible to simply transfer my love from one dead brother to a living one, or is Charles just a reminder of my lost love for Nick?

'When I first met Nick, he told me his name was Charles Temple.'

Wiping away a couple of stray tears, he looks surprised. 'Did he now?' he rubs his chin, deep in thought. 'That is interesting.'

'I only knew his real name after he was dead.'

He gives a pensive smile probably knowing the recollection will hurt. 'It goes back to our childhood. Although we were only half-brothers, we did look alike, and when one of us got into trouble, we'd swap identities, including our clothes, often avoiding punishment. It was bit more complicated than that, but we got out of many a scrape that way.'

'Were you often in trouble?'

Wistfully casting back in his memory, he laughs. 'Oh yes, we were a couple of terrors.'

'But why swap identities as adults?'

'We didn't, but just before I came to Africa, Nick was with HESEC and I with the Foreign Office and we each came across signs of corruption at senior levels within our respective organizations, but not the *who* if you see what I mean. So we agreed to use it as a code. The code was that if one of us got close to finding the *who* which could well put us in danger, we'd do the swap hoping to confuse the bad guys and let each other know we were onto something.'

'That's a bit complicated,' I frown. 'I'm not sure I fully understand, but whatever it was, it didn't work for Nick.'

'No, sadly it didn't. It could be that …,' he pauses, screwing his eyes in concentration, half murmuring to himself. 'Oh no! surely not!'

'Surely not what?'

He looks horror-struck as though something from the depths of his unconscious has flickered into his conscious mind. 'I think I've got it. Nick must have had a clue that I was alive and knew that if a certain person in the Foreign Office found out that I was back in the UK, they'd have a bloody fit – you see, I was supposed to be dead.'

'And that *certain person,* you now know to be Sir Alfred Beauchamp.'

'Absolutely, that bastard Beauchamp, my boss of all people, knew that I too had to be eliminated.'

'But what was it you knew that was so damning to him?'

'Ha, it's a long story, but basically it's to do with international aid channelled through the Department for International Development, known as DfID and the Foreign Office.'

'What is?'

'It's like this,' he sighs. 'The UK is very generous with its aid to Africa but, in return, the tradition was that British companies would get some of the contracts that this aid was financing. That's how it had been until a couple of years ago when suddenly, it all dried up. Our aid was being handed to foreign contractors, mainly Chinese. A Parliamentary committee sent me out, undercover, to find out why we were losing out all the time.'

'And you found out.'

'Yes, I did. I found that with the direct involvement of Beauchamp, British companies were being rejected in favour of Chinese. I sent a report back to the Parliamentary committee and then, a couple of weeks later, there was an attempt on my life, and the would-be assassin confessed to that before I killed him.'

'You killed him! Oh my God, but, there again, I guess you had to.'

'Damn right I did.'

'But this still doesn't add up. Your family was told by the Foreign Office that you'd gone missing and presumed dead.'

'But I'd been assured they would tell my parents that I was working undercover.'

'Well, they didn't.'

'The bastards. I guess they thought I'd been murdered as per their instructions.'

'It looks like it, anyhow, how did you end up being a prisoner in Guinea?'

Heaving another sigh, he shakes his head. 'I'm not a hundred percent sure, but thinking about it now that I've got more information, the Chinese mining outfit in Guinea must have fallen out with Beauchamp and they were holding me as some sort of pawn. If they didn't get more UK aid money, they'd release me so I could publically blow the whistle on Beauchamp - if that makes any sense.'

My mind's reeling, stunned at everything Charles is telling me and also that an important man in the Foreign Office could be so corrupt. 'I still can't get my head round it all.'

'Penny, listen to this theory, when Nick went around calling himself Charles Temple, the word would get back to Beauchamp. Hey, here's a question, were there any Foreign Office people at that New Year's Eve party you went to?'

'Yes, Paula's boyfriend for one.'

'That's it,' Charles punches his pillow. 'That's what happened, but oh fuck,' he puts his face in his hands and sobs, 'They murdered the wrong man, Nick was not the target.'

He takes my hands and puts them up to his face, the tears rolling down his cheeks. Gently, I put my arms around him as he reaches around my waist and we hug each other. His body is racked with sobbing. He is about to add to this tragic saga when there's a sudden knock on the door. Dr Kit walks in.

'Your driver says you must leave now, Miss Lane.'

Getting my breath back, I check my watch, it's eleven thirty. 'Yes, I must go.'

Ignoring Dr Kit, Charles says, 'Come and see me again, please Penny.'

'Yes, of course, I'll do my best, but it'll be tomorrow morning.'

Adele, being careful with her head bandages, greets me with a quick hug when I arrive back at Reggie's house. 'Noah's already here and we're sitting in that strange sunken hole in the living room. And hey, how did you find Charles?'

Was this a leading question or am I just feeling self-conscious? 'Oh, he's doing well,' I try to sound nonchalant but feel my face flush.

'Oh – my - God, look at your face!' Adele mocks. 'Please don't tell me you've fallen for him already, you tart, you've only just met him.'

'Don't be silly.' Scornfully, I brush off her insinuation. 'We talked, that's all, anyway,' I bluster, aware of the smirk on her face. 'Let's join the others.'

Teasingly digging me in the ribs, she follows me through to the living room. Reggie and Noah stand as we go down the few steps into the conversation pit. Plates of sandwiches are already on the centre table, along with a jug of lemonade and drinking glasses.

'I trust, dear lady, that you found our kinsman to be in fine fettle and that laggard, Dr Kit and his *frau* nurse are fulfilling their duties.'

'Thank you Reggie, Charles seems to be well on the mend and Kit says he should be well enough to fly back to UK in a few days.'

'Excellent news.' Adjusting his monocle, he gestures for us to be seated and hands the refreshments round. 'Before I pass the floor over to Colonel Tofa, I thought you may be interested in the latest newsflash from the BBC World Service. It appears there was a major accident at the N'Zera copper mine in Guinea when a store of explosives unexpectedly blew up, causing a landslide and destroying the mine road system.'

Adele laughs. 'So, they're calling it an accident, thank God for that. No mention of we terrorists from Liberia. Hopefully, the Samlians will escape any reprisals.'

'Indeed, let us hope so,' Reggie says. 'The report goes on to say that because of the explosion, the toxic tailings flowed back into the base of the mine, thus making it unmineable – that's my word,' he chortles. 'So the Samla tribe has achieved what it wanted, leaving the Chinese investors and corrupt Guinean officials extremely distraught.'

'And out of pocket,' Noah adds smiling.

Reggie raises his animated eyebrows. 'Without a doubt, like stuffed turkey-cocks I would hazard. Now, after that joyous news, I ask the good Colonel here,' he raises his glass of lemonade in Noah's direction, 'To bring us up to date on all matters military.'

Noah pauses a second to gather himself. 'Before I go into that,' his voice is noticeably sombre, 'I went to West Point slum this morning and I'm sad to report that Bambara died two days ago. It isn't a complete surprise because he was very sick when we saw him. His wife and child have already returned to their village and will be very difficult to trace.'

'Oh, poor man,' Adele's voice cracks with emotion. 'We owe him so much. It was Bambara who told Nick where Charles was being held.'

'Yes,' Noah confirms. 'The only other relative we know of, Mr Elkin, isn't expected to see the day out.'

'And we have a reward for Bambara,' Adele says. 'Well it's Penny's really, from the sale of one of the diamonds, so what happens to that?'

'May I make a suggestion,' Reggie fiddles with his monocle. 'It is, of course, very sad news about our two Mandingo heroes but handing over a large sum of money was never a good idea. Whoever received it would have no more than diddly-squat by the end of the week. A better solution, dear ladies, would be to use it to improve the lives of the slum dwellers in West Point, say a Bambara Clinic for example. The Colonel and I could organise it but I do feel this matter should be left until the impending military dangers have been addressed. Please continue with your report, Colonel.'

'There is still no military movement at Baros's diamond mine,' Noah says. 'Heavy rains are already falling in the mountainous northern regions of Liberia which will shortly swell the Mano River and flood the roads which the rebel army will need to use to get their heavy weaponry onto the Freetown Road, before heading for Monrovia.'

'Rains already,' I exclaim in surprise, 'I thought they weren't due for over a month.'

Noah shrugs. 'Weather patterns change and it's not unheard of for them to start early.'

'But that is even more reason for Baros to mount the attack on Monrovia right now,' Adele reasons. 'He's not the type to sit on his backside and do nothing. He won't give up his mine without one hell of a fight.'

Noah nods in agreement. 'The generals I talked to this morning are just as mystified. Almost all the Liberian army is now positioned at intervals on the Freetown Road, nervously waiting for the attack to start.'

'And there's one other urgent thing we mustn't forget, Colonel,' Reggie frowns. 'And that's potentially a second force to carry out a coup. What's happening to that cargo ship full of high-tech weapons and Chinese soldiers?'

'It's been radioed to anchor five miles offshore until further notice.'

'Mmm, I wonder if it will? There's nothing the Liberians can do if it ignores the order.' Reggie shakes his head, putting down his untouched glass of lemonade and calls for his steward to bring a bottle of whisky. 'I'm beginning to feel very nervous. Maybe we're missing something, something important, and all the generals are doing is waiting for Baros's army to attack. Tell me, Colonel, what can possibly be done to stop either of the coups from being successful?'

Noah is ready with an answer. 'We've studied dozens of examples of African coups and the successful ones have been quick, starting with killing the president. This creates a vacuum of power and someone has to step in and take over that power, move into the Executive Mansion, broadcast on TV and radio, and close the airports. Once the people see images of the dead president, the person behind the killing becomes leader because he has the strongest juju. Believe me,' he looks slightly embarrassed. 'As a nation, we believe in the power of juju.'

'So where is the President now?' I ask.

'In the Executive Mansion and it's my job to make sure she's safe,' Noah retorts forcefully. 'I'm the head of the Presidential Guard and, as you all already know, my men were trained by Nick Holbrook and the British SAS, with this situation in mind.'

'That's good to hear, Colonel, but what will the army do if there is a coup?'

'It's hard to say. Some would definitely support it but,' he pauses, deep in thought. 'We mustn't forget that many senior officers in the army served under Jacob Marcam, like me for example.'

Chapter Thirty
March 4th

Feeling pleasantly cool and refreshed, I gradually wake from the best sleep I've had in ages. We are sharing a bedroom but, unlike the Cleopatra, this one is blissfully air-conditioned. Adele is tossing and turning in the next bed and grunts as she turns over.

'Are you awake?' I whisper.

She exhales noisily. 'Just about.'

'Were you able to sleep with all those bandages on your head?'

'Only if I lie on one side,' she grumbles. 'If I turn over, it fucking hurts.' Groaning, she sits up in bed and her half-covered face breaks into a mischievous grin. 'Hey, Penny, what's all this between you and Charles? You went all coy last night when I asked you.'

I sigh. 'It's hard to say.' Taking a deep breath, I add, 'I had this extraordinary feeling. He looks and sounds like Nick and it's probably crazy but I think there was something between us, something special.'

'Ooh, maybe it's love at first sight. Do you think he fancies you?'

'Oh, I don't know,' I laugh. 'He was, of course, pumped full of drugs which may have affected his senses, it might have also affected his eyesight. We were only together a short time and my head and probably my heart as well, was all over the place and now I'm confused, trying to work out if I'm still thinking of Nick?'

She purses her lips and gives a little whistle. 'Well, that does sound interesting.'

Signalling that I want to change the subject, I tell her about Charles's theory that Nick was murdered on the orders of Beauchamp, because he had adopted the guise of Charles Temple.

She gives her half exposed chin a rub. 'Mmm, no, I don't think so, we're pretty certain Nick was killed for the location of the Limarni diamond mine and it was Thrimby, not Beauchamp, who was behind his murder.'

'But it now looks that Thrimby and Beauchamp are working together.'

She frowns. 'Could be, but that conundrum will have to wait for now. The first thing I have to do after breakfast is go to the clinic, so you can come with me.'

'Good, I promised to see him again.' I don't mind that she's still grinning like the proverbial Cheshire Cat. 'It's all a bit puzzling about the coup though, isn't it? Why is Jaro waiting? When we met him, he seemed a macho-man of action. In fact, Action Man himself.'

'I agree,' Adele nods. 'But as Reggie said yesterday, there's something not quite right, we're missing something but what is it? At least Noah is monitoring things. I think he's very good, in fact, he and his men were fantastic in Guinea.'

'Ah yes, that reminds me, I haven't heard yet how you rescued Charles.'

She makes herself comfortable on her bed, stretches and yawns. 'I know, so much is happening at the moment, I'll make it brief, okay?'

'Yes fine.'

'Well, we were lucky to team up with the Samla tribe as many of them had worked at the mine and knew the layout and how to avoid the guards.'

'It's a good job I wasn't there,' I joke, 'I'm no battle-hardened junkie like you.'

She smiles. 'You're probably right. Anyhow, Noah's men had night vision equipment and we easily cut through the security fence. Under cover of darkness, the tribesmen made their way to the building storing the mine explosives and, as a diversionary tactic, they blew it up. Some bloody diversion! There was this almighty bang which caused the landslide the BBC reported, we were at least a hundred yards away but were blown flat on our backs, the noise was deafening and you can imagine there was bloody chaos everywhere.'

'Just about.'

'Luckily, the Samla had already told us that Charles would be in the guard hut, and I can't tell you how amazing it was when I actually saw him, but it was a hell of a shock as the poor chap was locked in a soddin' cage, like a wild animal.'

'My God!'

Her face has that steely look again. 'I shot the fucking lock off and brilliant Elkin helped me with Charles who was too weak to run on his own. Our vehicle was only fifty yards away but before we reached it, the guards spotted us and opened fire. That's when we were injured. Noah's lot returned fire so we could get to the plane. I think you know the rest.'

'Wow, you must have been terribly frightened.'

'Terribly frightened!' she mimics sarcastically, 'Penny, I was scared shitless ... until I saw Charles.'

'As if he was coming back from the dead.'

'Something like that,' she nods. 'But, by the time we freed him, I suddenly found I was enjoying the excitement, even the chaos and danger, it gave me an incredible buzz, that's until the guards opened fire.' Closing her eyes for a moment, she relives that dreadful moment. 'But I hadn't taken into account how bloody brilliant Noah's men would be. They saved us.'

'I'm glad I wasn't there though, the baby would have taken a very dim view of it all. But how can we ever repay Noah?'

'I asked him more or less the same question but he brushed it off saying he was doing it in Nick's memory. He owed him one.'

After being closed for two days, business is back to normal at the Marguerite Clinic. The usual crowd of beggars gathering outside and the inside packed with the sick and infirm, waiting patiently in the hot, humid atmosphere smelling of eye-watering disinfectant. As before, we avoid this area and walk through Reception to an air-conditioned room. I can't help but feel guilty - why should we be so privileged?

Politicians talk about the gap between rich and poor in UK but they should come to Liberia to see what that really means.

At Reception, a nurse arrives to take Adele for her treatment. I'm about to ask to see Charles when a flustered Dr Kit rushes out of a side ward and, seeing me, comes to a standstill.

'Oh, Miss Lane,' he says abruptly, 'Mr Elkin died just after you left yesterday.'

'Yes, I heard.' I pause in respect. 'Where's the body now?'

'Gone. Within an hour of his death, the Chief of the local Mandingos came with four men and a van, and took him away. They said he'd be taken to his village for burial.'

'But why so quick?'

He gives me a look, plainly questioning my English naivety. 'Miss Lane, in the tropics, the heat makes them go ...they have to be buried or cremated very quickly.'

'Oh yes, of course.' I wait for a second before asking how Mr Temple is doing. 'Will he be fit to leave soon?'

'I'd prefer him to stay for a couple of days to finalise his course of antibiotics, but then I could discharge him as long as he stays in a clean, comfortable place. He still needs a lot of rest. If you want to see him, he's in the same room.'

Blood is pumping through my veins. Will I still feel the same when I see him again? Am I reading too much into our meeting yesterday? Maybe the affect of drugs will have worn off by now and he'll be ... I don't know, indifferent. What's wrong with me, for God's sake? Heart pounding, I knock gently on his door and go in.

Sitting in an armchair next to the bed, he uses the frame to pull himself up. Slowly opening his arms wide, he smiles, 'Penny Lane, what do you think of these?' He's wearing shocking-pink pyjamas and a shiny, almost fluorescent emerald green gown. 'Dr Kit lent them to me this morning.'

I laugh. 'Sunglasses would help.' I speak with an ease I wasn't expecting. 'But they are unique.'

'Uniquely bloody awful,' he laughs back. 'But they're clean, which is the main thing.'

'How are you today?'

'I'm better than when you saw me yesterday.' For some reason, his arms are still out wide. What does he want me to do, rush into his embrace? 'And,' he continues, 'I've also had a hot bath, the first in ages, ably assisted by a pretty young nurse.'

'You must have enjoyed that.'

'Oh yes,' he grins. 'Why don't you come and smell the *new me*?'

I hesitate. There's a palpable silence as we look into each other's eyes. I don't know what's going on in his head but, feeling surprisingly composed, I walk slowly towards him placing my hands on his waist, his arms loosely encircle me, our bodies barely touching. Resting my head lightly on his shoulder, I give a loud theatrical sniff. 'At a guess, I'd describe the smell of the *new you* as *Eau de Carbolic* with a delicate touch of *essence of dettol*.'

He chuckles. 'Yes, it's something like that but so much better than the shitty smell I had before. His tone softens, 'anyway, putting scents aside, I'm glad you came. I thought about you last night, you and Nick, poor Nick.'

'Does it upset you to talk about him?'

'No, strangely enough, it's sort of okay.' He blinks his watery eyes and I can feel his sadness reaching out to me. 'It's like he's still here and if I look over my shoulder he'd be there, smiling that smile of his.'

I fight back my own tears. 'I feel the same although I've had a couple of months to get used to it.' Gently pulling away from his embrace, I look directly into his face and tenderly smooth the hair off his forehead and wipe a stray tear away. 'Charles,' I say his name softly, 'I've been thinking over what you said about Nick being murdered because he was using your name but I'm not sure you're right.'

'Oh, why's that?'

'Adele and I are certain that Nick was murdered for the location of a diamond mine and his boss, Sir Desmond Thrimby, was prepared to kill to get his hands on it. Now it seems that Thrimby and Beauchamp are collaborating with the Chinese, not only in the misuse of British aid, but also to grab what we've been told is the biggest diamond mine discovery since Kimberley and it's actually here in Liberia. We think Nick was killed because of that.'

He searches my face. 'Are you sure?'

'As sure as we can be. We hope to find out more because both men are here in Monrovia at the moment, along with a Chinese man who's got a cargo ship full of weapons and soldiers due to arrive any day. They plan to take the mine by force and then operate it for their own benefit. They will mount a coup and assassinate the President in the process.'

'Bloody hell.'

I jump as the door suddenly bursts open and Adele barges in. 'Break it up you two, we have to go now, all of us, it's urgent.'

'But Charles can't go,' I snap. 'He can hardly stand and is still getting treatment.'

'Oh yes, he bloody well can,' she retorts vehemently. 'Dr Kit is packing his medication and sending one of his nurses with us to Reggie's. There's been a development and all three of us have to go now, right now. They're bringing a wheelchair to help Charles to the car.'

As the Rolls glides through the gates of the Grosvenor-Smythe's residence, the front door is flung open by Reggie. 'Well done, everyone, it's good you've made it so quickly.' James and the nurse lift the wheelchair out of the trunk and help Charles into it. 'I'm delighted to meet you, Mr Temple, welcome to my, shall we say substitute clinic,' Reggie gestures towards the door, 'I trust you'll be well cared for by charming Nurse Biyoyowei.'

'I'm sure I will, sir,' Charles's voice shows signs of fatigue. 'And thank you very much'.

'Think nothing of it, dear fellow, it's my pleasure. We'll get you settled first and by then, I hope Colonel Tofa will have joined us. But please don't be alarmed, I've asked you here as a precaution because you'll be safer than in the Marguerite Clinic.'

I want to ask *why* but keep my mouth shut while the nurse skilfully navigates Charles's wheelchair to the ground-floor bedroom. Like two sheep, Adele and I follow, worried that he's looking drawn after the twenty-minute car ride. Nurse Biyoyowei plumps up his pillows and as Adele turns to leave, I stealthily give him a crafty wink.

Clearly knowing the nurse well, Reggie booms. 'Oh, Nurse Biyoyowei, there's a rather pleasant little ante-room where you are most welcome to reside until Mr Temple has sufficiently recovered. I trust you are agreeable to that.'

Her beaming smile confirms the arrangement is more than acceptable. 'I will also attend to Miss Holbrook's head wound,' she says, touching Adele's arm.

'Thank you, Nurse, that will be first-rate.' Reggie ushers Adele and me into the living room, pointing at the sandwiches and lemonade laid out on the table in the conversation pit. 'I've been trying to contact Colonel Tofa on my cell phone for the last hour,' he dramatically waves the instrument at us, 'But I can't get a blessed signal. Some reprobates must have switched off the transmitters.' He places the offending object on a side-table. 'Miraculously, however, my landline is working, in fits and starts that is, and I was able to leave a message for the Colonel to get in touch immediately. So I hope he'll be here shortly.'

Desperate to know what's going on, I ask. 'What's happening, Reggie, what's so urgent?' my voice full of apprehension. 'Has the coup started?'

He opens his palms out as a calming gesture then, vigorously polishing his monocle, slowly settles in his seat. 'I don't think so, dear ladies, not at this moment, anyway.'

Adele speaks up. 'But Reggie, something critical must have happened.'

'Of course, you're right, and I'm not going to lie to you, there is a dangerous situation developing but I was hoping the Colonel would be here so I could tell you all together.' He leaves us hanging in limbo as we hear a vehicle screeching to a halt outside, followed by some muffled orders and, much to everyone's relief, Noah strides purposefully into the room.

After briefly acknowledging our presence, he says, 'I'll have to be quick as I'm due at the Executive Mansion for a meeting with the President and the army chiefs of staff.'

Like an aging thespian performing in repertory, Reggie glances heavenwards. '*Thank the powers that be* that you're here, Colonel, and the answer is yes, I have become privy to a couple of extremely important events which you may not know about, and will affect your military planning.'

Noah looks pointedly at his watch. 'As quick as you can, sir.'

'Yes, of course,' Reggie takes a unenthusiastic sip of lemonade which makes him grimace. 'First, I have a reliable harbinger in South Africa who informed me that three men were detained outside a maximum security prison in Durban. It appears that they were trying to *bust* an incarcerated ne'er-do-well out.'

Adele and I exchange puzzled glances not understanding the significance of this news. Annoyingly, whether for dramatic effect or not, Reggie pauses to polish his monocle once again. Noah gives an irritated sigh. 'Then forty minutes ago,' Reggie continues, 'My chappie enlarged on the story saying that the men are mercenaries. Not only that, but the local constabulary arrested the pilot of a small plane waiting at a nearby airstrip. The prison in question is where Jacob Marcam is detained.'

'Ah,' I yell with excitement. 'That's it, yes. Baros told us he'd sent mercenaries to get Marcam out of jail.'

Noah sits motionless, staring at the ceiling as if the answer can be found in its decorative white plasterwork. 'Of course,' he exclaims. '*That's* why Baros has been waiting, he wanted Marcam to lead the coup.'

'That's what I thought,' Reggie says. 'So will Baros still carry out his evil deed?'

'Yes, Baros has General Tabo to lead the men. Tabo fell out with President Poltara months ago. He was trained in America with their Marine Corps - he's very good.'

'So when do you think the attack will start?'

Noah massages his temples, presumably, trying to grasp the full implications of the situation. 'It'll be the moment Baros hears about the failed jail attempt. He can't delay any longer now that the rains have started. In fact,' he looks anxious, preparing to leave. 'It's possibly underway now, and that's why saboteurs have destroyed the cell phone masts.' Heading towards the door, he says, 'I'll begin plans to move the President out of harm's way.'

'Please wait, Colonel,' Reggie says. 'There's one thing more.'

Looking annoyed, Noah stops in his tracks for a second time.

'I asked Bachir Gemayel at the Cleopatra to listen-in on phone calls made by his two British VIP guests. One of them phoned their chum, the Minister of Mines and told him they'd signalled the Shenzhen Yong, the Chinese ship, to ignore orders from Liberian officials and dock at the port as soon as possible, using force if necessary.'

'Goddamn it,' a look of alarm crosses Noah face. 'Did they say when that would be?'

'Sometime tonight, I think Colonel, probably in the early hours.'

'Hell, bloody hell,' Noah growls, 'I'll immediately order the diversion of troops and heavy weapons to the port, they may be able to stop the ship docking, or at least delay it.'

Preparing to leave once again, he turns to face us. 'It would be wise for you to stay indoors for the time being. Do you have extra guards?'

'*Oh yes, Colonel,*' Reggie asserts, 'I've lived through two civil wars here without a scratch. I have a safe, well-stocked basement, and my own private security team outside. I'll make sure they're on twenty-four hour watch.'

'Excellent,' Noah nods and heads for the door.

But something's niggling at the back of my mind. We're still missing something, something important. And now it suddenly hits me as though a slow burning fuse in my head suddenly ignites. 'I've got it,' I jump up yelling, 'Noah, you've got it wrong, we all have.'

Exasperated, he glares at me. 'Penny, for goodness sake, I've got to go.'

'Stop this nonsense, Penny,' an equally annoyed Adele commands, 'Noah knows what he's doing. Baros's men are probably already on the Freetown Road heading for Monrovia.'

319

'You're WRONG, WRONG, WRONG,' I shout. 'Jaro's far too clever for that. No, it's just dawned on me, *HIS ARMY IS COMING BY SEA*.'

Angrily, Noah shouts. 'They can't come by sea, they'd need a ship for that, I'm going.'

'Noah stop.' My heart's pounding and I'm almost breathless with tension as I run in front of him holding my arms out wide. 'They don't need a ship because they've got boats. Noah, believe me, *they're coming by sea*.'

The same fuse must have just ignited in Adele's head. 'Of course, Penny's right, they have boats.'

Ignoring us both, Noah grabs my arm to push past but I persist, my voice racing away at top speed. 'Noah, when we were at the mine, we saw a fleet of small vessels on the Mano River, larger than speed boats and big enough to carry soldiers.'

The scowl on his face partially fades and his eyes narrow as though deep in thought. 'Carry on.' His voice calmer now.

'Baros told us that they use the boats to get supplies from Sierra Leone during the rainy season, when the roads are flooded.'

Noah turns to Adele. 'Did you see these boats, if so, how many, what size?'

'Yes I did,' she screws up her eyes deep in thought. 'About eight of them, forty or fifty feet I'd guess.'

'But are you sure they could navigate the rapids near the mouth of the Mano River?' Noah's stare is unflinching. 'They're a barrier to shipping unless - unless they've dynamited a way through.'

'They must have,' Adele answers animatedly, 'Otherwise they couldn't use them.'

His meeting at the Executive Mansion temporarily forgotten, Noah's brain seems to go into overdrive. 'Several years ago,' he says, 'The Government bought and paid for twelve twenty-three meter coastal patrol boats but,' he smiles contemptuously. 'They never arrived. There was a huge scandal at the time, but soon forgotten amongst all the other corrupt activities. These boats were to be equipped with missiles, torpedoes and rocket-propelled grenades.'

He pauses, taking a deep breath. 'Now, if Jacob Marcam got them and kept them hidden on the Mano River then, my God, they could sail along the coast all the way to Monrovia, up the Mesurado River, bypassing the Liberian army on the Freetown Road.'

Reggie adds. 'If they destroy the two bridges, the army would be cut off.'

'The clever bastard,' Adele says. 'But Noah, what about the President? You told us she'll be the main target, *if* she's still at the Executive Mansion, could they reach that?'

'She's still there and, this gets worse, the mansion backs onto the sea. They could launch missiles and a landing party could be in the building within minutes.' Looking shell-shocked, Noah glances at his watch. 'I've got to go, it's nearly two o'clock so we've got four hours of daylight. The first thing I'll do is order the UN helicopter to go up and see what's happening.'

There's so much we all want to ask, but it'd be foolish to delay Noah any longer. After he rushes out, closing the door with a bang, we hear his vehicle speed away. The three of us look at each other in a state of suspended shock, temporarily speechless.

Eventually breaking the silence, Reggie calls urgently to his steward. 'Bring my whisky and whatever these two ladies want.'

'I think Noah will do it,' Adele ventures, accepting a glass of lemonade from the steward. 'Don't you, Reggie?'

'Yes, my dear, I do. Getting to know the Colonel over the past few weeks,' he takes his first gulp of whisky and gives a satisfied nod. 'He's grown in my estimation and I like the cut of his jib, obviously been well trained by your brother. And, Miss Lane, if your conjecture about the boats is correct *and* our bold young warrior sallies forth and defeats the Armada, then the whole nation will be in your debt.'

'Oh, I don't think so,' I reply. 'But whatever happens, whether by land or sea, people are going to die, and for what? For a diamond mine - pure, unadulterated greed.'

'Ah, yes, avarice, the root of all evil.' Reggie raises his glass and muses. 'When I behold the havoc that greediness wreaks, who cares what damage to our souls we bring.' Bowing, he drains his glass. 'And now if you'll excuse me, dear ladies, I'm about to retire for my daily forty-winks before the skirmish starts. I don't suppose the Colonel will be able to put a stopper on things for a few hours yet but, once the blue touch-paper has been lit, there'll be very little sleep for any of us. *Alia lacta est*.' And with that, he heads towards the staircase.

Adele asks, 'What was all that rubbish he said?'

'Another of his mangled quotes,' I laugh. 'But anyway, maybe we should rest too.'

She agrees but thinks we should tell Charles and Nurse Biyoyowei of the latest situation. Adele gives me that *knowing look* of hers. 'You can tell Charles and I'll ask the nurse to change my bandages.'

Reflecting on my next move, I try to bring Charles's face into focus, or is it Nick's? 'Hey, what are you waiting for!' Adele gives me a start as she pokes her head out of the nurse's room. 'Don't worry, I'll be around if he screams for help.'

'Oh ha, ha.' The sound of her mocking laughter fades as she closes the door.

I take a deep breath, exhaling slowly as I hesitantly enter Charles's room. Sitting up in bed, he smiles warmly. Damn, my legs go weak. Whatever possesses me, I can't begin to imagine, but my guardian angel seems to have taken control of my body and I find myself propelled towards him, kissing him directly on the lips. He doesn't stop me but, there again, how could he with his head pressed back against the pillows. When I pull away, feeling embarrassed, I ask lamely, 'How are you?'

Cocking his head to one side, he laughs. 'Pretty good, thank you'. His face reflects an inner calm and the tension inside me evaporates. Still grinning, he says, 'And you are Miss er?'

'Lane,' I laugh back, 'Miss Lane.'

'Ah yes, it's all coming back to me now.' He pulls me towards him and we kiss again, more intimately this time.

Chuckling, I step back. 'And you are Mr ...?'

'To tell you the truth, I'm not sure, my mind's gone completely fuzzy.'

He's funny, a good sense of humour, I like that. Butterflies, pulse racing, heart pounding well, I feel all of them. Dare I dream he's the one? Calm down girl, he's still recovering from gunshot wounds and I'm pregnant which, to say the least, limits the start of a meaningful relationship. It nags me that I still think about Nick even at the moment when my body is telling me to forget. Disciplining myself, I get down to business, however difficult. 'Actually, Charles, I've come to tell you that the coup we're expecting could start at any time and we might have to shelter in Reggie's basement.'

He frowns, but looks amused at the same time. 'Is that how you always pass on bad news, with a kiss?'

'Yes, I'm well known for it.'

He holds both my hands. 'So seriously, is it all to do with the diamond mine?'

'Yes, it is, Professor Jaroslav Baros's diamond mine - Limarni.'

Charles purses his lips and gives a silent whistle. 'Remind me again, who are the protagonists in this coup.'

'Number One is Professor Baros whose rebel army is poised to march on Monrovia. He knows that if the government takes over the mine, he'll get nothing even though he discovered it in the first place.'

'I can see his point,' Charles nods. 'The government will kick him out and then, probably, be tricked by some foreign outfit, probably Chinese, and they'll end up getting peanuts.'

'You're already way ahead of me,' I say grimly. 'Because the second protagonists are the Chinese supported by your boss at the Foreign Office, Beauchamp, and his fellow conspirator, Thrimby. They've got a ship full of weapons and armed Chinese soldiers due to dock shortly. They want the mine whatever it takes.'

'Bloody hell,' he crinkles his forehead. 'And what about the Liberian army and the President, do they know there are two separate groups planning military coups?'

'They do now because of Noah.'

'Oh, of course, good old Noah, I'd still be locked up in that hellhole if wasn't for him.'

'He is a good man but Reggie's not sure how effective the Liberian army will be when the fighting starts.'

Adele and I spend the next couple of hours mooching around the living room or strolling aimlessly in the garden. To top it all, I'm not feeling well, a headache and stomach cramps. It such a bizarre situation to be in - here we are, in these tranquil surroundings whilst soldiers just down the road are preparing for battle. Eventually, we are joined on the terrace by Reggie after his *overly-long* forty winks, re-filled whisky glass in hand.

'Waiting, dear ladies, is the hardest part.' He absent-mindedly runs his index finger on the moisture running down the outside of his glass and vainly attempts to smooth down his bushy eyebrows. 'In the past thirty years,' he continues 'I've been through the vagaries of this kind of farrago twice, so I'm a seasoned old hand at waiting for urgent dispatches from the battle front.'

Carefully holding onto her glass, Adele gloomily plonks herself down on a terrace chair. 'Reggie, when do *you* think we'll hear anything?'

'Hmm, hard to say. I was hoping the Colonel would telephone us with a brief update. I'm sure he would have done if he could, but I've just checked my landline and unfortunately, it's dead. So we are twiddling our thumbs, incommunicado, so to speak.'

'But he has our satellite phone number,' Adele says excitedly, 'So he might try that.'

'Ah, of course.'

Puffs of high cloud drift across the late afternoon sky and the scents of frangipani and other exotic flowers hang heavy in the air. 'Time to go inside I'm afraid, ladies,' Reggie announces, 'Before the mossies think we're their evening meal.' He studies the sky and sniffs the air. 'I think we'll have rain by this evening, probably only a shower or two, but you never know, it might dampen the ardour of some of the more belligerent combatants.'

As if his words were a prophecy, we hear the first explosions in the distance, followed immediately by rapid small-arms fire.

'It's kick-off time, opening salvos I expect.' Unruffled, Reggie calls for his steward to bring a whisky. 'From the sounds of it, I'd say it's the far side of Monrovia so we needn't do anything yet.'

My tummy's beginning to feel worse and the headache starting to throb. I don't say anything to the others, hoping it'll go away as quickly as it came.

'Come upstairs,' Reggie suggests. 'It's getting dark and we'll get a better view from the roof terrace. There are no mossie blighters up there, either.'

A series of detonations join the heavy guns and the crack-crack of rifle-fire. Halfway up the stairs, our satellite phone rings and Adele quickly answers. 'It's Noah,' she whispers, holding the receiver tight to her ear, pulling a face as she struggles to hear. She grunts occasionally but doesn't have time to ask questions before the line goes dead.

'He's close to the fighting.'

'Yes, yes, but what did he say?'

'Well, Penny, you were right, the rebel army is coming by sea. The UN helicopter spotted several boats heading towards Monrovia from the Mano River, although the pilot and spotter disagreed about the number. They were spaced out, probably heading for different targets but they couldn't stay up longer because two of the boats shot at them so the pilot high-tailed it back to Spriggs Payne.'

'Did the Colonel say where they were attacking first?' Reggie asks.

'No, but one of the Mesurado bridges is down and they're defending the second one. The Executive Mansion has been attacked but Noah has already moved the President.'

'That, at least, is good news.' Reggie's glass is empty but it must be a sign of his concern that he doesn't immediately call for another. 'Keeping President Poltara safe may well stop the coup succeeding. Oh, and another thing, did the Colonel mention the Chinese ship?'

'No, Reggie, he didn't have time.' Adele wipes sweat from the part of her brow free of bandages. 'But the airport is closed. He said something about ... is it the Framlinton River?'

Giving a sharp intake of breath, Reggie bellows, 'Great Balls of Fire, it's the Farmington River. One of Baros's boats must have gone on ahead. Damnation! The Farmington runs into the heart of the Firestone Plantation and yes, by golly, part of it runs by the airport.'

Apprehensively, climbing the final steps, we walk out onto the roof terrace, dazzled by bright yellow explosions tinged with luminous green and blue flares we can see in the distance. Tracer bullets fly in all directions.

BOOM. We almost jump out of our skins as one enormous explosion erupts followed a few seconds later by an ear-shattering sound and a blast of hot air. Night is turned into day illuminating the whole area, a brilliance so bright we have to cover our eyes.

'Holy Sons of Thor,' Reggie gasps. 'What on earth is that? It's like Hiroshima.' Several more explosions and flashes shoot high in the air. 'By jingo, it's out at sea, look, you can see the reflection in the water.'

Suddenly, a severe pain shoots through my stomach and I lose all interest in everything around me. Clutching my belly with both hands, my vision blurs and another sharp pain strikes as I collapse on the floor, curling into a foetal ball.

'Oh my God,' Adele turns, 'Penny, you're covered in blood.' She gives Reggie a thump on his arm, yelling to get his attention. 'Has she been shot?'

Groaning in agony, my dress wet, I pray for the agony to go away.

'Oh hell, it's the baby, isn't it?' Adele shouts. 'I'll get the nurse, don't move.'

Reggie, left on his own, with me, bloodied and groaning on the floor, hovers around. 'Can I er ...' he gives a token cough to clear his throat. 'Can I help at all?' I mutter a weak "no", probably not heard above the din and then the clatter of footsteps rushing up the stairs heralding the arrival of Adele and Nurse Biyoyowei.

'Make space,' she orders loudly and, gently holding me round the shoulders, asks where the pain is. 'You call me Matilda, it my name,' she says, then under her guidance, I do some deep breathing while she lightly massages my stomach, the pain subsiding a little. Aided by Adele, she manages to haul me to my feet. All the time, the racket continues around us.

'She not stay here,' Matilda shouts at the others. 'We get her downstair.' Ignoring the gunfire, she orders Reggie to get Mr Temple out of bed. 'He can walk so we use his room.'

Looking a little perplexed to be taking orders instead of giving them, Reggie hurries to do her bidding. The staircase is narrow so Matilda leads, helping me take one step at a time with Adele taking part of the strain by holding onto me from behind. Each jolt sends a sharp pain into my belly. Sweating from every pour in my body, I don't know if it's sweat or blood; what I do know is I stink to high heaven. We eventually reach Charles's room and I'm half carried to the empty bed.

'We get her to the clinic,' Matilda says holding my hand tightly. 'She urgent needs doctor, could be baby miscarriage.'

My heart sinks, then another sharp pain makes me cry out.

Reggie appears at the door. 'We can't go to the clinic,' he states emphatically.

'We must,' Matilda insists. 'Look at her, she bad.'

'Sorry, but no,' Reggie firmly reasserts his authority. 'I'm sorry Miss Lane but you'll have to stay here. Every conceivable medical centre in and around Monrovia will be filling up with wounded soldiers.' He almost bristles. 'They go into battle high on drugs or under some Juju spell, smothering themselves in blood, believing it'll protect them from being shot. Chaos will reign at the Marguerite Clinic and you would be in even more danger and get no treatment.'

The realisation that he speaks with experience subdues Matilda. 'Yes, sir, but no doctor mean,' she lowers her voice hoping I won't hear. 'May lose baby and,' she tries whispering even more quietly, but I still hear, 'Miss Lane life in danger.'

Oh shit. I'm worried sick now and the pain is not decreasing. Through the corner of my eye I can make out

Reggie thrusting out his shoulders as if preparing for battle. 'In that case,' he declares, 'The mountain will have to come to Mohamed. I will go to the clinic and bring Dr Kit here. Oh, and Miss Lane, do you know your blood group?'

'I'm 'O' positive,' I whisper. 'But the pain, please get me something for the pain.'

'Of course, my dear lady, I'll do my very best.'

'But Reggie,' Adele butts in, 'Shouldn't someone else go?'

'Possibly, Miss Holbrook, but I've got James, my bodyguard driver, and I'll take a couple of my well-armed security officers from outside. They'll act as my Proetarian Guard. Now then, Nurse Biyoyowei, make a list of the medicines and equipment you need, and if Dr Kit hasn't already scarpered, I'll bring him here, even if I have to drag him by the scruff of his scrawny neck. If he's not there, I'll, well, get another.'

I notice Reggie's managed to get another glass of whisky which he drains in one gulp. 'This my Juju,' he laughs, and with a *v for victory* wave, marches majestically out of the room shouting, '*Carpe diem.*'

I lie on the bed, feeling very sorry for myself, while Matilda carefully uses scissors, cutting away my stained dress and underwear. She wipes away sweat and blood before wrapping me in clean sheets and towels. 'You got gown to wear?'

'Leave that to me,' Adele says. 'I've got the very thing, I'll be back in a sec.'

'Matilda,' I plead, 'Please don't let Charles see me like this.'

'He no see you, he sharing room with Missie Adele. How you feel now?'

'Not too good, I'm still in pain and feel dizzy.'

'You dizzy 'cos you lose much blood, and I can't give you nothing for pain until doctor come.'

'But that could be ages,' Adele returns carrying a loose fitting gown. 'Can't she have pain killers, I have plenty?'

'No, only water,' Matilda takes my hand in hers. 'Do your best to hold on.'

I try to smile. 'I'll let you know if it gets worse.'

During the time everyone's been fussing over me, the sound of explosions and gunfire seems to be louder. I'm frightened, no, petrified. If a doctor doesn't come soon, or can't, or won't, it could be curtains for me. 'Matilda,' I ask anxiously, 'How long will it take Mr Grosvenor-Smythe to bring a doctor?'

'Oh, e' hard to say with all the war business.'

A thunderous explosion shakes the house, rattling windows, doors, and causing the lights to flicker. The air-conditioning unit gives a couple of hiccups before kicking back into life. A security officer bangs on the front door calling. 'Everybody go basement, one time.'

'Oh God,' I cry out, desperately trying to keep my panic under control. 'What's next?'

'Stay calm everyone.' Adele's bossy character comes to the fore. Toma, Reggie's steward, peers round the door. 'Ah, Toma,' Adele says sharply, 'I want to see the basement.' They scurry off with her snapping at his heels telling him to hurry. She's soon back. 'There's plenty of room and it's secure. Matilda, you get Charles and take him down, then come back and we'll manage Penny between us.'

Biting my lip trying to mask the pain, Matilda and Adele support me to shuffle along the corridor, squeeze through a heavy metal door and then negotiate steps into the basement. There are no windows but it's brightly lit by three neon strip-lights and two air-conditioning units cool the air. Down here, the noise of fighting is deadened. I give an involuntary shudder as they lay me on a sofa already covered with sheets. Charles, still wearing the hideous gown from the clinic, is sitting in an armchair in the far corner, he smiles and waves. The move down here has made the pain in my belly worse and I sense that I'm losing more blood, my thighs are wet and sticky, my head's spinning and I'm feeling faint. I almost laugh at my own vanity, if I'm going to die, I want to look my best for Charles to remember me, not covered in blood and guck with my face and hair a mess. I think I'm going mad.

'Right, listen everyone,' Adele stands in the centre of the room. 'We will be safe here until the fighting stops. Toma and I have done a quick recce and in a small kitchenette there's tinned food and water, as well as sheets and blankets. An emergency generator is in a solid bunker so we shouldn't run out of power.'

'But Penny needs the doctor,' Charles points out.

'I know that, Charles,' she replies irritably. 'Reggie only left half an hour ago. It'll be some time before he gets back with a doctor.'

'But can't Matilda help, she's a nurse.'

'For God's sake, Charles, she already is. Just sit there and shut up.'

While a highly agitated Adele paces round the room, Matilda asks me, 'Any change?'

'No,' I whisper. 'Still dizzy, but I'd love a cup of tea.'

'Toma, you go make tea,' Matilda orders.

Dizziness sweeps over me in waves, I think I'm hallucinating. I have this image of drug-crazed soldiers bursting in and I'm the only one unable to run away. I blink my eyes a couple of times - the room seems to be going round and round, faces and voices go blurry and ... now it's dark, silent, my mum's shrouded face smiling at me. She's speaking but there's no sound.

Coming to, out of what seemed a dream, I'm aware of things happening to me and there are new voices. Struggling to open my eyes, I have a vague image of Dr Kit kneeling at my side, his words echo inside my head, all jumbled up. I'm lying flat and things have been attached to my arms and I feel the prick of an injection in my thigh. 'I'm cold.' I hear my own words but don't know if anyone else can hear me. 'Tea,' I say, 'I want tea.' A feeding cup of hot liquid is placed between my lips and I manage to swallow a couple of times before coughing, the liquid spurting out and burning my chest.

'How you feeling?' It's Dr Kit by my side.

I look around, my vision much clearer. I'm rigged up to a drip in my arm. 'Am I okay?' I ask. Although still weak, I can tell my voice is much stronger.

'You're doing fine,' he says. 'Your blood pressure is ... a bit low but the bleeding has stopped. I'll leave the other drip in for a couple of hours to make sure you're completely hydrated.'

'And the baby?'

He pauses before answering. 'I'm not sure. These are not ideal conditions, you need to be in hospital. My examination indicates that well ...it's my best guess, the placenta could be in the wrong place or damaged, but this can be treated in a hospital. I've given you an injection to prevent early labour as well as steroids to help the baby's lungs.'

'Does that mean the baby's alright?'

Again, a moment passes before he answers. 'I'm just about to do an ultrasound scan but it's only a basic portable machine, a leaving present from the hospital in Berlin, but it should give me a better idea of what's going on.'

Making sure my dignity is intact, Matilda applies some cold jelly to my stomach and Kit's machine, a bit like my parents' old gramophone, kicks into life. He makes adjustments to some knobs and dials and it hums as the screen flickers into life. 'It's working,' he says excitedly. 'Now nurse, here the Zauber.'

The monitor is at the wrong angle for me to see but Matilda smoothly runs the Zauber, or wand in English, over my belly for a few seconds. I hope it's a magic wand. There's total silence in the room as though everyone is holding their breath. Out of the corner of my eye I can see Adele gripping Reggie's arm, Charles by his side. Kit makes a few frustrated grunts as he twiddles more knobs and says, almost to himself. 'Ah, I'm getting a picture. Nurse, move it over a bit ... er up a bit.'

'I can see a heart beating,' Matilda shouts. 'Is that right, Doctor?'

Kit doesn't answer. Why? Is it for dramatic effect or serious medical reasons. I can't stand it. 'Is my baby alright, damn it, Kit, tell me.'

'Look, Penny,' he takes hold of my hand. 'I can only tell you the baby is alive, it's got a strong heart beat but, beyond that, I can't tell. Not now, not here in Liberia, you need to fly to England immediately.'

'But the airport's closed,' Adele says.

'What do you mean, closed?'

'There's a bloody war on, for God's sake,' Adele hollers at Kit. 'The airport was the first thing they closed.'

His face changes from apprehension to dread. 'In that case she'll probably ...' he stops. This infuriating habit of his, long pauses before replying to a question, is doing my head in.

'*She'll probably what?*' I summon up what little strength I have. 'Finish the sentence, do you mean *she'll probably* die or lose the baby. Is that what you're trying to say?'

'Well,' he gets his first word out, then finds an itch on his chin that needs scratching. 'Well no,' he eventually answers, 'I didn't mean anything like that. You're stable at the moment and I've given you a tranquilliser to help you rest. The bleeding seems to have stopped, which is good, and your blood pressure is just about within range, but ... '

'Ha, I thought there would be a *but*.'

'Miss Lane, the stark truth is that if the bleeding starts again,' he shakes his head. 'Well, the clinic's in a mess and there's no chance of getting to the blood stocks there.'

'Blood stocks!' Reggie declares loudly, 'God, man, if you have blood in the clinic we should go and get it right away.'

'Please, Mr Grosvenor-Smythe,' Kit almost grovels, 'I must stay here until the fighting's over. You saw how the soldiers were smashing up the clinic looking for drugs. If I go back, they'll probably kill me.'

'You pathetic, snivelling poltroon,' Reggie snarls, his face growing red with anger. 'You've got the chance to redeem yourself and, by all that's holy, I'll make sure you do. Get to your feet before I kick your fat butt all the way to the car.'

Another grovel from Kit makes Reggie even angrier and he grabs him by the collar, dragging him out of the basement. 'Peckers up everyone, we'll be back as soon as possible and,' giving a cheery wave, says, 'We'll bring all the supplies we can.'

'But you be target for soldiers,' Matilda says to Reggie.

'Not a chance, Nurse Biyoyowei,' he snorts. 'I've got my own security men and two large *stars and stripes* on my vehicle and no-one, but no-one, whether drunk or drugged, will shoot at Americans.'

With that final statement, he pushes Kit roughly through the basement door, slamming it closed behind him.

There's a stunned silence before Adele laughs. 'Good old Reggie, saved by Uncle Sam instead of St George.'

'Yes,' Charles attempts a cheery voice. 'He's right that every Liberian has an in-built admiration for America. It's in their DNA. Isn't that right, Toma?'

'Yes boss,' Toma beams. 'We like America too much.'

Although I'm still dizzy, the pain is less intense and my body is starting to relax, it's probably the tranquillisers kicking-in. I know everyone here cares about me, but right now, it's my mother I need. Poor mum and dad still think I'm, well, un-pregnant and on a carefree holiday in Spain. They're in for one hell of a shock. I pray silently to myself that I'll live long enough to see them again.

Adele quickly changes the subject. 'Anyway, Matilda, while we're waiting, what about Mr Temple, what can you do for him?'

'Mr Temple wounds heal good,' she smiles. 'His temperature and blood pressure fine, but he also need English hospital. Instead Adele, I change your dressing.'

'Thank you, Matilda,' Adele lets her clean and replace the bandage on her head. 'We owe you so much. All we have to do now is keep Penny stable until Reggie returns, hang on in there, Penny Lane, we're all rooting for you.'

'I think it help if Miss Lane has food,' Matilda says as she checks the drip feed. 'Like omelette.'

'I'll do that,' Adele quickly moves into the kitchenette. 'Are there eggs, Toma?'

'They upstairs, Missie.'

They leave the basement and Charles comes over to sit next to me. 'I wish there was something I could do to help,' he gives an affectionate smile and strokes my hand. He glances at his watch, 'Reggie will be back soon and he's certain to bring supplies with him, he's an amazing chap.'

'Yes, I know.'

Charles moves aside as Toma appears with a tray of food. Matilda starts to feed me some small pieces of omelette when an excited Adele almost tumbles down the stairs clutching the satellite phone in her hand. 'Hey everyone, I've just spoken to Noah, he thinks the hostilities are almost over and it's only a matter of time before the word gets through to those still fighting. And listen, there's very little noise outside now.'

'Oh my God,' Charles exclaims. 'If it is over, then who won?'

'I'm ... oh shit, I'm not sure.'

'Not sure! What do you mean? Is it Noah and the government who's won, Baros's army or the Chinese? It must be one of them.'

Adele's face is a picture of confusion. 'It was very bad line and Noah said he's rushed off his feet, but he'll come round here. I think he said in the morning, and explain everything. But he did say we shouldn't worry.'

'Well in that case, it must be the government forces who won - is it?'

'I've already told you I'm not sure,' she snaps. 'But ah, just a second, as he was about to hang-up, I asked him about the airport.'

'And?'

'He thinks it will be open in two or three of days.'

'That's fantastic,' Charles shouts. 'You hear that, Penny?'

I close my eyes with a sense of relief just as a stabbing pain shoots through my guts. 'Ow.' I clutch my belly with both hands, 'Ow.' I'm wracked with a new pain, my body stiffens and my brain is going blurry, I'm sinking, faces are spinning, voices distort and I drift away down a long, dark tunnel.

CHAPTER THIRTY-ONE
MARCH 5th

Where - what? Oh, God ... what's happening? Slowly coming to, through fuzzy layers, I'm aware of my breathing, whew, I'm alive and, oh, what about my baby? There's a faint droning filling the space between my ears. I shake my head but nothing happens. In the dim light, I can just make out Matilda, head back, gently snoozing next to my bed. Doing my best to look round, there's no sign of Reggie nor Kit nor, for that matter, the others. Why aren't they here? Did Reggie get the blood for me? How long have I been out? Hang on, the pain in my belly - it's almost gone. I try and speak but only a gruff animal-like noise escapes from my lungs.

Matilda stirs, a low light comes on next to her chair. 'How you feel; has pain gone?'

Saliva has drained out of my mouth, I can't swallow.

'Water?' she asks, 'I get you water?'

I nod. She holds a glass to my lips and I sip several mouthfuls before waving it away.

'That better?' Clearing my throat, I whisper, 'Thanks Matilda, I think the pain has gone.'

'That good, I now wash you while others still sleep.'

'Matilda, is my baby - you know?' I'm terrified of hearing her reply - bad news.

'Everything good, Missie, no miscarriage.'

A sense of relief sweeps over me. Maybe I'll ... no, maybe *we'll* make it after all. 'And Mr Grosvenor-Smyth?'

'He upstairs, Missie. It quiet now 'cos the fighting business finish. He bring blood. I give you two units and there no more bleeding, your pulse good and long sleeping make you better. There two more units in the fridge, just in case.'

'Is Dr Kit here?'

'No,' she gives me more water to drink and waits for me to finish. 'Dr Kit taken by soldiers at clinic. He stay there to treat injured soldiers, there too many.'

Ruefully I smile but say nothing. It probably serves him right.

Running water splashing in the kitchen must have woken the others. Lights go on making me cover my face for a few seconds.

'How're you doing?' wiping away sleep, Adele sits on the side of my bed but moves out of the way when Matilda approaches with a basin of water.

'Fine, I think. What time is it?'

'That's wonderful, you had us so worried. Oh! the time, it's nearly five-thirty and getting light. I'll go and organise some breakfast.'

Charles approaches but only has a chance to squeeze my hand before Matilda starts my ablutions. 'I'm in the way,' he smiles, 'I'll go with Adele.'

She gives me a thorough wash and helps me into a clean gown. 'You can sit up now. You feel better?'

My arms feel bruised but that's the least of my worries. 'Yes thank you Matilda, you've been wonderful.' I'm surprised my voice sounds strong and my woozy head has almost cleared.

'Try standing 'cos if you feel good, I help you upstair.'

I'm just about to take the first doddery steps when a vehicle screeches to a halt outside, and I hear voices in the entrance hall.

Adele pokes her head around the basement door and shouts, 'It's Noah, can you make it, Penny?'

Determinedly, I reply, 'We're on our way up, if you'll give us a hand.'

There's silence in the living room as Matilda and Adele sit me down in the nearest armchair. I must look a mess, but I'm alive and to hell with my appearance.

'Well done, Penny Lane,' a beaming Reggie gives a *thumbs-up* sign. 'You look marvellous.' A chorus of agreement cheers me up no end. Reggie, standing erect with thumbs anchored to the armholes of his waistcoat takes centre stage.

'The estimable Colonel Tofa. My dear fellow, you are exceedingly welcome and although I'm sure you've had very little shut-eye over the past few days, we appreciate your coming here to enlighten us on the events of the last twenty-four hours.'

Fatigue clearly showing on his face, Noah stands facing us. 'Thank you sir. In case the announcement hasn't yet been broadcast, I can tell you that Martial Law has been declared throughout the country, as well as a dusk to dawn curfew. Before getting some rest, I had to come here first as there wouldn't have been a successful outcome if I hadn't been tipped off by Penny that Baros's rebel army was attacking from the sea. Knowing this, we were able to make last minute adjustments which almost certainly led to the failure of the coup.'

'Bravo, Penny Lane,' Reggie laughs. 'Now then, my dear chap, what is the *successful outcome* you mentioned? Is the coup over and have the government troops won?'

Noah shakes his head. 'A settlement has been reached. In effect, General Tabo has conditionally surrendered, along with the rebel army'.

'Conditionally? Is that as opposed to an unconditional surrender?'

'Exactly.'

'Conditional surrender!' Reggie thunders, bristling with indignation. 'Never give in to the aggressor, Colonel, under any circumstances.'

To my surprise, Noah isn't intimidated by Reggie's challenge and in a composed voice replies, 'We have accepted some conditions from General Tabo, the first is that there must be no mention of the word *surrender*.'

'What!' Reggie almost explodes. 'Good God, man, so they haven't surrendered at all.'

Shrugging off Reggie's outburst, Noah continues, 'Instead, it's called *an agreement*.'

Still agitated, Reggie demands, 'And what exactly does *agreement* mean?'

'It means that the government has decided to go along with this. It will save more bloodshed and, after all, both sides in the conflict are Liberian. Also, when General Tabo realised we knew about the boat attacks and President Poltara had been removed from the executive mansion, then their cause was more or less lost.'

'And what, Colonel, if I may be so bold, are the other *conditions*? And by thunder man, I hope you've not given away too much.'

Noah's face betrays the irritation he must surely be feeling. 'No, we haven't.' He gratefully accepts a glass of water from Toma, then takes a deep breath. 'Many of Baros's men were reluctant conscripts anyway. The second condition is that they should be allowed to return to civilian life with their families, without any charges against them. With regard to the full-time soldiers, many of whom used to be government troops, we agreed to General Tabo's *third condition* that they could rejoin the Liberian army, but under new officers and at lower ranks. He, himself, will take the lesser title of Captain.'

'And is that it?' Reggie's eyebrows shoot up and down in unison. 'Three conditions?'

Noah frowns. 'Yes sir, just the three.'

'And will it work?'

'We believe it will because the threat to the government was always from Baros and his rebel army with, shall we say, some followers on the fringes of government. He's now a lost cause and his status went up in smoke when Jacob Marcam lost his appeal. To make matters worse, Baros's gang of mercenaries failed to spring Marcam from jail in South Africa.'

'Well then,' Reggie shakes him by the hand. 'Under the circumstances, Colonel, I think it's an acceptable settlement.' He then qualified his praise. 'But I hate the word *agreement*, it's, I don't know, too lame but, there again, you're probably right because if nothing else, all my years in Liberia taught me that saving face in any dispute is of paramount importance.'

'But hang on a moment, gentlemen,' Adele sharply butts in, Reggie having dominated all the questioning so far. 'That's not all, what about the Chinese? What happened to their ship full of weapons and soldiers?'

With a faint smile, Noah answers, 'Gone.'

'Gone? What do you mean, gone? Has it sailed away?'

'No, nothing like that, in fact it *blew up*. We aren't sure how but our best guess is that against Government orders the ship, completely blacked out, was approaching the port when it suddenly exploded in one massive blast.'

'A sort of spontaneous combustion?' Reggie asks flippantly.

'No, I don't think so,' Noah smiles politely. 'But the enormous explosion flattened most of the structures in the port area which must have deafened half the population.'

'That's what we saw and heard from the roof terrace,' Reggie says. 'It was like an atomic bomb.'

'Yes, probably,' Noah nods. 'We know from General Tabo that two of their boats disappeared at the same time, one of them armed with torpedoes so, whether the boats saw the ship and torpedoed it, or whether they collided by accident, we'll probably never know.'

'And what about survivors?'

'We have men combing what's left of the port and the surrounding coastline right now, but as the explosion was so huge, I don't think there's much chance.'

'So it's over,' Reggie booms. 'Game, set and match.'

'No,' Adele interrupts for a second time. 'No it isn't, what about Professor Baros?'

'Late yesterday, an army detachment went to the mine area completely unopposed. Baros has disappeared and his South African second-in-command is certain that he's gone for good. Baros had told him he'd gambled and lost but he'd live to see another day. Limarni diamond mine is now under the control of the Liberian government.'

'That's wonderful news.' Everyone turns to look at me as these are the first words I've spoken since coming into the living room. 'Nick would be so pleased.'

'Indeed, Penny,' Noah acknowledges. 'It was Nick who saw the promise and the danger of Limarni in the first place.' He gives me a worried look. 'Aren't you well, have you been injured?'

'No, not injured, but I've had a sort of haemorrhage and lost some blood. But thanks to Matilda and Reggie, I'm slowly recovering. But Noah ...'

'Yes.'

'There's still something extremely important we want to know. What's happened to the architects of all this trouble, Sir Desmond Thrimby, Sir Alfred Beauchamp and Mr Chan.

'All under control,' Noah replies. 'Before coming here, I contacted Bachir Gemayel and he confirmed that all three of them were still at the Cleopatra, getting ready to go to the airport. I instructed him to make sure his security guards keep them there and I immediately sent two of my best men to help. In fact, when I leave here, which is now, I'll see they're arrested.'

'But won't they be protected by some sort of diplomatic immunity?' I ask.

'No, definitely not. When they arrived, I checked their entry details and both of them came in as business associates of Mr Chan and the Sino Mineral Company. So under Martial Law, I will have them taken into custody.'

'Oh, I'd love to see that,' Adele laughs. 'They must be three of the most evil men alive. To see them arrested, humiliated, and thrown into your worst jail would be fantastic, please film it, Noah, and stick it on YouTube.'

He laughs and says he'll do his best.

Even in my weakened state, I still manage to seethe. 'Those three men, not forgetting of course, the late un-lamented Hal, with their insatiable greed, were behind everything. The fighting and loss of life, Nick's murder and the numerous assaults Adele and I suffered.'

'That's right,' Adele agrees. 'They and the Chinese organised another coup, or tried to, and the death toll is probably already in the hundreds. I'll only be able to get the rest of my life back together when I know they are suffering. I want revenge.'

'I'll do what I can and I'll make sure the President knows everything about them.'

Still looking worried, Noah turns to me again. 'I'm sorry you're not well, Penny, you of all people, our Liberian heroine.'

'Oh no, no, I don't want any of that, please. It was just luck that Adele and I saw the boats on the Mano River and then, when you explained it was nigh-on impossible for the rebel army to reach Monrovia by road, it was only a matter of putting two and two together.'

'That's just your English modesty,' Noah muses. 'Is there anything I can do for you, anything at all?'

'Yes, Noah, there is. Adele, Charles and I need hospital treatment in London so, how soon will the airport be open and can we be on the first flight?'

'Of course, we expect to have full control within three or four days and I'll find the first suitable flight out, making sure you have priority.'

CHAPTER THIRTY-TWO
MARCH 10th

'Well, my dear, your last day in Liberia.' Looking a little down in the mouth, Reggie clamps down his eyebrows and vigorously polishes his monocle. 'Will you miss any of this?'

We are sitting together in his back garden where the rays of the early morning sun shine through fan-shaped traveller palms onto the sweet smelling frangipani, oleander and vivid bougainvillea blossom. Glancing up, bright yellow weaver birds catch the light flitting from tree to tree, chattering to each other as they weave their elaborate nests.

'On a day like today, here in this beautiful setting, oh yes, I'll miss this as well as the beach at the Cleopatra and the rest of this extraordinary country.'

'It is rather splendid, isn't it?' Reggie replaces his monocle with a well practiced half twist.

'But it's hard to blank out what's happened. The coup attempts and fighting, Baros, the Chinese and all the dreadful poverty. I'll remember the *highs,* definitely, but do my best to forget the *lows.*'

Swinging round in his chair, he crosses his legs. 'And, of course, dear lady, my job offer will always be on the table for you. When the dust of war has settled ... it'll take six months or so, this country will be inundated by the World Bank and hoards of Western donors beating down my door demanding my estimable services, shovelling money in as if there's no tomorrow. I'll be worked off my feet.'

That's very kind of you, Reggie but I'll have a baby by then.'

'Of course, but both of you will love it here and be better cared for than under the NHS, I'll see to that.' He eases back in his chair. 'Please don't say no, not yet, anyway. What, with my looks and your brains,' he chortles. 'Or probably the other way round, we could make sure the money reaches those who need it, to alleviate poverty, as they say.'

Sighing, I tenderly place my hand over his. 'I might - oh, Reggie, this is awkward.'

'Awkward, what do you mean?'

'If my female intuition isn't totally up the spout, and if he doesn't come to his senses, I might have a partner, Charles.' It's strange hearing me describe him as that. It's the first time I've used it.

'And why would he change his mind? He's totally smitten, *depereo*, I saw it myself.'

I squeeze his hand, 'I hope you're right. By the way, he phoned last night, he's doing well and has been checked into one of the special government recuperation centres in Hampshire for a week, just to be sure.'

'Bully for him. The Foreign Office chappies are pulling out all the stops after what they put him through, and whisking him off by air ambulance shows how important he is to them.'

'Yes, it was Sir Alfred Beauchamp's replacement who arranged it.'

His voice takes up an enthusiastic edge. 'I'll tell you what, my dear, it would be doubly brilliant if you both came back to Liberia. Charles is a splendid fellow, what with his knowledge of the British Foreign Office and Africa and then you with your language skills and not forgetting my expertise in all things Liberian, we could form a partnership.'

I take a few seconds before answering. 'That would be something, wouldn't it?'

'My prediction is, my dear, that with a fair wind billowing our sails, this country will boom. Now that Marcam and the opposition has been routed, there will be no need for UN peacekeepers, and tourism will take off.'

'Tourism, here?'

'My contacts at the World Bank and EU have already indicated they will provide soft loans to fund the infrastructure.'

'That would be amazing.'

'Indeed. Liberia is the same distance from Europe as the Caribbean, but the beaches and scenery here are much better, and the long dry season in the winter is when the weather-weary Europeans are desperate for a laid-back lifestyle in the sun.'

'What an interesting idea,' I say. 'The Cleopatra would be a perfect place for a holiday.'

'And Western tourist entrepreneurs are desperate to find new destinations, especially as the Caribbean is getting chock-a-block. The potential here is staggering.'

'Excuse me sir,' Toma quietly appears from the house, 'Miss Lane's bags are in the car.'

'Yes, of course, it's time to go but this is not goodbye, dear lady, as you will all be at our London pad on 21st April for Coralie's birthday bash. You promised.'

'Of course we'll be there, we're looking forward to it.'

'Good,' he gently places his hand on my shoulder. 'Now James will take you to the Cleopatra to pick up Miss Holbrook and the rest of your belongings, and then on to the airport where Colonel Tofa has arranged VIP priority clearance.'

As I prepare to leave, I feel quite emotional and want to throw my arms around this amazing man and hug him, but that would only embarrass him, he's not the huggy type, too British by far. Instead, he takes my hand and gives it a gentle kiss. *'Bon voyage*, my dear,' his voice breaks with emotion. 'Take care, I'll ...' fussily, he jiggles with his monocle. 'As you know, I'll be here for two more weeks to help settle Axel Van Damme into his management of Limarni Diamond Mine and, after that, I'll be on my way.'

Sitting comfortably in the Rolls as James carefully drives me to the hotel, I take stock of my situation. Most importantly, I'm back to reasonable health after Matilda's nursing care and five days of rest, but I can't help worrying about the baby and the sooner I get checked out the better. Thinking about my darling Charles, I'm glad he flew out two days ago to start his recuperation, I can't wait to see him again. Can we really be in love after only knowing each other such a short time? I know I certainly am. And our other amazing friend, Noah, confirmed the situation here has normalised amazingly quickly. But God, I'm dreading telling my parents I'm pregnant, they're in for the shock of their lives. I haven't got a job to go back to either but that's the least of my worries, Axel said he could easily get ten million dollars for the three diamonds Nick left me, wow, I'm a millionairess! James glances in the rear view mirror to see what I'm giggling about, then grunts as he slows down seeing that the hotel gates are wide open. The only guard is curled up in a chair seemingly fast asleep, not even flinching as I slam the door. Bachir won't like that. Otherwise, everything is calm and peaceful. A slightly salty, refreshing breeze comes from the ocean and the waving palms rattle their rhythmic tune.

Strangely, Reception is empty and there's no sign of Adele. Noah had said that all the guests had run away when the fighting started. Walking along the corridor towards our old room, I pass the empty bar and dining room. In the eery silence, I call out, 'Adele, are you ready?'

I take two steps into the room then freeze into a horrifying paralysis. I hear a loud scream, it's me. A manic fear, beyond anything I've ever encountered stops me in my tracks. Adele, her eyes wet with anger, is balancing on a chair on the tips of her toes, a noose tight around her neck, her wrists and ankles tied and tape across her mouth.

Sitting nonchalantly on a chair next to her, casually smoking a cigarette, is Jaroslav Baros, his clothing stained with sweat and red earth, a smear of dried mucus on his upper lip. He's holding the end of a rope which is attached to the leg of Adele's chair.

'Careful, my sweet,' he holds the palm of his hand out at me, grinning cruelly. 'One tug, the chair go, she swings,' his accent, guttural and harsh. 'She dangle till she die.'

My whole body seems to have turned inside out. Pressure builds in my chest, his words swimming in my head. I cry out in jagged gasps, 'Let her go, for God's sake, Jaro, what are you doing? What do you want?'

He finishes one cigarette and lights another, blowing a couple of smoke rings in the air. His eyes are on me, searching, testing. 'I want you, Penny Lane, my whore, I want you.'

Paralysed, I stand frozen to the spot while uncoordinated, chaotic thoughts wiz around inside my head. If I say or do the wrong thing he'll pull the chair away. 'Let go of the rope,' I croak, 'Please Jaro, we can talk.'

'Talk!' He rages, looking from Adele back to me. 'You lost me my Limarni mine and you, Penny Lane, you promise to stay and be my woman but you run away. And now Limarni gone so you get punished.'

'Jaro, please believe me,' my voice quaking. 'We did keep the location of your mine secret, even though villains beat us up, look, we already told you that, they were kicking shit out of us and we almost died, but we kept your secret. It wasn't us who lost you Limarni.'

'What you mean?' he tightens his grip on the rope.

'You can't keep a big diamond mine secret forever, it was never going to happen.' My fear is gradually turning to anger and the rage puts some strength back into my voice. 'It was bound to get out sooner or later, one of your workers or maybe your South African friend, greed makes people do these things.'

'No,' he snarls. 'Not my men.'

The noose is gradually tightening around Adele's neck as she struggles to balance on her toes. 'It wasn't us, Jaro,' something in me takes over. 'You horrible, nasty bastard.' God, what am I saying? I'm risking Adele's life. Heart pounding, I take another deep breath. 'You're not a cold blooded murderer, Jaro, so let go the rope and cut her down.'

We stare at each other, unblinking, for what seems ages. A massive, shiny black cockroach scuttles across the floor and disappears under Adele's chair. No-one moves.

'If you'd not been so greedy,' I cry. 'If you'd gone into partnership with the Liberian government, you'd still have part of the mine so put the rope down.'

'Wow,' he growls. 'You some plucky whore, Penny Lane. I knew it. You come with me.' With his free hand, he holds up a canvas bag and jiggles it up and down. 'You hear that? Ha, I not leave with empty hands,' he sniggers. 'In here, I got diamonds, thirty million dollars, easy, you be rich whore if you come with me now.' He jiggles the bag again.

I'm frantic but there's something about his posture which makes me think he's beginning to waver, so I jump in, 'Jaro, I am not coming with you.' I hold my breath.

Giving me a look which is hard to read, he says, 'One - last - chance.'

'No.'

'Then I pull rope.'

'No you won't.'

'How you know?'

'I've already told you, you're many things, Jaro, but you won't murder Nick Holbrook's sister in cold blood.'

In a gloomy, almost sullen way, he shakes his head from side to side. 'Okay.' Letting go of the rope he says, 'Sadly, Penny Lane, I leave you now, but we meet again. You won't forget me.' Going over to the terrace rail and giving me a backward glance, he vaults over into the gardens, half singing, *"Penny Lane, you're in my eyes and in my heart"*, his voice fading as he moves away. *"Here beneath the blue Liberian skies ... Penny Lane."*

EPILOGUE

News Bulletin: *BBC Africa Service.* 5<u>th</u> March
Martial law has been declared in the West African country of Liberia following an attempted military coup. Our correspondent in Sierra Leone reports that rebel soldiers attacked the capital, Monrovia, at dusk on 4th March, but government troops soon took control and the rebel leader, General Wesley Tabo, surrendered his forces at 0800 hrs, this morning.

Coinciding with the attack on Monrovia, witnesses saw a large explosion a mile offshore, and the same government spokesman said that a foreign owned-fishing vessel was hit by a lightning bolt during a fierce, electrical storm. There are thought to be no survivors.

Liberia is still recovering from two lengthy civil wars between 1989 and 2003 which decimated the country's infrastructure, and left 250,000 people dead.

- - - -

Newspaper Article: *The London Daily Tribune,* 10<u>th</u> March
The Liberian government has withdrawn its ambassador from the People's Republic of China following evidence of widespread corruption by Chinese Government controlled mining companies. There has been no response from Beijing.

A spokesman for the Liberian Government said the Minister of Mines, Mr Sami Obeng, has been relieved of his position and faces bribery charges connected with granting several concessions to Chinese companies.

- - - -

<u>Newspaper Article:</u> *The Liberian Echo,* 12<u>th</u> March

Mr Axel Van Damme has been appointed to the General Manager's position at the new Limarni Diamond Mine in Cape Mount County, which is wholly owned by the Liberia Government. Mr Van Damme, an international expert in the development of diamond mines, has vast experience in South and West Africa.

The Limarni Diamond Mine has been registered with the International Diamond Trading Authority and sales of rough diamonds to the world markets will be handled by the newly-created Liberian Diamond Exchange.

- - - -

<u>News Bulletin:</u> *BBC Africa Service,* 20<u>th</u> March

Tragedy in Liberian Jail. Two senior British officials, Sir Alfred Beauchamp of the Foreign Office and Sir Desmond Thrimby, director of Heath Security's X Division, being held in Liberia on suspicion of involvement in the attempted coup earlier this month, were found stabbed to death in their cells at the Monrovia maximum security jail last night. Investigations are underway by the Liberian Police Force. The British High Commission in Sierra Leone has lodged a complaint with the Liberian Minister of Foreign Affairs saying that this was a dreadful incident as the evidence linking the two men to the coup was spurious and had no basis in international law. The Liberian Ambassador to the Court of St James in London was called to the Foreign Office to give an account of the two deaths.

- - - -

<u>Wedding Invitation.</u>
Mr and Mrs James Lane
of 69 Jessie Terrace, Reading
Invite Mr and Mrs Reginald Grosvenor-Smythe OBE
to witness the wedding of their daughter
Penny
to Mr Charles Shelly Temple
son of Mrs Katherine Holbrook and the late Lieutenant
Colonel Arthur Temple, of Poole Dorset
at St John's Church, Ham, Surrey
at 3.00 pm on Saturday 20th June

- - - - -

<u>Birth Announcement: *The London Daily Tribune*, 7th
September</u>
  TEMPLE. – On 3rd September, to Penny (née Lane) and
Charles, a son, Nicholas Reginald Noah, 8lbs 12 oz. Mother
and child in excellent health.

- - - -

<u>Newspaper Advertisement, *Liberian Daily Echo*, 25th March</u>
  Mr Reginald Grosvenor-Smythe OBE, Chairman of TnC
Consultancy Services of Paynesville, Monrovia, welcomes
two new executives to the firm. Mr Charles Temple,
an experienced management consultant with several
years' know-how in sub-Sahara Africa, will expand the
international contacts, and Mrs Penny Temple, multi-lingual
interpreter, will assist the firm in dealings with foreign aid
and development agencies.

- - - - -

NEW DIAMOND MINE DISCOVERY IN ANGOLA

A Government spokesperson in Angola announced the discovery of a new diamond mine in the S W region of Angola, which is expected to produce over one million carats per year. The government has entered into a partnership agreement with the discoverer the mine; Professor Jaroslav Baros.

Lightning Source UK Ltd.
Milton Keynes UK
UKOW04f0117231217
314941UK00001B/41/P